DOLLEY

DOLLEY

*A Novel of Dolley Madison
in Love and War*

Rita Mae Brown

BANTAM BOOKS

NEW YORK   TORONTO   LONDON   SYDNEY   AUCKLAND

DOLLEY

A Bantam Book / June 1994

Book design by Ann Gold
Map designed by GDS/Jeffrey L. Ward

Library of Congress Cataloging-in-Publication Data
Brown, Rita Mae.
  Dolley : a novel of Dolley Madison in love and war / Rita Mae
Brown.
   p.   cm.
  ISBN 0-553-08890-4
  1. Madison, Dolley, 1768–1849—Fiction.   I. Title.
PS3552.R698D65   1994
813'.54—dc20   93-44429
                                                       CIP

Published simultaneously in the United States and Canada

Bantam Books are published by Bantam Books, a division of Bantam Doubleday Dell
Publishing Group, Inc. Its trademark, consisting of the words "Bantam Books" and
the portrayal of a rooster, is Registered in U.S. Patent and Trademark Office and in
other countries. Marca Registrada. Bantam Books, 1540 Broadway, New York, New
York 10036.

PRINTED IN THE UNITED STATES OF AMERICA

BVG   0 9 8 7 6 5 4 3 2 1

To
Lady Bird Johnson

Not all the soldiers were in Vietnam.
This one was in the White House.

Fearlessness is better than a faint-heart for any man who puts his nose out of doors. The length of my life and the day of my death were fated long ago.

Anonymous lines from For Scirnis

PREFACE

*I*first met Dolley Madison in 1949. I sat on her grave. I had no intention of being disrespectful to our most-loved First Lady, who at that time had been dead one hundred years.

Although not yet in grade school, I had been reading voraciously and loved history to such an extent that I was rapidly emptying the shelves of the public library. That summer Mother, who didn't give a fig for history, dragged me to Mount Vernon, Monticello, and Montpelier. I have always thought this journey was an especial demonstration of Mother's affection for me. On the other hand, our little trip provided her relief from her ever-critical mother-in-law. As I look back, it's fine with me if Mom killed two birds with one stone.

Back then Montpelier was owned by that marvelous horsewoman Marion duPont Scott. At any rate, the big house was not available to visitors but the little Madison family graveyard was. We disembarked at Montpelier Station and hiked to the cemetery someways distant. My little legs were tired and I plopped on the first cool, inviting spot.

"Get off that grave this instant!" Mother commanded.

That's how I met Dolley. As I brushed off my skirt, I worried that I'd sat on her head. Mother, as I have said, evidenced no interest in history but as we stood there, she rattled off about Dolley's being a Quaker and, of course, about her courage during the destruction of Washington by the British. Clearly, this was proof of Dolley's power. Even Julia Ellen Buckingham Brown knew about her.

Once I earned enough money to buy a farm in central Virginia, twenty-five years after this visit, I became a regular visitor to the Madison graveyard. It's one of my favorite places to eat lunch, and while Montpelier was privately owned, it was blissfully quiet. Now that the buses come through, I have to time my lunches more carefully. Defiantly, I lean against Dolley's medium-sized marker. So far my mother's shade has not materialized to chastise me. No doubt she is in heaven discussing gardening with Dolley herself. Or giving orders.

The research for this novel, apart from Mother's lecture, began eight years ago. I won't wear out your patience with the miseries of trying to piece together the facts when most of the records had burned to ashes and when most survivors had been too exhausted to write down what they saw when they saw it. Of what did get recorded, well, there is always the problem of deciding how accurate or truthful the writer was. So many wrote after the events occurred, and they wrote with their eyes on political office. Others penned apologies for their behavior during the crisis and tried to pass it off as history. Even those who told the truth could discuss only what they had experienced. They didn't know what was happening over the next hill or around the next river bend. In short, our ancestors endured extraordinary devastation. If they couldn't collect themselves via writing in the aftermath, who can blame them?

Nonfiction is for the facts, fiction is for emotional truth. I have done my best to comply with the facts. You will, however, find much of the truth. Whatever errors and faults are within these pages are entirely my own and are no reflection on my assistants.

Someday, tomorrow perhaps, a curious child will open an old trunk in an attic and discover a treasure of letters and diaries from 1814 that will put my work and the work of historians upside down. So be it. Whatever the facts may yet turn out to be, I will ever believe that something of Dolley is captured here—or perhaps Dolley has captured me.

As always,
Rita Mae Brown
Nelson County, Virginia

MADISON'S CABINET
1814

VICE PRESIDENT
Elbridge Gerry

SECRETARY OF STATE
James Monroe

SECRETARY OF THE TREASURY
Albert Gallatin (in Europe as a peace commissioner)
William Jones (Secretary of the Navy), acting Secretary until Campbell's appointment
George Campbell, appointed February 9, 1814
Alexander J. Dallas, appointed October 6, 1814

SECRETARY OF WAR
John Armstrong, resigned September 3, 1814
James Monroe (Secretary of State), acting Secretary until following appointment

SECRETARY OF THE NAVY
William Jones

ATTORNEY GENERAL
William Pinkney, to February 1814
Richard Rush

SPEAKER OF THE HOUSE
Henry Clay (appointed to peace commission, resigns as Speaker
    January 19, 1814)
Langdon Cheves, appointed January 19, 1814

CHIEF JUSTICE OF THE SUPREME COURT
John Marshall

Throughout his presidency, James Madison would experience difficulty with his Cabinet appointments. So many men trooped through his Cabinet over the eight-year span that to be appointed was more a cause for mourning than for celebration.

THE CHARACTERS

DOLLEY PAYNE MADISON Born and raised a Quaker, she was cast out of the Society of Friends when she married James Madison. She is forty-five years old in the first part of this novel (1814), turning forty-six on May 20, 1814.

JAMES MADISON At sixty-three he is shouldering the miserable task of waging a war he never wanted. He was neither a great orator nor a charismatic leader, but the force of his intellect and his calm manner pushed him to the forefront of American politics, a position relinquished only on his death.

HENRY CLAY Thirty-seven in 1814 and already Speaker of the House of Representatives, he is like a jungle bird of electrifying plumage; when Clay was around, one just couldn't look at anyone else. Henry played to win. He wanted the war with Britain and by God, he got it.

JOHN C. CALHOUN Muscular, tall, a man of ferocious intellect, he is thirty-two in 1814. He is at the beginning of a career that is perhaps one of the most tragic in American history.

DANIEL WEBSTER Thirty-two in 1814, darkly handsome, an orator of spellbinding, theatrical proportion, he, too, is at the beginning of a career that will dominate American politics for four decades. He is bitterly opposed to the war with Britain and contemptuous of James Madison. Webster, Clay, and Calhoun will be locked into alliances as well as rivalries for the span of their long lives.

ANNA PAYNE CUTTS Dolley's fair-haired younger sister has one thing that Dolley lacks: many children.

PAYNE TODD Dolley's surviving son from her first marriage to Quaker John Todd, who died of yellow fever in 1793, he is twenty-two in 1814. Since 1813 he has been in Europe and Russia with the peace commissioners, and although he does not appear in the pages of this novel, he is vital to Dolley's life.

LOUIS AND LISEL SERURIER The minister from France is handsome, observant, deeply admiring of Madison. He can't understand why the American people do not realize what a great man Madison is. A servant of Napoleon, Serurier watches the European drama unfold with a sense of impending doom. His wife, Lisel, beautiful and savvy, adores Dolley and understands that Dolley's true brilliance resides in her ability to hide her knowledge, something a European queen would never have done.

ADMIRAL SIR GEORGE COCKBURN Arrogant, ruthless, and intelligent, he ravages the Chesapeake Bay from 1813 to 1814. This British officer brags that he will capture Washington and James Madison with it.

BRIGADIER GENERAL WILLIAM WINDER The United States officer charged with the defense of Maryland, Washington, and northern Virginia, he is short of troops and short of brains but not short of a sense of responsibility.

JOHN ARMSTRONG A Secretary of War whose behavior bordered on the criminal, Armstrong wanted to be elected President in 1816. It didn't occur to him that if he failed at his appointed post, there might not be a United States and he would be President of nothing.

ELBRIDGE GERRY At seventy years of age, this ailing veteran of Massachusetts politics could spot a crook before anybody else could—after all, he learned his trade in the Bay State.

JAMES MONROE A young hero in the Revolutionary War, he is capable, dedicated, and not afraid of combat in the War of 1812. As Secretary of State, he is being groomed by the Republicans to succeed

James Madison as President in 1816. He detests Armstrong. It's mutual.

FRENCH JOHN (Jean Pierre Sioussat) He acts as Dolley's major-domo. After years as a sailor, with a body covered by tattoos, he jumped ship in Baltimore. It was a leap of faith and probably the best thing he ever did for himself.

SUKEY Young, voluptuous, and rebellious in her own way, Sukey is Dolley's personal servant. She is a slave to her passions as well as a slave to James Madison.

UNCLE WILLY This chatty, fabulously colored macaw is much adored by Dolley. Her son gave her the bird and Willy keeps her company while Payne is in Europe. Like his mistress, Uncle Willy does not like to be alone.

JOHN RANDOLPH A thrillingly brilliant man tormented by his own demons, he hates Jefferson and by extension Madison. He does not appear in the pages of this novel, but the threat of his mischief disquiets Dolley.

THE CITY OF WASHINGTON Eight thousand inhabitants brave the pestilential summers and the raw, damp winters of this sorry little village. It is protected by a beggarly guard of five hundred Regulars and an untrained militia. The mayor, James Blake, mindful of his duty, tries to get provisions from Congress. The congressmen go home, glad to get out of the city. Blake and his militia face an army of British soldiers, well hardened by Wellington in the Napoleonic Wars. James Blake loves his city and does all a man can possibly do under the horrible circumstances.

THE FEDERALIST PARTY Tempting as it is to think of them as proto-Republicans, they were and they weren't. The Federalists, whose stronghold was New England, emphasized tradition and stability even at the expense of individual liberties. They believed in a strong central government and the rule of an intelligent, socially responsible oligarchy. Not that anyone quite put it that way—even Alexander Hamilton was prudent on that issue—but their party line was that the cream would rise to the top. They believed in leadership from above, which would be passed down to the people, not the other way around. They worshiped at the shrine of private property. They especially thought that leaders should be free to make decisions without consulting the public. They disliked the concept of political parties because they felt partisan politics created bitter and unnecessary divisions. This would open the door to venal men who could appeal to the rude emotions of the multitudes. An interesting statement of their philosophy was printed in the *Connecticut Courant* on April 23, 1813: "Political problems do not primarily concern truth or falsehood. They relate to good or evil. What in the result is likely to prove evil, is politically false; that which is productive or good, politically is true."

There were many gifted, compassionate, high-minded men in this party more than capable of leading the country. Their opposition to the war, an opposition grounded in short-term economic gain, led them to question the foundation of the Union.

THE REPUBLICAN PARTY Actually, they were called Republicans or Democratic-Republicans. During 1814 they were usually referred to as Republicans, but they were far closer to our present-day Democratic Party, which is keen to claim them as ancestors since Thomas Jefferson was their leading light. They distrusted a strong central government. "That government governs best which governs least." They believed that leadership should be cultivated in all the classes. They presented themselves as the party of the masses, but there were few poor men as leaders in the Republican Party. Then, as now, politics is a rich man's vice. John Randolph always claimed that the real source of his hatred for Jefferson, and by extension Madison (whom he regarded as Jefferson's pygmy shadow), was that when Jefferson became President, he abandoned his principles and sought power for himself.

In manners and dress the Republicans tended to be less formal than their Federalist counterparts. They also cut their hair short.

In one of those sidelights of history, the Federalists wore their hair in queues and a proper gentleman needed to have his hair dressed every day. Consequently, most barbers were Federalists. This newfangled notion of short hair cost them business.

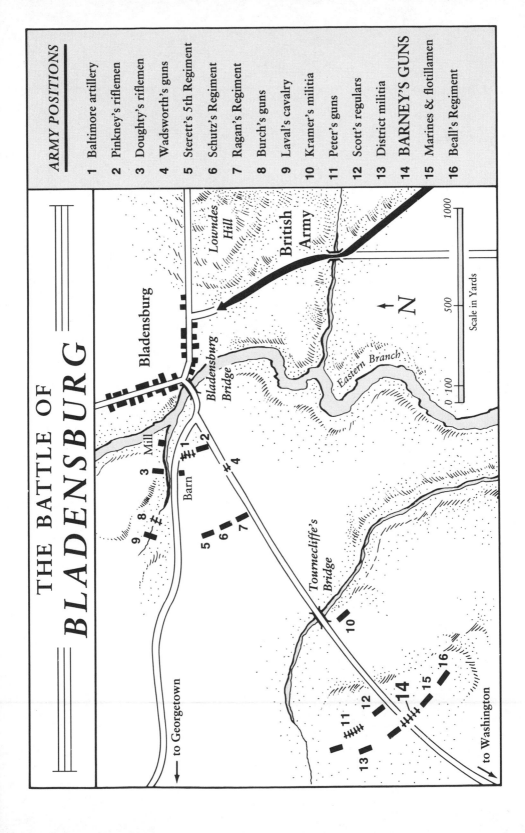

THE BATTLE OF
BLADENSBURG

ARMY POSITIONS

1   Baltimore artillery
2   Pinkney's riflemen
3   Doughty's riflemen
4   Wadsworth's guns
5   Sterett's 5th Regiment
6   Schutz's Regiment
7   Ragan's Regiment
8   Burch's guns
9   Laval's cavalry
10   Kramer's militia
11   Peter's guns
12   Scott's regulars
13   District militia
14   **BARNEY'S GUNS**
15   Marines & flotillamen
16   Beall's Regiment

Lowndes Hill

Bladensburg

British Army

Bladensburg Bridge

Eastern Branch

Mill

Barn

Tournecliffe's Bridge

to Georgetown

to Washington

N

Scale in Yards

0 100   500   1000

DOLLEY

PROLOGUE

4 June 1781

*I*t's curious how the color red jumps right out at you. The wing of a darting cardinal carries the eye aloft until it disappears into the trees. Odd then that the disciplined line of red-coated British soldiers marching through Hanover County, Virginia, went undetected on that hot summer day. Maybe they weren't undetected. Maybe the residents spied them and ran like hell. Or perhaps the hardworking farmers figured if they kept to their business, the British would keep to theirs. Why fire on farmers? No doubt, too, a few shrewd entrepreneurs traded with the enemy at night, far from prying eyes. It could be that some of those Hanover citizens sounded the alarm and protected one another. What is certain is that no one galloped ahead of the advancing column to warn John and Molly Payne.

The Paynes were Quakers and opposed the war. They opposed all war, even one as justified as an exhausting struggle for independence from Great Britain. Wearing plain clothes and using "thee" and "thou" when they spoke set them apart as much as did their determined insistence that no human being had the right to take another's life. The Quakers deserved what might befall them. At least, that's what the neighbors said. After all, if this grinding war was won, wouldn't the Quakers benefit from freedom from the British Empire just as much as those who bled for it?

Molly Payne's cousin, Patrick Henry, considered a bigmouth by some Virginians and a hero by others, owned the house she and her husband rented near Scotchtown.

Now that General Charles Cornwallis had plunged into Virginia after his depredations in the Carolinas, and Colonel Banastre Tarleton was raiding and burning along the James River, Patrick Henry was conveniently elsewhere. Just like a politician, his enemies said.

Molly Payne ignored the insults that were hurled at her firebrand cousin Patrick, whom she loved, and at her Quaker household. She performed the endless chores of farm life and of raising six children despite the threats and insults of neighbors, some of whom would ride into the fields to bait and torment John and her two eldest sons, Walter and Temple, who worked with their father.

Henry had said, ". . . give me liberty or give me death!" And on this clear, early summer day, death was moving toward the Paynes.

Dolley Payne, at thirteen, was stuck in the house helping her mother air out the bedding. She resented Walter and Temple for being out in the fields with their father. Anything was better than being stuck in the house. Isaac, eleven, adored his older sister, so she put that adoration to work. Coughing, he ended up shaking most of the bedspreads out the window.

Mother Amy, robust and smart as a whip, called from downstairs in her deep African contralto. "How you doin', chile?"

"Fine," Dolley replied as she watched Isaac choke on dust.

Dolley heard Mother Amy's footsteps retreat from the stairs. She also heard the whinings of Lucy, aged three, and Anna, aged two. Children were such a bother, Dolley vowed never to have them. She wasn't going to get married either and she did not keep this opinion to herself. Mother Amy rolled her eyes when Dolley protested her many views. Molly Payne, like most mothers, couldn't resist being drawn into battle by her oldest daughter. The more she lectured Dolley on the appropriate goals of a young woman, a member of the Society of Friends, the more Dolley disagreed with her. Her father didn't even try to argue with his determined offspring.

Mother Amy walked back to the stairs. "It's awfully quiet up there."

Dolley appeared at the top of the stairs with pillowcases draped over her arms. "We don't want to give Mother a headache."

Mother Amy put her hands on her hips when the black-haired,

blue-eyed girl stood before her. Little Anna toddled after Amy, who looked up at Dolley. "Uh-huh. You better be shakin' your tail as well as those bedclothes, girl, or I'm gonna come on up there and you gonna wish you was somebody else."

"Yes, Mother Amy."

Molly Payne walked into the hall. "Art thou sassing Amy?"

"No."

"Where's Isaac?"

"Helping."

"Dolley, thou hast tricked thy brother into doing all the work. Now that's not fair."

Dolley held up the pillowcases like trophies. "I am too working, and thou said when I finished I could go outside and pick strawberries. I hate being inside and thou talk about fair. It's not fair that Walter and Temple get to work outside and I get stuck in here. It's . . ."—she searched—"not Christian."

"What?" Her mother's eyes grew larger. "I am eager to hear thy disputation, Dolley Payne. So eager that I am about to climb up these stairs, tired as I am, lest I miss a single syllable."

"Dolley! Dolley! Come here!" Isaac hollered.

"In a minute," Dolley casually called over her shoulder, ignoring the urgency in her brother's voice. Isaac could be urgent about a butterfly.

He pounded out of the bedroom, screeching to a halt next to his sister, whom he much resembled. Isaac's lip trembled. "Redcoats! Coming up the road."

Dolley turned on her heel and raced into the room. Molly and Mother Amy hurried up the stairs. Two little pairs of feet could be heard trying to master the steps to follow the adults. Anna started to wail.

Dolley, hanging out the window, saw an unending line of soldiers moving smartly with a mounted officer at its head. She didn't know how to tell rank in the British Army but she knew he was important. If nothing else, the fine-blooded horse he rode bore ample testimony to that.

Molly wedged in next to her daughter as Mother Amy, taller,

3

peered over their heads. Isaac ran to the other window. "Oh, my God." Molly's hands flew to her mouth because of what she saw and because she had taken the Lord's name in vain, an unbearable sin, so strict was her faith.

"Momma, the Redcoats are turning off the road and coming up the hill," Isaac reported.

Dolley leaned farther out the window and shook her fist. The British were too far away to appreciate this youthful gesture of defiance.

Molly pulled Dolley out of the window. "Dost thou want to get killed?"

"Thee've got no business here. Thee can just get on thine ships and go back where thee came from!"

"Dolley, hush up!" Her mother held her arm so tightly that it hurt.

"I'll run get Father," Isaac offered.

"It's too late," Mother Amy replied.

"They're in the back fields. They can't get here even if you run fast as Mercury," Dolley said as she began to understand that their situation was critical. The British had turned off the road and started marching up to the house. This was not a diversion on their part. The Paynes were their goal.

"Amy, take the children with thee to thy quarters. I am confident the British will not harm children."

"They killed all the livestock, even the foals and calves, down along the James River," Dolley blurted out, making the association in her mind between foals and children.

Molly quietly said, "They won't harm children." She put her hand on Amy's broad shoulder. "Go on now, Amy."

"I ain't leavin' you." Amy squared herself and crossed her arms. "They comin' for you, they got to go through me."

Lucy and Anna were now squealing their heads off. Isaac's eyes nearly popped out of his head.

Molly, voice deep with emotion, commanded her servant and friend, "For the love of God, Amy, save my children."

Tears rolling down her cheeks, Amy snatched up Anna and Lucy like loaves of bread. Isaac moved along with Amy. He was an obedient child.

Dolley seemed frozen next to her mother.

"Thou, too." Molly stared into those eyes, as cobalt and clear as her own.

"Mother, we can fight them together." Not a hint of fear showed in Dolley's lovely features.

"I'll not fight anyone and neither will thee, but I will for the first time in my life raise my hand to thee if thou do not do as I say this instant."

"Mother, I can't leave thee."

"Thou can and thou will!" Molly shouted, then pushed Dolley toward the back door, through which Amy had just shepherded the children.

Dolley dragged out the door, following Amy. Carried along by Amy, Anna started to sob. Lucy picked up the chorus. Amy put them down and shoved them toward her own door like baby chicks.

Lucy toddled inside. She loved Mother Amy's cabin. Anna balked. Isaac ran by her, grabbing her left hand as Dolley grabbed her right. Anna's little fingers squeezed Dolley's hand.

As Anna lurched through the door, Dolley released her hand and quickly shut the door.

"Dolley!" Amy shouted.

Dolley hesitated for a moment, then ran back toward the big house. She ran to escape the fear in Mother Amy's voice and the censure.

The door to Mother Amy's cabin opened. Isaac peeped out and that quickly Amy collared him, shutting the door hard.

Dolley didn't turn at the sound. She reached the back of the house and moved with stealth around the side. For once she was glad of her drab Quaker clothes. No one would notice her.

Her heart banged against her chest, her breath was ragged. She thought she might explode with excitement. She felt giddy, wild almost.

She could hear the soldiers now, their queer accents filling the air, a swirling dust cloud engulfing them as it drifted toward the house.

A beautiful baritone called out. "Henry! Patrick Henry, show yourself, traitor to the King. If you don't come out, I'll ride in after you and relieve you of the burden of your miserable life!"

The officer, extremely handsome, perhaps thirty or thirty-five, halted his column at the front steps. No answer met his call.

Dolley slid back along the house. Her mother was still inside. Dolley quietly opened the back door and tiptoed in. If her mother heard her, she didn't turn to see her but instead stood strangely still in the center of the hall. As the front door was open to catch whatever breeze there might be, she could see the officer far better than he could see her. Dolley stayed at the back of the hall. She was partially obscured by the stairwell.

The officer spurred his horse, which leaped up the steps, clattered one stride over the porch, and trotted into the hall. The officer drew his sword over his head. Dolley's throat tightened. On seeing Molly he reined in his horse, not easy because the animal grew nervous inside the house. His sword arm was ready to strike.

"Where's Henry?"

"He is not here, sir. I am his cousin." Molly betrayed no fear. Her very calmness affected him. If she'd been terrified, he would have known what to do.

"Coward. He ran away!" The officer blustered.

"And thou canst do the same. Look what thou hast done to the floor!" A note of rage vibrated in Molly's pleasant alto voice.

His arm wavered, then he dropped it. He stared hard at this good-looking woman who defied him. Defied him and didn't even take a backward step when his horse twitched in front of her. She reached up and grabbed the horse's bridle. He could have ridden her into a pulp; yet in that moment she was stronger than he. She released the bridle, released it as though she were giving him the gift of freedom. Crimson-faced, he turned and rode back out the door, again clearing the steps with a leap. The column swung around to follow its handsome Mars, who never looked back at Molly Payne standing in the doorway.

Dolley watched her mother watching the enemy depart. She felt lifted up as a bolt of energy shot through her adolescent frame. Her mother was invincible. *She* felt invincible.

Molly's gaze dropped to the floor. She got down on her hands and knees to see how badly those iron-shod hooves had cut into the heartpine.

Wordlessly, Dolley moved up the hall to join her mother on her hands and knees.

"Dolley . . ." Molly didn't finish her thought. She studied her daughter, who was rapidly transforming into a woman. She knew Dolley had disobeyed her and risked her young life. She wondered if Dolley realized how lucky they were. Even if the officer had spared them, he could easily have put the house, the outbuildings, the crops, to the torch.

As the glossy black curls bent over the indentations in the floor, Molly knew how alike they were. For all the surface differences of this mother and daughter, underneath they shared a drive, a tremendous will, not just to survive but to triumph.

Molly thought of her other children. She knew in her heart that some of them lacked that will and she didn't know why. How is it that one child is born with the fire and another glides along or is smashed on the rocks of life? She loved them all, fiercely. She prayed silently for her brood but when she looked at this one, she knew Dolley needed few prayers. She was the strongest of the litter.

She stood up. "Go tell Amy that we are safe."

"Yes, Mother." Dolley hurried to the door. She felt her mother's eyes on her and turned. For a moment she looked at her mother not as her mother but as another woman.

Molly smiled. "Go on, Dolley."

Dolley ran back and nearly tore the door off its hinges. "We're safe. Mother has run off the British!"

Mother Amy shouted, "Praise Jesus!" Then she cuffed Dolley on the ear. "Don't you no never give me a scare like that!"

As they walked back to the house, Isaac asked, "What'd thee see?"

"This big, handsome man rode right into the hall and drew his sword on Mother . . ." She paused for her words to have their full effect and so that Isaac could contemplate his misery at not having been there. "And Momma didn't budge an inch. She told him to get on out of her house. And he did." She drew a deep breath. "He just wheeled his horse around and jumped the stairs. Isaac"—she pulled him next to her—"I believe she would have killed him if he hadn't done what she said."

PART ONE

*W*hat a liar and a hypocrite I've become. Tomorrow Jemmy and I host our New Year's gathering, to which all of Washington is invited, and I must pretend that all is well and getting better.

All is most certainly not well and indeed getting worse.

Little sister Anna says that thirteen is an unlucky number, and in 1814 all will be right. I laughed when she told me that because our dear, departed mother would have scolded her severely for holding on to superstitions.

Mother would have scolded me, too. The Society of Friends, whose strictures she followed with such conviction, abhors war and will do nothing to help in its prosecution. Perhaps it is better that she is not here to see her daughter as wife of a wartime President. Then again, she endured my being cast out of the Society of Friends when I married James, so perhaps she could endure my current situation.

Curious, how whenever I think of Mother, I also think of Mother Amy. She found ways to soften Mother's rules as well as ways to infuriate her. Mother Amy carefully selected her head rags. The more brilliant the color, the more she liked them, and oh, how Mother would complain of the luxury of the world that had extended even to the dress of Negro servants. Mother Amy would hum and go about her business. She'd tell me that God enjoyed many things that Quakers did not.

The older I get, and I am getting older, the more I realize that Mother Amy may have been the most sensible person I've ever known. What a sin it is, what an abomination, that one human being should own another.

The Southern legislators are using slavery to keep the war fever running high. The latest rumor is that the British may foment a slave rebellion.

Such a froth of speculation! Anna says, why bother to discover the truth of the situation? The rumors provide such constant entertainment.

I do have Payne's education to look forward to in the coming new year. He promises he will attend the College of New Jersey as soon as he returns from accompanying Albert Gallatin on the peace commission in Russia. It now costs three hundred dollars a year to attend the college. I fear the enticements of the town of Princeton, New Jersey, will surely surpass the cost of enrollment. Who can afford such an education these days?

These cheap tallow candles smoke something fierce. My eyes are smarting and my head is, too. I can't seem to put my thoughts down in sequence tonight; they're flying in and out of my head like bats.

A good night's sleep will clear my head and I will continue this on the morrow, God willing.

D.P.M.

*T*he road in front of the White House looked like chocolate pudding, its peaks and valleys frozen in the January cold. A huge gouge in front of the President's mansion resembled a bomb crater.

Curly-haired Daniel Webster, a first-term representative from the state of New Hampshire, had proclaimed Washington The Great Dismal, but then Northern congressmen had never liked the city, while Southern and Western congressmen seemed to enjoy themselves thoroughly.

The Madisons shared New Year's Day with everyone. Even the critical Northern senators and representatives trudged through the frozen muck to celebrate the coming year and to share fervent hopes that the cursed war would end.

Those wishing to make a dashing impression might rent a carriage or arrive on horseback, but most walked. The city, exorbitantly expensive, soon taught all but the most profligate that they would have to budget while living in the nation's capital.

The simple, elegant door to the sandstone building, painted white, remained open as throngs of people jammed inside; no one seemed in the least hurry to leave. The food, the wine, and the company were enticements to all save the most misanthropic. Besides, what better place for gossip and intrigue than at a party hosted by the President and his wife?

The Marine Band boomed in the anteroom, causing the elderly Vice President, Elbridge Gerry from Massachusetts, to remark that he hoped they could fight better than they played.

Dolley Madison glided from guest to guest. She adored being surrounded by people. Whether they were friends or foes of the Administration, her humor and tact never seemed to be affected.

Most of the guests, including the Cabinet members, who should have known better, assumed that Dolley was the warm heart of the Administration while James provided the cool brain. Only James Madison and Edward Coles, who was Dolley's cousin and the President's private secretary, knew that when Edward became seriously ill the year before, Dolley had assumed his duties. She was better informed than anyone in the room save the President. Her genius lay in disguising the fact.

Anna Cutts sensed her older sister's political acuteness, but she never probed. Eleven years younger, she felt as much Dolley's child as her sister, since Dolley had helped raise her.

Anna watched the shiny black curls shake with laughter as Dolley said something to Henry Clay, who at thirty-seven was a dynamic Speaker of the House. She then moved on to the dainty wife of Dr. William Thornton, the man who had designed the Capitol and had been appointed superintendent of the Patent Office by President Thomas Jefferson, a post he still held.

Mrs. Thornton thought herself an expert on fashion, believing that her French heritage dictated an innate sense of style. Although Mrs. James Monroe, having recently visited Paris, considered herself the repository of current style, Anna Maria Thornton somehow stayed one jump ahead of Elizabeth Monroe. Now Anna observed Mrs. Thornton silently appraising Dolley's pink satin gown enhanced by thick ermine. The great, white velvet turban with its ostrich plumes wiggled before Mrs. Thornton's envious eyes as she and Dolley chatted. Yes, a few ladies wore elaborate headdresses on the Continent, but Dolley had given the turban her own personal stamp. Mrs. Thornton, believing herself to be the understudy for the job of President's wife, as did most women in the room, was quietly determined to eclipse the First Lady in attire. To date, not only had she not succeeded, but Dolley, with her uncanny sense of fabric and color, outshone her.

James Monroe, Secretary of State, was mired in a discussion with John Armstrong, the pompous Secretary of War. Despite his fashionable wife, Monroe refused to abandon silk stockings, breeches, or his tricorn hat. Anna thought he looked ridiculous. To those Republicans who cared for power, he also looked like their next presidential candidate when Madison's term was over.

Dolley cheerfully finished with Mrs. Thornton and whirled over to her sister.

"I don't know who's more ambitious in this town, the women or the men," Anna giggled.

Dolley smiled. "I expect Mrs. Thornton is the moon to her husband's sun."

Anna accepted the delicious punch a waiter presented on a silver tray. She whispered, "How much did you have to pay for the extra waiters?"

"Thirty-five cents."

"That's not so bad."

"Not so good either, but I was lucky that the senators from the Carolinas and Georgia were willing to let their servants work here today."

"Congress really ought to give you more money."

"Congress realizes that last year our debt was some five million and this year my husband thinks it will double."

"You could live in a tent to economize."

Dolley laughed. "Before this war is over, we might have to. Can't you just envision it? French John in a tent?"

Just then the majordomo, French John—Jean Pierre Sioussat, born in the city of Paris and now in the prime of his exuberant life—strode through the room with Uncle Willy, Dolley's turquoise-and-yellow macaw, on his shoulder.

"Madame, Uncle Willy wishes some champagne." French John bowed very low and Uncle Willy walked across his back, much to the amusement of Rufus King, the distinguished senator from New York, rumored to be a likely candidate for the presidency in 1816 for the Federalist Party—the party whose sole purpose seemed to lie in opposing James Madison and anyone else who did not put the economic interests of the North first. Senator King, bald on top, combed the curly hair on the side of his head forward. It lent him a noble, Roman air so long as he wasn't exposed to a strong wind.

"Uncle Willy may have some of mine." Dolley gaily allowed the bird to drink from her glass.

"Even the animals of the earth worship you." Senator King held up his own glass. He meant it. There were few people who didn't like Dolley. Even vitriolic John Randolph, the former representative from Roanoke, Virginia, and a bitter foe of Madison's, liked Dolley, and he hated women.

However, recognizing Dolley's unusual ability to bring out the best in people did not deter the President's enemies from using her against him. New England newspapers were hinting that Dolley was having an affair with the French minister, Louis Serurier. They also hinted that James Madison was impotent; after all, Dolley had borne two sons by her first husband and yet no children by James. Those Puritan Yankee traders thrilled to sexual secrets under the guise of rooting out scandal. Dolley loathed the rumors but prudently never responded to them. It would only add fuel to the fire.

A rustle among the crowd and a rush to the door let Dolley slip back to her husband for a moment. Never comfortable in large groups, the President stood like a statue while people paid their respects.

"Your usual triumph." James squeezed Dolley's hand.

"Don't count your chickens—the party's not over yet. John Armstrong still has the opportunity to offend someone before we blow out the candles."

"Most likely it will be me," James whispered.

"You know what Mother Amy used to say." Dolley leaned closer to her husband's ear.

"Dolley, I'm always suspicious when you attribute a phrase to Mother Amy."

"She was a loquacious woman."

"She . . ." James smiled. He never could get around Dolley. "Well, dear, what did the philosopher of Hanover County tell you?"

"The higher a monkey climbs, the more you see its red behind—and how John Armstrong believes he's climbing!"

The President laughed out loud, unusual for him. Onlookers strained to catch tidbits of the conversation.

Not far away two Southern senators, James Brown from Louisiana and John Taylor from South Carolina, were calling the roll of United States victories in the year just past. The list was short. The war was long. Those who had trumpeted a quick victory when it began in 1812 were now conspicuously silent.

Mobile, Alabama, had been recaptured, and General Henry Dearborn and Captain Isaac Chauncey had burned York, the capital of Upper Canada. Young Captain Oliver Hazard Perry, after three bloody hours on Lake Erie, had defeated six well-made British ships and won Erie back for the United States.

Those were the bright spots in these last, grinding twelve months. The worst problem was that an arrogant British Navy still blockaded the coast, bombarding whatever city or town captivated its interest. The British were shrewd enough to blockade New England only rarely, encouraging that disaffected section to trade with them. But the Chesapeake Bay particularly fascinated the British, and they also felt compelled to visit the mouth of the mighty Mississippi. Great Britain considered herself invincible on the seas. After all, she had savaged the French, teaching Napoleon to stick to land warfare. What damage could a puny former colony inflict on the great empire?

Yes, there was the slight embarrassment of losing the War of Independence to General George Washington, but times had been different then and the English told themselves they hadn't sent their best, they'd had other preoccupations in Europe. This time the United States was going to be taught a lesson in international manners.

That Great Britain made curious claims as to what constituted the borders of the United States and impressed American seamen for the war against Napoleon seemed natural. To them. They had even stolen John Lewis, George Washington's great-nephew, who escaped from the British ship and swore to kill them all one day. But then everyone considered John slightly unbalanced. Relatives and friends hoped his hatred would fade and he would apply himself to a profession.

While the two Southerners, Senators Taylor and Brown, hinted that things might go better if Secretary of War Armstrong was removed, they prudently changed the subject and bowed as Dolley and the President joined them. Dolley's husband raised an eyebrow. Dolley took the sign and put her arm through Senator Brown's. She steered him away, giving Rufus King of New York his chance to speak to the President—and all the better that Madison's supporter Senator John Taylor was there, with James Monroe joining them. Senator King opposed the war. He disliked the party started by Thomas Jefferson, the Democratic-Republicans, of which Madison was the head. But King was a man of honor and knew that once you were engaged in a war, you saw it through to the end, at least politically. What one did in private was, well, what politics was all about: deals and counterdeals.

Dolley led Senator Brown toward the food. "Is it true that you've become a victim to the new dicing game? It must be very exciting."

"Hazard." Brown shrugged, using the French name.

"Craps." Dolley's ostrich feather dipped a moment.

This made the Louisiana senator laugh. "Well, yes."

"And is it also true that the Theatre d'Orleans has grilled loges for people in mourning?"

"The entire theater's been rebuilt at the cost of one hundred eighty thousand, Mrs. Madison. It is surely the most sumptuous theater in the New World."

"Befitting our most exciting city. I do want to visit New Orleans. The British, too, are drawn to its charms. I think I'll visit once their interest cools."

Senator Brown cooed, "Ma'am, a few little bandy-legged men in red coats are no more bother to my constituents than are mosquitoes."

Just four days before, Sir Edward Pakenham had attacked New Orleans with the help of Indian allies, but his foray was more trouble than it was worth, serving only to give notice to Mississippi River towns that they, too, would soon be ravaged like the hapless villages of the Chesapeake.

The focus of the crowd had shifted to the arrival at the front door of the resplendent French minister and his equally dazzling wife in a gilded coach drawn by four horses, whose individual value was more than the average yearly income of an American citizen. Four footmen, gleaming with gilt, braid, and even gold swords, attended the energetic, dashing Louis Serurier. The Frenchman glanced down at the cavernous hole at his feet and then gracefully leaped across, hands in the air, to the cheers of those who jammed onto the front porch to behold his progress. The footmen carried Madame over the crater.

On entering, Serurier immediately found Dolley, now talking to the Russian emissary, André Daschkov.

"Your Beauty." He bowed low. The bemedaled Russian nodded his leonine head to Serurier, then turned to give Elizabeth Monroe the benefit of his attentions. Elizabeth's smile froze on her face. Daschkov had a wicked reputation with women and Elizabeth was exhaustingly proper.

Dolley held out her hand for Serurier to kiss. "You are a flatterer."

"I can't call you Your Majesty." He bowed again.

"Ah, but my enemies do." She lowered her voice.

"Ignorant asses." His voice dropped, too, then rose. "May I compliment you on the largest pothole in the city of Washington."

"Since we are the First Citizens, it's only proper that we have the best pothole."

The Secretary of War, John Armstrong, said, "And that is precisely why the British will never march on Washington despite their puerile boasts. With our roads, they'd never make it."

Those around them laughed, soon returning to the lifeblood of politics and parties: trading favors, paying back betrayals, and keeping score.

The wine flowed freely, an act of hospitality bitterly criticized by faithful Quakers. Not only had Dolley so forgotten her religious upbringing that she wore fancy clothing, she even served spirits. Dolley never answered her critics, but the Quaker barbs hurt.

The French minister lowered his voice again. "Monsieur Armstrong imagines himself an American Napoleon who will one day become President. He has forgotten the necessary ingredient for such a comparison."

"Which is?" Dolley's deep blue eyes reflected the brilliant candlelight.

Serurier tapped his temples. Dolley laughed as Rufus King and other Federalists noted her animation in the company of the handsome Frenchman and exchanged sharp glances.

She propelled Serurier toward her husband, then walked over to Madame Serurier instead of waiting for Lisel to approach her.

French John scowled as Dolley smiled broadly at him, knowing full well why he disapproved. She had cast protocol to the winds in going to the younger woman.

"Mrs. Madison, French John will scold us both." Lisel Serurier laughed. "I was trying to make my way to you but ran into many obstacles."

"All male." Dolley winked. "You are the most exotic beauty Washington has ever seen. The poor dears don't know what to do with themselves when you descend upon us."

"They're only talking to me because you're occupied." Madame inclined her head. "And don't forget, Uncle Willy is more exotic than I am."

"But not nearly so well spoken." Dolley laughed. "He curses in your language, you know. French John taught him."

"I do that sometimes myself."

Both women laughed.

Born and raised in Haiti, Madame Serurier, at the age of seven, had saved her parents from a slave rebellion by appealing to the insurgents' compassion. Moved by the child's courage, they allowed the family to survive. Many in Washington believed her to be a Creole. Pedigree meant much to such people, and the less power they had, the more it meant.

However, as Louis Serurier was the only French minister in the entire New World, few dared to cross him or question his wife. It put the pedigree worshipers in a curious position, having to accept on equal terms a person who might carry a drop of African blood in her veins. Madame Serurier enjoyed their discomfort. It appealed to her sense of humor.

Madame whispered to Dolley, "Here comes the Vice President. Do you think we can escape in time, or will it be too obvious?"

"His sight is still good. It will be obvious."

Both women sighed, for Elbridge Gerry could talk. Then they beamed smiles on him as he approached.

The crowd grew noisier. Cheers for 1814 raised the roof.

The festive air was tinged with a maniacal quality. The human animal dances the wildest on the edge of the grave.

*T*he house, quiet in the early hours of the morning, after the last guest had staggered home, seemed to shudder in the deepening cold. James Madison sat before the fire, too tired to get out of his chair and go to bed. Dolley, moving from room to room as she closed up the house, tiptoed closer in case he was asleep.

"I'm awake."

"So I see. Anna and I thought you looked splendid tonight. Those Federalists searching for a crack in your armor didn't find one." She sat next to him. "You haven't any."

He put his hand over hers. "What a terrible liar you are, Mrs. Madison. They're like a pack of Hamlets, calling up the ghost of Washington. I don't *look* like a wartime President. I don't look like George Washington."

"I didn't hear one person mention George Washington's name. After all, Jemmy, he's been dead fourteen years."

The light played on James's weary features. "They don't have to mention his name. He'll be the measuring stick for every President to come." He sighed. "I miss him myself, even if we did drift apart at the end."

"We all miss him, but you're a wonderful President." She put her other hand on his shoulder as she stood beside him. "I thought the way you maneuvered Rufus King over to William Thornton very handsome. They were so enchanted with each other they forgot to woo their opponents."

"Two Federalist windbags. I wish Thornton, who for all his chatter is a remarkable man, would desist from playing politics. He's too . . ." James groped for the word.

"Obvious." Dolley supplied it.

"Not a fault of Louis Serurier's, however." He smiled. "Nor

Henry Clay's. I suppose Clay is the other extreme. You know, I stood there tonight and I watched the young men. I don't envy them. I thought to myself, 'Who will be their Washington? Who will be above party politics?' And you know, my dear, not a one, not a one." His stomach growled.

"Are you hungry? I will never understand how you can be near all that food and not eat."

"How can I talk to someone with my mouth full? It looks undignified."

Dolley pulled him up. "We'll take care of that."

They walked down the darkened hall toward the kitchen. Hanging in the dining room was the Gilbert Stuart painting of the first President. Washington stood with one hand on his sword and the other hand outstretched, beckoning—an ambiguous message, or a warning. Neither Dolley nor James glanced at the somber likeness of Washington. They hurried into the kitchen, where coals glowed in the huge fireplace. Dolley found a broomstraw, touched the tip to an ember, and lit a candle. Breads were piled on the table, along with cold meats wrapped in damp, thin towels, as were the butter and pastries.

"Here, try this." She put buttered bread and some of the meats before him and poured a glass of robust French wine.

James, although almost sixty-three, was blessed with good teeth, and he chewed the meat with pleasure. "Speaking of Washington, I do miss his wine cellar. Mrs. Washington set a good table. I always thought that's what hurt John Adams, you know. Too frugal. Cost him a second term."

Dolley tossed a log on the fire to ward off the chill.

"It is a vice with Adams. I don't know how Abigail bears it. But you know, Jemmy, that's New England. They're forever accusing Virginians of being spendthrift—the whole South, in fact. Senator Taylor tells me that when John Calhoun's lady joins him, they'll entertain like royals. That will send the New Englanders into new fits of frugality and censure. They worship money so much, they can't bear to part with a penny."

"And when might we expect this dazzling entry into the social lists?" James's gray eyebrows rose; his fork was poised in front of his mouth.

"At present the rising star from South Carolina considers Washington too 'primitive' for his wife." Dolley sipped from his glass. "A tired excuse. Once the war is won, Floride Calhoun will show up fast enough."

"And if the war is lost?" James would never breathe such a thought to any but his wife.

"If the war is lost, John Calhoun's political career is lost with it."

"And mine, too, the great difference being that I am old and he is young. He'll be bitter. I'll be—"

"We won't lose the war," she interrupted. A commotion drew her attention away from the subject. A muffled giggle was followed by hurried footsteps. Dolley rose and peered back into the house. She squinted and could make out two receding figures. "Sukey!" she called out. There was no answer. The other figure, powerful and male, quickly disappeared. She heard a door open and close and then hoofbeats.

"What's she doing up at this hour?" James asked.

"Not her work, I can assure you."

Sukey, as gorgeous as she was lazy, provoked Dolley more than Dolley liked to admit.

"I often think we should send her back to Mother."

"Your mother has more servants"—Dolley carefully avoided the word *slaves*—"than she can feed now. Besides, would you bedevil your mother's last years with Sukey?"

James laughed and changed the subject. "Now I'm wide awake. If you hadn't made me eat, I would be in my bed asleep." He sighed in mock distress. "Now I shall have to stay up with you and ring in the New Year." He took her hand and kissed the back of it, then turned it over and kissed her palm.

1 January 1814, Saturday
New Year's Day

*T*he day was a triumph, but I must remind myself why it is important to create these social extravaganzas. My thoughts return to the children orphaned by the war and to the women left young widows. I was once a young widow. I wish it upon no woman.

Everyone attended except for those too feeble to walk. The war hawks turned out in full force, but then, so did the Federalists.

Henry Clay, impeccably dressed as usual, appeared older to me tonight. I noticed that his hairline is receding. Or maybe it's me. For some reason everyone looks older. I notice the crow's-feet around eyes, the slight downturn of mouths once upturned. Clay, surrounded by supplicants as well as enemies, could barely move. I wanted to speak to him in private but it will have to wait. Perhaps getting this war, which he wanted so badly, is aging him.

Suffice it to say that I, too, am showing my age, and again I credit the war. My hair stays jet black, for which I am grateful, but if I weren't just a bit plump, the wrinkles would be plain to see.

Well, I'm not losing my vision. Anna is, and she is so much younger. Well, she's not actually losing her sight, but I observe that she's beginning to hold papers farther and farther from her face when she reads. Apart from that she remains as lovely as ever.

When I was young, I don't think I noticed people's age as much as I do now. Odd. I wonder why?

Louis Serurier was as delightful and amusing as ever. Strange, I feel as though I've known the Seruriers all my life.

How different from the last French minister, General Louis Marie Turreau, with those ferocious black mustaches. They bent each time he passed through a door! His face was as red as a Harvard beet. An unfortunate word, for he mercilessly beat his wife, a most intelligent and generous woman who managed to keep her good humor despite her loathsome spouse. I seldom spent a moment in her company but what I cracked my sides laughing.

The fierce general disported himself amongst the whores of Washington with such alarming frequency that I doubt there is a single one in Washington who has not been visited by that loathsome man—or by Mr. Clay either, for that matter!

Why marry a woman if you're going to betray her, and if you're going to betray her, why beat her? The fault is not hers. Not all horrors are the horrors of war. I sometimes think the worst we do, we do behind closed doors.

Thank God both my husbands were tender, decent men. For a woman who never wanted to marry, I hit sevens when I cast the dice.

Senator Brown was explaining craps to me, and if you roll seven or eleven, you win the pot. I do love games of chance and I've lost too much money playing cards. My New Year's resolution is, no more cards. Of course, dice are different from cards and—no, I mustn't even entertain the thought, although I'd love to see Elizabeth Monroe's face if I suggested a genteel game of craps at our next Dove Party. Usually my distaff Cabinet meetings are pleasant, but sometimes, when Mrs. Monroe sees fit to tell us how things are done in New York, I count to ten. It's been a very long time since she lived in New York. How odd that she and I have known each other for years and yet we've never become close, and I've known Madame Serurier but a brief time and feel that she is almost a sister.

I miss my darling Payne terribly, and I haven't heard from him in months. I hope Jemmy and I did the right thing by allowing him to go to Russia. I'm curious to hear about the Czar. They say Alexander is a handsome man, robust and blond. What sufferings those people have endured. Remarkable as Bonaparte may be, it is hard to think of his Russian foray as anything but a celebration of death.

How can Napoleon continue? He knows only victory. I should think it would dull the senses.

I'm so tired I can't hold up my head.

Until the morrow, God willing.

D.P.M.

*T*he wood grain in the smooth dark table appeared to vibrate before James Madison's eyes. He touched the wood. The papers on the desk in front of him refused to budge. The message was no illusion. The wood grain wasn't vibrating, but Mr. Madison's head was. His pocket watch told him it was three o'clock in the morning. Everyone had gone to bed. He could be alone with his worries.

Even though he knew better, it was only human to hope, especially at the turn of a new year. At the start of 1813 he had replaced his Secretary of War with John Armstrong, but Armstrong was not proving to be much better than William Eustis.

The coastal blockade was driving the New England states to new pitches of commercial fury; yet even while they wept and wailed about lost profit, a sentiment the President certainly understood, they sold goods to the enemy, an action he deplored. The representatives from New England and New York, ever sensitive to the sound of a falling dollar coin, skillfully deflected investigation of what some called treason.

Rufus King appeared to be a mediating influence between Federalists and Republicans, but he needed to hold on to his Senate seat the same as anyone else did. New York politics was a dogfight.

No nation with seventeen ships, three of them frigates creaking with age, ought to declare war on a nation possessing one thousand warships, bristling with guns of fabled precision.

No nation with six thousand Regulars in its Army ought to declare war on a nation whose Army was like a splendidly ordered infernal machine, a machine true and tested by the Napoleonic Wars. The United States officers were either aged Revolutionary veterans, as creaking as the frigates, or young men who had never fired a shot at an enemy and, more telling, had never withstood the shot fired back.

Madison hoped his fellow Republicans Henry Clay and John Calhoun were happy. They had lusted for this war. They had forced his hand. Oh, how the shine of ambition glowed on their young faces, each man believing his destiny was to be President. Well, the presidency was more a curse than a prize. Madison had watched the highest office in the land age Washington, Adams, Jefferson, and now himself. He hadn't been very young when he entered the office and now was in his sixties. The presidency could kill a man.

Lack of good fighting men could well kill the infant nation, although at least Lieutenant Colonel Winfield Scott had captured Fort George and General William Henry Harrison looked bellicose. There was an officer patrolling the South, Andrew Jackson, who was aggressive. All was not lost on land, but by and large the Army was shabby, its leaders worse.

The irony of this war was that the few celebrated victories were on the waters against perhaps the greatest naval power the world had ever known.

That was no comfort to the people of Buffalo.

Nor would there be any comfort for the President tomorrow when he would ask for the court-martial of Brigadier General William Hull. Better to see if there's discussion within the Cabinet than to order to court-martial outright. That would seem high-handed. Hull had surrendered Detroit on August 16, 1812, without a shot being fired. Although his men were not even outnumbered, Hull had heard of British General Isaac Brock's alliance with the Shawnee chief, Tecumseh. Fearing the possibility of superior enemy numbers, he caved in without a fight. What did Hull think, that ten thousand Indian braves would spring up overnight? The sorrow of this mess was that Hull had been a good officer in the Revolutionary War.

Congress needed a scapegoat, and Madison, in the eyes of the Federalist Party, fit the bill. But relations between the Federalists and the Democratic-Republicans, called Republicans by most people, were so rancorous that no Republican President could have repaired them, or so Madison believed. Now his enemies would say he was using Hull as his scapegoat. After all, the President was the commander in chief and he had picked the coward. Maybe Hull was just too old. Maybe Madison was too old.

On the surface of it, a court-martial had nothing to do with party politics. But there would be someone with something to lose, and someone with something to gain. There always was.

George Washington, towering at six feet four in his boots, had enjoyed good relations with Congress during his presidency. James Madison considered the likelihood that George Washington was the only United States President who would ever enjoy good relations with Congress. As for himself, he was faced with a body of men in which even some malcontents of his own party schemed against him, and lately it seemed as if their number was swelling. The balance of seats, narrowly held by the Republicans, ensured constant fighting in both houses and no comfort for James Madison. While he had been reelected in 1812 by an electoral college vote of one hundred twenty-eight to DeWitt Clinton's eighty-nine, he had never known the ease of a clear majority in Congress. He was constantly accused of being ineffectual in working with the legislature, an arena in which he had excelled as a young man.

Wouldn't John Randolph, the supreme Republican dissenter, steeping in his own bile down in Roanoke, thrill to the news of Buffalo? The President thought a moment. Randolph would take no pleasure in the miseries of the people of Buffalo, but he would rejoice in the miseries of the President. John Randolph loathed Madison almost as much as he loathed Jefferson. James Madison hoped that out of Congress, Randolph would cause less mischief than he had when he was in office. With Randolph, one could never be sure.

Years ago, when John Randolph strode into Congress with his pack of hunting dogs and unleashed them on the delegates, Madison had decided he was deranged, though capable of brilliance. Now he was convinced that the genius had withered and Randolph was quite mad, seeing an incipient autocrat in every President. The President was also convinced that Randolph, in some sly way, was making contact with Madison's bitterest Federalist enemies in New England —men who had been Randolph's own enemies. Randolph was more obsessed with bringing down Madison than with coming back into politics himself. Well, if the two should coincide, so much the better for Randolph. He was convinced that Madison was leading the Republicans away from their—meaning Randolph's—principles. The purity of his party meant more to Randolph than did winning the war, whereas for Madison winning the war meant life or death.

The President had no proof, not a scrap, that Randolph was up to anything, but he was wary. Pray God Randolph didn't make an alliance with DeWitt Clinton. The mayor of New York wielded considerable power. Clinton thought Randolph mad, too—Madison knew that—but madmen can be useful. Even though Clinton was no Federalist, his goal was to break up what he saw as the Virginia dynasty. Then, too, Madison's administration had refused DeWitt Clinton's motion for his pet project to build a canal linking the Hudson River with Lake Erie. Clinton was passionate about that canal. Not that Madison held any animosity toward his former presidential opponent; he didn't, but Clinton was a New York man and New York was seeing more of this war than its people imagined it would.

Would there be a state left untouched before the war was over?

John Armstrong, secure in his belief, which was unsupported by fact, swore the British would never drive toward Washington. The Secretary of War felt the theater of conflict would remain in the Great Lakes and perhaps the Mississippi.

Could Madison replace a second Secretary of War so shortly after removing the first one?

The gray sleet poured down harder. Madison got up from the desk to look out the window. The weather accentuated his misery. If the United States lost this war, its back would be broken. No foreign nation would feel compelled ever to consider its welfare. The strain of the war, the defeat, and the mounting debt might then force an internal crisis. If the United States cracked open to form new, smaller nations, the states of the Union would be picked off, one by one, by the great gilded vultures of Europe.

The United States had to win this war.

How?

*B*uffalo has been burned. And so the war continues like a bloody dye spreading over our country. Even if the flood recedes, I worry that a deep stain will stay in our hearts.

Jemmy is so exhausted I fear he'll make himself ill. The nation can't afford that. Neither can I.

I don't think any other man could take the strain. I marvel at my husband. He remains steadfast in his desire to prosecute this war. A peace treaty with favorable terms would be "most agreeable." Agreeable! It would be a gift from God. But short of that, we will press on.

His face was ashen when he told me. The bleakness of the day, the constant sleeting rain, reminded me of a day when we were living at Montpelier. The rain poured and poured and Jemmy and I—I can't remember why—couldn't bear being trapped in the house. So I dared him to chase me around the portico until we had run a full mile, and he did. We laughed so hard we fell into each other's arms just as Mother Madison came out to see what the ruckus was about. We told her, she laughed too, and then we all three ran around the portico.

Jemmy smiled when I recalled that day. Then he chased me around the room and I chased him back and Uncle Willy squawked at the top of his considerable lungs. French John and Sukey rushed in. Uncle Willy saw he had a larger audience and took full advantage of it.

Sukey thinks we're not right in the head. There was no need to explain our running to French John. He brought us a little sherry to "ward off the chill," as he put it. Sukey, relieved not to be given a chore, left to flirt with Paul Jennings. Being mulatto, he is light-colored and quite a handsome lad. But Paul, at fifteen, is no match for Sukey and she flaunts her power over him. She shouldn't torment him so.

I've noticed this last month that Sukey has been more insolent than ever. I had hoped she would be married by now. She is of age, and if she found a good partner from a neighboring plantation, Jemmy would do all he could to arrange the marriage. She evidences no interest in the prospect. I like to think that marriage settles people, but the truth is it settles some and scuttles others. My sisters and I made good marriages, but I have seen many friends languish in theirs. They proved to be part of a mismatched team. When one horse is pulling both along, no good can come of it. I have also noticed that the woman usually pulls more than her share. Jemmy and I pull together.

No one could believe that at twenty-six I would marry James Madison, who was forty-three. I couldn't love any man more than I love my James, although I did love poor John Todd. I always knew Jemmy was of the highest intelligence, but he has an inner strength; these terrible times have allowed me to see that in him and to love him more, though I would have thought it impossible to do so.

Uncle Willy, cloth over his cage, has a great deal to say. I can't write with his carrying on. He's rocking the perch and throwing seeds all over the floor. Sukey will complain tomorrow.

I do love that bird because Payne gave him to me. When I look at Uncle Willy, I think of my son, but quite apart from that, Uncle Willy reeks of personality.

I believe God meant for us to love all living creatures.

Until the morrow, God willing.

D.P.M.

The faint winter light changed from deepening blue to Prussian blue. Anna, mindful of costs, lit the tallow candles in the hall and tiptoed into the parlor to light the expensive beeswax ones. Dolley and Henry Clay, engrossed in conversation, barely noticed. Anna tiptoed out. Her boys were at a birthday party and Dolley's namesake, Dolley Payne, almost two and a half, was sound asleep upstairs. At least Mr. Speaker and Dolley enjoyed some quiet.

". . . Western states should be another country." Clay leaned back in his chair. "It's this shortsightedness that will cost the Federalists the future."

"Only if we win the war," Dolley swiftly replied. "Then it's natural for our energies to shift from the Atlantic to our interior and that's where the next fight will be. Of course, if you and Mr. Calhoun can continue to work together, the South and the West can outvote New England."

"I see we've been thinking along similar lines, Mrs. Madison." He reached for his glass of port. "I'm delighted, as always."

Dolley smiled. She knew that Henry Clay was devoted to her husband and therefore he was dear to her. "New York is the key," she said. "Will New York throw her weight with our own developing commercial interest or will Europe sing her siren song? I don't know, but I know that DeWitt Clinton is nobody's fool and I continue to hope that Daniel Webster is."

"Ah, a Webster-Clinton alliance. Well, Webster is a bright hope but bright hopes fade. There was a time when Josiah Quincy looked the coming man, and he'll never, ever return to Congress."

"Don't underestimate Webster, young and new as he is to Congress. He has greatness." Dolley had taken Black Dan's measure. "And he hates what they call the Virginia Cabal, which means he hates my Jemmy. We must find a way to trim his sails . . ." Her voice trailed off as she thought. "Perhaps the key is his opposition to the war, which is bringing him such attention."

"You are a gambler, Mrs. Madison." Clay's light blue eyes brightened.

"Well, I know better than to cut cards with you." She laughed, then her voice grew earnest once more. "I don't know how much of a gambler I am but I *can* read a map."

"Ma'am?"

"Virginia, Pennsylvania, and New York. One of those states will emerge to control the Atlantic coast. If Benjamin Franklin were alive, I'd say it would be a dogfight between Pennsylvania and Virginia."

"I regret I never had the opportunity to work with Franklin."

"A rollicking sense of humor—you share that with him." Dolley knew Franklin well. "But you have a boldness, Mr. Speaker; some will call it arrogance. I have never seen a man grasp a situation so quickly and act with such speed—when it suits you."

"And when it doesn't?" Clay, like everyone, was fascinated to hear someone else's view of himself.

"You're as capable of intrigue as a Byzantine."

"Is that a compliment, ma'am?"

"Today it is." She merrily pointed her finger at him.

"Then I am in the right company for today and every day." He meant it.

"Thank you."

"I believe, Mrs. Madison, that you are trying to steer me toward a course of action once these hostilities are—over."

"Oh, you give me too much credit."

"Well, I give you credit enough to know that Virginia needs strong ties with New York because you believe, as I do, that DeWitt Clinton will move heaven and earth to create a pathway of some sort into the Western Territories, a cheap pathway. Then all that lumber, wheat, and cattle will pour into New York State, and her manufactured goods will flow back into the Western Territories. Unfortunately, Virginia's face is set on her glorious Revolutionary past, if you will forgive my being so blunt."

Dolley, who hoped this wasn't true but feared that it was, offered no argument. "Time will tell. But these conflicting monetary interests are poisoning our ability to make war. I know you have tried to find common ground—"

"I might as well get blood out of a turnip." Clay shifted in his seat. "Do you know, that violent Federalist, Laban Wheaton, actually came up to me the other day and said he hoped I'd run as Vice President in 1816. And then he quoted John Randolph and said that since the office of Vice President was a tomb, I ought to take advantage of it."

"Laban Wheaton is a blistering idiot."

"And he's drawing Webster into the circle of Federalist senators. Do you know what else he asked me?"

"After wishing for your death? I'm not sure I want to know." Dolley's hand fluttered to her throat.

"He wanted to know if you replaced Ned Coles as your husband's secretary when Ned was so ill last year."

"What did you tell him?" Dolley leaned forward slightly. This was a secret she shared only with her husband, Anna, Clay, and, of course, Ned.

"That if he were in need of your services, he should apply to you directly." Clay slapped his thigh.

Dolley enjoyed his riposte but ruefully added, "A woman playing politics. They must never find out. They'll use it against Jemmy. Make him appear—you know."

"Fear not."

"Oh Mr. Clay, we've got to protect the President. He is surrounded by treachery, even in his own Cabinet. He works himself to the bone and for what? To save us all, including the very Federalists who want his hide. Do they think they will fare better under the Prince Regent? Do they want to become subjects again? Subject. The very word makes me sick. Is freedom that frightening, or are they so shortsighted they would sabotage our war effort to continue their trade with England? They'll use me against my husband. They'll stop at nothing to make him appear ridiculous and weak. And meanwhile men are dying. And we've got to wrest a vote from these very men for more soldiers and more money to prosecute this war—more death to end death." Dolley, shaken after her outburst, gratefully took the glass of port Clay poured for her.

As she drank, he put his fingers together and rested his chin on them. "This war is my doing. You're too kind to accuse me and the other war hawks. And I confess that declaring a war with a Senate vote of nineteen for and thirteen against does seem like folly. Even in the House, where I had more support, it was seventy-nine for and forty-nine against. So—"

"Don't accuse yourself." Dolley spoke firmly. "At first I was against this war, but I now believe that it was inevitable. If we didn't fight it now, we would fight it ten years from now. Either we are a sovereign nation or we are not, and we may have to fight Europe yet again."

"Yes." Clay's voice was low. "Until they leave us alone. Until we can trade freely with any nation we choose."

"And so we need a foreign policy that is backed by deeds, not words."

Clay leaned forward and patted Mrs. Madison's hand. "You were right to insist that I force Calhoun to put Webster on his Foreign Relations Committee. Poor Crisis."

"Beg pardon?"

"Crisis Calhoun. That's what I call him—behind his back, of course."

"You are funny, Mr. Clay."

"He's a good man. But now he is saddled with Webster day in and day out."

"And Mr. Webster keeps talking and talking, and on a committee where everyone listens." Dolley smoothed a fold of her dress. "Soon the entire Federalist Party will see him as their hope. He's the youngest among them. We've got him on the right committee, now we've got to find his Achilles heel."

"Umm."

"Does he borrow money?"

"He does, ma'am."

"Does he repay his debts?"

"Occasionally."

Dolley laughed. "Ah well, as that applies to almost everyone in the service of our government, perhaps we'd better look elsewhere." She paused and cleared her throat. "Ladies?"

Clay inclined his head. "A weakness but not a notable weakness. Not like myself, madame." He smiled broadly, then turned his palms upward like a supplicant. "I am not strong enough to resist the enchantments of your sex."

Dolley smiled at him. Bold, yes, Clay was bold. Most men would lie through their teeth before admitting such a thing. "An understandable—"

"Vice. But do know that I hold my wife in the tenderest regard and she will never, ever hear of my feet of clay."

"Then why do you tell me?" Dolley caught his play on words.

"Because you already know." Clay met her eyes. "Little escapes you, Mrs. Madison. A highly intelligent woman without your discipline would use such things for her own advancement, or even amusement. You use what you learn to protect your husband and because you love your country. I will hide nothing from you." He grinned again. "You'd find out anyway." He paused. "I shall apply myself to Webster's Achilles heel."

"I will, too." She glanced out the window. Dots of light in other windows provided the only relief from the darkening gloom. "Sometimes I think politics is no more than a gathering of treacherous feudal chieftains." Then she sat up straight. "No. Forgive me. We will yet pull for the common good."

Henry Clay discreetly left by the back door, and Dolley sat alone in the parlor. Anna finally joined her.

"Tired?" the younger sister asked.

"Exhausted. Thank God for Henry Clay, and John Calhoun, too."

"What about Mr. Monroe?"

"Yes. James Monroe is a patriot, always and ever. Jemmy knows that, even if he feels such reserve toward him. Regardless of their past political differences, Jemmy knows Mr. Monroe has courage. He served in the 3d Virginia Rifles and was wounded at Trenton. A young hero, as was John Armstrong."

"I wonder why he didn't pursue a military career?"

Dolley shrugged. "I expect that's why General Armstrong loathes him so. James Monroe left the Army in 1778 to study law—some say politics—under Thomas Jefferson. John Armstrong stayed in the Army, even during the awful times when they numbered barely twenty-five hundred. Here it is, thirty-six years later, and he has to face James Monroe again. He can't bear to hear a single military suggestion from Mr. Monroe."

"Does Jemmy know you've been meeting with Mr. Clay?"

"Of course not; what kind of question is that?"

"Women playing politics—you know the kind of trouble that can stir up."

Dolley jumped out of her chair. "My own sister!"

"Your own sister who wishes to protect you."

"Me? What about the President?"

"That's just it, Dolley. You'll be used against him if you're found out."

"Well, I am damn well used against him even if I sit and do needlepoint."

"Don't swear at me."

"Don't tell me what to do," Dolley fumed, her beautiful complexion turning scarlet.

"We have our sphere. Men have theirs."

"You don't believe that." Dolley put her hands on her hips. "I've seen you politicking with the best of them for your dear Richard."

Anna stammered, "Only because I asked Dr. Thornton for—"

Dolley interrupted. "Dr. Thornton? Oh, come, Anna. I've seen you make a beeline for senators and congressmen when you needed them."

"It's not like that."

"We all play politics."

Anna shouted back at Dolley. "Just don't get caught."

"I won't if you don't talk." Dolley wheeled on Anna. "I saw the face of our enemy. You were off with Mother Amy. Our mother saved our lives, Anna. I am telling you the British will throw us in the dirt and kick us senseless if they can. If we lose this war or make a bad peace, we'll wind up like Canada and I, for one, have no desire to be part of Britain's Commonwealth. England thinks only of England and she despises anything she sees as weak. She squeezed us dry when we were a colony and she'll do it again if she can. She'll do it to any colony."

Dolley's voice dropped. "There is nothing I wouldn't do to save this nation. And if you're my sister, you're going to get right in there with me and play politics, too."

After a time Anna found her voice again. "What do you want me to do?"

"Spend time with Anna Maria Thornton."

"Oh, no." Anna's face fell.

"He's a Federalist and she can't resist telling what she knows."

Anna swallowed hard. "Anything else?"

"Forgive me for losing my temper."

3 January 1814, Monday

*H*ad a spat with Anna. She finally saw things my way, I think. Came home and threw the dice Senator Brown gave me.

I've been practicing in secret. If Jemmy thinks I'm gambling again, he'll be cross with me. I think I do it to relieve my worries about money. I always imagine that I will win the pot.

Mother, her face scarlet, tried many times to stop me from the fripperies of the world, as she called them. But Mother Amy taught me how to hide my little toys from Mother, including a pretty necklace Grandmother Payne gave me. Her maiden name was Anna Fleming. A pretty name, and she was a lovely woman who relished wearing the finest clothing. She was horrified when her son John married my mother, a Quaker, and then became one himself. I wore the necklace under my collar and no one would have known except that Isaac and I got into a fight. He grabbed for my neck and got the beads instead. He ripped the necklace off and then felt so bad about what he'd done, he promised never to tell Mother. He never did. Poor Isaac. I think of him often. I've lost so many of the men in my life, starting with my brothers—Temple to disease, Isaac to violence, and Walter just disappeared. Well, I don't want to think about all that right now. Did I lose my thoughts again? Gambling, that was it.

Well, wagering lends a spice to any activity, especially a horse race, and I can see how intoxicating this dice game can be. Better than cards because you have less to remember.

As a child, whenever I did something wrong, I would have to recite whole passages from *The Book of Discipline*. This was to guarantee that I would repent and correct the error of my ways. But all it did was guarantee that once I was out of my mother's house, I would never again read *The Book of Discipline* or any other religious tract.

I once asked Anna and Lucy—before she married Thomas Todd and moved to Lexington, Kentucky—if Mother scared them. They both agreed that Mother could be a stern disciplinarian but that I, being the eldest daughter, bore the brunt of it. With each child, especially the ones born after the War of Independence, Mother grew more lax.

Now that I am older, I often wonder how Mother felt that not one of her nine children who survived to maturity elected to remain a strict Quaker. Once we had made our decisions, though, she never spoke of it again and did her best to see us happy. I think that's what surprised me most.

When Lucy ran off at fifteen to marry George Steptoe Washington, the Society of Friends removed her from their rolls even though he was President Washington's nephew. Mother continued to attend meetings, saying that Lucy had her own life to live and that was the end of it.

Dear George. He died too young. Consumption. What a cheerful, kind man he was. I thought Lucy would never recover from the blow. She refused Thomas Todd so many times, a lesser man would have given up. I think Lucy's marriage on March 31, 1812, was the last time we've been truly happy in this presidential house.

At least Lucy is in Lexington, far away from the constant battling. If we applied ourselves to fighting the British as intensely as we fight one another, I believe this war would come to a speedy conclusion.

It's Lucy who always says I look so much like Mother that if she blinks, she thinks she's gone backward in time. Mother always said I looked like her mother, whereas Anna looks like Father's mother. Whenever I glance in the mirror, I realize all too well that I am not going backward in time. Mirrors, which Mother regarded as instruments of vanity, were not allowed in our house. Mother may have been right about that.

This morning I rose early as usual. Sukey dropped my curling iron on my dressing gown. Sukey blamed the dressing gown for being voluminous. The smell of burning fabric sent Uncle Willy into a fit. The macaw's noise made Sukey all the angrier, and she said none of this would have happened if I didn't insist on getting up so early. I replied that if she didn't stay up half the night, doing heaven knows what, rising would be easier for her. She picked up the iron and left. She declined to return. I spent the day with my hair covered up with one of my turbans. I look much better with curls emerging from the turban, but I told my visitors today that I was feeling very Turkish.

That reminded me of Sidi Suliman Mellimelli, the grand emissary from the Turkish Empire, with his eight-inch black beard and his twenty-yard turban. His progress was announced by his four attachés, his Negro servants, one of whom carried his four-foot pipe. An Italian band heralded Mellimelli's every arrival. The Italians have a gift for music. Unfortunately, these Italians did not, which is perhaps why they were driven to find refuge in Turkey. I imitated Mellimelli's walk, which made Anna laugh when she visited today.

We needed to laugh, to take our thoughts from Buffalo. Few others share our concern. A mood of false gaiety has descended on Washington. It's as though nobody cares about anything but fashion, parties, intrigues, and gossip.

Older people say Philadelphia was like this during the Revolutionary War, but as we didn't move there until 1783, I never saw that.

I had intended this diary to be a record of politics and life, to be hidden away until long after my death. It would never do for our friends or foes to realize how much I know. Yet I sit down, reach for my quill, and begin to prattle. I can distinguish the past from the present and the dead from the living, but when I sit here, the dead are as alive to me as the living.

I have never much believed in spirits, but their spirits do inform me. I am the sum of what they have taught me and what I have learned on my own.

Perhaps it's my age or perhaps it's this war, but Mother and Mother Amy follow me like shadows. At the moment when that cursed Redcoat, sword drawn, insolently clattered into our house, I thought he would kill Mother, but her anger saved her. It saved us all.

I have often wondered if I have the courage of my mother.

I rolled the dice. Seven! This could become a habit.

Until the morrow, God willing.

D.P.M.

*T*he uneven, frozen road was slippery. Walking tested one's sense of balance.

Dolley and Madame Serurier walked along gazing in shop windows. Although the cold made Dolley's nose run, she felt so cooped up indoors she was happy to be outside.

"Just one decent ladies' apparel store, just one." Dolley sighed.

Madame Serurier, not wishing to be rude, offered, "Perhaps after the war some fashionable shops, no?"

"Oh"—Dolley kicked at a clod, nearly slipping in the process—"I sometimes fear Washington will forever remain provincial."

"Even Paris was provincial once," the younger woman said.

"That was a thousand years ago. Lima, Peru, is more cultivated than Washington. And it will never be a ladies' place, really."

"They say that Charleston is beautiful. Philadelphia, too, is sophisticated?" She voiced this as a question.

"Naturally, I take great pride in the city of Philadelphia." Dolley smiled and continued. "You know, I have few regrets in this life but I do regret not having traveled. I envy you that. It's such an education. I would love to see Paris and now that my son is in St. Petersburg, I am quite curious about Russia. A grand tour. Florence. Rome. I suppose I'd relent, after hostilities are concluded, to see even London."

"One day."

"Not with my husband though." Dolley pursed her lips. "James says, 'Why exchange the familiar discomforts of home for unfamiliar discomforts elsewhere.' He swears the only purpose of coaches is to bruise one's bones. If he could walk to France or perhaps ride, he might consider it." She lingered before a tobacco shop, the sweet aroma wafting out onto the street even on this crisp day. "I'm being picky. My poor husband hasn't been free of the cares of state since he was a young man. He has spent his whole life in the service of this country, you know, and while I know we need him, I sometimes wish we could—oh, I won't even say it. I'm being selfish."

"Fly away?"

Dolley pounced on the idea. "Yes, and after we'd seen the Old World, I'd love to see our New World. Quebec and, oh, Mexico, and well, I won't go on. But I am fascinated with what we are doing here, whether we speak Spanish, Portuguese, English, or French. What an experiment. That's why this war is so critical, Madame Serurier. I know you appreciate that, but some of my own people don't. The New World must be left alone. We can't be drawn into those Old World conflicts and—no, I'd better not say it."

"Mrs. Madison, you can say anything you wish. No one can hear us, and I do not labor under the delusion that the government of my country never makes a mistake."

Dolley looked at her with gratitude. "What a delight you are." She then spoke in a lower tone. "In 1804, when Great Britain threatened to blockade the coast from Ostend to the Seine, we paid little attention. Two years later this paper blockade stretched from the Elbe to Brest. All bark and no bite. Then the Emperor, not to be outdone by the British bombast, issued the Berlin Decree. Now let me see, that was . . ."

"November 21, 1806. All trade between Great Britain and the Continent was over. Not a spool of thread could pass from British to Prussian hands—Napoleon smacked the lion on the snout."

"Then came the Order in Council. By now we were paying attention because Great Britain declared that every port and colony belonging to France or her allies, and I emphasize allies, were going to be blockaded. Of course, we knew even Britain and her mighty Navy couldn't bottleneck every single port on either side of the Atlantic, but she could certainly capture any ship she believed suspect. Which she promptly did. Then Napoleon issued another decree, and well, it slipped from bad to worse. If France wasn't stealing our ships, anybody's ships, the English were. Being a neutral country just means both antagonists feel free to abuse you. What could we do?"

"You could have declared war on France."

"Never." Came the firm reply.

Lisel Serurier half smiled. "I am the wife of the minister of France. You could hardly say otherwise."

"And whose wife am I?" Dolley laughed for a moment. "The United States will never declare war on France."

"Pray, why? We stole your ships, too."

"But you helped us during the Revolution."

"And when those people are gone, do you expect the new generations to honor that alliance?"

Dolley stepped over a small chasm and then gave her hand to help the younger woman over. She was so nimble that Lisel was put to shame for a moment. "There we are."

"Thank you."

"What was I going to say? Oh, I should hope our children and grandchildren have some sense of honor, but more to the point, France's goal is not the same as England's. Your ambitions are in Europe. England, you see, wants no rivals anywhere on this earth, and any nation that develops into a manufacturing nation will be her enemy. We are such a nation."

"London as Rome. A Pax Britannica." Lisel's light laughter was enchanting. "You think?"

"I do." Dolley sighed. "Perhaps every nation has its moment, as every dog has its day. I myself will never understand why we can't learn to share with one another and live in harmony. We say we're Christians but we march over one another's land, we steal, we kill. And even in victory one may be impoverished."

They walked arm in arm for a while. Then Lisel Serurier spoke. "I am so glad not to be alone. I ask myself these same questions. I thought I was the only one, and I feel this wave crash over me, the sorrows and the foolishness of the world. I want to tell Louis but somehow—I can't. Can you talk to your husband, Mrs. Madison?"

"Yes, I can, but not now—not now."

They continued to pick their way among the rivulets and small icy patches, two distinct individuals who had arrived at a moment of perfect understanding. They walked so far they found themselves at

Eighteenth Street and New York Avenue, admiring the Octagon House Dr. Thornton had designed for a friend. Across the street stood a dwelling made even uglier by comparison. It seemed disproportionate and pretentious. They looked at this house, then at each other, and laughed.

*H*ell was a Cabinet meeting, and James Madison marveled that he had spent his entire life in political meetings of one sort or another. When he was younger, he had assumed they would become easier. Alas, the opposite had happened.

The room was either too hot or too cold, and the President kindly took the coldest seat at the table while allowing Elbridge Gerry, his Vice President, to sit with his back to the fireplace. Even so the older man was shivering, his nose inflamed, his eyes runny. James wished Elbridge better health. He needed him even if he was a Harvard man. They had met as young men united in throwing off the British yoke, and now, as old men, they faced the same deadly task.

William Jones, the Secretary of the Navy, was finishing his report: ". . . that being said, there remains the problem of revenue. Surely there must be methods above and beyond being supplicants of Congress."

"Thank you, Mr. Secretary. We are fully aware that you labor under a double burden, having assumed the duties of Secretary of the Treasury, and this administration remains grateful."

"Any word from Gallatin?" John Armstrong bluntly asked.

"Nothing new." Madison's face stayed impassive, although at that moment he could have pushed Armstrong out of his chair. The reference to Jones's predecessor as Secretary of the Treasury was an insult that escaped no one in the room. The antipathy between the Secretaries of the Navy and of War fattened like a mushroom in the dark.

Armstrong gleefully used any moment to humiliate the man he considered a potential rival for the presidency. Since Armstrong seemed to believe the British would be content simply to march about their former colonies and then withdraw, he assumed that after the

45

war was won—how did not occur to him—he would be the shining star of salvation. America liked to elect military heroes.

What amazed the President was how transparent Armstrong was even to him, and Madison knew he was not the best judge of character, a trait he deplored in himself. He believed either too much or too little of what a person told him.

Albert Gallatin, the talented former Secretary of the Treasury, languished in Russia. Czar Alexander had offered to mediate between the United States and Great Britain, and Gallatin, a Swiss who spoke impeccable French, a necessity at the French-speaking Russian court, was the best choice as peace commissioner. In May 1813, with Dolley's son, Payne Todd, in tow, Gallatin had left for the Colossus of the North. Deprived of Gallatin's Midas touch, the Republicans soon felt the blows of the Federalists, who hammered away at them about the national debt, escalating war costs, and diminishing trade.

Albert Gallatin, overflowing with sound methods of raising revenue, did so with such ease that no one realized how arduous the task was. William Jones now understood Gallatin's true gifts and had full occasion to repent his former ignorance.

The President knew Jones was swimming against the tide and did everything he could to assist him. But James's greatest kindness was that he didn't expect Jones to be Gallatin.

He cast his eyes around the room. Following precedent, he had selected his Cabinet on the basis of geographic representation. He had already lost one Vice President—George Clinton, DeWitt Clinton's uncle—to death, and he was beginning to worry about Elbridge Gerry. He could work with Gerry even though they weren't especially close. They knew each other's strong and weak points. He could work with Monroe—the Secretary of State was his most able Cabinet member—but he had to force himself to do it. As for the other men, well, he could blame no one but himself, and the absurd festering rivalry between John Armstrong and William Jones only compounded his woes.

Those woes intensified because the Federalists, after the fact, refused to accept Albert Gallatin as a peace commissioner. They said they wanted him back in Washington because he was so valuable. Michael Lieb, the Federalist senator from Pennsylvania, led the skillful campaign of arm-twisting and promises, that lifeblood of legislative politics.

Given the time it would take Gallatin to return from Russia, the Federalists could weaken Madison's administration even more. James Madison, through Clay, had heard the remark Lieb made to Webster about his administration: "It's like an old Chinese vase. Fill the cracks with water and bring on the freeze." Webster had replied that New Hampshire men flourished in the bitter cold.

The one consolation James Madison enjoyed during his titanic struggle with the British and, unfortunately, with his own countrymen—the Federalists—was that no one accused him of being Thomas Jefferson's creature. He had finally laid that myth to rest.

That he worked hand in glove with the red-haired third President for the majority of their lives did not mean he couldn't think for himself. He thought well enough to frame the Constitution. But Jefferson had been smooth, personable, and fond of attention in a way that Madison was not. Madison wasn't a mole, he thought to himself, but people treated him like one whenever Jefferson was around. Now that Madison was President, Thomas Jefferson had retired to Monticello and did not meddle in James's affairs. Even Madison's most severe Federalist critics gave up on this tactic, except for John Randolph—a Republican who was acting like a Federalist in James's estimation. Randolph, ensconced on his estate, still fulminated that Madison was the puppet, Jefferson the puppeteer.

James glanced again at Elbridge Gerry shifting uncomfortably in his seat. Gerry, infuriated by Armstrong's snide question, blew his nose louder. But he would not confront Armstrong unless Madison gave the signal, which the President did not.

Mr. Madison, capable of great subtlety when the occasion demanded it, now spoke to give his Cabinet a demonstration of the same. "Mr. Armstrong."

"Mr. President." Armstrong's dark tenor voice caressed the listeners, a voice so different from the President's thin, reedy one.

"I am confident that you will continue to raise troops and that the coming of spring will herald a renewed attack against the British. We *will* drive them from our shores."

Armstrong swept his hands toward the other Cabinet members in an expansive, confident gesture. "The Army is offering a recruiting bounty of one hundred twenty-four dollars with happy results." He smiled, showing his excellent teeth.

What the Secretary of War forgot to mention, and he was thick-headed enough to think the President did not know, was that his plan for conscription had failed. Not that this was entirely Armstrong's fault; the New England states flatly refused to ante up the men. The miseries of fighting this war had fallen on the shoulders of Southerners and Westerners.

James's only motion, the only betrayal that he was moving in on Armstrong, was one tap on the table with his right forefinger. "I am so pleased to hear of your happy results." Elbridge Gerry knew something was coming but not what. He stopped coughing as Madison continued. "Given your success with recruiting, I ask that you direct your attention to the accumulating evidence against Generals James Wilkinson and Wade Hampton. As you know only too well, sir, these gentlemen are entrusted with the crucial task of cutting off Canada's supply lines."

"What accumulating evidence, Mr. President?" Armstrong stiffened, since he had replaced General Henry Dearborn with Wilkinson and then put Hampton in charge of Lake Champlain. Then in a fit of pride Armstrong had traveled to Sackets Harbor on Lake Ontario to coordinate a combined attack on Montreal, to be led by his hand-picked generals.

John Armstrong believed the force of his personality could overcome the deadlock between Wilkinson and Hampton, who detested each other. If the Secretary of War had gathered more information about these two generals before appointing them to their present juxtaposed positions, he might have prevented the ludicrous mess that followed.

Hampton, secure with four thousand men, bumped into four hundred sixty British soldiers. Hampton's men scattered like rabbits.

Wilkinson, with even less provocation, then retreated to Plattsburgh. Armstrong, once back in Washington, acted as though both his generals had maneuvered a brilliant retreat in the face of a deadly foe.

The President, not a military man, could count. Four thousand versus four hundred sixty looked like good odds to him. To everyone's amazement, including his wife's, Madison let it ride. He also heard that Armstrong was bribing officers with promises of higher rank. He let that ride, too. How would it look to the enemy if he replaced his Secretary of War after so recently appointing him? A long discussion with Elbridge Gerry confirmed his own point of view that such a move, at the time of the Wilkinson-Hampton embarrassment, would embolden the British.

The President waited, too, because the court-martial of General William Hull would expose the Army to more ridicule and loss of faith. Armstrong paid little attention to that issue because he had not appointed Hull. It didn't occur to him that as Secretary of War he inherited the mistakes of his predecessor. Armstrong should have defended the Army with vigor and shrewd public relations after Hull's ignominious surrender at Detroit. Instead he acted as though the drama with Hull, which would take months to conclude, had nothing to do with him.

He couldn't take that tack with Wilkinson and Hampton. They were his appointees.

"The accumulating evidence, sir, would seem to indicate cowardice in the face of the enemy." James sat still as a stone as he spoke.

So did everyone else except Armstrong. His face reddened, he shifted in his seat, then found his voice, a trifle higher. "What is it you wish me to do, Mr. President?"

"As I said"—James's voice was as cold as the room—"I wish a full inquiry initiated by your office, sir. Of course, if you are too overwhelmed by current affairs, I will appoint someone else to bring this affair to light. Ah, yes, you asked for accumulating evidence." Madison pushed a stack of papers toward Armstrong. "These are copies Ned Coles made for you of testimony gathered by combatants —perhaps that is the wrong word." He allowed himself the hint of a smile. "I am certain this will help you get started—that is, if you accept the responsibility for such an inquiry, and I repeat, I do understand the strain of your office."

Elbridge Gerry wiped his eyes not because of the wretched cold he suffered but because if he hadn't cried those tears of laughter, he would have torn apart the room with his guffaws.

Armstrong put a good face on it. "I will do all in my power to resolve this issue." He reached over and took the papers.

After the Cabinet meeting James Madison walked into the hall. The small figure of Richard Cutts, holding his mother's hand, captured his attention. He waved to the child and Anna and then returned to his office.

James wondered if the frail little fellow would live to manhood. So many died young. His mother always said if she could get a child to seventeen, he'd live to be seventy. Madison had seven more years to fulfill his mother's prophecy.

4 January 1814, Tuesday

Little Dickey came today with his mother. He's still so listless although a perfect tiny gentleman. With five children Anna's kept busy, but she spends most of her time nursing Richard. It reminds me of when we were small. If one of us was sick, Mother, like a broody hen, hovered over the sick chick, leaving the rest of us free to do as we pleased. I can't say that I prayed for my brothers and sisters to be taken ill—that would have been too wicked—but I admit that I took full advantage of an illness when it occurred.

I have been blessed with one surviving son and he is healthy. The single sharp sorrow Jemmy and I have known—that we never had children—has lessened.

Well, my sisters Anna and Lucy and departed Mary, bless her soul, have had enough children to compensate for me.

Monsieur Serurier paid me a visit today. He brought cut bone for Uncle Willy and confided that Napoleon believes in horoscopes. They are all the rage in France. I said they're all the rage here, too, although few will admit to their fascination. I don't believe in them myself, but for some people, I suppose it is better to believe in the stars than to believe in nothing.

Paul Jennings complained to me that Sukey gives him orders "left and right. I'll not be the slave of a slave!" He declaimed this with all the passion of fifteen years.

After he left to accompany French John to the market, I called in Sukey. Really, we should rename her Sulky. She denied everything. She said Paul sassed her and lolled about—this from Sukey, who only breaks cover if you put the hounds on her! I take a deep breath and count to ten when she tosses her head and puts her hands on her hips. Today I had to count to one hundred. I told her that Paul was young and to remember that.

She said, "You're old and I remember that. What do you know about menfolks?"

"More than you think," I replied. I was so angry I left the room. Oh, what I'd give for Mother Amy to take a switch to this arrogant girl.

French John returned from the market and groaned that the price of potatoes has risen to fifty cents a bushel—a ten-cent rise, just like that! Someone is getting rich off this war and it isn't the President. Jemmy's salary is twenty-five thousand dollars, which sounds like a princely sum, but we must dip into our own pockets to make do.

Jefferson acquired hideous debts in the service of his country— well, because of that and also his passion for building. I'm afraid the same will happen to us. I don't bring it up to my husband, for he has enough to worry about; but I did get a letter from Mother Madison and she's worried, too. In her eighth decade and her hand is as firm as a girl's, her mind's like a razor, and her eyes are good. She still believes she has some dread disease. Every time she learns of the symptoms of a new contagion, she quickly acquires them. She'll out-live us all.

Foul as the weather is, I couldn't stay inside, so I asked French John to accompany me to the stables. My gray horse, which I loved, has died, and we bought a pair of sorrels. Jemmy, while no great horseman like Washington (but who could match him?), possesses a keen eye for horseflesh. I didn't think these horses were much when we acquired them, but they've blossomed into beautiful animals. I wanted to hike up my skirts and just ride. What a scandal that would cause!

Madame Turreau had a luxurious satin riding habit. Publicly I'd join her in the carriage, but sometimes we'd meet outside the city limits and I'd get on my gray mare and off we'd go. How I miss Madame, and I wonder how she fares in France, which is hovering on the precipice. They are a volatile people. I worry for the Seruriers also. If Napoleon loses power, what will become of them?

Whoever decided that women shouldn't ride astride? Absurd, but then social conventions rarely carry the weight of reason, although I do obey them. There's enough to contend with in this life without engendering an explosion over petty issues. Still, when no one is looking, I do as I please. If only I could find another Madame Turreau to ride with me. Perhaps young Madame Serurier would be so bold.

French John gave me a full report of what he hears is going on in Congress. So far, nothing. Will they fiddle while Rome burns? The nation needs a proper defense, not posturing. The Federalists fight tooth and nail not to vote one more penny to our defense. England encourages their antiwar fervor by removing the blockade at New York City, for the most part. This allows the New England ports to keep trading. The older I get, the less inclined I am to like anything English, but I must admire their vulpine skill in arousing dissension within their enemy.

Thank heaven for French John, a born chatterbox and a master at gathering information. His position here at the presidential mansion also makes it easy to obtain news of the goings-on in Washington. Jemmy hears official sources. The news from unofficial sources is more truthful, and besides, I can stomach only so much flattery.

Anna told me that she and Richard must tighten their belts. His shipping losses are dreadful. The man has lost a fortune to the British, yet his spirits remain high. She laughed and said at least she wouldn't get fat this year, although I detect that she's gaining weight. Enough to make her the picture of health.

Richard is such a handsome man and he and my sister make a dashing pair. Jemmy and I do so like Richard, even if he is a Harvard man. We worried when he lost his congressional seat from the Maine district of Massachusetts because he supported the war. That, combined with the financial drain of the war, encouraged Jemmy to appoint Richard Superintendent General of Military Supplies. Charges of nepotism flew like flies, but Richard has proved to be an excellent public servant as we knew he would. His work takes him away from home a great deal, however, and both he and Anna will be glad when this war is over, if for no other reason than the sheer pleasure of being in each other's company!

Jemmy looks after my family as well as his own. He truly loves my sisters and we try to care for my brother John, but he appears and disappears and, I'm afraid, is a woeful victim of drink. Jemmy gave dear Mary away in marriage, and Anna, too, because both sisters love him so much and of course John is so unreliable.

Anna's as blond as I am dark. People never believe we're sisters until we start talking. We sound alike.

Not a word from my son.

I wish by some miracle I could lay hands on fresh roses. The drabness of winter preys on the emotions.

Until the morrow, God willing.

D.P.M.

*D*olley laid her quill in a brass tray on her desk, poured sand on her paper, allowed it to soak up the excess ink, then carefully tilted the diary pages to let the sand fall back into a small bowl. She closed her book and pushed herself away from the desk. Outside, the wind whistled low. She glanced out the window but could see no snow.

Time for bed. As she walked from her room she noticed King George racing across the hall ahead of her, ducking into James's study, and then racing out. Curious, she followed the cat's path.

When Dolley stuck her head in the door, she saw that James was startled. He must have fallen asleep while reading dispatches from Europe, and King George's mad rush through his study had no doubt wakened him. Papers were scattered on the floor.

Dolley knelt down cautiously, for her back was stiff, and retrieved the papers. "Here, sweetheart, you're the only head of state whose dispatches are carefully read by your cat." She handed her husband the stiff papers, which were scratched in places and bore a few teeth marks.

He inspected the damage. "There must be something, some smell that attracts her. She also enjoys sitting on paper, no matter where it is. The paper can be of the smallest proportion but if it's paper, George will sit on it."

"Well. I'm sure it's a difficult job, being the President's cat."

James started to say that the cat belonged to the cook, but King George must have known they were talking about her because she sauntered back into the room and sat before the ebbing fire. "My father loved cats."

Dolley smiled. "Good farmers always love cats."

"It will soon be thirteen years since Father died, and sometimes, Dolley, I blink and thirteen years is just that, a blink. Other times I try to reach into my past and I feel it receding out of my grasp, not necessarily receding from memory, but out of grasp."

Dolley stirred the fire and wrapped her shawl around her shoulders more tightly. She leaned over to kiss her husband's cheek, which showed a fine white stubble. "Darling, I know exactly what you mean."

His eyes twinkled for a moment. "You aren't old enough to know exactly what I mean, Mrs. Madison. No matter how old I get, you will always be so much younger and I can reflect on the envy of other men that I have such a bride."

"Jemmy, it's not like you to be a base flatterer."

"Alexander Hamilton could never understand how you selected me out of all those beaux in Philadelphia."

"I didn't really have beaux, Jemmy," she blushed. "I was a young widow with a tiny son. If you keep this up, I'll know you've been spending too much time with Henry Clay."

"Is he—?"

She interrupted, laughing. "No, he's just the most notorious flatterer in the nation." She paused a moment to notice King George, eyes half-closed, rocking back and forth in front of the fire. "Do you ever wonder what would have happened if Aaron Burr hadn't killed Alexander Hamilton ten years ago?"

The President cupped his chin in his small, beautifully formed hands; he liked brain games, as he called them. "Well, they both wanted to be President."

"Doesn't everybody?" Dolley sighed. "Here, forget those papers, it's too late to work. Let's pull our chairs in front of the fire. I hardly get to see you and I relish every moment."

Happily distracted for a moment from his cares, James stood up and turned his chair around, then moved one over for his wife. "What would have happened if Burr hadn't killed Hamilton? I think Hamilton's intellectual inflexibility would have grown more pronounced with age." He thought a moment. "Regardless of his policies, he and Burr would have run afoul of each other because they were natural rivals."

"Like Webster and Calhoun?"

"And Clay." James rubbed his fingers. "In good time we'll have a triangle of rivalry."

"Clay and Calhoun work hand in glove. I'd like to think they will continue their association over the years"—she paused—"but time changes people." Dolley noticed her husband rubbing his hands. "Do your joints hurt again?"

"I'd rather it be bitter cold than damp." This was Madison's way of saying yes.

Dolley reached over and began massaging his fingers. "Well, what I think is, had there been no duel, Aaron Burr's inclination for grand schemes would still have weakened him . . . like poor Light-Horse Harry Lee after the war. He bristled with schemes and he spent his dollars before he made them and then, of course, he never made them. These land dreams." She shook her head. "Everyone thinks he can go West, buy land, and become John Jacob Astor."

"That's what Washington did."

"Jemmy, Washington was a surveyor. He saw the land first."

"That's true," said Jemmy, who hadn't thought of that. "What would have happened to Hamilton?"

"Alexander Hamilton and John Adams and later John Quincy Adams would have battled over leadership of the Federalist Party. Mr. Hamilton would have called up the ghost of Washington at regular intervals, too. He would have made more trouble for you and Mr. Jefferson because he was so brilliant. But on the other hand, we all lost that brilliance. Many roads lead to Rome."

"And he did serve Rome even if I sometimes disagreed with the way he served it, to continue your figure of speech, my dear."

"Does that feel better?"

"Your touch always makes me feel better." He smiled at her. James possessed a curious smile, oddly childlike and infectious. He stared into the fire, then looked up when she spoke again.

"You haven't heard anything about Payne? Nothing in the latest batch of dispatches?"

"You know I would come to you the instant I learned anything. He's seeing the courts of Europe, he's young—he's having the time of his life." (The President didn't say, "And he's running up debts that I am paying in secret.")

"I know, I know. I think I will feel a little better when he's living in Princeton."

"I will, too. I think if more young men had the opportunity to attend the College of New Jersey, our nation would benefit. When I leave this burden behind, I intend to pay more attention to education. What are the young men in the Western Territories going to do? They can't all travel to the East."

"Here, give me the other hand." She took his left hand. "If this room were warmer, your fingers wouldn't ache so much."

"I do feel better in the summer."

"Is there anything in the dispatches about Napoleon?"

"No. But I don't think he can remain in power. If he is displaced, the British will end the war. If their stated reasons for the war are really their reasons"—he smiled a slow smile—"then they'll stop."

Dolley said nothing because like her husband, she believed that the British bombast about trading with the enemy—meaning France—and their failing to pay duties to Britain was a smoke screen, as was a host of other charges. "The British will end the war when the subjects of the Prince Regent tire of paying war taxes."

The embers glowed an iridescent coral and yellow. A purple-blue hue radiated from the deepest part of the logs. The low crackle and the deep purr of the dozing cat created an aura of peacefulness.

"My dear"—Jemmy broke the silence—"if disaster should befall me in this war, if I should die in office, I want you to return home to Montpelier. Go home to Mother and see to it that Payne finishes his studies."

"No," came the swift and resolute reply.

"No, what?" came the equally clipped response.

"You aren't going to die in office."

He sighed, then chose his words carefully. "I certainly hope not. We are, however, in a war in which the enemy is apparently carrying out his depredations unmolested. Should Washington be the target of his nefarious designs, well, no one knows what the future may bring. If God in His infinite wisdom sees fit to remove me from this earth, I don't want you to stay here. I want you safe at home."

"No." She shook her head, her glossy curls also shaking. "Jemmy, Elbridge Gerry can't run this country. His health is failing. His lady wouldn't be able to perform the functions expected of her either. I would have to stay on until a stronger couple succeeds. I couldn't walk away from my post in time of danger any more than you could walk away from yours."

"I was elected for such travails. You were not, and there is no need for you to expose yourself to harm or to deplete your finances in the service of your nation. I will not be leaving you a rich widow, Dolley. Now listen to me."

"I am listening to you—I'm not agreeing, that's all. I think of finances as financies." She paused because he didn't catch her play on words. "Finances, fancies—financies."

"Ah."

"Now it's your turn to listen to me. Just because I wasn't elected doesn't mean I don't have obligations. It's my country, too, and should you leave us, God forbid, there will be a time of troubles quite separate from the war. There are different kinds of leadership, you know, and once I am certain that the new people can carry on, I will fly home to Montpelier as though I had wings on my feet like Mercury."

"The new people had better be James and Elizabeth Monroe."

"Not until 1816."

"Not until we win the war. We won't have a party, much less a candidate, if we lose." He exhaled deeply. "Might you press a little more lightly? You won't lure me to your side by force, you know."

In her intensity, Dolley had massaged his fingers with unusual vigor. She stopped and apologized. "Oh, dear."

He withdrew his hand and wiggled his fingers. "No harm done." Then he laughed.

She reached for his hand, took it in her own, and kissed it. "I'm sorry. Why don't we consider each other's points carefully before we continue this discussion?"

"Dolley Payne Madison—and you portray Clay as a finagler."

Tears suddenly spilled from her eyes. "I hate it when you talk about dying."

He reached for her other hand. "I didn't mean to upset you. I'm sorry. You know I like to plan for things—all manner of things. Your welfare is uppermost in my mind and always will be."

"I know. But let's not speak of dying, Jemmy. There's so much living left to do." She lifted her chin as he wiped away her tears. "And we will win this war. God will not turn his back on our nation, not after what we've accomplished here. We are an infant in a world of giants, and I can't believe God let us fight so hard for our birth only to abandon us now to the British just as we are beginning to walk."

James wrapped his arms around Dolley and leaned his gray head against her cheek. He truly hoped God would shelter them, but his mind, that rational instrument of grandeur, wondered, "To what God do the British pray?"

*H*oping to give Madame Serurier an appreciation of the mechanics of democracy, Dolley escorted her to the gallery in the House of Representatives. What it gave both women was an appreciation of a good heating system. The gallery on this Wednesday morning was cold as a tomb, and apart from a few lobbyists, the women were alone.

Henry Clay, poised above his colleagues in his Speaker's chair, looked warmer than they did. His sandy hair kept falling over his high forehead, and his dark coat, well cut, accentuated his trim figure.

William Bradley of Vermont freely pulled from a bottle of liquor and passed it to his neighboring peers.

Dolley noticed Webster was drinking, too.

"How unique," the French minister's wife observed, unique being a euphemism for odd.

"The cold, I expect."

"It must be quite *froid* in Vermont then." Lisel touched her nose and cheeks, indicating that Bradley's florid, heavy-drinker's complexion was apparent even from the distance of the gallery.

"Well—yes." Dolley smiled at Lisel's quickness. "Also, they seem half-asleep today. We'll have to come back when there are fireworks."

Madame Serurier surveyed the assemblage. At that moment she couldn't imagine fireworks.

Dolley, as if reading her thoughts, pointed out Laban Wheaton of Massachusetts. "He called Mr. Clay and his war hawks 'fawning reptiles'—a phrase he borrowed from a former representative from Massachusetts. Not only is he splenetic, but poor Mr. Wheaton lacks imagination, too."

"Ah, yes. We have such men at home, too." She sat on her hands in a vain attempt to warm them. "These New England men, a thorn in your side, no?"

"In this war, yes. During our Revolution, no. You see, my dear, New England can't grow. They know that. The South, too, is trapped by her boundaries. So New England fears the West, which can grow and grow and grow."

"And what of the South?"

"They have made alliances with the West."

"Ah . . ." Madame Serurier grasped the situation instantly. "But alliances shift like sand."

Dolley nodded in agreement. "Perhaps this one won't because whatever the South's faults, its leaders understand that whoever controls the Mississippi controls the West."

"Pardon?"

"The river. New England, you see, shows no concern over the British navigating the Mississippi River after the war. Westerners know if we permit British ships on that river, we'll have to fight a third war with Britain because someday they'll block our expansion or try to claim the territories for themselves."

Madame Serurier gave up on her hands. They were tingling cold no matter what she did with them. "Odd to think of a nation still growing, like a child. You haven't reached your full height yet."

"Not by a long shot."

*D*espite the burning of Buffalo, or perhaps because of it, Dolley's Wednesday night levee sparkled more than usual.

The guests ate, drank, and heaped compliments on the turbaned head of Mrs. Madison. French John, with Uncle Willy on his shoulder, Paul Jennings, and Sukey were pressed into service because the few waiters employed couldn't handle such a large crowd. Sukey was practicing her French, spoken with French John's accent, on André Daschkov, the Russian minister. She showed more interest in serving him than in serving the others. Sukey moved with a grace that drew men's eyes as surely as her beauty did.

James Monroe, not normally an ebullient man although an approachable one, chatted amiably with Washington's mayor, James Blake.

Louis and Lisel Serurier floated about in their splendid clothes like iridescent dragonflies. Their very presence underscored the roughness of the Western gentlemen and ladies, although the Southerners were well dressed.

Anna and her husband, Richard, laughed with Massachusetts Senator Christopher Gore. That took discipline on Anna's part, since Gore had mercilessly attacked the President on the Senate floor. Dolley's sister couldn't understand how men spent their days fighting each other politically, then exchanged civilities at night. They all knew that the President's wife insisted there be no political factions at her Wednesday evening gatherings, merely friends. If men wanted to fight again the next morning, well, go to it, but Wednesday evenings were dedicated to banishing the cares of state and the cares of life.

Henry Clay and his high-spirited secretary, Henry Carroll, offered Elizabeth Monroe a slice of salty Virginia ham. Clay laughingly said he'd offer her some Kentucky whiskey but he knew Mrs. Monroe would have none of that. It was part of Clay's way with women to intimate that they were far more unconventional and daring than they truly were. Elizabeth glanced around to see whether her husband was near enough to overhear, and then she blushed and laughed.

Dolley noticed. For all of Elizabeth's pretensions, Dolley did like her and sensed that Elizabeth's withdrawn nature must make it difficult for her to mingle. That she forced herself to do it was testimony to her dedication to her husband's career. Perhaps the reserve existed to hide her shyness. Elizabeth Monroe was quite unlike Anna Maria Thornton, who was making a beeline for Serurier, probably to inflict on the Frenchman news of her husband's latest ideas. Anna Maria, although French by birth, was ardently patriotic when it came to her American husband. Recently, he had become interested in creating artificial ice. Before that, William had concocted a scheme for African colonization.

Henry Clay separated himself from Elizabeth Monroe and Henry Carroll to join Dolley for a moment.

"Thank you for paying attention to Mrs. Monroe."

"My pleasure."

"Do you like crowds, Mr. Clay?"

"Love them. I can get far more accomplished in a crowd than in my office."

"Me, too." Dolley was beginning to feel that this man, in his prime at thirty-seven, was a kindred spirit. "And what better place to tell a secret."

"Tell," Clay whispered, his eyes full of excitement.

"Webster's Achilles heel is as plain as day. Probably that's why I've missed it until now."

"And . . . ?"

"Ambition."

Clay rubbed his chin. "Most politicians entertain some ambition."

"The presidency." Dolley's tone rose.

Clay's light blue eyes clouded over for a moment. "Do you think he is—aware of this ambition?" He had too much faith in Dolley's intuition to doubt her.

"No . . . but it's there and we must help him find it."

Clay started to protest that a prideful Webster would be that much harder to combat, then remembered that it was Dolley who discreetly suggested Webster be placed on the Foreign Relations Committee. "I will find a way."

"One other small suggestion, though I'm certain you've already thought of it. I hesitate to mention it because you'll see that I am truly a turtle to your hare."

"Mrs. Madison, out with it." Clay cocked his head.

"Tie Webster to his party. Party, first. The United States, second."

Clay nearly whistled. No, he had not thought of that although in time he would have. Most Americans would indeed think twice before casting their vote for a man who put his country second, no matter how admired he was. People wanted a President above regionalism, above the narrow concerns of party. "This will, of course, redouble his efforts against the war."

"I know."

"He is brilliant."

"I know that, too, but we will *win* this war, and he will forever wear the stain of not battling the enemy." She paused, then became unusually solemn. "Politics are cruel. The times are cruel. I hate to hobble such a gifted man. I hate even to think of such—"

Henry Clay put his finger to his lips. "Shh. Don't, Mrs. Madison. Your heart puts you at a disadvantage in such matters. Believe me, he would do worse to you. And his attacks on your husband have been remorseless."

Dolley still felt guilty and Clay spoke again. "Dear Mrs. Madison, you are not responsible for this man's character. The Fates reveal who we are and what we are soon enough."

Before she could reply, William Thornton slapped Clay on the shoulder. "A word, Mr. Speaker . . . although I know no man willingly leaves Mrs. Madison's company."

Dolley smiled at Thornton as he pulled Clay to him.

"Sevens and elevens," someone whispered in Dolley's ear. She turned around to see the senator from Louisiana give her a tobacco-stained grin.

"Don't you ever tell, Senator Brown. My husband would give me a tongue-lashing that I couldn't bear." Dolley reached in her pocket and brought out the dice, only to replace them quickly. She'd taken to carrying them wherever she went, turning the cool cubes over and over in her fingers. It produced a calming effect, and Dolley needed to appear calm. She was far more worried than she wanted anyone to know.

Her first concern was Jemmy's health. After that she worried about the war and she fretted over Payne—her son could at least have written her. Dickey Cutts, almost four years old, tugged at her heart, too—he was so weak—and then she missed her sister Lucy, that indefatigable chatterbox, off in Kentucky. Mostly she worried about Jemmy, but underneath, something else stirred, too.

Dolley had set aside the more rigorous aspects of her Quaker faith. She would never quite forgive the Society of Friends for disowning her father when he went bankrupt. She expected them to disown Lucy when she married George Steptoe Washington and she thought it silly, but to cast aside John Payne, her father, a hardworking, principled man who had suffered much for his faith during the Revolutionary years—that was cruel. When she herself was disowned years later for marrying James Madison, an Episcopalian, she barely noticed. She wondered if the residue of what was good about the faith still anchored her life. Obviously the caveats against gambling, socializing, and wearing fashionable clothes had never truly reached Dolley; to look at her, one would never suspect she had endured such a strict upbringing. But the admonition never to take another human life remained with her even if she was powerless to stop the war. The longer the war continued, the more she sought diversions.

"Did you hear that I won five hundred dollars from our esteemed Speaker of the House? He can't roll the dice to save his soul." Brown gloated, interrupting her thoughts.

"No? I hear he's a wicked cardplayer."

"That man could cut cards with the Devil." Brown lowered his voice. "And before this war is over, he might have to."

Elizabeth Monroe swept over to them then. Brown bowed to her and joined Senator Rufus King, the center stone in a necklace of Federalists. Even in casual conversation the New Yorker outshone the others. His ferocious hatred of slavery inspired likeminded people but made Southerners laugh. King hated the fact that since the Negro counted for three-fifths of a white man, the South got 60 percent more representation because of its Negro population, even though those Negroes were never represented politically. Moral indignation is the plumage. Look to the bird. So people said, but King, a deeper man than that, chipped away at slavery whenever and wherever he could. The Southerners resented it, yet most of them knew slavery would drag them down. While all but a few fanatics admitted this, none knew, economically, how to extricate themselves from slavery.

Well trained in Louisiana hospitality, Senator Brown circulated among the crowd. Dolley watched him make special efforts to be pleasant to the Federalists, whom he despised. If men could make such efforts socially, then why not politically? Common cause was woefully uncommon.

Dolley turned to see Anna Maria Thornton bearing down upon

her. Even from across the room it was hard not to notice the jewels that adorned the doctor's wife.

Mrs. Thornton's earrings must have cost a king's ransom. Dolley shrewdly appraised the bright sapphires. The blue gems were usually either too pale or too muddy, but these, set off with diamonds, gleamed a rich marine blue. Jewelry was to women what rank was to military men.

"Mrs. Thornton, you shine in those sapphires." Dolley praised her as she reached them. Elizabeth Monroe simply stared at the gargantuan stones.

"My William says women are silly to be so taken with mere rocks under pressure. That's what he calls sapphires, diamonds, rubies, and emeralds. You know William, he has such a practical turn of mind . . . until it comes to horses. He's as silly about horses as he says I am about precious stones."

"A vice I do share with your indefatigable husband," Dolley confessed. "What about you, Mrs. Monroe?" Dolley saw Elizabeth hesitate, so she added, "Not that you have vices, my dear, but surely you love horses."

Mrs. Monroe cleared her throat. "I've learned to appreciate them. Mr. Monroe appreciates a good horse. He says the best judge of horses is Light-Horse Harry Lee. Now I doubt Mr. Lee can even afford a horse."

"He has the best eye for women, too." Mrs. Thornton couldn't resist.

"Well, he was always gallant but not"—Dolley weighed her words—"a cad."

"Like Daschkov," Mrs. Thornton whispered.

Both Dolley and Elizabeth leaned toward Mrs. Thornton, drawn by the irresistible force of gossip. Mrs. Thornton adjusted her careful coiffure, relishing the moment. Then she continued. "Now mind you, he is handsome in a brutal, Slavic fashion. That deep baritone voice. Oh my"—her hand fluttered—"but I've heard from friends now in Russia that mothers never left a daughter alone with him for even ten minutes, and, of course, he must have enriched the entire race of gypsies."

"What do you mean," Elizabeth Monroe whispered, "gypsies?"

"Oh, Mrs. Monroe. Forgive me. You *are* sheltered." Anna Maria Thornton couldn't abide the thought that this prim woman might be First Lady. She herself would make a better one. "The gypsies in Russia, indeed throughout most of central Europe, provide music and, shall we say, *comfort* for men who can pay for such exotic delights."

Elizabeth pursed her lips in disapproval.

Dolley laughed. "Mrs. Thornton, I shall be very careful never to leave you alone with André Daschkov."

Young Matilda Lee Love, blessed with fine, straight teeth and a perfect figure, walked over. She was the mistress of Rokeby Plantation, a large estate near Washington, across the Potomac River in Virginia. Despite her youth, she was renowned for her hospitality and good sense. "You all are as merry as grigs."

"Matilda, sweetheart." Dolley addressed Mrs. Love by her first name, which let the other two ladies know she was dear to Dolley. "I take it as my mission to keep Mrs. Thornton from the clutches of that rascally Russian."

Matilda turned her head to see where the broad-shouldered fellow was. "Ah, yes." She then turned to observe Mr. Thornton. The comparison was not favorable. "Mrs. Thornton, perhaps some clutches are more, uh, bearable than others."

Dolley doubled over. "You are wicked!"

Matilda inclined her head. She liked being thought wicked. Mrs. Thornton smiled. She would not lose ground before these two. After all, she was a woman of the world.

"Mrs. Love, you are aptly named."

Matilda hooted with laughter. "Oh, my dear Mrs. Thornton, if only I had done everything I was accused of."

"And I!" Tears ran down Dolley's cheeks, she was laughing so hard.

Even Elizabeth Monroe was laughing, although she wasn't sure she should be.

"What does the Bible say?" Mrs. Thornton struggled for the

exact words from the Old Testament. " 'Who can find a virtuous woman? for her price is far above rubies.' "

"Sapphires." Matilda pointed to Mrs. Thornton's necklace.

"You know," Anna Maria Thornton said thoughtfully, "I really don't think William bought these because of my virtue. He bought them to keep me quiet. He says I talk too much."

That did it. The ladies swayed in merriment. Maybe Mrs. Thornton did talk a stream of nine words at once to you, but she knew it, and somehow that along with her slight French accent made it all right.

As she caught her breath, Matilda held on to Dolley's arm for support. "I tease you mercilessly but you are virtuous."

"Virtue is not habit-forming," Dolley saucily replied, setting them off again.

Lisel Serurier could not stand being left out. She hurried over, leaving a congressman from Connecticut in her wake. "You ladies are having a good laugh, no?"

"Yes," Elizabeth Monroe added.

Matilda gave her the details and soon Madame Serurier was glancing at Daschkov conspiratorially. "I think he puts padding up here," she whispered, pointing to her chest.

"No!" Mrs. Thornton seized on the detail.

"We all have our little tricks." Matilda raised an eyebrow. "Remember John Randolph trying to lower his high voice by—?"

Mrs. Thornton interrupted. "Well, he's insane. Truly. Just yesterday my William was making notes for better treatment of the insane."

"Spending a lot of time in the congressional gallery, no doubt." Dolley was feeling devilish.

"Why, no . . ." Then Mrs. Thornton got the joke.

Madame Serurier caught Dolley's eye and laughed. Her laughter sounded like a harp glissando. Madame felt closer to Mrs. Madison than to other American women, who seemed drab and one-dimensional to her. She had once confided to Dolley that trying to make conversation with an American lady forced her to expand her vocabulary on the weather, child care, and clothing. Accustomed to the courts of Europe, she expected bracing discussions of politics, the arts, and the world. She valued Dolley because she also enjoyed such discussions. Yet Madame observed how the President's wife avoided detailed political topics in public. The more she knew of America, the more she appreciated Dolley's tactics.

Mrs. Thornton complained that the British had driven down cotton and tobacco prices. Madame Serurier listened intently. Mrs. Thornton ventured a bit out of the safe realm, but not too far. Madame Serurier expressed her concern and sympathy, as did Mrs. Madison, yet neither woman had ever heard a convincing explanation of how the British devalued Southern goods whose prices had started to slide before the war. Commerce, like the wheel of fortune, rolled and rolled. When it was up, everyone decided their unusual intelligence had created good fortune; when down, the bad fortune was always somebody else's fault.

This fault was laid at James Madison's door by the Federalists. Out of the corner of her eye Dolley observed two of her husband's more outspoken enemies putting their heads together. In the absence of John Randolph, Michael Lieb, senator from Pennsylvania, had snatched the mantle of hostility for himself, although he could not match Randolph's rancor. While he ate from the President's table, he managed to suggest to the other guests that Madison was a fool. According to Lieb, James Madison had been lied to by the French and believed them. He'd been lied to by the British and believed them, too. Napoleon promised not to sell off the United States ships he had seized, then sold them anyway. The only reason the United States went to war against Britain instead of against France was that the British had been stealing longer.

Christopher Gore was a good Federalist, giving Michael Lieb his full attention. Gore was pro-British, and the Boston bankers were still lending money to Britain. Gore would never offend a Boston banker, and if some of that money financed Britain's war effort—well, he didn't know about it.

Dolley edged closer to overhear.

Gore listened to Lieb recalling how the British minister to the

United States, with his pretty American wife, had promised to back down over shipping rights. The minister even hinted that British ports in the Western Hemisphere, closed to Americans, would be opened. He lied outright but he had fooled Madison. His replacement, Francis James Jackson, far less attractive a liar, was soon recalled to the motherland to save him from death at the hands of the irate Americans.

Gore laughed. "They recalled him before our President had ample opportunity to believe him, too."

"That gave Clay and Calhoun the last straw to break the camel's back." Lieb lowered his voice as he saw Clay approaching.

"Gentlemen."

"Mr. Speaker."

"It's black as the Devil's eyebrows outside—or Daniel Webster's."

They smiled at this while the mayor of Washington joined them. Clay put his arm around James Blake's broad back. "Jimmy, when are we going to get some street lamps?"

"We've got three on Pennsylvania Avenue."

"Those were put in nearly fifteen years ago." Gore, fussy about his clothing, fiddled with his coat sleeve.

"And you congressmen didn't leave the great city of Washington any money to maintain them," Jimmy Blake replied.

"I thought the citizens whose homes are graced by these torches of freedom from the night paid for their own maintenance." Clay finished his drink. He needed another.

"Does that mean we have only three rich families in Washington?" Lieb asked with good humor.

James Blake smiled a tight smile. "We have rich folks aplenty, but they keep their money in their home states. Washington is left to fend for itself. I am quite sure you have street lamps all over Philadelphia, Senator."

Henry Clay laughed. Good for James Blake. Why, they'd both have another drink.

Clay and the mayor left the two Federalists to chat with Dolley, who had now taken over the tea-pouring duties from Anna. Every lady present knew one brought the teacup to the pot, never the other way around. When the duty became arduous, Dolley would enlist another lady to take over for a while, always a feather in that lady's cap. It was important for the husbands to see their wives honored.

Dolley laughed at Clay's recounting of James Blake's remark. Her turban wobbled, and Clay quickly placed his hand on the brilliant jade material.

"My dear Mrs. Madison, I don't want you to lose your head."

"I imagine the British would sing at such an occurrence." Dolley reached up to straighten her headdress.

Uncle Willy screamed whenever he heard his mistress laugh. He screamed a lot that night.

"French John, give him some cake. He can't holler when he's eating."

"Did you teach him not to speak with his mouth full? My children haven't yet learned that lesson." Clay smiled.

Minister Serurier walked over and held out his teacup.

"Tea?" Dolley questioned. The minister usually enjoyed stronger drink.

"Perhaps it will settle my stomach."

"A smooth Kentucky bourbon will help that." Clay offered a sip from his glass.

"Mr. Speaker, I marvel at the wonders of the New World: Turkeys. Red savages. Bourbon. Had you concocted this elixir later in your history, it would have been called Napoleon, or Bonaparte, *n'est-ce pas?*"

"I never thought of that." Clay's features relaxed for a moment. "Whatever we call our liquor, two facts remain: we will forever be indebted to the French people for their assistance during our first war with Britain and"—he held up his glass—"our spirits are strong."

"I think, monsieur, that my people and your people will always have a common enemy in England."

"One other." Clay nodded.

"What?"

"The stupidity of the narrow-minded and the greedy."

"Ah yes." Serurier passed his cup to Dolley. "But they exist in every nation. At home we bestow honors upon them. They spend so much time brandishing their prestige, they haven't time to meddle in politics."

"The genius of a Bourbon, Louis XIV." Dolley referred to the Sun King, who had perfected the art of deflecting political ambition into social ambition.

"Do you ever wish your husband could be King?" Serurier asked.

Dolley considered a flippant answer, disregarded it, and said, "The four-year term of our presidency forces a man to waste time planning for his reelection. Even if our President is granted two terms, it's difficult to plan and even more difficult to enact those plans. Whatever one builds can be dismantled by the succeeding President, especially if he is from the opposing party. So, plans of state resemble a patchwork quilt rather than an organized design. This is our great weakness and yet, Monsieur Minister, a king is even more vulnerable than a president for he rarely hears the truth. Since a king holds the position for life, those around him tiptoe—after all, they could be banished for his lifetime. To make good decisions, one needs the facts, flattering to oneself or not. We can only pray that those who do succeed us can appreciate the wisdom of our good decisions and have the wit to correct our failures."

Both Clay and Serurier were silent for a moment, then Louis reached out for his now-filled cup. "Mrs. Madison, you have settled my mind. Now I do hope this settles my stomach."

A sly smile crossed his face. "Do you know that George III conceives of himself as a teapot?"

"Then we'll just have to empty the pot, won't we, sir?"

5 January 1814, Wednesday

I'm too tired to commit much to paper this evening and too lazy to sharpen my quill. On the surface, the evening was a success, yet the Federalists are sharpening their claws. That they want a Federalist

President elected in 1816 is as it should be. Such is the nature of politics. But if the war continues to go badly for us, they will hog-tie Jemmy if they can.

Had a good talk with Henry Clay. What would I do without him?

James Monroe has received communication from England. Jemmy says one could hardly call it a peace offering. I meant to mark that down the other night but it slipped my mind. If only we had some victories! Then we could construct a peace on favorable terms.

I believe that James Monroe is a good Secretary of State and I know Jemmy does also, but he will never quite trust him. I say bury the past, but Jemmy can't forgive Monroe for allying himself with Patrick Henry against him. The decades haven't erased Jemmy's reserve toward Monroe. I think men cling to these grudges in a way women do not. But then, were I running for office, or holding one, perhaps I would feel differently.

Monsieur Serurier told me that George III, when he went mad, once imagined he was a teapot. Since the Prince Regent remains in charge, perhaps George is still bubbling. Yet, what a terrible thing. I can't find it in my heart to wish insanity on the King. Patrick Henry was Mother's cousin; when I was a child, his wife, Sarah, lost her mind. Cousin Patrick had to confine her to a downstairs room and sometimes tie her up for fear she would hurt herself. I fear insanity more than I fear death.

Perhaps that's why I fear Randolph. He has been mercifully quiet. Daniel Webster, Lieb, and Gore are more present dangers but they are rational men, misguided but rational.

Can't hold up my head.

Until the morrow, God willing.

D.P.M.

A wind like a knife slashed off the Potomac into Henry Carroll's bones. Clay's secretary would make his first stop far out on New York Avenue, a desolate road. Two small but neat houses shivered in the darkness. If there were more homes out this way, Henry Carroll never saw them. This wasn't a fashionable area, nor was it a fashionable distance from the Capitol.

He knocked on the door, painted a deep blue. French John opened it, revealing a household full of lively progeny and a pretty wife. Henry tipped his hat and handed French John a letter to be given to Mrs. Madison.

"Won't you come in, Mr. Carroll?" The swarthy man spoke in his ineradicable French accent. French John was sincere and, like Dolley, was a genuinely hospitable person.

"Thank you, Mr. Sioussat. I'm still making the rounds."

Henry retraced his steps, moving faster as the cold gnawed through his coat and gloves. His nose dripped from the chill. A high wagon with red-painted wheels swayed in the frozen ruts of the road. Two muscular mules pulled the load of firewood. The driver could have been fat or thin. He was so bundled up, Henry couldn't tell. The fellow stopped when Henry flagged him. He didn't recognize James Smith, a free Negro, until he climbed up in the wagon next to him and Smith unwound the scarf covering his face to say hello.

He pressed twenty-five cents into Smith's mitten, a good piece of change, and asked Smith to take him to Georgetown. He had wanted to save the money, but the cold was so fierce he decided it would be better to ride. Henry Clay had given him two dollars for tonight's errands, and one of the best things about working for the Speaker of the House was that he never minded if Carroll found a cheaper way to do something and pocketed the savings.

"Going that way, Mr. Carroll, going that way."

Henry hung on to the sides of the wagon as it violently hit ruts and mudholes. He was glad to reach Georgetown and get back on his feet.

Henry hopped off a block from the boardinghouse where Senators Christopher Gore of Massachusetts, Jeremiah Mason of New Hampshire, and Rufus King of New York, and Representative Daniel Webster from New Hampshire, took lodgings. He leaned against a building, back to the wind, and waited. One man passed him, drunk as a skunk. He wouldn't do. Two representatives walked by, hunched over against the cold. Carroll turned his head. They didn't notice him. Finally a boy, perhaps fourteen, scurried along carrying an unplucked chicken. Henry laid his hand on the youth's arm, pointed to the boardinghouse, and gave the boy twenty-five cents. "Twenty-five cents to walk across the street."

"What, sir?"

"Just take this letter over there."

"Yes, sir!" The happy fellow snatched the money and the letter and ran across the street.

Henry smiled and then walked to John Calhoun's lodging house, which was not far off.

Most secretaries to senators and representatives wrote in a similar hand. Since there was no signature on the letter he had just had delivered to Daniel Webster, the New Englander would not know it came from Henry Clay.

The brass knocker of Calhoun's boardinghouse, called the War Mess by his enemies, barely gleamed in the pitch of the night. A haughty, high-yellow servant, Tosh, dressed far better than Henry Carroll, opened the door. Recognizing Henry, he smiled politely and said he would fetch Mr. Calhoun. Henry handed him a letter and said there was no need to disturb the master. The butler bowed low and allowed as how he would deliver the letter. Henry touched his hat and left.

A haggard John Calhoun, bent over his desk studying a map of

Europe, blinked when the butler quietly knocked. He took the envelope off the silver tray and dismissed Tosh.

John Calhoun opened the letter and read its contents:

> I expect your full support.
> Henry Clay

6 January 1814, Thursday

*T*oday I had the strangest experience. I walked over to Anna's to
see whether Dickey had improved, and when I turned into F
Street, I thought I saw Aaron Burr. Were he in town, I'm sure I would
have heard of it. The man is alive and yet a ghost, a figure from a
Greek tragedy, doomed to live forever in the shadow of his victim,
Hamilton. *Sic transit gloria.*

It was Aaron Burr who introduced Jemmy and me. He knew
Jemmy from the College of New Jersey in Princeton, where Aaron's
father (also Aaron Burr) was president. Aaron Burr introduced me to
Jemmy in Philadelphia, where I also knew Alexander Hamilton, of
King's College. Everyone liked everyone then. How fresh and hopeful
we are when young, and then God works His will upon us, or perhaps we do it ourselves. I remember once, when talking to Clay, the
name of Burr crept into the conversation; Clay just sighed and said,
"The mighty fall, the rest just grow older."

I keep thinking of the orphans in Buffalo. It's wicked-cold here.
Buffalo must be a frozen hell.

French John brought me a letter from Henry Clay. One sentence:
"Paris has shot his arrow at Achilles."

I suppose politics has always been fussing, fighting, bombast, and
false bravado. It seems to provide a theater for strutting banty roosters. Truly, it's a wonder anything ever gets done.

And it's so expensive. The treasury is empty and my pantry is
bare. I have been successful in keeping our money woes from Jemmy.
He frets over his mother's managing Montpelier in such distressing
times. Even with a good crop the market is far from certain, and every

day our currency's value dips. How much longer can I give merchants here promissory notes? At least Mother Madison can barter.

Heartache is one terrible worry. Money is another. I don't know which is worse. Oh, I'm just saying that because I've got empty pockets now. Sometimes I can't see any farther than my nose!

I can't pull myself up today. Usually a visit with friends or a prayer will lift my spirits, but today I feel like Mother Amy, who when sad would say, "I gots the low blood."

I gots the low blood.

Until the morrow, God willing.

D.P.M.

"Mommy!" Five-year-old Walter ran into the room. "Tommy says I can hab his soldier."

Curly-haired Tommy Cutts hastened into the room to remove the little lead soldier from Walter's white-knuckled grasp. "Did not."

"Walter, it's have, not hab."

"See, Mommy says I can hab it!" Walter crowed.

"I said no such thing." Anna stood up with a rustle of material. "Jimmy, Jimmy, where are you?"

James, the eldest at eight and a half, reluctantly entered the room. "Yes, Mother."

"I told you to watch your brothers. Aunt Dolley and I are busy. Now where's Dickey?"

"He's asleep."

"And Dolley Payne?"

"She's asleep, too."

"Where are they asleep?"

"On the floor."

"Why didn't you make them get into bed?"

"You didn't tell me to."

At that moment Anna could have cuffed him. Dolley stifled a giggle, which made Anna want to smack her older sister, as well. A wail from Walter indicated that Tommy had seized his lead soldier by force, not negotiation.

"That does it! I want you boys in your room and if I hear so much as a peep, a whisper, I can tell you the names of three boys who are not getting sugar cookies."

"Oh, Mother." Jimmy loved sugar cookies.

"Jimmy, you put Dolley Payne in her bed and Tommy, pick up Dickey."

"He's too heavy," Tommy fudged, for little Dickey was thin as a reed.

Anna advanced on Tommy, who prudently took a step backward. "One more word out of you, Thomas Cutts, and you're going to wish you were somebody else. Now get, all of you!"

The boys scattered and Anna, flushed, sat down with a plop.

Dolley shook her head, "I haven't heard that expression since Mother Amy."

"What?" Anna was still steaming.

" 'You're going to wish you were somebody else.' As I recall, that was followed by the swat of her broom."

"You used to say that to me when I was little. You were besotted with power."

"That's always the lament of little sisters," Dolley replied.

"Lucy agrees with me."

"Two against one. No fair." Dolley laughed, and Anna joined in.

Anna sighed and leaned back in her chair, putting her feet out. Dolley pushed a small hassock over for her. "Thank you. I've been on my feet all day with those rascals. If only this city would get a good school. The children are cooped up in the winter and if they're going to be wild Indians, I prefer they be wild somewhere else." She sighed again, then changed the subject. "Sukey spends more time prancing about your levees than Mrs. Thornton. She flirted openly with André Daschkov as well as casting her big, beautiful eyes on Senator Brown from Louisiana. That girl is wild as a rat."

"Oh, Anna, you always did have an imagination for that sort of thing."

"No, I don't. You just can't see what's under your nose. You never want to see what's unpleasant."

"What's so unpleasant about a beautiful slave girl flirting? I can't see that it's so awful."

"She ought to be better behaved. And she's pouty."

"You discipline her. I can't keep after her all the time and perform my other duties. Which reminds me, James and I were sitting up talking the other night. I could scarcely believe I had my husband to myself for a few moments—"

Anna interrupted. "I know what you mean." Then she laughed. "But every time I do get Richard to myself, I wind up with another wild Indian."

Dolley put her feet up on the hassock also and tapped her sister's foot with her own. "Many are the women who would pray for such a complaint."

Anna raised an eyebrow. "Dolley, I didn't mean that the way it sounded."

"I know. Anyway, I wasn't talking about myself. I was talking about those women, some of whom we know, whose husbands aren't interested in them anymore. The men use their homes like a boardinghouse."

"A legion of women, I'd say. Poor things." Anna shook her head. "Maybe they shouldn't have gotten married in the first place."

"It's all a crapshoot, isn't it?"

"A what?" Anna's eyes grew larger.

"Uh, a crapshoot. Dice. Seven or eleven and . . . now, Anna, don't frown. It's not a vulgar expression, it's a sporting expression. I was merely making a parallel to the fact that marriage is a game of chance." Dolley folded her hands in her lap.

"Are you gambling again?"

"I most certainly am not."

"You know that affliction runs in our family."

"Oh stop, Anna, you sound like Father. Any time one of us did something he disapproved of—and think how many things he disapproved of—he'd say, 'That's just like my mother.' Fond of gambling, fond of fripperies, or whatever. I thought Grandmother Payne quite grand myself."

"I wish I could say I remembered her clearly. After all, I'm named for her."

"She loved society, loved to laugh—and oh, Anna, her clothes! The most exquisite silks. She never could understand Father but then he could never understand her."

"How did you learn to play dice?" Anna was not to be put off by reminiscence.

Dolley reached in her pocket and pulled out the white cubes. "A little bird taught me."

Anna reached for the dice but Dolley withdrew them. "Let me see them."

"Don't tell Jemmy."

"I won't." Anna felt the two cubes drop in her hand. She turned them over in her fingers. "Is this what the Roman guards used when they cast for Christ's robe?"

"I wasn't there. I'm not that old."

Anna didn't want to laugh at what might be regarded as a mild blasphemy, but she did. "Well, all of Mother's religious efforts failed with you." She thought a moment. "With me, too, I suppose. She was too strict. They're all too strict. If the Society of Friends would enjoy dancing and music and clothing, they would attract more people than they do with their severity. I can't say that I ever found anything in their teachings that wasn't—helpful."

Dolley reached out a cupped hand and Anna dropped the dice into it. "I guess I would have to agree, although I'll never forgive them for casting out Father. Oh, I never told you what Jemmy and I were talking about. I was telling him that Sukey is getting out of hand, and then I reminded him that my father, being a good Quaker, freed all his slaves, and do you know what Jemmy said?" Anna shook her head and Dolley continued. "He said, 'And your father went bankrupt.' That was so unlike Jemmy."

"He's tired, he's besieged, and he has only four friends in Washington: you, me, my husband, and Henry Clay."

"The other night he was talking about dying. He told me if he died in office, I was to go to Montpelier."

Anna's face darkened for an instant. "He's just—"

"I know, I know." Dolley waved her hand to stop her sister. "Tired. It's not the British I fear so much. They aren't going to shoot Jemmy. Kill their prize when they could capture him? Never. No, Anna, it's these fanatics. What if someone walks up and shoots him?"

"Assassinate Jemmy?" The thought was so horrifying that

Anna's hand flew to her mouth as if to shut off the thought. "Put a guard around the presidential mansion."

"We can't do that. Then we'd be no better than the kings and queens of the Old World. The President must be available to his people. Think how it would look. Think what it would mean—that we are afraid of our own people, and a president afraid of his own people ought not to be governing the land."

"Perhaps in certain situations men are not governable." Anna's emotions spun around inside her. "Didn't the Romans elect a temporary dictator in perilous times? Cincinnatus at the plow—the citizens came to ask him to lead Rome against an invading army."

"I remember. And I still say we can't post a guard, and Jemmy wouldn't hear of it even if I begged him. The Father of the Constitution hiding behind soldiers. Wouldn't the British papers bleat and holler over that?"

"Ours aren't much better."

"Well, no." Dolley thought a moment. "I've always wondered why bad news sells papers."

"You can pick up the news and know that someone is worse off than you are." Anna heard a yelp in the back room. "Well, there's the first peep."

"More like a howl, I'd say."

The two sisters rose and tiptoed to the boys' room, where they were greeted by the spectacle of Tommy and Walter tied back-to-back. A handkerchief filled Walter's mouth, but Tommy must have managed to spit his out because he was the one yelping. James jumped in surprise when his aunt and mother descended on him.

"James, what is this?"

"You told me to keep them quiet."

7 January 1814, Friday

John Randolph's pen, dipped in venom, has found its mark. Anna told me today that she heard from Mrs. Thornton that Randolph has begun writing, with monotonous frequency, to his boon companion, the president of the Bank of Virginia. I know Dr. John Brocken-brough, and he is an honorable man even if he is a dear friend of John Randolph's. I believe he's the only man that unhappy soul has never turned on.

Dr. Brockenbrough, being a Virginian, would rather win the war than lose, but bankers, fearful creatures that they are, seem to be more Federalist than Republican in hue. If Dr. Brockenbrough shares these letters, which will multiply like rabbits, with his financial com-peers, the contents will certainly find their way into the hands of New England's bankers. If William Thornton has heard of the letters, I can be sure they are well on their way toward wide distribution. Daniel Webster will make good use of them. On the surface, Randolph and Webster never would agree on anything. But loyalties have shifted. Party politics are shifting, too. Randolph's brilliance feeding Web-ster's budding oratory—horrible thought!

We don't know what is in those letters, but they won't deal affec-tionately with my husband.

Oh, Randolph, decrying the pains of pestilential society, how he wants to be free of society. He says he wants to be alone but everyone knows where to find him.

I must get French John to see if he can't find out more about this.

I received a letter today from my sweet Lucy. She won't be spend-ing the rest of the winter or the spring in the capital this year. If only she would. When Lucy, Anna, and I are together, we can find the humor in the worst of situations, and this is the worst of them. But with a houseful of little judges, as she calls her children, she thinks she must stay in Lexington this winter. She promises that she is going to make up for this self-denial, though, and visit for the entire season next year. Won't that be merry?

What good times we've had. And when sister Mary was alive—well, as Anna used to say, the more the merrier, and then she'd tweak Mary. Now Mary's gone and all my brothers, too, except John Coles Payne, trying to do his duty in this war as an assistant quartermaster. John is so much younger than I, we never grew close. And the drink-ing—well, that's painful to bear. He stops and sometimes goes with-out alcohol for months. If he married, perhaps a wife would steady him. Mother used to say that a man without a woman was like a ship without a rudder.

I have observed that drinking seems to pass through generations in families and I find it peculiar that Mother and Father did not drink, yet John does. I still believe that's what killed my Isaac. Under the influence he offended someone, and he was shot the next day as he left his house. That was January 1795, and my older brother, Temple, died that same month of sickness.

As far as I know, neither of my grandparents drank to excess, although William Coles, Mother's father, fully appreciated celebrations; but I never knew of his drinking on a regular basis.

I am very grateful that not one of us girls is so afflicted or my darling Payne, either.

So many deaths in January and October, too. Cruel months for me.

On this day in 1790 I married John Todd. He courted me for three years and I didn't want to get married, but there didn't seem to be anything else I could do. Once I was married, I was glad he had been so persistent. He was twenty-six years old and I was twenty-two. It's hard to remember being that young.

How handsome John was and how unconcerned with the follies of this world, as a good Quaker should be. I was never too successful at that, and he would chide me for being pulled in the direction of worldliness. Then he'd laugh out loud and pull out a ribbon for me. He could never refuse me anything.

I thought all marriages were as happy as my own, and then I learned that some of my dearest friends were savaged by their own husbands. They bore these blows in silence, but blackened eyes and bruises are difficult to conceal. I know John would never have taken a hand to me, but if he had, I would have hit him back. A Quaker is never supposed to strike in violence, but there's enough Irish blood in me to do so. I want to believe that peacefulness creates peacefulness, and yet my experience of the world leads me to other, more sorrowful conclusions.

I never knew how much I loved John until I looked at the husbands of my friends, and I guess I never truly knew how much I loved him until he died. October 1793. We had less than four years together. Our son died then, too. Mother died in October 1805. Mother Amy died in October 1792, which broke Mother's heart.

Why is it that we don't realize how much we love others until we lose them? If only I had told John how much I loved him. He told me in a thousand ways and none more convincing than his ride back to Gray's Ferry, only hours from death, riding all the way from Philadelphia so that he could see my face one last time.

May God forgive me for not knowing what I had in John Todd. May God forgive me for not telling him that he was worth the whole lot of men in Pennsylvania. Instead, I wept on his grave.

May God forgive me now. I hope in remembering my first husband I am not in some way taking from my second. But I learned, and I tell Jemmy every day that I love him. In the beginning of our marriage he used to blush. I believe now that it fortifies him. I tell him each night before falling asleep, and if he works late, then I leave a note on his pillow or notes on his desk since sometimes he will awake in the middle of the night and go to work.

If there is another world beyond this world—I fear I do not have the easy assurance of other Christians—if there is, I long to meet my John Todd again to thank him from the bottom of my heart for teaching me how to love and be loved.

Until the morrow, God willing.

D.P.M.

A rare sunny day pushed the temperature up into the mid-fifties. Dolley, Madame Serurier, and Anna seized the opportunity and rode to the outskirts of town in Madame's carriage, accompanied by French John astride one of the sorrels. Madame Serurier's driver, in clothes so exotic that he was the envy of all, carried on a lively conversation with Jean Pierre Sioussat.

Both men had been promised to the Church and had endured the spartan rigor of a Roman Catholic education. French John escaped the fate planned for him when he pushed a corpulent priest out of a church window and followed this rash act by running away to sea.

The driver laughed at French John's account and said his own exit from Mother Church, barren of such drama, occurred because he cried so piteously when his mother came to visit him that she freed him from his bondage.

French John asked him if he had seen the execution of Louis XVI, and the driver, glum for a moment, replied that yes, he had seen it and could perfectly recall the sight of the King's head held high before the bloodthirsty mob. The blood still gushed from the severed neck and the eyes, wide open, bulged as if in horror at the spectacle to which it contributed. Remember it? He would never forget it.

French John nodded. In January 1793 his own father had held him up high so that he could see. That October he had also seen the Queen beheaded. He didn't care what the crowd screamed; he pitied her.

Delicacy forbade French John from accurately describing how he had become an American. He was serving on a French frigate bound for Baltimore to fetch the unhappy Jerome Bonaparte back to his brother, Napoleon. Jerome had married Elizabeth Patterson, reputed to be the most beautiful woman in the New World, and saw no need to hasten back to the cauldron of European troubles.

When Baltimore hove into view, French John decided without a moment's reflection that this was where he belonged. When the night watchman lit his pipe, French John slid down a rope and swam to shore. That was in 1805 and he had no regrets.

As for the British pigs, let them come. He would smack them on the snout.

The Seruriers' driver agreed. To be French meant to despise the British.

Dolley poked her head out the window. "I do wish you'd speak in English, French John; you know how my French wobbles."

"Mrs. Madison, you would be bored to hear this tale in English."

"You've never bored me for an instant."

"Because to be in your presence brings out the best in every man." He swept his cap in a grand gesture.

The driver laughed. French John's importance grew in his eyes.

Dolley's majordomo smiled. As the ladies chatted, he asked the driver if he had heard anything of European news. He especially wanted to know about the Emperor, whom he pretended to admire. Truthfully, French John preferred that Napoleon should conquer rather than be conquered, but as an American he wished most of all that Americans would profit from whatever happened across the ocean.

"Ah, well, you know," the driver said, "in the beginning the Emperor swept all before him, but his enemies have studied his tactics. He has taught them how to fight him."

"Napoleon is a military genius."

"*Oui.*" The driver agreed. "No man will ever equal Napoleon but . . ."—he glanced around to see if Madame Serurier was listening and she was not—"France has been fighting for years now. How many more men can we lose? How much more money can we spend? Men do not fight for free, even in the service of freedom."

French John wondered what would happen to the minister and his wife if Napoleon was defeated. The forces of reaction would reinstate fat, idiotic Louis XVIII. Would the Seruriers be recalled, imprisoned, killed? Far better for them to stay here. He kept these thoughts to himself.

He had seen much of the world. America lacked polish, and the Westerners were little better than savages, but he had made a good life for himself in this country, a life he could not have duplicated in France.

No matter how sophisticated the country of his birth, neither France nor any other European nation could stay out of war with its neighbors. He hated the British. He hated this war and he prayed to Great God Almighty that America would win and then have the sense never to become embroiled in a European conflict. A thousand years of culture. Two thousand years of culture. Great Rome and Paris and Vienna and London. Yet all they could do was drag one another into rivers of blood. America was so big. Whole sections were just waiting for bold people to settle them. Why, this nation didn't need other countries. Europe could go to hell.

"French John."

"*Oui,* Mrs. Madison."

"How come you're so quiet now?"

"I want to hear what you ladies are saying." He leaned back toward the passengers. "You know, women used to rule the world until they got men to do it for them. I am hoping I'll learn something."

This was met with peals of laughter, an antidote to the tensions building in the city.

8 January 1814, Saturday

*R*ode into the country with Madame Serurier and Anna today. Anna eats everything in sight. This sounds familiar.

Madame delighted me as usual.

French John, who rode along, told me the driver is losing his enthusiasm for war and by inference we can assume that the French people are, too.

He also told me that Henry Carroll delivered a letter to him informing him that the House of Representatives might prove high entertainment in the next week. The maneuvering for votes has begun in earnest now. We must have more troops. I gave him permission to attend if he wishes.

Sukey and Elizabeth Monroe's servant, Toffey, exchanged harsh words, and Sukey won't tell me the cause except to say that Toffey is dim-witted. According to Elizabeth, Toffey accuses Sukey of using her position to boss the other servants, and she hinted darkly that Sukey is a creature of unbridled passion.

There's a war on, and the wife of the President and the wife of the Secretary of State waste their time mollifying their servants. I know what Mother Amy would do but I haven't the heart. I don't believe in taking the strap to anyone—I wonder sometimes, if I had, would my Payne be more disciplined?

I don't want James to get wind of Sukey's behavior. He takes these things to heart and he'll go over to the Monroes' and try to put things right.

Slavery, the worm in the apple! When my father freed our slaves, I thought that would be the end of this issue for me. James feels the same as I do, but he won't free his slaves as long as his mother is alive. Mother Madison can't manage a five-thousand-acre estate alone, and James can't afford to hire enough help. We can't manage the estate either. I put it to my husband that we may have to sell some of our land—indeed, a great deal of our land.

He said, "We'll cross that bridge when we come to it." That made me laugh because Jemmy rarely uses the little clichés that make communication so much easier for the rest of us.

Mother Madison mentioned in her letter the other day that she had heard the British were threatening to march inland. For spite they intend to pay her a visit. So much the worse for the British. Mother Madison does not shine on trespassers.

In a housecleaning fit today—Uncle Willy waddled along at my feet—I uncovered a book on rabies sent to me some years ago by its author, James Thacher, a physician from Massachusetts. I remember that I wrote and thanked him, but I wondered if Dr. Thacher was making a sly comment on my temperament. Uncle Willy has chewed the corners and made a few deposits on the cover. The bird is becoming a literary critic.

Until the morrow, God willing.

D.P.M.

10 January 1814, Monday

*T*he cook performed miracles tonight. We gave a dinner honoring Mr. and Mrs. Monroe. Forty attended. It's impossible to find anything now other than fresh meat, but jams, jellies, and the ever-serviceable potato, in a variety of guises, made up for the lack of green. I had to borrow money from Anna because the butcher refused to extend my account. Anna has so little money I hated to do it, but I'll rummage through my things. Surely I can find something to sell. Naturally, I'll pay my debt to Anna first.

Mother Amy used to say you can't sit down to eat if there isn't something green on the plate, but then Mother Amy could consume a gallon of collards steeped in pork fat. She was one of the healthiest women I've ever seen.

I made Sukey stay out of sight because of her recent troubles with Toffey.

Madame Serurier commented that she thought my practice of having small dinner parties to honor various people a splendid idea, but that she couldn't understand why the President sat in the middle of the table while Ned Coles and I sat at the ends. I told her that Jemmy, not the most comfortable man in large groups of people, enjoys himself much more if he doesn't have to be in charge of passing the food about. She also confided that the first time she sat at our table, she was amazed to find all the courses on the table at once. I told her frankly that it cut down on the number of outside waiters I must hire. When I told her my operating budget, she nearly swooned.

I explained to her that Ned Coles is my cousin and as the President's secretary, he is delighted to perform the duties of the head of the table. The Federalists attacked Ned, too, saying he got the job because of family connections. Is there anyone in Washington who *doesn't* have employment because of family connections? Last year, with Ned desperately ill, I discovered how good a secretary he really is. Naturally I didn't inform Madame Serurier of that.

Ned is so deeply opposed to slavery that he has told both Jemmy and me that as soon as this war is over, he will be moving to one of the Western Territories, probably Illinois. He intends to free all his slaves and start anew. Freeing the slaves will leave him close to destitute, but he says he doesn't care about the money. He cares more about his soul.

Jemmy has asked James Monroe to act informally as a liaison between himself and the House of Representatives. Albert Gallatin performed this service and with his absence on the peace commission (he has still not been approved!), James's relations with the House are languishing. Tactfully, I suggested to Mr. Monroe that he enlist John Calhoun to help him perform this duty. I did this privately, of course. And since I, and everyone else, believe that James Monroe will be the Republican candidate for President in 1816, this will send Floride Calhoun to her husband's side as soon as she gives birth and is able to travel. She now awaits this happy event in Bath, South Carolina.

Calhoun, who really is a handsome man, needs the softening influence of his wife. He is even worse at small talk than Jemmy is. And what is so curious is that among family and dear friends, my husband is a lively conversationalist and truly funny. Once at Thomas Jefferson's house, Jemmy made a witty remark and Jefferson, not the most easily humored of men, began laughing. Well, the sight of Thomas Jefferson laughing made Jemmy laugh even harder, and he tipped back in his chair and fell out the window. Beautiful as Monticello is, I have never thought those three sash windows practical. What a pity that the public will never see Jemmy's humorous side.

The Federalists began a campaign in the House today. They're howling against the war and most especially the embargo. I don't believe they'll stop until each and every Federalist speaks. In this city, the wolves gather at noon.

Until the morrow, God willing.

D.P.M.

A driving rain illustrated the flaws remaining in the unfinished Capitol. The north wing, completed seven years ago in 1807, leaked like a sieve. An unpainted, long wooden shed connected the two wings of the building. It, too, leaked.

Dolley, Anna, and Madame Serurier dodged raindrops to squeeze into the gallery. From time to time a wet plop alerted them to the dolorous fact that the roof over the House chamber was not as tight as it should be.

Down below, Daniel Webster looked as though he was drenched by the storm. His black curls hung limp, his great black eyes flashed, the sweat rolled down the sides of his face. Only the purple-bordered toga was missing.

Henry Clay, from the rostrum, endured Webster's first great speech. Dolley looked around the chamber as Webster continued his merciless attack on the poor prosecution of the war. All around her, journalists scribbled on their pads. Webster, shrewdly, turned from time to time to address the gallery. He was now ripping into the embargo and the non-importation acts, which he believed, as did every Federalist, had created the severe depression.

When he finally sat down, the Federalists erupted in an uproar of delight. They leaped out of their seats to surround their young lion.

People shouted from the gallery. Madame Serurier watched this raucous demonstration with interest.

Anna cupped her hand around her mouth so that Dolley could hear, "If only we could answer his attacks!"

Dolley reached over and squeezed her hand. She said nothing. She would play patience.

"*D*aniel Webster sees himself as an apprentice to the future," James Madison wryly noted after listening to the Secretary of State's report on Webster's fiery denunciation of Administration policies.

As soon as the roof-rattling speech had concluded, John Calhoun informed James Monroe, who then informed the President, who had already been informed by his wife. The President kept that to himself.

"He certainly promotes his opinions with extreme eagerness, although to date, they are a reflection of Federalist principle. We've heard it all before." Monroe rubbed his cleft chin, which gave him a pronounced masculine appearance. "He simply says it with more flamboyance."

"Acting." Madison twirled the quill in his hand, then stood up from behind his desk. He began pacing. "I suppose politicians *are* actors. 'All the world's a stage, . . .' Well, at least he didn't call me Napoleon's lackey."

"No." James Monroe remained on his feet while Madison walked back and forth.

"Mr. Secretary, please sit down. I appreciate your honoring protocol, but you should not be discomfited because of my habits." As Monroe reluctantly sat down, James Madison continued. "Congress must appropriate more money for troops or suffer the indignity of a surrender, which will be placed at the Federalists' doorstep. In fact, they'll hail it as an act of reason. We've got to find money for Mayor James Blake as well. Washington's militia . . ." He paused in his pacing and shook his head. "Secretary Jones appears to grasp the situation whereas Armstrong does not, but I can't ask the Secretary of the Navy to oversee a militia."

Monroe nodded. A former Army man, he understood the rivalry between the Army and the Navy. The city was woefully undefended. What passed for a militia was no more than a raggle-taggle band of older men. No weapons had been issued to them and each man was expected to purchase his own uniform.

What compounded the difficulties was that both the President and his Secretary of State thought that military suppliers were delivering an inferior grade of materials, delivering them late, and charging unfair prices. Richard Cutts, struggling with the task of procuring supplies, needed his own army to keep the manufacturers honest.

Madison clasped his hands behind his back and squeezed them too hard, hurting his sore joints. He frowned, then recovered lest James Monroe think he had displeased him. "I have heard that Daniel Webster calls me a little pygmy."

"I haven't heard that," Monroe lied.

"What is Clay doing during these attacks?"

"He's playing possum."

"At least he realizes this is not a military interlude, which is how the Federalists are treating the war. I must have more troops and more money. There is no cheap war!"

This outburst startled James Monroe, who had known the President since they were young men. No matter how tense the situation, how close the race, Madison did not raise his voice, lose his temper, or display any outward sign of concern other than a tightening of his facial muscles and a harder set to his mouth. "We have a narrow margin in both Houses. I am certain we will get more troops," he told the President.

"Oh, I know that"—Madison's voice vibrated with irritation—"but the numbers will be whittled down. Benjamin Franklin once said to me, 'An old dog remembers old tricks.' He was talking about himself. Well, for the life of me I have been trying to remember some old tricks and I can't."

"Your mind is above tricks, Mr. President." Monroe was sincere in his compliment.

Madison stopped pacing and finally sat down. He cast his clear eyes on his Secretary of State and for a moment was silent. "Thank you."

"We do find ourselves in perilous times, but we have endured perilous times before." Madison held his breath, waiting for Monroe to raise the specter of George Washington, but Monroe did not mention him. "I have searched my mind as to why this crisis is so different from the War of Independence." Monroe paused, then leaned forward. "The political parties were not fully formed, not as strong as they are today. Factionalism wasn't as pronounced. It is hard to imagine Republicans and Federalists agreeing on any issue today, no matter how trivial, for we see governance from opposite sides of the spectrum. Without a strong majority in either the House or the Senate, we—the Executive and his Cabinet—are condemned to endless squabbling. If we cannot create some common ground, I fear that the leadership of this country will devolve to the business interests."

"DeWitt Clinton." Madison nodded after listening to Monroe's slightly stilted manner of speaking, as awkward as his attire. He knew that his Secretary of State could become a good President, and yet he realized he had never overcome his anger, created decades ago when Monroe, as Patrick Henry's minion, opposed him for office. "And fortunes will be made in the West. I don't know how that will affect Congress in years to come. For those of us born British subjects, I think our sights will ever be on the original thirteen colonies."

"Burr understood the West. He was unusual in that respect, whether he intended to create a separate nation out there or not."

"Clay understands." Madison drew in his breath. "And our enemies in Europe understand."

"It is a great curiosity to me that a body of men sitting in Parliament on the River Thames can divine the meaning of the American West, and men from New England cannot."

"Mr. Monroe, are you hungry? I've lost track of the time and I would be gratified if you would join me for refreshment."

As the President called out for French John, James Monroe asked, "Did you hear that Daniel Webster and Laban Wheaton asked Clay to dinner the other night?"

"That would be an interesting dinner."

"Well, as it happened, Henry Clay had another engagement but he did say, 'Whoever sups with the Devil must use a long spoon.'"

When French John brought in the cold meats and hot coffee, Madison, smiling, carefully inspected the spoons before handing one to James Monroe.

11 January 1814, Tuesday

Daniel Webster gave a lauded speech today against the war, against non-importation, against, by inference, my husband. Perhaps I should say the Federalists lauded him. There was such uproar when he concluded, I feared I would go deaf.

Henry Clay, biding his time, will attack party and person soon. Mr. Webster might as well enjoy today's glory.

We have learned that there is a famine on Nantucket Island. Our people are suffering horribly for this war—in Buffalo, the entire Chesapeake, and now Nantucket. Jemmy is blamed for it, of course, but you can't fight a war without suffering. The good Lord knows we suffered in the last war.

I pray while I do my chores. I pray as I walk from room to room, as I visit the stables or see Anna. I pray from the moment I awake until I close my eyes at night. Dear God, grant us a victory so that we might end this war and our country may flourish. God doesn't seem to be interested in my prayers. Mother would fight the urge to thrash me for even thinking that I am not heard. God's wisdom is greater than our own. I know that, but what I can't fathom is why innocent people must suffer. If it distresses me, a poor mortal, should it not distress God?

I struggle to find my Inner Light, as the Society of Friends puts it; I used to believe I possessed this Inner Light. When Jemmy and I first married, he would try to understand. He read everything written by members of the Society of Friends. He would be so puzzled when I would tell him you don't reach the Inner Light with the mind, but through opening your spirit and your heart. How difficult for my husband, that most intellectual man.

And now, how difficult for me.

I find no good in suffering and murder and I feel that my Inner Light has been extinguished by the brutality of the British, or perhaps by my own weakness of faith.

How is it that faith was so easy for my mother and so difficult for me? She had seen a war and yet she never wavered.

I search for answers and I trip over more questions.

Until the morrow, God willing.

D.P.M.

"What you really want, Mr. Clay and your pack of hyenas, is to swallow a mighty chunk of Canada whilst Britain fights for her very life against the Mars of France." Laban Wheaton gulped in air, then roared on to accuse Clay and the Republicans of slithering at the feet of the President and leaving their "filthy slime upon the carpet of the palace."

Wheaton howled, he hooted, he snarled, and he finally sat down. He also lifted much of his speech from his Federalist idol, the ousted Josiah Quincy. Since Congress had been nearly swept clean with the last election, Wheaton figured no one would notice. Those who did hear Quincy's echo were too furious to care where the verbiage originated.

Clay, shrewdly, had elected not to encourage his party to reply after Webster's magisterial speech, but now the time was right. Calhoun leaped out of his seat as did the other war hawks. "Mr. Speaker! Mr. Speaker!" Each vied with the other for the Speaker's attention. Each wanted to be called on to take the attack at last.

Clay shouted for Langdon Cheves to take his place over the Speaker's gavel. The din in the chamber lessened as the representatives from these disunited states watched the Speaker step down from his post. Cheves seized the gavel and pounded hard on the rostrum. "Gentlemen. Gentlemen, come to order, please!" The uproar would not abate.

Henry Clay stood in front of them under the rostrum. He held up his hands. The body quieted while Langdon continued pounding the gavel. Clay turned his bright eyes on Langdon, who put down the gavel.

Dolley, fascinated by Clay's control over this body, watched his every move. French John had told her today would be the day; Henry

Carroll had so informed him. Carroll had stashed food and liquor near the rostrum and with other Republicans in preparation for a long siege.

Finally, in a voice that would roll back the tide, Henry Clay spoke.

"I have endured these coarse assaults of party malevolence long enough." A huge cheer went up from the Republicans. "You"—and he pointed to the more prominent Federalists—"have obstructed a bill to raise more troops, you have obstructed bills to raise revenue for those troops, you have refused to assist us to conclude this war.

"My esteemed colleague Laban Wheaton, from the proud state of Massachusetts, is quite undone by the embargo. Was it not this same honorable and intelligent gentleman who, during Thomas Jefferson's administration, supported Josiah Quincy's move to impeach the President? This, too, over an embargo. The vote was one for and one hundred and seventeen against. Mr. Wheaton, in the face of overwhelming odds, saw fit to part company with Josiah Quincy, who for good or for ill stuck to his guns. Well, Mr. Wheaton, you and your party are abandoning our troops in the face of overwhelming odds. Perhaps it becomes a habit. And I am quite moved by your tender regard for Great Britain in your phrase 'fights for her very life against the Mars of France.' The United States of America is fighting for her life against the Mars of Great Britain, or should I say Neptune since she possesses the greatest Navy the world has ever seen? How is it, Mr. Wheaton, that you have more tender regard for our enemy than for your own country?"

Wheaton's face became empurpled.

Clay's voice shifted from withering sarcasm to a quiet, reasonable tone. Those who had seen the Speaker at work knew him to be his most incisive and dangerous in these quiet exchanges. Clay glanced up at Mrs. Madison, then directly at Daniel Webster. "Mr. Webster, the idol of New Hampshire, instructed us that the war originated because of poor Republican leadership. That it is an unjust war. Ah, allow me to state to Mr. Webster that I am unaware that my party has any influence in the English Parliament. We did not inspire them to make war upon us. England stole our ships, imprisoned our seamen, and then forced us to pay punishing duties for remaining neutral during yet another European war. Pray, how could our leadership be responsible for these violations of our sovereignty? He declares the war has unjust cause. That our leadership created this war. If we have unjust cause, then I would beg to be educated by Mr. Webster as to what constitutes a just cause.

"The Republican Party is dedicated to the interest of America, and we wish to transcend party lines to end this grievous war! We did not impound British ships. We did not impress her seamen. We did not inflict upon her outrageous penalties for trading with other nations. How could the Republican Party have caused this war? How could the United States have provoked such a conflict? We did not, sir. Britain is at fault. We ask to be left in peace. We do not seek war." Clay's voice rose, clear and deep. "We did not start this fight but by God we will finish it!"

Dolley heard the light net, so light that Webster never felt it, being cast over his head. No one but Dolley and Clay caught the faint whistle through the air as he cast. He had said, in so many words, that Daniel Webster put party before country. In the heat of the acrimonious debate, only Dolley heard Clay's thunderous, accusing whisper: party above nation.

12 January 1814, Wednesday

James Monroe and Brigadier General William Winder, nephew to the Maryland governor and now charged with the defense of Maryland, Washington, and northern Virginia, each suggested to my husband that we need more troops for the eventual defense of Washington. John Armstrong insisted it was unnecessary, but Jemmy was able to raise the issue in Congress through Mr. Monroe and John Calhoun. The fur is flying!

In answer to the incessant bombast of the Federalists, Henry Clay stepped down from the rostrum today and took the floor. When I left, he was still speaking. Clay has promised Jemmy that he will get us more troops before he leaves for Europe. I do hope he will give me word of Payne, since my son must be too busy to write.

Little Dickey is sick again. Anna says he's caught a cold. I offered to nurse him, but Anna is sure this will pass.

Another ball at the Navy Yard this Saturday. I never learned to dance as a girl, having been forbidden, and I feel I'd be so clumsy if I tried to learn now. But I do love balls. Everyone looks so splendid.

James Smith stopped by today to see if Uncle Willy would like some sunflower seeds he had saved especially for him. Uncle Willy did not wait for my answer but assaulted the man the instant the seeds were in his hand. I would like every slave owner who complains that Negroes won't be able to fend for themselves to meet James Smith. Hardworking and thoughtful, James Smith is as good as any white man.

Until the morrow, God willing.

D.P.M.

13 January 1814, Thursday

*H*enry Clay continues. I couldn't get over to the House today, but French John brought me word that Mr. Clay is still standing.

Winter returned with a vengeance today. Our January thaw is over.

Jemmy and I poured over Mother Madison's report on Montpelier. She needs another team of horses. We haven't the money, but if we don't have the horses, we won't get enough acreage plowed and then the crop will be less than what we need to make money.

I told Jemmy that I know where there's a good team for sale. I'll send Paul over to Senator Brown's. He'll find me the horses at the best rate, and I think Madame Serurier will help me sell a necklace discreetly. Jemmy will never know. Paul, young though he is, will never tell. He's a good lad and industrious. If only he wasn't so infatuated with Sukey.

Very late. Hosted a large informal gathering of the Western representatives. No one will ever accuse them of being dull.

Until the morrow, God willing.

D.P.M.

14 January 1814, Friday

*H*enry Clay finished today, so weak that Henry Carroll came onto the floor and, with John Calhoun's help, assisted him in walking out of the chamber. For three days he fought back the Federalists.

Clay's final burst over the chamber was, "I want freedom of trade. I want freedom from Europe. Let Europe look to Europe. Let America look to the future!"

Many a Federalist eye stared at the floor during these last three days, so French John has told me. But in a few days or weeks they'll be hammering against the war again—against Jemmy.

Clay leaves soon for the peace commission. Gallatin and Clay, our two most able men, must languish in Europe! Well, I suppose someone must treat with the British. If only it were I. I'd give them a piece of my mind.

If we had men like Clay commanding our Army, I believe things would be quite different, despite the bragging of that pompous goat, Rear Admiral Sir George Cockburn. He's going to drive us from Washington. He's going to capture us and send us back to England with foolscaps on our heads. Is there no one to chase this man out of the Chesapeake?

I feel confident that after Clay's effort Congress will vote for more troops and more money, but will it be enough? John Calhoun can take over the floor work in Clay's absence.

I shall miss Mr. Clay. John Calhoun has a good heart, I'm sure, but he has none of Mr. Clay's warmth or wit. Well, I'm going to have to work with John Calhoun, which won't be easy. Not only is he cold, he lacks Clay's subtlety, especially where women are concerned. Calhoun, so virtuous, would never stray from his wife, but he puts little value on a woman's mind. Clay, that marvelous combustion of brilliance, gambling, and whoring, is quick to make use of any good mind—even a woman's. I just know I shall wear myself out trying to get Calhoun to see my point—without upsetting the masculine apple-cart!

French John brought me a letter written by John Randolph. He purchased it from a Maryland representative who wished to remain anonymous. I won't let Jemmy see it. Randolph states that the Prince Regent's speech on the opening of Parliament was a "model of dignity." Surprising, for I have never heard anyone refer to the Prince Regent as dignified or even intelligent. Everyone knows those Hanoverians are dumb as stones. Then the "Baron of Roanoke" continues and attacks James by saying, "Mr. Madison's rant was well suited to the meridian of Washington." Comparing James's speech with the Prince Regent's! If that was not enough of an insult, he further states, "I cannot conceive who it is that writes the speeches of the English Vitellius—Lord Liverpool, most probably; but I wish he would lend his aid to the American." The Prince Regent as Vitellius!

I fear Randolph's sarcasm far more than Wheaton's splenetic foaming at the mouth.

Who else has copies of this letter and how many more are there? More will be forthcoming, I can be sure of that.

For a wicked instant I am sorry I stopped the Randolph-Eppes duel. So much for Christian duty.

I must trust to a higher power. God must have some purpose for John Randolph. I know I am at a loss to find it.

I will give John Randolph credit for one thing. When the war hawks started beating their drums in 1811 and 1812, he disputed them in the House. But that was the extent of it. This fascinates me. The Federalists are now a solid antiwar party, but they never formulated their arguments and sentiments until <u>after</u> my husband made the decision to go to war. Isn't that like bolting the barn door after the horse has run out?

What prevented them from sitting down and presenting their case to Jemmy? A peculiar lassitude must have come over them.

We know that upward of twenty million dollars has been invested in New England textile mills. Because their President is an agricultural man, a Virginia man, do they really think he wants a war to harm their investment, to see the mills fold? Do they think he lies awake at night dreaming of schemes to destroy New England for the benefit of the South? My husband is above petty regionalism, which is more than can be said for the Federalists.

I'm too angry to think straight.

Until the morrow, God willing.

D.P.M.

Sheets of hard-driven snow covered the doorways of Washington. The temperature plummeted below zero. A man couldn't see his hand in front of his face. Neither man nor beast stirred on the streets.

Dolley stared out the window, Mayor James Blake at her side.

"Mayor Blake, please be our guest tonight. I hate to think of your venturing out in this."

"I haven't far to go, ma'am, and my missus will worry. I thank you so much for hearing my troubles."

She walked the mayor to the door. He was powerfully built, short and quick-moving. She waved goodbye to him, turned, and nearly ran into Sukey, who had tiptoed up behind her.

"You startled me." Dolley stepped back.

"Miz Madison, Paul's brought in wood. I don't know if it's enough.

Dolley followed Sukey to the back of the house. The locust and good cherry had been stacked against the kitchen wall. The snow swirling outside would have covered the pile if it had remained in its usual spot.

"That's fine but to be safe, in case this storm goes on, let's only have fires in the President's office and my drawing room."

"What about the bedroom?"

"Start the fire late. The same for the one in your room and Paul's, too."

As Dolley walked back to her drawing room, she noted that Sukey had been pleasant. Good. Bad enough to be trapped in the house during a storm. Trapped with a pouting Sukey would pluck her nerves raw.

Mayor Blake, frantic over the lack of defenses for Washington, had come to Dolley as a last resort. She told him the President shared his concern but was blocked by Congress. Dolley suggested that the mayor organize a committee of trusted men to make plans—just in case. He could expect no help from Congress by way of money or troops. He agreed that a citizens' committee was better than nothing, but he was crestfallen. So was Dolley, but she hid her anxiety. The mere mention of defending the city shot through her like an electric current.

As far as she knew, the only shield between Washington and the British was winter—winter and Commodore Joshua Barney, the fifty-four-year-old daredevil who baited Rear Admiral Cockburn into chasing Barney's few gunboats with the British fleet.

Barney hated the British. He had suffered in a British prison after being captured in hand-to-hand combat during the War of Independence, but he made good use of his year. He tried to learn everything he could about the British Navy so that when he escaped, which he did, he could use it against them.

Dolley wondered where the Revolutionary War hero was hiding out during this storm. And she wondered how long this winter would last. With spring the British would march, and not even the courage and cunning of Barney could hold them all back.

*D*olley lowered her head. The ice bits swirling in the wind were like cold needles against her skin. She could feel her face reddening.

Staying inside would have been prudent but she was restless. The windows, closed and shuttered against winter's mighty rages, meant that after a while the air inside the house became stale. The heavy curtains, expensive, nonetheless soaked up the tobacco smells. The windowpanes rattled. The downdrafts blew smoke, ash, and sparks out of the fireplaces.

She needed fresh air no matter how cold. With a wicker basket on her left arm she could have been any lady in the city venturing out for provisions. True, most women of substance had servants to perform these routine chores, but some wives insisted on visiting the market themselves. Setting a good table, a necessity in any national capital, proved of paramount importance in Washington because there was little else to do. Setting aside gambling, whoring, and cockfighting, few entertainments existed that were suitable for ladies as well as gentlemen.

Dolley hated to wear heavy socks because then she needed to wear larger shoes. No lady wanted big feet. She cursed her petty vanity, however, because her toes were so cold they throbbed.

The chandler's sign swung in the wind, its hinges squeaking. She hadn't intended to buy anything special, but seeing the shop, she thought purchasing two dozen beeswax candles an excellent idea to ward off winter's dark.

"If I'm ever rich," Dolley said to herself, "I'll only burn beeswax candles and I'll have fresh flowers in every room."

She pushed open the door and gratefully stepped inside to the warmth. Hanging from the rafters, on wooden X's, were tallow and beeswax candles of every color, shape, and size. Lovely brass holders, polished and gleaming, lined the wall shelves. A few of the candlesticks had handblown glass sheaths to protect the flame from drafts or as one walked from room to room.

A stout man, balding and wearing a tight-fitting tunic of heavy, boiled wool, greeted her. "Madam."

"Hello, Mr. Mauer." Dolley removed her bonnet.

"Ah, Mrs. Madison, I didn't recognize you. What a nasty day for a lady to be out."

"Indeed, but it felt as though the rooms of the house were shrinking."

"Ah, yes, I know that feeling. Are you looking for anything in particular?"

"Two pounds of beeswax candles. White."

Mr. Mauer walked, with a limp, to one of his hanging bunches. He carried a stick, a bit like a shepherd's crook, and neatly lifted off one dozen candles. Then he lifted a second dozen, tied together at the wicks, and cut off four candles. "Anything else for you?"

"I think not."

"I'll wrap them for you. I'll find something here to keep the ice off. You've not too far to go if you return home."

"Thank you so much."

He hummed as he rolled the candles in an old red-and-white towel. Dolley put her basket on the counter and he placed the bundle in the bottom. "Thirty cents, Mrs. Madison."

"Oh . . . haven't we credit, sir?"

"No." Mr. Mauer put his hand back in the basket—just in case. "I suspended that January first. You're so far behind, you see. I can't afford to give merchandise without prompt payment."

Dolley flushed. "Of course. These are hard times." She opened her small purse and counted out the change. She had just enough.

"Mrs. Madison, I know you and your husband bear the burdens of state, but could you"—he cleared his throat—"do your best to make up this debt?"

"How much do we owe?"

"Fifty-seven dollars and twelve cents, madam."

Her eyes widened. "I had no idea. I am sorry. We're terribly far behind. I'll go right home and see what I can do."

"Thank you. I hope I haven't offended you."

"No." She smiled. "I'm the offender. Good day, Mr. Mauer."

It seemed colder when she walked outside again. She hurried to the presidential mansion and slipped in the back door.

Sukey was sleeping by the fire in the kitchen.

"Sukey!"

Sukey's eyes opened and then widened. "Yes, ma'am."

"You sleep as though you've been up all night."

Wary, the beautiful woman shrugged. "Cold weather makes me tired."

"Doesn't feel cold in here." Dolley handed her the basket. "Put a dozen of these on President Madison's desk so he'll see them tonight. Put the rest on my desk, please."

Sukey glided down the hall.

Alone in the kitchen, Dolley absentmindedly tapped her nose as she thought. Then remembering where she had hidden the money, she walked into the pantry. An old molasses tin on the top shelf hid the booty. She stood on a rickety chair, grabbed the tin, and reached inside. Barely five dollars rewarded her efforts.

She combed through each room, looking in pots and drawers, anyplace where she might have stashed change. Her purses yielded the most. Dumping the contents on her bedspread, she quickly counted sixteen dollars. Adding in what she'd gathered elsewhere, she had the princely sum of thirty dollars and eighty-one cents.

She wrote a note to Mr. Mauer, informing him that this was an installment on her debt and she knew the balance remaining was twenty-six dollars and thirty-one cents.

She copied down the sum and slipped it in the cubbyhole of her desk where she kept her envelopes. That way every time she had to write a letter, she would be reminded of the debt.

She called for French John.

"Please see that Mr. Mauer, the chandler, receives this today." She handed him the bills and coins tied up in the red-and-white towel in which Mr. Mauer had wrapped the candles.

"*Oui.*" French John gave her a quizzical glance that sent his mustaches as well as his eyebrows rising upward.

"It has come to my attention that we have not settled all our household debts from last year and—and don't tell my husband."

"Never. Don't worry, Mrs. Dolley." French John called her that when he wanted to tease or cheer her. "God will provide."

"I truly hope so, French John."

"Did He not bring me to you?" He outstretched his arms. "And Uncle Willy. Are we not birds of a feather?"

She laughed. "French John, you most certainly are birds of brilliant plumage."

"Is not his English as good as mine?"

"And his French is better than mine." Dolley laughed again, forgetting her financial humiliation for a moment.

"What a pity that the United States does not speak the tongue of its ally instead of its enemy."

"Why, I'd never thought of that."

"French is so easy, and so beautiful."

"I should think whatever tongue we are born to is the one we consider easiest and most beautiful." As he pondered this, she motioned toward the red-and-white towel. "Regardless, money is the lingua franca of our day."

"Touché." French John smiled and departed on his errand.

15 January 1814, Saturday

I can't write with my gloves on. Even though Paul built a good fire, it's bitterly cold as soon as I stray six feet away from it.

It's still snowing, but the high winds have abated. One advantage of such a storm—Washington looks so beautiful.

Until the morrow, God willing.

D.P.M.

$\mathcal{T}$he snow had stopped early on Sunday morning, but no horses and few people moved through it. Since no one had expected a blizzard, or even a few snowflakes, no one had taken the precaution of preparing sleighs, smoothing runners, or soaping harnesses and leathers. Nor had Washington's blacksmiths changed the shoes on the horses. It was as though the city slumbered under a white blanket; the only clues of life were the smears of smoke streaming into the sky from fireplaces. Those with little wood would soon be blue from the cold.

Henry Clay was not only blue from the cold but wet from the knees down. He trudged to the presidential mansion, occasionally losing his balance as he made his way along roads that looked utterly alien except for a tavern's swinging shingle or a familiar door. Even the rooflines changed from slopes to curves. Icicles hung from windows, ledges, and roofs like diamond swords. Clay remembered, as a young man in Kentucky, another such ferocious storm. A man he knew but slightly opened the door to his house and jarred loose an icicle, which fell, point downward, and split open his skull. He died instantly. Not that Clay feared icicles. When your number is up, that's that, and between now and the time when his card would be yanked from the deck, Clay intended to wring every ounce of delight from life.

Paul Jennings opened the door when Clay knocked.

"Mr. Speaker, come in. I'll fetch the Missus." Paul ran off.

"Mr. Clay! You will catch your death of cold. Come with me." Dolley propelled him toward the living quarters. Despite his protests, she nearly pushed him into a seat.

"Paul, remove his boots. Let's see if we can't dry them out. Not too close to the fire—they'll crack."

"I wish they would; then I'd have an excuse to buy a new pair."

"Oh, and Paul, ask the cook to bring out anything he's got that's hot, and if there isn't anything hot, to make something up immediately . . . oh, and a hot toddy, too, would be most restorative."

"One or two?" Paul inquired.

"Three. Ask President Madison to join us in a few moments."

"Mrs. Madison, your attentions are more warming than the fire," Henry drawled.

"The tyranny of women, Mr. Clay?" An eyebrow arched and the corner of her mouth curled upward.

"If this be tyranny, then I shall revise my opinion of the same."

"Have you recovered from your ordeal in the House?"

"A good night's sleep put me right." He settled in the chair. "You know, I thought about your assessment of Webster, and before his philippic in the House, I had Henry drop off an unsigned letter at his boardinghouse. A simple thing designed to appeal to his ambition. The letter hinted that the states disaffected with the war ought to consider a convocation, and that in due course of time, after he turns thirty-five, he should be President. He'll forget the letter but he'll remember the idea."

Just then King George scurried across the room, a hapless mouse squealing between her jaws. She stopped under Uncle Willy's perch, stared up at the bird, who stared right back at her with an unblinking eye, and ran off into the hall.

Clay, who loved animals, laughed, and then laughed even harder as Uncle Willy sent up a timber-shivering holler, lifted off his perch, and went in pursuit of the cat. Uncle Willy was trailed closely by Dolley, who managed to catch the turquoise-and-yellow macaw and return him to his perch. He grumbled and paced from one side of the perch to the other.

"Uncle Willy sounds like John Quincy Adams." Clay smiled. "And I don't believe I have ever had the pleasure of meeting your extremely healthy cat."

Paul brought the hot toddies. "Master James will join you soon." Paul served Mr. Clay, then Dolley, and put the third hot toddy on the tea tray.

"Do you like cats, Mr. Clay?"

"I love them. I've always thought they should be the preferred pet in a democracy because they're so independent."

"I've never thought of that."

"What is your kitty's name?"

"She belongs to the cook, truthfully. I can't keep a cat in my quarters because it upsets Uncle Willy. You see how he is." Uncle Willy paced some more and stretched out his stunning wings for effect. "Usually King George stays in the kitchen, but this cold has driven the mice into the house, so George, who takes her work most seriously, is everywhere at once."

"*King* George?"

"Because she's so fat."

This made Clay laugh all the more. Dolley was a tonic to him. "Have you given her a throne?"

"She has a tiny feather bed the cook made for her. It's in the pantry, that magnet for mice."

"I take it George came to you under false colors?"

"No, the cook originally named her Georgianna after an elderly aunt. I never did find out what the aunt thought of that, but as time passed—or flew I should say, I don't know where it goes—Georgianna got fatter and fatter. Besides, Georgianna takes too long to say." Dolley turned Clay's boots around so that the backs could dry. "Would you like a throw for your legs?"

"That way you wouldn't have to see my feet."

Dolley brought out a handsomely knitted throw, which she handed to Mr. Clay. For whatever reason, George came back to peek inside the room. The mouse no longer dangled from her jaws. Willy spied her first and squawked.

"Desist, Willy." Dolley's voice was firm.

"I would have said 'hush.' " Clay smiled. He saw the cat. "I believe King George is requesting an audience with Queen Dolley."

Dolley followed the direction of Clay's gaze to behold King George sitting regally in the doorway. However, when she sat down, her obesity became embarrassingly apparent because her quite beautiful head was surrounded by pounds of flesh. It was hard to believe that the head and the body belonged to the same cat.

"You must have legions of mice." Henry started to laugh again.

Dolley took his point and laughed, too, as Uncle Willy shouted, livid because of the cat lurking in the doorway and because he wasn't the center of attention.

President James Madison entered amid the laughter and the squawking. He paused at the doorway, glanced down at King George and then up to his guest. "I see you're familiar with her majesty."

Henry Clay stood up. "Mr. President . . . a most impressive cat."

"Please sit down."

Clay complied. James thanked the Speaker for braving the weather and King George. He too turned the boots by the fire. Dolley excused herself, but both Madison and Clay begged her to stay. She ordered another round of hot toddies when Paul brought in the corn bread, jam, and three bowls of hopping John. Sukey carried the china on a tray. She returned to the kitchen for a pot of coffee, in case anyone wanted it.

The conversation turned to the Seruriers, and Dolley told the two men that Napoleon hated cats, so his officials were sure to have them removed whenever the great man paid a call. Madame Serurier had named her cat Madame de Stahl because she knew that Napoleon couldn't stand de Stahl, or indeed any woman with political opinions. She also did it to tease her husband. Theirs was a European marriage at its best. The Seruriers adored each other, but graced with civility, both had great freedom of action so long as each behaved with discretion. They knew, however, that the Americans were so prudish about dalliances, they could not possibly understand the Serurier's relationship. Serurier, as a minister to the Emperor, and his wife kept quite close to each other in America. They discovered they liked this rather bourgeois concept of marriage, and besides, dalliances took so much time.

Sukey quietly entered and placed the tray with coffee, cream, and sugar on a small side table.

Clay hinted that the Russian minister was often seen in the company of Lady M, unnamed but not unknown, who had recently taken to her bed with an attack of rheumatism due to an imprudent exposure of her beautiful shoulders. No one believed she was in bed because of rheumatism, however. The worst gossips in town, and there were many who vied for that title, counted the days. If the weather hadn't been so bad, Laban Wheaton would have been prowling by Lady M's door.

The vision of Laban Wheaton, gossip extraordinaire, patrolling the rheumatic's door made the Madisons laugh. Sukey, scowling, withdrew. The men didn't notice. Dolley did.

James Madison was relaxed and friendly with intimates. Clay wished the President could expand his personality to accommodate more people, but that was not and would never be Mr. Madison.

"We thank you again for your speech in Congress." Dolley's voice was congratulatory.

"Since I'm the Speaker, I decided to speak."

"For three glorious days—we are so grateful to you," Dolley replied. "Now, gentlemen, I know you two have many things to discuss."

Both men stood as Dolley rose from her chair. She turned Mr. Clay's boots again and left.

As the men sat down, Madison asked, "Will I get my hundred thousand men? I have only eleven thousand men in the regular Army. We are in desperate circumstances, Mr. Clay."

Henry breathed in deeply. "I don't believe Congress will vote you the number of troops you have requested, but I think that we will get far more than the Federalists were willing to give."

"Thanks to your efforts."

Henry enjoyed praise but felt no need to take full credit. "Mr. President, we are each doing what we can in this war effort. You know I rely heavily on John Calhoun in the House, and he never fails either one of us."

"Yes, I know. Nor does Monroe fail." Madison sighed. "My Cabinet, aside from Mr. Monroe and M. Gallatin, is . . ." His voice trailed off, then rose again. "The mistake for a President, I now believe after experience, is to pick Cabinet members along sectional lines. Far better to find the best man for the job than to try to please the South, the West, and New England with appointments." James Madison's clear eyes narrowed. "Do you have any idea how many men I will get?"

"At the very least, half the number you requested."

"Ah." Madison rested his head in the cup of his hand. He had hoped for more.

"The vote should come sometime next week or the week after, at the latest. The Federalists can't delay much longer and they know they haven't the votes. Our party is better organized now."

"Again, thanks to you." Madison shifted the subject, a trait to which Clay was accustomed. "They won't confirm Albert Gallatin for the peace commission, will they?"

"No. If the Federalists have to vote more troops and more money, they'll punish you with Gallatin."

"When you see him, tell him everything."

"I assumed he would be coming home."

"I wrote him informally, telling him to do what he thought best in the interests of our nation. I asked him to stay in Europe. He'll be a minister without portfolio, in a sense, except that I can't confirm him even as that. He's wellborn, which means everything over there."

What the President didn't say, but Clay knew, was that Gallatin would work tirelessly away from the public glare; since he was not officially a minister to the commission, he could bribe, cajole, and do whatever he needed to do. And Gallatin could wring money from a turnip. Whenever palms needed greasing, Gallatin would deliver hogsheads of grease, for he knew that peace isn't just negotiated; it's bought. Clay, in his position, could not possibly do that.

Madison continued. "Do you think John Quincy Adams capable of any subtlety at all?"

"As much as a bull." Clay smiled.

John Quincy Adams, James A. Bayard, and Jonathan Russell were the other peace commissioners Clay would be joining. Adams was quarrelsome, scholarly, and absolutely incorruptible and like his father, John Adams, and his father's cousin, Sam Adams, was a pain in the ass. Much as people admired the Adamses, no one wanted to be around them. But John Quincy would pounce on every point in the peace negotiations. Nothing would escape his scrutiny, and that made him valuable. If only he could curb his tongue.

The President and the Speaker talked for another hour, then Madison handed Clay an envelope. "I'm giving you this draft on my account. We both know that my wife's son has not yet, uh, settled down. I fear he has incurred debts. No word to Mrs. Madison, please."

"Of course."

"And one other . . ." Jemmy cleared his throat. "I have heard, informally, that Payne is quite taken with a young Russian lady of royal blood. To the point of proposing marriage. Have you heard anything of this?"

"No," Henry Clay truthfully replied.

"Then perhaps we can keep it quiet." Madison was encouraged that the scandal seemed to be contained. "I wonder how long before Daschkov gets wind of it?" Jemmy sighed. "Payne was foolish enough to entertain thoughts of eloping until the girl's father, a grand duke, put a stop to it."

"These Russian titles . . . Let's see, a grand duke would be brother to the Czar?"

"Exactly."

"A matter of delicacy then."

The President's face reddened. "It never occurred to Payne that his pursuit of love might jeopardize his country. It took all of Gallatin's considerable powers to put things right, but should any—how can I put this—loose ends be dangling, please use the funds to tie them up."

"I will."

"And don't waste your breath trying to talk sense to Payne. He listens, beguiles you, and then gets into another scrape. His charm, truly, will be his undoing."

"He'll grow up—in good time." Clay's voice was soothing.

Madison nodded more out of convention than belief. He brightened. "I heard you challenged Daniel Webster to a drinking contest."

"I did, sir."

The President's eyes lit up. "French John garbled the story."

"Webster backed out. He chided me and said, 'Mr. Speaker, you'll ruin your health.' And I said, 'And yours, too, given half the chance.' "

Madison laughed. "That's good. Oh, that's good."

The two chatted a bit more and then Clay pulled on his toasty boots to brave the snow.

16 January 1814, Sunday

*T*he stillness all around astonishes me. It's as though angels have covered us with their pure white robes and bade us be quiet. The only sound I heard today, apart from Uncle Willy and a much-needed visit from Henry Clay, was the sound of shovels in the snow. Tomorrow Washington will be dug out enough to permit a few noises, perhaps even some sleigh bells. Once the men can get back into the Capitol, there will be noises of another kind.

It's been such a pleasant day, I don't want to think about that.

I remember when I was small, Mother Amy would take me out in the snow and make snow pops. She'd make a snowball and then pour flavoring on it. I have never learned why she called them pops. I loved the cherry and the vanilla, too. Temple and I used to fight over them, and Mother Amy would laugh and tell us that there was enough snow to go around. Temple, two years older, liked to boss me around. He wasn't very successful, and I got us both into trouble with Mother when I hopped on one of the horses and jumped a ditch. I dared Temple to repeat my jump. He fell in the ditch and broke his arm. If he hadn't broken his arm, I don't think he would have told on me. But he did.

To think that he died at the age of twenty-nine, nineteen years ago. I hoped my first son, his namesake, would live, but I was cruelly disappointed. I hope the name Temple is not cursed for our family. It's a beautiful name. Sukey suggested once that I name the next horse I buy Temple. I declined but thanked her for the thought.

She and Paul Jennings, housebound, have been fighting like cats and dogs, and she is more sour than usual. I asked her what was wrong today; she shrugged and said, "Nothing." If she doesn't want to confide in me, fine, but I do take umbrage at her thinking me stupid.

I've been catching up on my correspondence and practicing with the dice. I wish I could find someone to play with who could keep his mouth shut.

Until the morrow, God willing.

D.P.M.

*A*lthough the worst of the storm had passed, a light snowfall kicked up again. James Madison and John Armstrong didn't notice the renewed snowfall outside the windows of the presidential mansion. Madison struggled not to pick up an andiron and brain his Secretary of War. Armstrong was trying to wriggle out of scrutinizing Generals Wilkinson and Hampton as he had promised to do. Madison wouldn't let him off the hook, so Armstrong was busy distancing himself from the inquiry and going to great pains to blur why he had made those appointments in the first place.

"However unwilling James Wilkinson was to fight the British, he was always ready to fight Wade Hampton." The President clipped his words. "You will bring me every development from the inquiry, sir."

"Yes, of course," Armstrong lied. He had no intention of fully informing the President. "If I might, Mr. President, I'd like to bring up the matter of postage—"

"No matter what becomes of this public outrage, you won't lose your franking privileges, so don't let that stop you from contacting everyone necessary for the inquiry."

"The postal service would seem to be fueled by a combination of mismanagement and greed."

"And I have heard the same of your department, Mr. Armstrong," Madison snapped back.

This rocked Armstrong because James Madison was usually not irritable or direct. "I will call out anyone who so charges me, sir."

"You'll do nothing of the kind. Fight the British. I can't afford my Cabinet officers' fighting one another."

"You can at least do me the courtesy of telling me who leveled such charges."

"I've misplaced my courtesy." A steely gaze met Armstrong's

eyes. "But the rumors about the War Department will compromise your future." Madison stifled a smile. All Armstrong ever thought about was the future. He didn't care about the present. "A vote for an epaulet. A commission is socially and politically useful, is it not?"

"Monstrous! But I will say, sir, that if I could sell off commissions to raise money for troops, I'd sell every epaulet, sword, and piece of braid in the country."

How neatly he turned the subject away from his real goal, the presidency. Yes, a vote for an epaulet made perfect sense. Madison smiled and appeared to be moved by this outburst. "I believe you would, and if the Federalists continue in their opposition, we may have to sell our very souls for more men." He rose from his chair and stirred the fire. He'd remember to pull the sash for Paul after the meeting. He wanted no interruptions.

"Did you expect such a public outcry over postage?" Armstrong clearly did not want to talk about the war, his department, or Wilkinson and Hampton.

"No, but when they start charging eight cents to send a single sheet of paper not more than thirty miles, I can't blame our citizens for being angry. I'm angry."

"The escalation did it." Armstrong leaned back comfortably in his chair, confirmed in his opinion, and he was right. "Every increase in distance brings a lamentable increase in postage, and who can remember the mileage rates? Because much of my correspondence goes to New York, I know that posting a letter between one hundred fifty miles and four hundred miles costs eighteen and a half cents. After four hundred miles you surrender your life savings." Armstrong snorted. "I can eat a decent meal for eighteen and a half cents."

"Not in Washington," Madison replied.

"Ah, yes, that reminds me." John Armstrong rubbed his chin. "Mayor Blake waded through the snow to see me. He's quite hysterical about the defense of the city. He pleaded for arms. That's all my department needs in these quarrelsome times. To give ordinary citizens guns and ammunition so that they can shoot themselves in the feet?" He paused, then drawled, "They don't have boots either. Blake would like boots."

"He is a conscientious public servant. Surely you can spare him something."

"Mr. President, I can assure you, Mayor Blake, and anyone else who is anxious: the British will never march on Washington. There's nothing here worth having."

"In military terms"—he caught his breath, then continued—"perhaps not, but the capital is the symbol of a nation. They might wish to humiliate us."

"Admiral Cockburn's sights are set on Baltimore. I'd stake my life on it."

Madison folded his hands together. "You have."

18 January 1814, Tuesday

*F*rench John has relieved me of chasing Sukey. With these eyes I saw her working.

I sent Paul Jennings out with a letter for Madame Serurier and one for James Smith. The roads are now passable despite a new dusting, so I hope James can bring in some timothy for the horses. Paul told me that our hay supply is dwindling.

Jemmy again spent time today discussing DeWitt Clinton with James Monroe. Originally, Jemmy thought, as did others, that Mayor Clinton would be replacing Federalists with Republicans in appointed posts. Instead, he rewards everyone who has given him so much as a penny. The result is that more and more men flock to the Clinton bandwagon, or should I say milk wagon?

Clinton denies this is what he is doing and says that he opposes the spoils system. He's merely trying to ensure that he gets cooperation from both parties in a split state during wartime. Rufus King, as would be expected, thinks otherwise.

If this tactic becomes common practice, our politics will degenerate into tribal warfare. They're perilously close to that already, but imagine what might occur if a man practices the spoils system and has great personal wealth. It could happen.

Better a John Randolph than a man with no principle other than his pocketbook.

I can understand ambition. I can't understand ambition tied to nothing other than vanity. Even Daniel Webster believes in something other than Daniel Webster, although I am not quite certain what that is. Time will reveal all—but will it matter?

When the snowfall began again today, I thought of my father. When we moved to Philadelphia from Virginia, he thought he would try a new business. I had recently turned fifteen and thought the city was wonderful. Most youngsters would have thought it awful, but to me Philadelphia seemed enchanted. But in the aftermath of war the dollar had been reduced to a shadow of its worth, and food prices shot up as the dollar dropped. The money Father made on the sale of the Virginia property dwindled, and in just over a year we were forced to move into more modest quarters. Father decided starch, which was much in demand but hard to find, would be the answer to his money troubles. So he started a starch factory, trying to extract his product from corn, potatoes, wheat, or any other grain he could lay his hands on. No matter how hard Mother, Mother Amy, my sisters, and I scrubbed, starch powder covered the floor, the table, and the chairs. It would drift up from the lower floor where Father worked. The fine, powdery snow made me think of that awful starch. Poor Father, he wasn't meant to be a businessman. There we were, squashed into this little house, and in the winter only one room was warm. It would be snowing outside and snowing inside. Maybe that's why I hate winter.

My husband surprised me today by mentioning how much he missed my flower arrangements. He complimented me, too, on my efforts to create gardens around the house, which looks as though it's been plopped in the middle of the road. Tom Magraw, my gardener, has been very helpful, but there's nothing any of us can do in the winter; Washington is still so uncivilized that no commercial hothouses have been constructed. On the southwestern side of Montpelier I had good luck bringing bulbs along early, and if glass wasn't so expensive, I'd like to build a small structure for forcing bulbs. Perhaps I could have success with an orange tree, but then I'd really have to be extravagant with glass. Well, it's a nice dream in the middle of winter. How kind of Jemmy to praise me. He said I was artistic and he envied me that.

I will be ecstatic when my husband's term of office is over. On top of every other happy consideration, we will see people who want to see us and not people who want something from us.

Until the morrow, God willing.

D.P.M.

$\mathcal{T}$wo beribboned heads, pretty heads, were bent over reams of paper covered with a bold, clear handwriting. The room, full of the glories of France—rich satinwoods dripping with ormolu, beautifully bound books, and heavy, exquisite curtains of blue brocade— provided a suitable setting for Madame Serurier and Dolley Madison. Dolley, never out of place regardless of her surroundings, seemed especially at home in these regal chambers.

Madame, through her own web of associates, which is to say a formidable number of men in the service of the Emperor, had acquired copies of many of John Randolph's letters. Dolley, who recognized Randolph's handwriting, knew these were not the originals but the style was unmistakably his. Prepared to doubt their authenticity, she now believed they were exact copies.

Madame simply stated that she had heard French John had been purchasing letters. Knowing how thin the presidential budget was, she was happy to share with Dolley the letters she had obtained. Louis Serurier knew nothing about this, and Madame knew that James Madison would know nothing of it either.

Dolley appreciated Madame's ability to maneuver, just as Madame appreciated Dolley's. Each thought that the other was the only woman in America willing and able to play politics.

Madame held up the most recent copy and read, her accent soothing the words. " 'I have been too long acquainted with the maneuvering of the sex, and especially of the lady in question, to be surprised at what you tell me: for which of my sins it is I know not, that I have sustained this long and heavy persecution (more hot and galling than the dreadful fire which killed nine of General Harrison's mounted riflemen), but I humbly hope that the penance will reduce

the "balance" against me (to speak à la Virginienne) on a final settle-
ment.' "

"He claims he can't stand women, and yet if one passes outside
his window, he knocks everyone over to get a look at her," Dolley
said. "He also thinks that every woman is interested in him and when
he does not return the warmth, she transforms into an avenging
virago." Dolley picked up another letter. "I know he is physically
afflicted, but still . . ."

"Has anyone ever seen this affliction?" Madame's voice rose, her
eyes danced.

Dolley couldn't answer, she was laughing too hard, and then
Madame joined in her mirth.

Not only had no woman ever seen the much-discussed shrunken
genitals of John Randolph, Madame had learned, no man had either.
Madame Serurier persisted, knowing how provincial Americans were
in such matters. What no one was able to ascertain was whether John
Randolph's genitals were truly minute or merely failed to function.
Whatever, his inability to enjoy life's pleasures and life's regeneration
had soured his brilliance into bitterness. The unhappier he became,
the more he resented the happiness of others, most especially conjugal
happiness. James Madison's marriage, which was the envy of everyone, drove Randolph to new excesses of spite.

And yet he shared his resources with shirttail relatives. He was
hardly a rich man. His wealth didn't approach that of the first President or even the diminishing wealth of his bête noire, Jefferson. Yet
he took care of the children of a Mrs. Dudley. He cared for Richard
Randolph's sons, Tudor and George, after Richard's lamented death.
Then, when a childhood friend died, he took in his two sons. All told,
John Randolph supported six fatherless children. Madame's first reaction when she heard that was to suspect Randolph of lascivious
purposes, but none of her sources ever found anything distasteful on
that subject. He was not a pederast but a tender surrogate father by
all accounts.

So there was good in the man. There was also danger. Madame
noted that in the letters, Randolph had evidenced good knowledge of

the struggle in Europe. He knew that Bonaparte had endured a defeat near Frankfurt and he knew that Pampelune had surrendered with forty-five hundred men. Randolph assumed that Lord Wellington had entered Bayonne. Clearly, John Randolph enjoyed excellent lines of communication with his country's enemy. Either that, or he was uncommonly adept at piecing together information and reading maps of Belgium, France, and Germany. Or both.

Dolley put down the letters. Madame carefully placed them in a folio, and the maid brought tea, much needed despite the fact that the temperature had climbed well into the forties.

After the maid left, Dolley said, "I am in your debt."

"Not at all." Madame was sincere. She wanted the United States to win this war, not only because she desired a defeat for their mutual enemy but also because she had learned to love this nation, crudeness and all. And she loved Dolley.

"As you must have surmised, our intelligence from the Continent is as thin as it is at home. If John Randolph has this information, we may assume the Federalists will soon have it, too, if they don't already. As Mother Madison would say, 'too little too late.' "

"And how is the esteemed Mrs. Madison?"

"She has recovered from a recent bout with good health."

Madame laughed. Nell Conway Madison's hypochondria was well known. "You are fortunate not to need intelligence the way we do in France. I begin to think that every fourth person is a spy either for our government or for the English."

"The English have the best spy system in the world."

"Because they are the most suspicious people in the world." Madame did not laugh when she said that.

Dolley sighed and put her teacup in the saucer. "My darkest fear is that John Randolph works in the service of Great Britain and that he will support the antiwar factions even if they were formerly his bitterest enemies."

"But they still *are*." Madame patted Dolley's hand. "Mrs. Madison—"

"Oh, do call me Dolley. I can't bear to be formal anymore." The letters had shaken Dolley. Randolph knew far more than she dreamed.

"Then, Dolley, call me Lisel. It's my childhood nickname, and I feel as though I have known you since childhood." Madame again patted Dolley's hand. "John Randolph is not a British agent. As much as he hates this war, he would not betray his country," the younger woman said to console Dolley.

"Well, the bankers in New England certainly are betraying it!" Dolley was shocked at her own outburst. A President's wife had to be cautious.

"Yes, but he is not a traitor. Think of how you know this man. He is insane, no? But surely not a traitor to the nation to which he helped give birth."

"No, I don't think he is, but Lisel, he knows so much." Dolley sighed, only slightly relieved by Lisel's words.

Madame clapped her hands as Madame de Stahl padded into the room. The cat immediately rushed over and leaped into her mistress's lap. Very loud purrs accompanied this. "John Randolph is a highly intelligent man. Extraordinaire."

"He is that. I think of that passage from Genesis 16:12: 'And he will be a wild man; his hand will be against every man, and every man's hand against him.' How can he not understand the necessity of this war?"

"Even brilliant men make mistakes."

Dolley wondered if Madame was thinking of Napoleon, too. "Do you remember life before the Revolution? In France, I mean."

"I was so little. I do remember Papa's telling me that the aristocrats had become so accustomed to privilege that they no longer understood power. As I have grown and observed the world, I know what Papa meant. People in power believe they will always be in power. If their wealth is intact, all they do is buy things and order the servants about, but they've lost the ability to distinguish between that and political power. The aristocrats had really lost their power before the Revolution. They danced in a charade. It may happen here, too, someday. I believe it is happening in England."

Dolley's eyebrows knitted together. "England under the Regency seems stable enough."

"Stable, yes, but the great lords frolicking on their huge estates don't realize that the textile manufacturer or the steel manufacturer they despise will one day take over the government. And commercial men think differently from"—she searched for the right expression—"from those with wealth in land."

"Power rests with money." Dolley sighed because she had so little of it.

"Yes and no. Power rests with money and energy. Those who have the energy and the will are those who acquire power. What of 1776? What of today? Your country is changing even as mine is."

"Change or die, as Mother Amy used to say." Dolley thought for a moment. "But the changes I see are . . . frightening. The generations of Washington, Adams, my husband—they thought only of the common good. These new men think only of what's good for them!" Then she said, "Oh, I think I'm just cross today. Reading those letters, those vicious attacks on Jemmy, has put me at sixes and sevens. Promise me, as soon as we get another warm day, we'll ride."

"I promise."

When she arrived, Dolley had given Madame the necklace she wanted to sell. Madame tactfully did not refer to it again. She wished that Dolley would not sell something so personal, but once Dolley was set on a course of action, nothing could dissuade her. How could a nation expect good leadership when the President and his wife lived from hand to mouth?

19 January 1814, Wednesday

*P*eople came out to my levee despite the bad weather. Henry Clay resigned today as Speaker of the House and will soon leave for the peace commission. Langdon Cheves is the new Speaker. He's a good Republican although not Henry Clay, but then who can match him?

Although he is not yet forty, I marvel at Henry Clay's ability to wrest concessions from opposing factions. Strong as he may be on any given point of view, he can see the other side, too. His mind is flexible. He will be a great asset at the peace talks even though he will need to bite his tongue and defer to Adams.

John Quincy Adams expects to follow in his father's footsteps and become President. Despite his contentious personality he displays such high intelligence and lofty purpose, I think he would be a good President even if his politics are different from ours.

I believe Jemmy is sending Henry Clay to Ghent to groom him for the presidency some distant day. If he can return with a signed and honorable peace, he will be lionized throughout our nation. Should we gain a respectable peace, it will help Adams, but Clay will be seen as its champion.

Perhaps I am wrong and my husband isn't worried about who will be President in twelve or sixteen years. We both worry about these younger men. They are so quick to press for personal advantage. I hope the years season them.

The main reason Jemmy is dispatching Mr. Clay to Europe, however, is that he believes Clay can hasten the peace. Jemmy puts the welfare of this nation before all personal consideration and affection.

I spent a lovely few hours with Lisel Serurier, who asks that I address her by her childhood name. What wasn't lovely was reading John Randolph's letters. If Randolph is so admiring of the English, I suggest that he move there.

I encapsulated his arguments as best I could for Cousin Ned and asked him to inform Henry Clay. He is also to alert the Speaker that my husband has not read the letters.

Ned has never failed me, or his President.

I discreetly asked Matilda Lee Love, who came by this evening, if she had heard much sentiment against my husband on the Virginia side of the Potomac. She said, in so many words, "No more than usual."

But then I always believe that people gossip less in the winter because they have fewer opportunities to socialize. This is one of my pet ideas. Jemmy's answer to it is that winter and our own Commodore Joshua Barney have prevented Rear Admiral Cockburn from committing his usual acts of violence in the Chesapeake, hence the lessening of criticism against him from those close to home—excluding Congress, of course.

I find myself becoming angry when I hear a New England accent. I'm being silly but I can't help it. I hope my feelings don't betray me.

My husband bears the burden of two centuries. The young people are different from us. They read different books. They have different ambitions and they expect much more than we ever did. They have heard of the Stamp Act, the Boston Tea Party, and the guns blazing at Lexington, but they didn't live through any of it and I believe they are getting tired of those of us who did. The past must seem like a play to them, more fanciful, more robust than life. But it <u>was</u> life. Our lives as well as our deaths. How many of us died? I don't think we'll ever know. Mother used to tell me to pray for the souls of the English and the Hessian soldiers; even though they were our enemies, God loved them. I didn't. I never did pray for the souls of those Redcoats who fell in battle. Wicked of me.

I don't remember the war as Jemmy does, but having been born in 1768, I can remember the excitement; Jemmy remembers the issues and the personalities. In 1776 he was a young man at the hub of the wheel, and now, thirty-eight years later, he is an old man, but still at the hub. The wheel spins faster. I thought life would slow down as we aged together, but exactly the opposite is true.

Is that why the young are so belligerent and so cavalier about our past? Do they believe time began with them and that it will never run out?

Time is an imp scampering through the waist of an hourglass. I used to laugh when Mother would flip over the hourglass and say, "The sands of time are running out." The imp is running away with my life, and I never knew I was a victim of theft.

I have tried to tell Payne how valuable even the minutes are, but to no avail. Payne exhibits the Coles bullheadedness that used to infuriate my father about my mother. He's so charming though, one always forgives him. He'll learn to respect time when he's ready. We all do. My husband was forty-three when I married him and I thought he was somewhat old. Now I'm forty-five!

When I was quite small, Mother Amy was about the age I am now, and I thought she was the oldest person on earth. Now I know that the oldest person on earth is really Mother Madison, bless her. Mother Amy would smile, her teeth stained from chewing tobacco, her earrings dangling, and she would say she was the Ancient of Days. Then she'd tell me some great truth. Upon reflection I realize that Mother Amy never really looked old, but I thought she was because that's what she told me.

Shocked as I am at my own age, I perceive that it has its advantages. In growing old you are torn from vanity and set free. People speak of the weight of the years, but I believe I am becoming lighter. True, the burdens of life have never been heavier, but I feel myself to be lighter. I can't explain it.

French John understands. I see it in him. He becomes more jolly and outspoken with each passing year. By now both French John and I have seen enough to know what's worth worrying about and what isn't. Truthfully, there's not much worth fretting over. Except this war.

I don't want to think about the war tonight.

Until the morrow, God willing.

D.P.M.

The children played outside while Dolley and Anna planned for Little Dickey's fourth birthday the following day, January 21. The heavy aroma of a roast filled the house, mingling with the rich odor of burning oak from the main fireplace.

"I don't think Jemmy can come tomorrow afternoon, but he's bought a wonderful miniature ship for Dickey and I've found him a sailor's hat. Actually, I prevailed upon William Jones. I told him if there wasn't one at the Navy Yard, to snatch one off a sailor's head."

"Dolley, you are always so thoughtful of my children—"

"I love your children."

"I know, but these presents are"—Anna groped for words—"warlike."

"No, they aren't. The sailing ship doesn't have any guns on it and a sailor's hat, well, don't be so strict."

"I'm not strict, but I don't want the children growing up thinking war is an acceptable Christian pursuit."

"Acceptable or not, both our husbands are in it."

"I know that, and mine is losing money hand over fist!"

"Well"—Dolley, having examined the bills that morning, was in no mood to hear her sister poor-mouth—"you know, James and I will be lucky to get out of Washington with the clothes on our backs. We don't have enough money to be suitably dressed, set a fine table, or entertain as the President should. And what about those lots Jemmy purchased? The market here never climbed as high as we had hoped it would and now it's plummeting. We are all suffering, and I know I owe you money, as well. I am endeavoring to secure some funds to discharge my debt."

"Jemmy is a rich man," Anna argued.

"You know better than that. Why, there are years when he hardly makes a penny."

"He has a lot more than Richard."

"He's a lot older than Richard, Anna. He's had more time to accumulate things and to invest. Richard will come along." She sighed. "And I hope to have your money soon. Really."

"I know that," Anna snapped. "We always pay each other back and our husbands are none the wiser. But I look around and I see no end in sight. Every day a dollar buys less. Every day whatever I need —milk, pins, a bolt of cloth—costs more. I can't keep the children in clothes. I don't want to wind up like Father. I couldn't go through the shame again."

Just then the children burst through the door, Dickey and Walter punching at one another like two tiny drunks.

"I'm gonna tear your thumbs off!" Walter bellowed.

His younger brother, one day from being four and already feeling more mature, bellowed right back, "And I'm going to blow you right out of the water!" This was followed by a kaboom sound.

Walter pasted Dickey, knocking him back. Unfortunately, Dickey cried and Walter's torments increased. "Fraidy-cat, fraidy-cat!"

"Am not!" Dickey took another swing and this time Walter socked him harder and bloodied his nose.

The other children, watching the fight, shrewdly melted into their rooms when Dickey's nose began to bleed. Anna leaped up, grabbed Walter, and fried his ears with a lecture liberally laced with punishments; the worst was that he was forbidden to come to Dickey's birthday party. That hurt. After all, Walter was five and was looking forward to the party games. He knew he was going to win some prizes. He was marched to his room while Anna carried the still-sobbing Dickey.

After much kissing and soothing, Anna gave the little boy a cookie and allowed him to sit in the kitchen with the cook, where he was sure to filch more sweets.

She returned to her sister, dropped in the chair, and wiped her flushed face with her hand.

"You ought not to protect Dickey. He has to learn to fend for himself."

"He's too small and weak. At his age James was half again as big."

"It doesn't matter. There's rough justice in child's play and if he doesn't learn to fight for himself, he's going to have a hard time in this world."

"Oh, do keep quiet, Dolley Payne! Your son is hardly an example of fending for himself. He sponges off everyone, he made a fool of himself in the militia, and—"

"He did not make a fool of himself in the militia! He's not cut out for military life."

"Apparently he's not cut out for any kind of life. I have yet to see him earn a dollar."

"He has to go to college." Dolley felt her own temperature rising.

"Then he can get himself to the College of New Jersey in Princeton. He has no business squandering time and money in Europe. You can't afford it!"

"Europe is an education in itself."

"I'd hate to think what he's learning," Anna snorted. "In the future I'll thank you to stay out of how I raise my children. If you ask me, Payne Todd has too much mother. My word, Dolley, you even dragged him along when you and Jemmy were first married."

"Jemmy loves Payne, and he didn't mind." Dolley was really offended.

"Mind? The poor man had no choice. It was weeks before he was alone with you."

"It wasn't that bad." Dolley's memory had glossed over that event.

"It wasn't that good. You had one child to fuss over. I have five and believe me, it's different. I don't want any of my boys turning out like Payne."

"If you weren't my sister, I'd smack you right in the face!" Dolley shouted. She stood up and hurried out of the house. She slammed the door so hard that the timbers of the house trembled.

Dickey, hearing the raised voices, emerged from the kitchen with the cook in tow. "Mommy, why was Aunt Dolley hollering? Is she sick?"

"No," Anna curtly replied.

"Did you have a fight, Mommy, like me and Walter?"

"No!" Anna boomed. "Aunt Dolley sees what she wants to see."

"Does she have bad eyes?" The child was confused.

"Dickey, Aunt Dolley likes to give orders. I am her little sister just as you're a little brother. I'm tired of her giving me orders, that's all. Grown-ups don't—fight."

"But Mommy, grown-ups are fighting the British."

"That's enough, Richard!" Anna's face reddened, and the cook grabbed the child by the wrist to drag him back into the kitchen.

20 January 1814, Thursday

*S*ukey has been the soul of cheerfulness since last night. She aired out my dresses voluntarily. I wonder what she's up to.

I called on Anna today, and the entire brood was at home. Little Dickey and Walter were engaged in a furious fight and Anna got up to stop it. Frail as Richard is, Anna can't go on protecting him. He must learn to get along with other children. He must also learn to stand up for himself and watch out for little Dolley Payne.

Our mother used to demand that we pray and forgive one another. Naturally, nothing was settled that way. When Mother's back was turned, Mother Amy would take us out behind the slave quarters and let us go at it. We learned.

Anna flew up in my face and accused me of protecting Payne, doting on him, making excuses for him, and said that she'll raise her children without any help from me.

Anna and I haven't fussed so at each other in years. I left. Otherwise I would have said something unkind in return. Having five children in the house between the ages of two and a half and nine frays the nerves, and Anna gets so emotional when she's angry that there's no reasoning with her.

I decided to walk home and sent Paul ahead with the carriage. At first I was put out with my little sister. I much prefer to tell her what to do than to have her tell me. The older-sister bully in me was coming out, although I am right about Dickey. As I walked off my anger, I considered her criticism. I did dote on Payne. I still dote on Payne. He looks so much like his father, and after John died—and our son within days—all I had was Payne.

I don't speak of that time, when I inhabited a continent of despair, yet it's with me. I probably did pour my grief and loneliness into love for Payne. Is it possible to love too much? I know it's possible to love too little, and I have observed the consequences of parents who don't want their children.

I realize Payne has not found his way in the world, which is one of the reasons we sent him to Russia. When he comes back, he will have received the valuable education of travel, and perhaps he will have found out what he wants to do with his life. Then we will send him to the College of New Jersey despite the hideous price of tuition, and he can acquire those skills necessary for a man to succeed.

I really don't think that my telling Anna to let the boys fight it out quite deserved her retort, and Payne was the brightest, most beautiful little boy. He has his father's features and build with my dark blue eyes and black curls. I believe he took the best of John Payne and me.

When Jemmy and I married, I was apprehensive about how my new husband and my son would get along, but Jemmy loved him like a father. He was so mild with him, rarely rebuking him—he was patience itself with the boy. I am not given to choleric outbursts but I can pitch a fit, as Mother Amy used to say, on rare occasions. The more Jemmy loved Payne, the more I knew I had the most wonderful husband. Not only did he provide me with companionship, steadfastness, and every comfort he could afford, he also provided love for a fatherless child.

Jemmy is a great man. History will so record him when people realize how he had to hold together the country, but it will never know that his true greatness was in his heart.

I have had more love in my life than most women dare dream of, and I am grateful for that love.

Lately, when I'm alone at night, writing in this diary, and my handwriting becomes increasingly illegible, or I rise early to set about my chores, I find myself going back to John's death. The Yellow Plague. I remember his anguish and his refusal to complain. It was God's will, he said. Then I think of those women widowed by this war. If they loved their husbands and sons as I love and loved mine, I pity them and pray for them and ask God why women must suffer so for the deeds of men. This war is a stain on all. All wars are grotesque blasphemies against God's greatest gift: Life.

Until the morrow, God willing.

D.P.M.

I patched it up with Anna today and Dickey had a nice party this afternoon.

Sukey remains helpful and bright. She told me that the latest fashion in Europe is a slightly lower-cut bodice than what we are currently wearing. Any lower and we'll be nude! I asked her how she came by this news, and she saucily replied that she has friends, too. I take this to mean she's been talking to servants working in European ministers' houses. She certainly isn't talking to Toffey anymore, for which Elizabeth Monroe and I are grateful.

Elizabeth brought her daughter, Maria, with her today when she came to call. I sent the child with King George—Maria loves cats—into the kitchen. French John saw that she was given a nice hot drink. I noticed Elizabeth was pale, so I wanted a moment alone with her. She is so circumspect it took me a good twenty minutes, but she finally relaxed enough to confess that the current political strain is fatiguing. She rarely sees her husband, who runs from meeting to meeting. I commiserated. I rarely see mine until the wee hours. He too is fatigued. One good thing, Mrs. Monroe does not question the necessity of the war, but then she wouldn't.

When Maria returned, she wanted to feed Uncle Willy. When she finished giving him bread, that terrible glutton wanted more, so he hopped onto the floor and tried to bite her toes. He frightened her, and I had to put him on his perch and take Elizabeth and Maria into another room. Uncle Willy, bereft of manners, is really a brightly colored pig. I do love the monster!

Until the morrow, God willing.

D.P.M.

22 January 1814, Saturday

*A*nna came over today to thank me for helping with Dickey's party. Since I apologized yesterday, she apologized today, and we had a good cry and talked of how we miss our darling Lucy.

I told her she was a good mother and except for coddling Dickey, she is. She replied that being a good mother isn't enough. You never know how your children will turn out, and you pray that the ones who survive will not become a burden.

Anna and I are as close as two sisters can be, and yet I continue to find facets of her being that are new to me. Anna's a thinker and I'm more of a doer. Since I've been keeping this diary, I am thinking more —more like Anna, I suppose. It's not natural to me. I believe that what's done is done and one must press on.

Why argue the matter? The difficulties will argue themselves. Just keep working, breathing, trying.

Not that Anna doesn't work hard, but she dwells on the complexity of things. Because she's my little sister, I'm afraid I underestimate her.

Still no word from Payne.

I did show Anna how to play craps. I shouldn't have but we needed to laugh. I told her I stopped playing cards because you need too many people and people talk. I don't wager to excess, but I do enjoy a bet. This way I can bet against myself, so I don't lose any money.

Money! Not one of the Paynes has evidenced a skill for making money. I can manage it and Jemmy never complains, although I did scare us both when I ordered some clothes from Europe and the duty, just the duty alone, came to two thousand dollars. If there were a hole in the earth, I would have crawled into it and covered myself up. My husband stalked off for the entire day, but when he returned that evening, he wiped away my tears and said that we'd find the money somehow; after all, I was the most beautiful woman in the capital and the public paid such attention to my clothes, I really had to be fashionable.

I didn't have to be that fashionable.

French John has taught Uncle Willy to say "Dolley's coming!" When he says this, he stretches out his feathers. I believe French John loves that silly bird as much as I do. He's also taught him to say *"merci"* and *"vive l'Amérique."* What a lovely surprise. It quite took away my worries about my conversation with Anna. Of course, Uncle Willy still swears like a trooper in French and in English.

I feel certain that the vote for more troops will come this week. I hope so. Not knowing is worse than knowing, even if the news is bad. I feel like taking a gun and drilling on the front lawn to shame those Federalists into supporting this war.

Until the morrow, God willing.

D.P.M.

23 January 1814, Sunday

*I*t turned bitter cold again early this morning. A light snowfall dusted the rooftops. This has been the strangest winter within my memory. The weather goes from warm to bitter cold and then back to warm. I think that today winter finally has us in its grasp and won't let us go until spring.

I hate winter. The only colors to assault my eyes are white, gray, brown, and more brown. Where are my soft pink roses and laughing yellow daffodils? The brilliant hummingbirds, like flying emeralds with ruby throats, and the sound of peepers in the night—oh, how I love the summer. When I was little, I would kick off my shoes and run barefoot to feel the warm earth between my toes. Mother would shout that I'd become splayfooted but I didn't care. Still don't. When no one's around here, I kick off my shoes. I'd even welcome a battle with beetles over possession of my roses or with rabbits over the garden.

A solemn heron lives at Montpelier. Mother Madison and I believe he is the soul of her husband, James Senior, coming back to check on the place and on us. He stands, one-legged, in the marshes, peering not only into the water but up at the house as well.

I can't imagine living without my husband. Mother Madison was sixty-eight when Mr. Madison died, and now she's eighty-one. Or is it eighty-two? At such an age, does it matter?

Mother Madison, not a woman to complain about life's hard blows—in contrast to her constant worries about her physical infirmities—once said to me that the first year after James Senior died, she thought she would die. She'd wake up in the morning and wonder why she hadn't managed to die in the night. A selfish feeling, for she had children to love although they were all grown. That year Franklin was born, a spindly, sickly colt whose mother's milk had dried.

Mother Madison determined that Franklin would live. Every morning she would stride down to the stables—her long steps leaving giant footprints in the dew because she'd slide—and she would order the stable boys to care for Franklin. She tired of their lack of mothering, so she took to giving Franklin the milk herself. Franklin today is a far cry from his former self. He stands sixteen and a half hands and is a shining blood bay. He's the handsomest fellow on the farm and follows Mother Madison about like a puppy. He's getting on in years. She swears that horse kept her alive and that when he goes, so will she.

I don't know where the will to live comes from. I have seen people go under for lack of it and I have seen people fight against impossible odds and live. I don't think anyone can live without someone or something to love, and Franklin seems to me as worthy of devotion as any human being.

Among children from the same family, some have the will and some don't. I have often wondered if my brothers Temple and Isaac lost their will to live. I know John Todd had will enough for twenty persons, but the fever proved too strong. Then there was my father, who wasted away a healthy man. Why?

My mother passed away in the full triumph of the Christian faith. She showed not a shred of fear toward death. I fear it. Oh yes, I fear it. I don't want to die. I want to live forever and I want to see yellow butterflies and calico kittens and pretty dresses from Paris, and I want to hear the laughter of my nieces and nephews and I hope, someday, my grandchildren. I want to watch the clouds sail across the bright blue sky and I want to make shapes out of them. When I'm too old and frail to ride, I can still walk into the stables to catch that rich, tangy horse smell and hear them grinding their oats. How can I leave this world? How can I leave my friends? Why must we die just when we are learning how magical life is? I don't believe I had sense enough to come in out of the rain until I was forty. I love everything more now than when I was young. I love the color of the green frog and I love the light in my Jemmy's eyes. I'm even getting used to my wrinkles. I don't care. I just don't want to miss anything. I don't want to die. I have not my mother's faith.

I was taught that life is a veil of tears, an illusion. The reward lies in the beyond. Then why did God make this life so sweet? Why should I deny his handiwork? Isn't that the same as denying beauty? The Society of Friends frowned on any expression of outward beauty. It's all one to me: life, beauty, laughter. The senses are not to be denied, they are to be fulfilled. I can find God in the deep purple of an iris as easily as in a church.

I feel as though I am waddling full of sorrow and I don't know why. I guess missing the summer is as good a reason as any.

Until the morrow, God willing.

D.P.M.

*T*hank God for Mother Amy, Dolley thought as she surveyed her dinner table. When they lived in Philadelphia, Mother Amy would take Dolley to the market and show her how to buy the cheaper foods and make delicious dishes out of them. Tonight was testimony Dolley learned her lessons. John Calhoun couldn't get enough of the corn relish Dolley had put up at Montpelier. The chicken, beets, and potatoes, in various guises, seemed to satisfy everyone this night.

The vote for more troops still had not been called on the floor of Congress. Each day the tension mounted. Perhaps that's why the gathering was so lively. She'd made a point of inviting the Federalists Daniel Webster, Laban Wheaton, and Michael Lieb along with Republican stalwarts Henry Clay, John Calhoun, James Monroe, and Elbridge Gerry, of course. William Thornton, although a Federalist, always enlivened her table.

Elbridge was romanticizing the hero of his youth, Samuel Adams. John Calhoun listened to the Vice President politely.

"Great man, great man—thumbed his nose at King George." Elbridge sipped his wine. "If that conflict taught me anything, it is that Europeans have no concept of the New World, none at all. Perhaps Talleyrand does."

"You know Chief Justice John Marshall, I be—" Calhoun didn't get to finish his question.

"A pompous ass and an obstructionist."

Dolley chimed in, allowing Calhoun to turn his attention to the guest on his right. "Mr. Gerry, you must write your memoirs. But I fear you will be prevented from this labor by your duties and by the fact that you can't resist a political Gordian knot—you've untied so many."

146

The Vice President glowed. "Why, I could write a book on gerry-mandering alone," he joked.

The guests laughed and Clay raised his glass to Gerry. "Mr. Vice President, it's always the best fruit the birds pick at first."

Another wave of laughter followed. As governor, Elbridge Gerry had been instrumental in the redistricting of Massachusetts. His enemies claimed the districts were cut up to favor his party. The new districts resembled a salamander slinking across the state, and Gerry's opponents called it a gerrymander. If the Vice President had redrawn the lines to ensure his own political base, he wasn't the first to do so, although his name had become synonymous with the process.

Dolley glanced over at her husband, seated next to Elizabeth Monroe—a deft move on Dolley's part. The President liked women and could communicate with them more easily than he could with men. "This day must have emigrated from Scotland," he said, referring to the snow and the sleet. He was rewarded by a large smile from the attractive Elizabeth for his attempt at humor.

André Daschkov, his wife, and the Seruriers were there to lend more charm to the gathering.

Daniel Webster thought he was informing the Russian minister about John Jacob Astor. Daschkov nodded as though Webster's remarks were news to him.

Webster's beautiful voice intoned. ". . . Astor, Parish, and Girard saved us in 1812 by putting their financial genius and reserves at the service of our nation. It's interesting that all those wealthy men were born in other countries."

"Ah, but that's the genius of your country, sir; you take the best from everyone."

Daniel Webster smiled. He knew that a true aristocrat, which Daschkov was, believed just the opposite: America was peopled by Europe's rejects and Africa's ensnared. "Astor is a fascinating man. Started out as a fur trader. He would walk into the frozen North himself and select the pelts. Of course, then he began buying land in Manhattan. Fascinating man."

"If the Republicans prove victorious," Daschkov slyly hinted, "then those businessmen loyal to the Administration will have the advantage."

"Quite so." Webster smiled but did not take the bait. If Daschkov wanted a Federalist to tell him the party's plans should the Republicans not prove victorious—should this war be lost—someone else was going to tell him, not Webster.

Far from the Seruriers' ears Michael Lieb, the Pennsylvania senator, was earnestly convincing Anna Maria Thornton that the states must exert their rights. "I do not believe the nation can be divided into military districts for the purpose of raising troops by conscription."

"And what is your plan, Senator?" Anna Maria Thornton egged him on so that she could report every word to her husband later.

"Each state has a militia, and the President, under certain circumstances, can call out that militia. But those states do not have to agree to send men if they are opposed to the, uh, circumstances. Mrs. Thornton, the states must uphold their authority against the encroachment of the national government. This is imperative." He lifted his chin. "If the national government can move men about at will, call men up at will, what is to protect us?" He cast his eyes to make certain the Seruriers were engaged in conversation. "The greatest evil of our time is the military despot."

"Ah, yes, I take your point, Senator." She smiled and couldn't wait to tell William.

Henry Clay sat at Dolley's right. When Lieb finished talking, Clay murmured, "I see his new tack is that calling up the militia is unconstitutional."

"He's powerful," Dolley noted.

"Power is not a permanent substitute for skill."

Dolley laughed. She caught her husband's eye and he smiled at her. How fortunate to be surrounded by such men, even those who were political opponents. She knew she could never be bored.

Paul glided in and out. He was helping serve tonight. Dolley noticed that Paul couldn't take his eyes off André Daschkov. The man wasn't that interesting. She wondered what that was all about.

She drew closer to Clay. "Will Calhoun call the vote?"

"Soon."

"Can he lead—really?"

"What do you think?" Clay already knew she had made up her mind.

"Yes. His mind is a ferocious instrument, but my fear for Calhoun is that what he doesn't know he hardly suspects exists."

"Brilliant but blind."

"Yes." She brightened. "But not on the war. His blindness will get him into trouble somewhere though. I don't know if I will live to see it, however."

"You'll live to be one hundred." Clay was emphatic.

"I wouldn't mind, as long as everyone I love lives that long, too." She hesitated. "I couldn't imagine life without my husband or my sisters, my Payne or you." She caught herself before revealing too much. "Even Black Dan. I want to see what happens to him."

Clay, a sentimental man, lowered his voice. "Mrs. Madison, to be included in your list of hoped-for immortals is more reward than I deserve."

She blurted out, "Isn't it curious how we go through life, and every now and then someone comes into our world, like an angel, and we know, ah, if things had been different, if—"

"If I had met you first, Dolley Payne Madison, I would never have let you go."

Dolley gasped at his boldness. "Flattery, Mr. Clay. Base flattery. I am a good deal older than you."

"The truth? You are the most alluring woman I have ever met. You aren't that much older than I. And, no, I haven't had too much to drink." He held up his hand. "No man can ever replace James in your heart, and small wonder, for you may be the only woman in Washington who has a faithful husband. I know my place, ma'am, but just once I wanted to tell you, just in case . . ." His voice trailed off. They both knew what "just in case" implied: if the war overwhelmed them both, if his ship never made it to Europe, if the British blasted them all to kingdom come.

24 January 1814, Monday

More snow. I refuse to give in to melancholy. I'm not going to write another word.

Until the morrow, God willing.

D.P.M.

"Give it back!" Sukey's voice ricocheted throughout the presidential mansion. "Give it back, you got no right."

"Enough!" French John's baritone threatened.

The bellowing reached Paul Jennings's ears, and the young mulatto trotted out into the hall only to be gruffly ordered back to his post by French John. Paul stared, bewildered, as French John, fingers clasped tightly around Sukey's wrist, dragged the woman along.

French John turned when Paul didn't duck back into the room. "Where is Mrs. Madison?"

"Last I saw her, she was talking to Tom, the gardener."

French John nodded and hauled Sukey along. Sukey wouldn't look Paul in the face. Paul noticed that French John's accent was very thick this morning, which meant that he was very angry.

Dolley, startled when French John located her, put down her needlework. She and her majordomo sensed each other's moods, often not needing to say a word. His face, dark with fury, belied his voice, which was quieter now.

"Mrs. Madison, I regret having to trouble you before your audience with the Western ladies this morning."

"What is the trouble then?"

French John, still clasping Sukey with his right hand, reached up to her neck with his left hand and pulled out a heavy, exquisitely worked gold chain.

"This."

Stunned, Dolley stood up and walked over to Sukey. Tears rolled down from Sukey's large brown eyes as Dolley took the necklace in her hands.

"This is extraordinary. The workmanship is exquisite."

"French," French John said with pride, and then as an after-thought, "or Florentine."

Sukey lowered her head.

"Where did you get this?" Dolley asked.

Sukey chose silence.

French John shook her hard. "Did you steal this, you lazy slug-gard?" He lost his temper and then regretted it because Dolley quietly shook her head.

"Sukey, please. I know you didn't steal this, but you must admit this is a curious set of circumstances." Dolley's contralto smoothed over each word.

"Missus, I ain't no thieving girl!" Sukey allowed herself a glare of Devil-pure hatred at French John.

"I know that with all my heart and soul."

"Don't you lie to Mrs. Madison, girl, or I'll take the whip to you, I swear I will." French John lost his patience again. "You tell Mrs. Madison the truth."

"French John, I believe Sukey and I can unravel this mystery." She winked at French John, who bowed and left.

He stalked down the hall dreaming of swatting Sukey's behind with a good cane switch.

Dolley returned to her seat and picked up her needlework. She calmly tipped the needle in and out of the fabric. Sukey remained standing. Dolley plied her with no further questions; she just contin-ued her sewing.

"I'm not a thief," Sukey cried again.

"I never thought you were. Now why don't you tell me all about it before there's more of a rumpus."

"I didn't steal it."

"So you said." Dolley's patience was genuine.

"André Daschkov made me a present."

Dolley glanced up from her needlework. She started to say some-thing but bit her tongue. Even Uncle Willy was unusually silent, and any drama generally sparked tremendous squawking from him.

Sukey continued after a long pause. "He likes me."

"So it seems. Has he given you other presents?"

"Yes."

"Well?"

"A bracelet and bolts of cloth."

"I take it, Sukey, these gifts are not the result of your conversational abilities."

Sukey couldn't tell if she was being mocked or not, but she was in no position to worry about a slight. "No."

"And how long have you been in Daschkov's company?"

Sukey shrugged. "Weeks. A month. I forget."

"You're a beautiful woman. That's a kind of power. I should think it would be almost impossible to resist that power . . . in your position." Dolley stopped her needlework and spoke directly to Sukey. Her gaze was unwavering, and finally Sukey met the deep blue eyes. "I am responsible for you. Perhaps I'm not doing a good job of it."

"I don't belong to you." A rush of emotion tumbled out of Sukey's mouth.

Dolley folded her hands together. "Yes, I suppose you're right. Legally, you belong to Mr. Madison."

"You don't own me. None of you own me. You just think you do. You can order me about. You can catch me if I run away, but my soul is my own!"

"And apparently your body is your own, too, up to a point." Dolley, moved by the outburst and the anger, tried not to be angry in return.

Sukey had expected a blast, and the sweetness in Dolley's tone undid her. She started to sob. Dolley rose from her chair and put her arms around her.

"Child, I didn't make this world and there are times I don't like it any more than you do. If I had the power to end slavery, I would. If I had the power to end this cursed war, I would. Sukey, I can't vote any more than you can."

Sukey put her head on Dolley's shoulder. "It ain't right, missus. It ain't right."

"No."

"Daschkov's rich. I want those pretty things. I want money."

"So do I." Dolley wiped her eyes. Sukey's tears brought up her own. "Sit down. Let's sit down and talk this over."

At first Sukey hesitated because it wouldn't do to sit down with the Missus. Sitting behind her or sitting along the wall waiting on her, that would do, but to sit opposite her, that was strange.

"Come on." Dolley led her to a chair.

Sukey dropped into it with relief. "My looks ain't gonna last forever. I got to get what I can whilst I got 'em."

"I quite understand." And she did, although Dolley did not approve of sex out of wedlock. But how could she hold Sukey to the rules that held for whites if the rewards were not the same for the African race? Then too, how many of the white race obeyed those rules? "You know I can't approve of what you're doing. I'd like to see you marry a good man, Sukey."

"I'll die before I marry." Sukey's lips clamped tight. "I'm not being the slave of a slave."

"I thought that, too. You have to meet the right one."

Sukey shook her head defiantly. "Never!"

"Do you care for Daschkov?"

"No. I don't care no more for him than a sack of hammers."

"Is he attractive to you?"

Sukey laughed. "No."

"Does he promise you things?"

"No, but he gives me stuff."

"Does it affect you that he's married?"

"If it don't bother him, it don't bother me none."

"I see." Dolley breathed deeply. "Does he ask you questions about Master James?"

"He wants to know who comes and goes in this house."

"Like Louis Serurier?"

"Yes'm."

"Do you tell him?"

"I tell him enough to throw him off the scent."

"Does he ask political questions?"

"No, but he ax me if I reads and writes."

154

"Sukey, do you understand why we are at war with Great Britain?"

"They stealing our ships and mens, too." She corrected herself. "Men." Sukey listened to the powerful whites speak. She was training herself to imitate that speech. That was power, too.

Dolley brightened. If thousands upon thousands of men in New England couldn't grasp one of the reasons for the war, a female slave from Virginia certainly had. "Yes. Do you understand that André Daschkov is a representative from another country? His primary concern is his country and only his country. If he can find an advantage in this war for Russia, he will seize it like a crow a June bug."

Sukey nodded that she understood, and she did. That Sukey was intelligent somehow made slavery even more hateful to Dolley. To waste this woman's intelligence, to waste anybody's intelligence, seemed beyond crime. It drifted into sin.

"Daschkov says that his estate is big as Rhode Island."

"Anything is as big as Rhode Island," Dolley laughed.

"He don't think much of us. He don't say it but I can tell."

"Europe doesn't think much of us, Sukey. That's another reason we're in this mess. Now listen to me. I can't live your life for you. Sometimes people do things that aren't right, but they may learn from those things and become better people. I like to think so."

"You think he's using me? Men don't use me. They thinkin' they do but they so dumb, Missus Madison. They easy as pie."

"For you." Dolley smiled. "Have there been other men like Daschkov?"

"Uh-huh." Sukey smiled. She relished her exploits like a hunter recalling the big game he's killed. She thought a moment, then leaned forward. "If Daschkov be for Russia, then Madame Serurier be for France."

"Madame Serurier is a personal friend of mine but politically, yes, she must be for France even if she disagrees with her husband, the minister."

"You trust her?"

"Yes. We both recognize where the line is drawn."

"You goin' to tell Master James?"

"I must. It's my duty."

"What do you think he'll do to me?"

"I don't know." Dolley drew her shawl around her shoulders. "Sukey, I don't expect you'll believe anything I say, anything any white person says. The Fates play tricks on us. They made you beautiful, a dusky Venus. They made you intelligent and then they made you a slave. I abhor slavery. I thought that by being a Quaker I was free of the stain of this terrible sin—but I'm not. We are all"—she searched for a word—"responsible. But I don't know what I can do except to tell you life is unjust, people can be cruel, and yet if you harden your heart, you will lose what little love there is in this world." She reached over and took Sukey's hand in her own. Dolley knew slavery was the worm in the apple of democracy.

25 January 1814, Tuesday

The court-martial of General Hull proceeds, casting an unfavorable light not only on the Army but on this Administration. John Armstrong has had no communication from the generals in the West Florida territory of Alabama or from Louisiana. He is taking this as a good sign, and Jemmy is taking it as something else.

My poor Jemmy. I added to his cares today by telling him of Sukey's affairs, most particularly the one with André Daschkov. I can be angry with Daschkov. I can't be angry with Sukey. She can't possibly understand how she may have compromised us. If only James would free his slaves!

How I hated to tell him about Sukey. He was dumbfounded. Truthfully, I was, too, when French John dragged her into my room, but being a woman, I can understand this situation better than my husband can.

His first thought was to dispatch her immediately back to Mother Madison. I said yes, we could do that, but Sukey, once roused from her lethargy, is a good lady's maid and she knows our routine. It would take some time to break in a new girl. He considered this and then told me that she could stay, but she absolutely must stop seeing Daschkov. Because he thought she had earned the necklace, he didn't tell her to return it.

What has made this especially painful for Jemmy is that he has always liked André and his wife. When we moved into the presidential mansion, the Daschkovs knocked on our door and, according to the Russian custom, presented us with two wine coolers: one filled with bread, the staff of life, and one filled with salt, the essence of life.

I asked Jemmy if he wanted me to tell Sukey that the affair must stop, and he surprised me by saying he would do it. She must understand the gravity of the situation and the harm she could do to us. I begged him not to become too angry with her.

He left the room. When he returned, his face was drawn, his lips tight. Sukey had cried. Jemmy can't bear seeing a woman cry, but he persevered and told her she was not just putting him in a delicate position but was putting herself in harm's way as well.

My dear husband. Even though she had done wrong, he thought of her welfare.

He paced the room. He wouldn't get into bed and the man was dog-tired. He said he knew in his bones that slavery was the greatest evil this nation would ever know. Not only must we free the slaves, we must send them back to Africa, to the land of their ancestors. He kept going for an hour. He feared that the westward expansion, though necessary, would also spread slavery. He knew that the West Florida territories couldn't get by without slave labor.

I beseeched him to come to bed. We could do nothing about slavery until after this war, and even then I felt uncertain about what we could do. Of course, I said nothing about freeing his slaves. I tried that early in our marriage, and now with this cursed war he couldn't possibly consider this course of action even if he were so inclined.

Wherever rice, cotton, or tobacco can be planted, there will be slavery.

Jemmy finally exhausted himself, crawled into bed, and I believe was asleep before his head hit the pillow. Then I couldn't sleep. It's three in the morning. This room is as cold as a tomb.

What can we do with slaves? Can we send them back to their

homelands? And how would slaves know their homelands? Their language is lost. When you look at Africans, you can see that they are as different from one another as an Irishman is from a Greek. I know this evil gnaws at Jemmy's conscience even as it gnaws at mine. He was so overwrought. I don't believe we should send our slaves back to Africa. They are Americans. I realize that they will never be allowed into society, but it is far better for them to remain here and make their way, painful and unjust though that way may be. Sending them back to Africa would be like sending me back to Ireland or Wales. I don't belong there.

Perhaps once the war is over, Congress could someday consider giving the Africans a territory. Congress would never give them the vote, even if former slaves could read and write, but if the Africans wanted their own territory under the protectorate of the United States, they could educate and govern themselves. Maybe it would provide some sense of justice.

I must try to go to sleep.

Until the morrow, God willing.

D.P.M.

26 January 1814, Wednesday

*D*aschkov and his wife attended my Wednesday drawing room. Such looks he cast at Sukey! I kept my eyes on Jemmy. This situation has upset him as much as his worry over the impending vote. Perhaps in a strange way it's a relief from the tension, or a safe conduit for the tension. I have never observed my husband in such a state of controlled anger.

He is furious with Daschkov for taking advantage of a slave, although with Sukey's exotic beauty she probably had the advantage. I remember Jemmy's outrage when the Federalists spread rumors about Jefferson and his slave Sally Hemings. Jemmy's mildness disappears whenever women are mistreated or a friend is abused.

And yet how many men slip off into the night down to the cabins? One has only to observe carefully the faces of slaves on many a plantation to see the mark of the master. My dear James wishes that all men were as honorable as himself. I do, too.

As if Daschkov's moonings and sighings weren't enough, Laban Wheaton had the audacity to cite me for spending $12,669.31 to refurbish the small sitting room and the large oval drawing room. I spent that money between 1809 and 1811 and I accounted for every penny, an accounting he has obviously memorized. French John overheard Wheaton, and when French John served him wine, he managed to spill it in his lap. I feigned concern and winked at French John.

Mrs. William Thornton overheard the conversation and whispered to me, "Men want to live in comfortable homes, and then they complain about the bills. You had to spend that money. Every woman knows that."

Madame Serurier still searches for a buyer for my necklace, which I do hope she finds quickly because James Brown knows of a good team of horses. Perhaps, too, I can placate some of our creditors

159

if there is enough left over after the purchase of the horses. Now we're in the depth of winter, but spring will be upon us and Mother Madison needs that team. When I begged Senator Brown to see if he could hold the team for me, he said he would hold them " 'til kingdom come."

Oh, I know Southern men slip down to those cabins, but then they flash that deadly charm. I don't know when I've met more charming or handsome men than the delegation from Louisiana.

Laban Wheaton leaned over his wineglass, calling the men brought into our country from the Louisiana Purchase the "ignorant hordes."

James Brown returned fire in a slow drawl. "I quite agree, Laban, I quite agree, we are ignorant of avarice, treachery, and small-mindedness." Then he smiled, and we waited for him to say that Laban Wheaton had flagrantly exhibited all those characteristics, but the smile proved more potent than a further attack. Wheaton retreated.

Daniel Webster paid his respects. He'll run to fat in his old age, which I shall not see, but now, in the bloom of manhood, what a handsome man and what a pity that he is a Federalist. I think of Federalists as such old men. I'm quite undone by the thought of a young one. I should think the young would want to go to the new territories. I know I would.

I can see the gleam in Daniel Webster's eyes. I've seen that kind of ambition before. If we should lose this war—and we will not!—then Webster might win his prize.

I think those New England fellows resent men like James Brown of Louisiana and Henry Clay because every time Western Territories are opened up, more men and more money are drawn into the West. Our energies will turn westward, inward, away from Europe. New England's face turns toward the Atlantic Ocean.

Of course, the fact that certain of these Northern businessmen have sunk fortunes into the timber in Maine and Vermont surely affects their politics. It's possible to ship lumber north and south on rivers and even across oceans, but how will they get it inland unless by wagon? The expense would be terrible. The West is not a market for them.

The Federalists are led by city men. The Westerners and most of the Republicans are country men, men who want to be left alone to clear land, plant crops, and breed cattle and horses. A Federalist probably sees more people in a day than a Westerner sees in a year. Being alone, I believe, creates an independent spirit. Webster and his kind perceive this independence as lawlessness. Perhaps the men of the new territories aren't as enamored of rules, procedures, and laws. I expect Mother Nature is their lawgiver.

Anna helped me tonight, as did Elizabeth Monroe. Anna stayed late and I told her about Sukey. Anna was horrified. When she recovered she shocked French John and me by saying that Sukey could prove very useful. Then she burst out laughing and so did I. We asked French John what he thought of such behavior, and he replied with a Gallic shrug of the shoulders, which made us laugh some more. Then he said, "Daschkov can't be as busy as he pretends to be if he has the time for three women. I can't keep up with the one I've got."

He must keep up all right, because he has more children than a cat has kittens.

Which reminds me: King George escaped from the kitchen, rushed into the drawing room with her tail fluffed out, and made off with a turkey leg during my party. French John started to chase her, but I told him to let George keep her prize. This made the guests laugh. Actually, I believe we were all glad of any diversion to keep our minds off tomorrow, most especially Jemmy and John Calhoun. Mr. Calhoun is so gaunt that he looks cadaverous, and he's an attractive man. He must not be eating or sleeping properly. I prepared a plate of food for him and then forced him to sit down with me for a moment. I wouldn't let him go until he had consumed every morsel. By no stretch of the imagination is Mr. Calhoun a jolly fellow, but with a bit of patience and pulling, one can lure him onto lighter subjects. He and Mr. Webster nodded politely to each other. Nothing more.

I asked Mr. Calhoun about his plantation, and for the first time I got more than a sentence out of him. He told me about the soils, his overseer's capabilities, his use of the rich bottomland for corn. He was proud of his wife's abilities as a manager and of being able to leave his land without a moment's worry with Floride in charge. He smiled and said he didn't know how she could be so beautiful and so intelligent. She was far better than he deserved. Then he blushed and apologized for bragging about his wife.

"Your youth and your love for your wife are refreshing, and I'd like to hear more," I said.

"After the war Floride will join me here, and, Mrs. Madison, you are the first person I want her to meet."

"I am honored," I replied.

Well, I am. I think John Calhoun and I will work together very well so long as he doesn't know we're working together!

A busy day. Sukey's still teary. I don't know what to do. Jemmy forbade her to see Daschkov and he's right, yet I hate to see her so miserable. If she's not in love with the man, then why is she so unhappy? Perhaps in those moments when she has a man in her power, she feels free.

I know women have to work around men as I will have to do with Calhoun, but I don't know that I have ever had a man in my power. I wouldn't like it. I don't want anyone to have power over me and I don't want power over anyone else. Jemmy has never given me an order, nor I him. Well, when I ran up those dreadful duty charges on the Parisian clothes, he gave me orders never to do it again, but we made up.

I had merely asked Ruth Barlow, who was then in Paris, to send me a few things, a few gloves and so forth, and to bill my husband. I had no idea she would send so much! Then the turbans were too big and I couldn't find anyone with whom I could exchange them. Well, the turbans weren't the problem. The ten-thousand-dollar bill, including duties, was the problem. In all the years of our marriage I think that's the angriest Jemmy has ever been with me. And yes, I did put in another clothing order to Paris last year, but I was much more precise and the costs will be reasonable. I can't go about in clothes everyone has seen a hundred times, or looking raggedy. It just wouldn't do.

At Montpelier it is different. I wear gray Quaker dresses, no frills, and Jemmy wears a simple shirt with the sleeves rolled up. He's outside as much as in. We look like the two farmers we are.

Did I take another detour? I fear I did. These Wednesday levees make me as chatty as a blue jay. Oh, I almost forgot, William Thornton found another racehorse. A 16.2-hand liver-chestnut colt with two white socks and a blaze. One white sock, buy him. Two white socks, try him. Three white socks, be wary. Four white socks, nary. Father used to say that and I have heard it many times since. I wonder where it comes from? Naturally, Jemmy can't buy this horse with Dr. Thornton. We haven't a penny, but oh, we've won some wonderful races together in the past. I must see the horse, and Dr. Thornton promises me a visit.

I'm nervous about tomorrow's vote. I'd roll my dice but I'm anxious. What if I turned up double sixes? I rolled them. Three. I kept going and got my three. Good!

Until the morrow, God willing.

D.P.M.

*J*ames Madison threw the newspapers across his desk with such force that he startled John Armstrong. "Lies, lies, and poppycock!" Madison's thin voice filled the room.

"I know that, Mr. President." Armstrong's voice dripped sympathy, but in truth he was enjoying Madison's fury.

The Secretary of War had asked the President for a private meeting after the levee. Armstrong lost no time in producing the Federalist newspapers and gossip sheets that insinuated Dolley Madison was having an illicit affair with André Daschkov. A few papers threw in Louis Serurier for good measure.

"I ought to call out each of these editors and hasten his departure from this life!"

"The President can't risk himself dueling, especially since you've been so opposed to the practice in the past," Armstrong replied in a silky voice.

"This nation has lost enough good men through dueling but oh, the satisfaction of it!"

"You could engage a good attorney." Armstrong nearly smirked as he said that.

"The law allows what honor forbids." Madison had always been suspicious of lawyers.

He stood up and began pacing, but Armstrong made no move to stand as his superior paced. "My wife will see these. I can't hide them from her," said Jemmy.

"No gentleman would mention it—"

"Oh, Mr. Armstrong, as my mother would say, this is 'scandal too good to be true.' Of course someone will mention it! I have to consider how to tell her"—he paused—"and right before this crucial vote. Those fimicolous vermin!" Madison surmised from the quizzical look on Armstrong's face that he didn't know what *fimicolous* meant. "Inhabiting dung, Mr. Armstrong."

Armstrong smiled weakly and nodded. "It will all blow over."

"Yes." James rubbed his chin. It greatly irritated him that he couldn't shave himself because one eye was nearsighted and the other farsighted. He liked being clean-shaven and the hint of stubble bothered him. "It will blow over, but think of the harm it does."

"Anyone who knows your good lady knows she is quite incapable of this."

"They've been whispering about her since the war began, but putting it in print—" Madison stopped pacing and directed his gaze at the handsome Armstrong. "Yes, it will blow over, as you say, but remember what happened to Jefferson in 1787 when he was serving as minister to France. He was across the Atlantic and could hardly defend himself. His enemies spread the rumor that he had taken his fourteen-year-old slave girl, Sally Hemings, as his"—he paused— "concubine. Those rumors are alive today. They will be alive when both Thomas Jefferson and Sally are dead. And now my dear wife, my Dolley, who is the kindest, sweetest, and most lighthearted woman I have ever known—laughter is her natural element, Mr. Armstrong, have you ever noticed? She is either laughing or she spins it out of other people." Armstrong smiled and indicated that he agreed with the President. "This good woman, who never harmed anyone, never even spoke against anyone, is enduring this filth— because she's married to me."

John Armstrong suddenly wondered what he would do if the newspapers printed something like this about his wife. Well, that was easy. He would call the fool out for a duel. He might lose his Cabinet post over it, but he would retain, indeed enlarge, his standing in the public eye. James Madison, as President, could not fight a duel. It occurred to John Armstrong for the very first time that a man surrendered a great deal of freedom when he became President. This revelation gave him pause. He didn't like the idea, so he blinked rapidly and started talking; he wouldn't think about it.

"Mr. President, well, you know what they say. For Mrs. Madison, the sun rises and sets upon you. She will weather this storm."

Madison sat down. "I know she will, but that doesn't erase the fact that I brought it upon her." He composed himself and then stood up again and reached out to shake Armstrong's hand. "Thank you for bringing this to my attention."

As French John showed John Armstrong out of the house and to his carriage, James Madison reflected. He knew that Armstrong had hated issuing orders for Hull's court-martial. Bringing the newspapers to Madison's attention was his way of getting even. Armstrong was quite unprepared for the President's outburst, though, and Jemmy thought that the man had left just a bit embarrassed at what he had done.

James put his hands under his chin, resting his elbows on the desk. He thought about the time long ago, when he still had light color in his hair and had attended the College of New Jersey. In April 1771 David Rittenhouse's orrery, or planetarium, was delivered to the college. The panels were supported by sturdy wooden legs, the heaven was blue, and the zodiac decorated the edge. When a crank was turned by Dr. John Witherspoon, president of the college, ivory spheres representing Mercury, Venus, Earth, Mars, Jupiter, and Saturn began to move around the brass Sun. As each planet had a slightly different orbit, it was fascinating to watch them dance around the Sun. The device was so cleverly constructed that a dial ticked off the days, months, years, and even the centuries.

So it should be with government. Each body had its place in the firmament. Government had to be a system of checks and balances. Louis XIV conceived of himself as the Sun King; he was the Sun at the center of France, and by extension, Europe. But in America the people were the Sun. Government existed to serve their needs. As the Father of the Constitution, James knew that better than anyone else did, but at that precise moment he was sorely tempted to attack the First Amendment. Did free speech mean this kind of slime?

He walked to his wife's private room. Dolley glanced up at him, then down again at the lace handkerchief she was mending. Her obvious nonchalance made him feel even worse.

"Ah, you know then." He folded his hands in front of him. "We should give these fellows a good thrashing!"

"Perhaps the British will do it for us," Dolley said, hastily adding, "That's an awful thought. I believe it's the only time I thought kindly about a British soldier." James looked at the subject of this abuse, the living target, and she smiled back. "Come, come, we have an important vote in Congress and a war to win. Neither of us has time for these flights of fancy."

"The reference to a 'female form seen leaving the President's house in the darkness of night' has to mean Sukey. Some reptilian newspaperman probably spent his nights spying on the house." Jemmy's tone was harsh.

"A snake stand out all night in the cold?" Dolley laughed. "Oh, Jemmy, these people paid someone to do it for them. They don't get their feet dirty or cold. Now you're all upset and I'm grateful that you wish to protect me, but there's nothing to worry about."

"I can at least draft a reply," James said stubbornly.

"Why dignify their ravings? You must put this printed poison out of your mind and get ready for bed. You need all your strength. Come on." She reached up for his hand then rose.

Jemmy put his arms around his wife. "This is my fault." He sighed. "I'm too agitated for sleep."

"I don't want to hear that kind of talk. This is not your fault. Politics is—you know." She kissed him. "Let's walk about. It's too cold to go outside, and I've been standing still chattering to everyone tonight. I need to move around even if you don't."

They walked through the rooms of the house, their shoes softly tapping against the grain of the wooden floors. Without speaking to each other, they found themselves in the dining room staring upward at the somber painting of George Washington.

"I've never thought it looks like him." Jemmy studied the figure.

"His complexion was florid—that part's right—but his nose was more pronounced and this makes his cheeks look puffy. Still, there is something of Washington there, something of his imposing stature and the majestic stillness he possessed." She slipped her arm around her husband's waist. "It must be quite difficult for a painter to capture a person. A painter who paints too true to life runs the risk of offending the victim; if too complimentary, the subject's friends won't recognize him. Let me put it this way: he looks enough like George Washington so that future generations can get an idea of him."

"I agree."

"Now I don't think there is any representation of you that I like. They don't portray your clear eyes, the way the color shifts sometimes, and I have always liked your eyebrows; they're—they're manly."

James burst out laughing. "You're painting with words."

"Well, you're handsomer than people realize."

He laughed again until the tears came into his eyes. "Dolley, you are the only person in the world who thinks that. Even my own mother never called me handsome."

"A mother never looks at a son the way a lover does. Of course she wouldn't say you were handsome."

"You're a terrible liar, Dolley Payne Madison, but I love you with all my heart and soul."

She was silent for a moment. "Jemmy, what do you think Washington would have done if the papers had rained calamity and dirt on Martha's head?"

"Flown into a rage. He could, you know. Not often, but I remember Hamilton's telling me that once, during the war, the general lost his temper and he just cleared the room, he so terrified his staff officers." Madison mused. "The longer he is dead the more he will be painted as a lifeless saint, and then when no one is left alive who knew him, they'll paint on the halo." James put his arm around Dolley's waist so that they were intertwined. He couldn't hug her and stand behind her to look over her shoulder at the painting because they were exactly the same height, both five feet six inches. "Yes, I think he would have flown into a rage, but like the good leader he was, he would have put it behind him and addressed the serious problems before him. He wouldn't forget though, and Dolley, neither will I."

"Did you like the painting Gilbert Stuart did of me?" Dolley inquired. It had been painted in 1804 and hung at Montpelier.

"Yes, but how can a man paint laughter?"

A sickly sweat shone on John C. Calhoun's face. Dolley, hurriedly leaving the gallery in the House of Representatives, noticed the man's pallor. Langdon Cheves banged the gavel to no avail. The uproar in the chamber must have sounded like the roar when Pandora opened her box. Republicans dashed from their desks to congratulate one another, while some Federalists sat grim and quiet and others congratulated one another for a compromise that could buy them time. Daniel Webster's eyes glittered like onyx. Laban Wheaton threw his papers on the floor and stalked out to the cloakroom.

Congress had passed legislation authorizing an Army of 62,773 men, an odd number that reflected the seesaw battle between Republican and Federalist. Madison's magical number of 100,000 had been whittled down enough to demonstrate the power of the Federalists, even though they were the minority party. As of that moment, the Army consisted of only 11,000 men.

The number of new troops would have been even lower if the Republicans, ably led by Calhoun, had not modified the embargo forbidding trade with Great Britain. This was done to relieve the famine on Nantucket Island, and it changed some critical Massachusetts votes.

Clay always said that politics was give and take, and Calhoun knew that his party must offer the Federalists something. Until a new Secretary of the Treasury could be ratified, John Calhoun would have to beg, borrow, and steal the money for those 62,773 soldiers.

Dolley dashed out to her carriage, French John at the reins.

"Won but compromised," she called up to him as she hopped in and closed the door before he could climb down to assist her.

She suddenly felt faint. A warmth and wooziness washed down from her head to her toes.

As the carriage pitched and rolled toward the presidential mansion, she realized the fear, the anxiety, was ebbing out of her. Her body had relaxed. The danger was over even though her mind continued to race.

She tipped her head back on the little cushion and looked outside the window. Washington alternated between cold and damp and steaming and damp. The climate was so miasmal that Clay had once said to her during one of her levees that it was probably healthier to be on the battlefield than to be in Washington. He had thought a moment and then added, "Especially if the commander is Hull."

She laughed out loud and couldn't wait to tell her husband of the vote.

"James," Dolley called as she stepped through the back door.

She hurried through the mansion, past the large painting of Washington, still calling her husband's name.

James emerged, his spectacles on his nose, papers in hand.

"Sixty-two thousand, seven hundred and seventy-three men," she said and stopped in front of him.

He sagged against the wall. "Not enough."

"It has to be enough, Jemmy." She reached for his hand. "It just has to do. You knew the Federalists would never give you what you asked for, what we need."

"I had hoped . . ." his voice trailed off, then gained vigor. "You're right. This will be enough."

"I can't believe God would bring us so far only to destroy us. We will yet surprise our enemy."

"If I had more generals with your enthusiasm, I have no doubt we would win this war." He covered his eyes for a moment, his hand trembling. "Dolley, sometimes I wonder, will the Union hold?"

"Husband," her voice was firm, "you are the answer. When the Articles of Confederation failed, you gave us the Constitution. You, Jemmy, you are the architect of this nation."

"No. There were many others—"

She interrupted. "James Madison, the others were like firewood without a match. You ignited them. The Constitution is your instrument, your creation."

He dropped his hand from his eyes. "My dear, your faith in me restores me even if you do give me too much credit."

"If it weren't for you, we would rush from crisis to crisis as do so many other governments. They've periodically refashioned themselves with the result that they're too exhausted to get anything else accomplished."

"Great Britain is stable."

"Yes . . . and at a very high price. You gave us order without a King, without a standing Army ready to march on its own citizens. We will endure this test. The Constitution will prevail and the Union will hold. It *will*."

"You're a lion, my love." He hugged her fiercely. "I married a lion. Oh, Dolley, I love you so."

27 January 1814, Thursday

Congress voted today to give the Army more men. Jemmy was much relieved when I told him. When Henry Clay and John Calhoun arrived after the vote, he spent hours with them. Getting Armstrong to use the new troops effectively may be as difficult as facing the British. Jemmy, like his mother, usually has a tendency to see the dark side. But today he's hopeful that Armstrong could suffer a streak of competence. For a change, I am less optimistic than he.

Anna and I celebrated by baking her children gingerbread. We've all but forgotten the lies the Federalist papers have printed about me. The cook fussed when we descended on the kitchen. Dickey is much better and Anna's spirits have returned to their usual ebullient state, although her husband's long absences are hard for her.

My spirits today should be as ebullient as my sister's. We've won more men. Dickey is healthy again. Anna is happy. If only I would hear from Payne; I keep telling myself that if anything terrible had happened to him, I would have heard by the fastest ship. Albert Gallatin would have seen to that. Anna comforts me and Jemmy teases me that young men rarely think of their mothers as often as their mothers think of them. Of course, I know that's true, but Russia is so very far away.

Madame Serurier says that "General Winter" is the only general who ever really defeated Napoleon in the field, and there is my son in the depths of a Russian winter. His world must be silver and white. Here it's returned to mud.

Mrs. Gallatin showed me a letter from her husband wherein he quoted Vasily Golitsyn, a most fascinating man. This Golitsyn, the favorite of Sophia, the Czarina or whatever she was called—well, actually, she was Peter the Great's half sister and she ruled for a time —anyway, in 1682 he wrote to her that his dream was of "peopling the deserts, of enriching the beggars, turning savages into men and cowards into heroes and shepherds' huts into palaces of stone."

Isn't that what we've done in America? Surely that is why we must continue this war. I am happy that Congress, after a knock-down-drag-out, voted for more men. Yet it means more killing. Why must we kill? Why can't men sit down at a table and settle their differences? Freedom and justice are such seductive words, but the older I get, the more I believe that no state can stay in power without threat of violence. Will there be a time when this nation, so dedicated to the pursuit of liberty, allows a standing Army, a large body of men who can be turned this way and that? May the people have the wisdom never to allow such a thing. Imagine such an Army under the influence of an American Napoleon. How easy it would have been for George Washington to keep the Army together and rule. He was more opposed to the military meddling in politics than any man I know. If only he was among us now. The British would be sent packing!

I must never let my husband know my thoughts on war. Jemmy hates it, too, but he doesn't hear the echo of my mother's voice.

The insults and outrages Mother and Father endured during the War of Independence—how did they bear it? Men rode up to my father in the fields for the nasty pleasure of baiting him. My older brothers were ashamed. It seemed to Walter and Temple that fighting the Redcoats was a worthy goal, but Father said that killing was killing and it makes no difference in the eyes of the Lord. If you destroy His handiwork, you violate God. Temple could never understand how an Englishman could be God's handiwork. Right now I'm not sure that I can either.

Over and over Mother and Father defended their beliefs when they were pressed, moved their household when they were threatened with being burned out. We talked differently from other people, using "thee" and "thou," and we dressed differently. As a child I used to think that we looked like a flock of gray pigeons. The only bright soul was Mother Amy.

But I think when that Redcoat rode up the steps into the hallway, Mother would have killed him if he had tried to harm us. She hid us for our protection and I believe she hid us so that we wouldn't see her true self. He could have struck her down with one blow but he didn't. Why? Because she exerted some moral force that even he felt? Because she wasn't worth killing? Because she was a woman and he was a gentleman? I have observed few gentlemen in times of war. Because hearth and home are still the sacred province of women and he knew he had trespassed? Or because, but for his red coat, epaulets, and saber, he was a Christian and he could not kill a defenseless person? The rules of war somewhat amuse me. In theory they sound noble, but in practice I expect they are often forgotten. Nonetheless, that haughty, bewigged, handsome Redcoat did not kill my mother.

But she would have killed him. I often wonder if she knew I was there. She never spoke of it.

In my heart of hearts I don't believe my father would have killed to save us. His Quaker principles meant more than his own flesh and blood. He couldn't live without those principles. When he violated the Society of Friends by going bankrupt, he shriveled up and finally died.

Despite Father's cherished principles, I think that my mother was the most Christian woman I have ever known. Perhaps there are times when one simply must kill and God will forgive, but killing in defense of one's family is different from going into the field to kill the enemy. Ah, I know all the arguments. I know that the enemy, that faceless mass, ultimately threatens one's family. Still, it doesn't seem right to me.

I wish I could put these concerns out of my mind. I often wish I had not been raised a Quaker, and then there are times when I wish everyone had been raised a Quaker.

Maybe it isn't just the killing. Maybe it's death. January is a sad month. I'll be glad to be done with it.

I sometimes think that my family and friends are like a flock of pigeons in the sky—turning, whirling, and slashing through the blue sky of Time until one by one we fall out of the air.

Until the morrow, God willing.

D.P.M.

PART TWO

I am so astonished and exhausted that I can barely write. I don't know quite where to begin. I awoke early this morning. I couldn't sleep, which is unusual for me, but these troubled times are affecting everyone, I suppose. The war god, Mars, is not smiling on us.

Anyway, the morning star shone brightly, the red rim of the sun had just peeped over the horizon, and I slipped out of bed, careful not to waken anyone, most particularly Uncle Willy. I tiptoed past my drawing room, which must be why I found what I found. Had I walked with a firm tread, I would have given warning of my presence. There was Sukey reading my diary. I could scarcely believe it.

"Sukey, what are you doing?" I asked.

She jumped so violently, she dropped the diary and then stooped to retrieve it. Her eyes were as big as King George's when she's stalking a mouse. She couldn't even open her mouth to answer me. I walked over and took the diary from her hands.

I repeated, "What are you doing?"

"Dusting," came the halfhearted reply.

"At dawn? Sukey, I may be a white woman but I am not a total fool. Now you tell me what you're doing going through my diary." I never thought to lock my desk. Jemmy would not read something so personal without asking. Then it occurred to me that Sukey couldn't read.

"Really, Miz Dolley, there's just so much mess with the windows being open and the heat and you put such store by this book that I—"

"Don't you lie to me or I will slap your face! What were you doing and who taught you to read?"

Sukey's lips actually quivered. "I can't read but so much."

"Well, how much then?" I seized her by the upper arm and just shook her like a rag doll. I was so angry.

"I can read my name."

"I expect you can read more than that. Nouns?" I remember as a child when I was learning to read that the names of persons and things were easy but the verbs were difficult.

"I don't know nothing about no nouns." Sukey's natural surliness was returning with full vigor.

"Names. Can you read my name?" Sukey nodded, so I continued. "And Master James?" She nodded again, and again at every name I could rattle off. She had obviously mastered "to be" and "go" but I was right, she hadn't progressed very far with verbs. "Who taught you this?"

"You can't make me tell."

I was furious. She put her hands on her hips and thrust out her ample bosom.

"I can make you tell and I will make you tell." I shook her again and when I grabbed her other arm, I dropped the diary. Well, Sukey is younger and quicker than I am, which also makes me want to spit. She snatched the diary off the floor and began ripping out pages and running away from me. I chased her but she had a head start, running through the house, tearing up pages with every step. I was afraid we'd waken Jemmy, but to my relief, if I can call it that, she bolted into the kitchen just as Paul Jennings entered through the back door. "Stop her, Paul!"

He did. She screamed and bit him, all the while shredding my diary. By the time I could get it back from her, she had destroyed nearly everything. I was so furious. I can't remember being that angry since I was a girl and Temple would goad me. I raised my hand to strike her. She flinched but was unrepentant. Poor Paul didn't know what to do, but he hung on to her. I couldn't hit her.

I made Paul push her into a chair and hold her there. He put his hands on her shoulders and she didn't budge. I expect, too, that she knew French John would be arriving at any moment and it would afford him enormous pleasure to thrash her.

"Why do you want to know what's in my diary?" I beheld the pathetic remnants in my hand.

"You talking ugly about me." She pointed to the pages.

"I am not."

"I seen my name and I seen André's name and"—she turned to look up at Paul—"I seen your name, too."

"So what?" Paul rejoined.

"Why is it so important to you, Sukey? A diary is where a person records the events of the day, the people she's seen, and what she is thinking about. Why does it matter?"

She buttoned her lip. Paul pushed her but she kept silent.

"You don't have to spy in my diary. I can tell you what I think about you."

"I can tell you what I think about you, too." She jumped on that idea. "You like Uncle Willy, full of noise and bright colors. You keep everyone hopping. You flatter everyone and you don't forget Master James. Everything you do, you doin' for him. You don't really like nobody."

"That's not true!" She shocked me so much I shouted. "I love people and yes, I love my husband first, something you'll not know, I fear."

"You don't like me." She was quiet now.

"No, Sukey, I don't. You're spoiled. You don't care about anyone but yourself."

"You think Paul cares about you? Any slave that cares about his master is a born fool."

"I do so care!" Paul gripped her with his powerful fingers.

"Sukey, you once said that to me before, in so many words, about men—that any woman who cares for a man is a fool. Why is love so frightful to you?"

"Love? Don't make me laugh."

I sighed. I was unexpectedly quite tired. "Do you want to go back to Mother Madison?"

"No."

"What do you want?" This threw her.

Sukey thought, then shrugged off Paul's grasp. I tipped my head and he released his hands, but he stayed behind her. "I want to be free."

"And that's the one thing I cannot give you. You aren't mine."

By now I realized that André Daschkov or another of her romantic victims had been teaching her to read. I found this fascinating because Sukey grumbled so much when she had to dust around papers. She never evidenced the slightest interest in reading, and she asked few questions. I wondered what had provoked her to make such an effort—and at some risk to herself.

"You could talk to Master James," she hissed at me.

"I have talked to Master James, you know that!" I started to lose my temper again. "He refuses to free or sell any slaves as long as his mother is alive. He plain won't do it, Sukey."

Paul observed me with curiosity. "You asked him?"

"Of course I asked him, Paul. I ask him once or twice a year. Every year. I'm a Quaker. We don't believe in slavery. We don't believe in war, and for the love of God I find myself in the middle of a war and surrounded by slaves. You make sense of it, I can't!"

My explosion sobered Sukey and caused Paul's face to crumple in consternation.

"Well," he said after deliberation, "I wouldn't mind being free, but Miz Dolley, I am never, ever, gonna leave you. I love you."

Paul said this with such simple dignity, with such true emotion, that I burst into tears. I couldn't help myself. I don't know what got into me. Then he worried that he had upset me. Sukey sat in amazement. Apparently she believes she is the only person in the world with feelings and was stunned to discover that we have feelings, too.

"I'm sorry." He lowered his voice.

"Oh, Paul, don't be sorry. I'm crying because I don't know when I've ever heard anything that touches me so. And here with all this— this mess. I don't even know if we're going to keep this country together. People act hateful to my husband and the papers are hateful to me and my family. For all I know, people have been hateful to each of you, as well." I regained my composure. "I will try to be deserving of your love, Paul."

"You like a mother to me." His deep brown eyes filled with tears, too. "I won't never leave you. No matter what, unlessen you tell me to go."

"Thank you."

Now Sukey was crying.

Paul couldn't believe it. "What you bawling about?"

"The newspapers. I know what's been in the newspapers about the Missus. They blaming her for what I done."

"They'd blame me anyway. They're looking for targets that can't fire back. Sukey, the war is going from bad to worse. The British are looting the Chesapeake again and Commodore Barney has fewer than a dozen gunboats and only a handful of men to try and stop them. They destroyed Fort Oswego, and the blockade now goes all the way up the coast of New England." I felt so drained, I sat down. "And those Federalists blame us for the loss of their money, not the British for finally blockading their ports. Sukey, ease your mind. If they didn't accuse me of carrying on with André Daschkov or Louis Serurier, they would have found other men. They even slander Anna. They'll do anything to hurt Jemmy."

"Do you blame me?" Sukey asked.

"No." I did blame her, though, for making trouble for herself over André. But I'd talked to her about that and so had James. It wouldn't have been right to discuss it in front of Paul. He couldn't help being in love with her. If Sukey had a brain in her beautiful head, she would realize that Paul, young though he was, was worth a bushelful of rich men, powerful men. It has always puzzled me, how a woman can pick the worst man possible when a good man is available. Not that she loved these men, but I still believe God meant for a man and a woman to care for one another, honor one another, and work together. As these thoughts raced through my head, I searched for something to say. I could think of nothing, so I dismissed them both and got on with the chores of the day.

Now, with the stars overhead, I wonder how I could have become so angry. I have been faithful in keeping my diary. Yes, I missed days here and there as the year progressed, but I was unusually disciplined, for me, and I was so proud of that. I guess losing my record of the political struggles and the war isn't so bad. Surely other people are keeping records, too. Maybe it's just as well that the litany of losses isn't spelled out by my hand.

We did have a few victories. In March Andrew Jackson crushed the Creek Indians at Horseshoe Bend on the Tallapoosa River in Alabama. There was a bloody battle this month near Niagara Falls at a place called Lundy's Lane. Neither side won. Vicious finance plagues us. There's not much left in the larder.

What saddens me about my torn-up diary is the loss of my personal memories. I don't know if I can recapture them. Maybe it's wiser not to try to remember but just to push ahead. All I have left of my diary is January.

Sukey can't realize, truly, what she has done.

We're all close to the boiling point. When Congress adjourned in the late spring and the population of Washington shrank accordingly, I think even the Sukeys of this town realized that we're but a handful against the British. What are a few ink-blotted pages against that fear? And how curious that Sukey wanted to know if I blame her. Perhaps she feared I would point the finger at her in some fashion and the newspapers would write about her. I don't know.

This war has caused a fatal looseness of social restraints in people regardless of their station. It's not just Sukey. Anna and I have been arguing more frequently than either of us could have imagined— about the fact that I borrow money, repay her, and then borrow again. About a change in the weather! We're like two banty roosters. Jemmy has lost weight. How he keeps his temper I don't know because he is the Federalists' whipping boy. The other night at my levee a very haughty lady, for whom I will do a great service by not mentioning her name, said to me in regard to my husband, "He must be thinking of the presidency." She implied that he was thinking only of his own reputation.

I replied, "I assure you, madam, he is not. He is thinking of the country." The idea that my husband would be so petty as to worry about how people, how posterity, will regard his presidency!

John Randolph, writing that Washington is Gomorrah on the Potomac, says a British cleansing might not be so terrible. Now I

<u>know</u> he's insane. He is also reputed to have said, "It's a pity they won't march as far as Monticello." Hate takes such effort, small wonder John Randolph is what he is.

I'm trying to collect my thoughts and they're still scattered. I feel as though I've been wounded. Those pages all over the floor—I felt a loss like physical pain. Vanity, I suppose. Why should I think that my musings are of any importance? Sheer vanity.

Yesterday a few summer squalls came through and cleared the air. Afterward the sky sparkled and Lisel Serurier and I hopped in her carriage for a drive along the river. It was such a pleasure to be in her company and to get away from here for a few moments. My only sadness was that my husband was chained to his desk. As we drove along, we found ourselves talking about the battles, the dead, the terrible toll of war. Thank God the Seruriers remain here, even though Louis XVIII is back on the throne. No orders have arrived to clarify their status.

I told Lisel that even with the British drawing ever closer, I am not personally afraid. I asked her what she thought of that because I don't regard myself as especially courageous.

She replied, "Since the French Revolution we have all become habitués of terror."

I have turned this over in my mind and I think there's a great truth in what she said. One becomes accustomed to the killing.

I remember even after the Reign of Terror in France, Jemmy remained distraught. Publicly, of course, he had to support France's overthrow of the monarchy, but no one imagined the horror that would follow. Once, when we were first married, we were talking about that terrible time and he turned to me—I will never forget the anguish etched on his face—and he said, "The guillotine casts a shadow even at night."

I think adding up the numbers of the dead, whether they rode in the tumbrels or fell screaming in Lundy's Lane, is somehow obscene, somehow a great sin. Those weren't numbers that died. Those were men and women. They had names. They had lovers. They had mothers and fathers, sisters and brothers, daughters and sons. They had homes, dogs, cherished gardens, and well-tended fields. Those weren't numbers that died. Oh, how we gloss over the evil of our deeds by removing the faces of our victims. I ask myself, "Where is God?" I don't know where God is but I know where man is. Man is behind the guns, firing away.

Until the morrow, God willing.

D.P.M.

1 August 1814, Monday

The crape myrtle is blooming today. I noticed as I drove through the city that white and deep cerise flowers splashed cheer everywhere. It was such a mild day that I was tempted to walk over to Anna's, but we are currently so unpopular that Jemmy requested I ride with Paul and French John. "Surely you don't think I will be shot?" I jested. Well, Jemmy's face turned white. I got in the phaeton. No more jests.

Anna, quite huge, should deliver next month. How she can care for a sixth child I don't know. Even little Dolley is a handful at three. Her birthday was July 13 and she's already looking forward to the next one. I asked Anna what name she and Richard had chosen for the baby. If a boy, Temple, she said, which brought tears to my eyes, and if a girl, Mary, for our dear sister. That brought more tears.

Poor Mary, not even thirty when she died. She and John Jackson so enjoyed each other and their home in Clarksburg. When she began to fail, she asked John to bring her over the mountains to Anna and me. Because the racking cough was so severe, she could no longer sit upright; John bought a buckboard, hoping that she could lie down for the journey. Before he could carry her to us, he was clubbed nearly to death outside the courthouse by henchmen of the criminals he was prosecuting. As he recovered, Mary and all their children except one died. He wrote me the most heart-wrenching letters, and I replied as best I could, for my grief, too, ran deep. I'm becoming a heretic. I see no reason why people must be made to suffer so.

I think Anna and I talked about Mary and both Temples so we wouldn't talk about what's in front of our faces. The congressmen left a long time ago. They had an excuse, of course—Congress adjourned. The residents of the city have made more than one reference to rats fleeing a sinking ship. We have only five hundred men in

185

Washington's ragtag militia and, I think, three rickety gunboats. Joshua Barney has gunboats out on the Chesapeake and the rivers feeding into the bay, but he's too far away to sail up the Potomac. James Blake, everywhere at once, rallies those citizens remaining. I always liked the mayor, but now I much admire him.

He dropped by the other day as I was feeding Uncle Willy, who brings crowds in the warm weather. The children gather at the window to see Uncle Willy flap his wings and screech. He's without shame. The larger the crowd, the worse his antics. The French he sputters is obscene. My French is poor at best, and, of course, the varmint never speaks French when Lisel Serurier is here. Then he jabbers in English. French John assures me that Uncle Willy is well mannered. I seriously doubt this. His attacks on King George are now accompanied by much verbal abuse. He screams, "Fatty, fatty, fatty cat." His best word, and French John's favorite, is "British," followed by a terrible sound I don't think I will describe. Trying and difficult as times are, it even makes Jemmy split his sides, and I never know when the crazy bird is going to say it.

Where was I? Oh yes. Well, James Blake dropped by to tell me that he's heard the Alexandria bankers are taking their money out of town. They're rowing it down the Potomac. To where, I asked, and he said he didn't know, but that there was an ugly rumor they would give it to the British if the enemy got that far upriver. We both agreed the story seemed far-fetched.

Far-fetched. Some New England governors, aided by New England congressmen, are planning a meeting to question the war. Is that far-fetched or traitorous? They think Jemmy doesn't know about it. He does, and he told me there is nothing he can or would do. Any state or group of states can meet whenever they please. Jemmy must be correct about the ability of the states to convene, but to do so in order to question a war in progress? I wonder, where does one draw the line?

Sukey is moping. She appears chastened after yesterday's uproar. I keep remembering things I wrote about in my diary. My birthday, May 20, was truly a wonderful day. Jemmy had a new saddle made for me and it's beautiful. My nieces and nephews made me little presents and sang to me. My son did not forget my birthday. He wrote me a wonderful letter of his accomplishments in Russia, and now he's in Ghent with Henry Clay and John Quincy Adams. Here I am edging closer to fifty and my son has his whole life before him—yet I wouldn't take back the time. My years are my true wealth.

Anna embroidered a pillowcase for me. She has such a fine hand. I don't.

What a wonderful day my birthday was, and I wrote page after page in my diary.

I can't think about losing that diary to Sukey's spitefulness. I'll become angry all over again.

Thinking of Sukey makes me think of André Daschkov. He has been helpful of late. He even offered to seek out Cockburn and treat with him. Naturally, Jemmy and the Cabinet declined.

Mother Madison reports that the new team of horses is working well; the truth is, I don't even miss my necklace.

Mother Madison also says she has heard John Randolph is having money woes. Aren't we all?

Armstrong still asserts that the British are simply doing what they did last year, marauding. No one believes him but himself.

Mother Amy used to say that trouble came in threes, as did good things. Since not one awful thing has yet happened to me or to this city, I am waiting. I feel trouble coming, just as one can smell the turn in the air before a thunderstorm even though there's not a cloud in the sky. Somehow waiting is worse than knowing.

I did manage to read Lord Byron's *Bride of Abydos*. How I don't know. Lord Byron is fortunate that he does not depend on me for his literary reputation.

Until the morrow, God willing.

D.P.M.

2 August 1814, Tuesday

The one good thing about this summer is that the crater in front of the house has been filled. But now it's a giant dust mushroom. If one doesn't know it exists, one falls into it, sending the dust billowing upward. If the Romans could build roads that lasted for nearly two thousand years, I don't see why we can't do the same, or at least get rid of the potholes.

The Secretary of the Navy and the Secretary of War bellowed at each other at the tops of their lungs today. I heard them clear at the other end of the house. When the meeting was over, Jemmy said to me, "If only they evidenced as much hostility toward England."

What started the row was William Jones's report that he was making preparations to burn down the Navy Yard should the British march on Washington. To allow such a store of munitions and supplies to fall into enemy hands would be as bad as the capture of the city itself.

John Armstrong jumped to his feet and shouted that even considering burning the Navy Yard was absurd. He stated that the British target was Baltimore, is Baltimore, and always will be Baltimore.

Jones replied, "Then why haven't they taken Baltimore?"

Armstrong said, "Because they haven't had the men. They want to make sure they have superiority in numbers."

Jemmy said calmly, "They will shortly."

Both belligerents were silent then. Jemmy did not elaborate and Armstrong was foolish enough to ask, "How do you know?"

James Monroe stepped in and chastised him. "The President's word should be quite enough."

Is Armstrong so stupid that he doesn't realize Jemmy is privy to information to which he is not? The utter arrogance of the man! To make it worse, he is a College of New Jersey man. Oh, how this upsets my husband.

Monroe attended William and Mary, of course. Jemmy declined to go to this college; he thought the College of New Jersey would offer another view, an opportunity to experience another region. Much as he loves Virginia, one can have too much of it, or of one's mother. The College of New Jersey was a good choice for Jemmy.

Poor Elbridge Gerry sat through this uproar, gasping for breath. Jemmy has pleaded with him to return home for the summer because Washington's climate can only exaggerate his discomfort.

Elizabeth and Maria Monroe were with me when the commotion occurred. We adjourned to the back gardens, and still the ruckus could be heard. Elizabeth's only comment was, "Your roses appear a haven for beetles." Indeed.

I underestimate Mrs. Monroe. After all, eleven or twelve years ago, when her husband was in Europe negotiating the Louisiana Purchase, she managed to obtain Madame Lafayette's release from La Force Prison.

Ah, the French. And now the great man, Napoleon, is like a beached whale lifted mercilessly by each tiny wave.

Nothing from Payne since right after my birthday. I'm sure he is using his time on the Continent to learn from those older civilizations and to find his true calling in this life. I'm much relieved that he is free from the Russian cold.

I still don't know why he is signing his letters to Jemmy "John Todd." He's always been Payne. John Payne Todd, but he's never been called John for an instant.

Jemmy carefully suggested that we send Anna to the country until she delivers her child. There are many friends in northern Virginia and Maryland who would be happy to have her; she's such delightful company. I told him I'd broach the subject.

I miss Senator Brown. With Congress adjourned, he has returned to Louisiana to do whatever he can to prepare for the British invasion there. He's certain it will happen. And I surely do miss Henry Clay. He's as slick as quicksilver and as shiny. I miss John Calhoun—"Crisis," as Clay calls him. I even miss Daniel Webster.

The city grows continually thinner as though wasting away from some horrid disease.

I think I'll play with my dice. Something to take my mind off this clammy sensation of dread.

Until the morrow, God willing.

D.P.M.

A steady drizzle kept the temperature down. The dust settled on the roadways, the roses turned their huge heads toward the liquid refreshment, and a young couple ran laughing between the raindrops. French John, a side of mutton heaved over his shoulder, walked toward the kitchen. His rolled-up sleeves displayed a vivid array of tattoos, gathered in most of the ports of the world.

James Madison observed the life outside his window. He envied the people their simple lives, or perhaps most lives only appeared simple but were complex on closer examination. Close examination was where Madison excelled. Never a man to jump to conclusions or rush to a decision, he enjoyed the laborious process of studying an issue thoroughly. He could be thorough without becoming lost in detail, a trait he liked in himself. However, events now moved so rapidly that he no longer had the luxury of taking his time to make a decision. This war and his Cabinet were teaching him that not making a decision is in fact making a decision, usually the wrong decision. He was going to inspect General William Winder and his troops.

James Monroe agreed to ride with him. Armstrong was worse than useless. He was dangerous. So Madison's only course, at present, was to ignore his Secretary of War and take matters into his own hands. If the United States could survive the summer, then he would attend to Armstrong. Would Madison himself survive the summer? He used to worry about dying, but he'd seen so much of it that if he were to die now, better it be in the service of the nation he founded and loved than as an old, irritable man gabbling in a feather bed.

The only mistake he and his generation may have made was in putting the capital where they did. As a compromise between North and South, it suited neither particularly well. North and South. He'd address that issue after the war, as well.

His personal mistakes haunted him. Armstrong had been aide-de-camp to General Horatio Gates during the Revolutionary War. Armstrong enjoyed good relations with General Washington, and Madison respected the general's judgment of men. But Gates's other aide-de-camp, James Wilkinson, was now proved as idiotic as Armstrong, and Madison wondered if General Washington was as wise in military matters as he had assumed. The Revolutionary War was decades ago, though. These men were young then. He was young then. Or was he? James Madison, for a moment, couldn't remember. Of course, even then there had been talk about Wilkinson, who was too close to Benedict Arnold, and Armstrong and Wilkinson were thick as thieves.

Was he an ineffectual leader, or were men naturally greedy and lazy? Madison reviewed his sorry relationship with Congress during his first and second terms. The victory of being voted more men at the beginning of the year was supplanted by the reality of having to find them and pay for them.

Could they fight the British in a large land battle? The Americans fought well enough under Jacob Brown and Andrew Jackson, but they were at the far reaches of United States boundaries—one in the North and the other in the South.

What worried Madison most were the ways in which the United States goaded the British. Yes, it was Britain's fault that the war began, but after it had started, he received reports, confidential reports, which disturbed him greatly.

The small town of York, in Canada, had been wantonly burned on April 30, 1813. The building that housed the legislature was reduced to a charred rubble. The official reports, like most official reports, were to be instantly disregarded. What James Madison discovered, through sources he trusted, was that American soldiers, out of uniform, had set torch to the town. York was an important place to the Canadians. Revenge would not be impossible to understand. You burn our legislature, we'll burn yours.

Of course, the British had set fire to the barracks and public buildings of Detroit in September 1813. The score ought to be even.

But then, the American militia, under George McClure, had wantonly destroyed Newark, on the Canadian side of the Niagara River. A renegade, Joseph Willcocks, was blamed for inciting the militia to this disgusting act, which sent defenseless women and children into the snow with no shelter.

So the British turned around and savaged Buffalo and Black Rock.

Surely, that should have brought an end to this absurd destruction, but no; Abraham Marble, one of Joseph Willcocks's followers, burned every home, barn, mill, and public building for a distance of some thirty miles along the northern shore of Lake Erie. The victims were also robbed of everything they owned.

If Madison ever got his hands on Willcocks or Marble, he personally would shoot them.

There was no doubt in his mind that the British were coming. The only question was when.

If this war ever ended, a good-sized standing Army would be a necessity. Getting the American people to accept that would be extremely difficult, but militias were ineffectual and undisciplined. Even his own wife feared a standing Army. She never said so but he could tell.

The whole history of Europe struck fear in the heart of any thinking man. Military leaders would arise and take over governments or throw nations into internal chaos, while legitimate kings and parliaments would fight for their lives. A strong President would be a safeguard against a military despot, but a strong Congress was an even better safeguard—there might be times in the future when Congress would protect citizens from their own President. If the safeguards were in the system rather than dependent on personalities, America would be free from that disruptive pitch and roll so common to other nations. Madison felt confident that once he and his peers had accomplished that, the nation would be free from military coups.

The highly intellectual James Madison was driven by ideas and by the construction of whole systems. To think that the British might smash his entire life's work was an anguish so grave he could scarcely conceive of it.

He ached now because he had to go back to the living quarters, where Dolley would be bent over her needlework or her correspondence, humming while Uncle Willy cracked sunflower seeds. She would be worried when he told her he'd be joining the Army, so to speak.

He remembered what she wrote him once in a love letter years ago when her knee became infected. It was the first separation of their marriage and both were wretched. He kept all her letters to him in his desk, even the notes she put on his pillow or hid in his pockets. He walked over to the desk and pulled out one of the drawers containing her letters. He touched the envelopes. "Our hearts understand each other," she had written. He knew she would understand.

3 August 1814, Wednesday

*M*y husband insists that he ride out with General Winder. I offered no argument. How could I? He is the commander in chief. He had this war pushed on him and he despises it as much as I do, but he will do his duty, and oh, dear God, he's so frail. What if the enemy should recognize him? Mr. Monroe will accompany him, but he isn't a young man either.

Jemmy hasn't told me exactly when he is going to do this, but soon, I should think.

The only two persons left in the city attended my levee. Well, it seems like two, but James Blake was there, the Daschkovs, my dear Seruriers, Anna, the Monroes, and of course the Vice President. The surprise was that both John Armstrong and William Jones appeared. No doubt they thought they had to put on a good face after their intolerable behavior. Elbridge Gerry talked to me at length. He recalled his youth during the Revolutionary War and reminded me, that war was not universally supported either.

I don't know how I managed to be cheerful during the evening, because all I could think of was Jemmy's riding off to discover the enemy. It should be Henry Clay and John Calhoun, not my husband!

French John told me he has heard that John Randolph is inquiring about buying a house in Washington. Neither of us can believe this. I thought Randolph was experiencing financial difficulties. How can he buy a house here? French John also told me that an acquaintance's house in Georgetown sold for nine thousand dollars. The prices these people are getting! How did a house in that area, so muggy, ever fetch such an exorbitant price?

Fortunately, Jemmy acquired a few lots in the city before becoming President. Selling them will keep us in our old age, although the lots will prove useless if people don't want to buy them.

Matilda Lee Love was also here this evening. She said there must be over one hundred houses now in Georgetown, but the imagined profits from the sale of these houses remain just that—imagined. She too was amazed that a house had just sold, and for such a price. Nothing else has been selling. Then she laughed and declared, "We could depend on the good men of Washington to defend their city if for no other reason than to maintain their property values."

Dickey has been running a fever and so has French John's youngest daughter. Summer is the fever season here, and one can't be too careful, but it is especially hard on the little ones and the elderly. Anna, as always, is patience herself.

I received a letter from Henry Clay. Payne is fine. The British have not appeared at Ghent for the negotiations. Of course not, I thought, they're all on the Chesapeake. I should write Clay that. He'd find it amusing. The gall and arrogance of the English! We cross an ocean while they have merely to cross a channel, but they keep us waiting.

I know it's sinful, but I pray to God for a great victory in arms just to put them in their place.

Tonight as I write this, a silvery mist enshrouds the house. A pale circle, a hint of light, indicates where the moon must be. I expect giftzwergen to creep out of the mist, to frighten Uncle Willy and me with their evil. I remember as a child hearing about these poison dwarfs. Mother Amy used to tell us the most bloodcurdling stories. The giftzwergen punished people for their misdeeds but also for the sheer deviltry of hurting someone.

She scared Temple and me half to death with the story of a military ball back in the days when Virginia was being settled. The ball was given at the governor's mansion in Williamsburg. Carriages lined the streets and candles glittered through the windowpanes. An arrogant young British officer, despised by all but terribly handsome, had broken the heart of a Tidewater belle and then was cruel enough to laugh at her expense. He danced with every lady that evening, and when he visited the punch bowl, a little, well-dressed man, a dwarf, smiled at him and pointed to a dazzling beauty quietly sitting along the wall. The officer, smitten, immediately asked her to dance. They danced every quadrille and minuet that night. Her brown eyes sparkled and her golden hair caught the light. The officer couldn't take his eyes off her, and the little man leaned against the wall, enjoying the sight.

At the end of the ball the young gallant asked the beauty if he might escort her home. She said yes but that she would need to ask her guardian. She inquired of the dwarf and he said he would be delighted to ride in the officer's sumptuous coach.

She was chilly, so the young man wrapped her in his officer's cloak.

The cool night air brushed their cheeks, a relief from the heat of the ballroom. As they came to a crossroad, the dwarf asked the coachman to stop. He hopped out of the coach and held up his tiny hand. The young lady took his hand and gracefully glided down from the coach.

The officer, confused, begged her to allow him to take her to the door. She smiled and said, "No, I want you to remember me in the starlight."

He asked where she lived and she answered, "Not far."

He beseeched the dwarf, who replied, "We live in the cottage Rosedown. Come, Rebecca."

In an instant they were gone, she still wearing his cloak. He didn't call her back. It would be an excuse to visit.

The next day the officer returned to the crossroad and followed west. Shortly he came to the cottage called Rosedown. He dismounted and knocked on the door. An older, but good-looking, woman answered. He asked for her daughter and she replied that she had no daughter. He told the lady about the previous night and how he had danced with Rebecca. Her face blanched. She silently pointed to a graveyard, then quickly closed the door.

He walked to the graveyard and on top of a grave, neatly folded, was his officer's cloak. On the headstone were the words "Rebecca Rice. Born April 9, 1698. Died January 12, 1714." He heard the dwarf laughing in the woods, and he lost his mind. They say he danced himself to death.

Mother Amy's voice would drop low and then she'd fold her hands and stare into the fire. Oh, how that scared me and oh, how I loved it.

As I grew older, I'd catch her changing the names. One time it was Elizabeth Haldane and another it was Meredith McLaughlin. Each new crop of Paynes would hear that story.

I've always been able to remember names and faces. Jemmy says he doesn't know what he'd do without me.

Apart from telling wonderful stories, Mother Amy never told me anything that wasn't true. She used to say, "Sickness comes in through the mouth and disaster comes out of it." I have had ample, melancholy opportunity to observe the accuracy of that over the years.

When I'd become frightened, she'd pat my head and say, "Fear seeks a place to rest in all of us. Cast him out! Cast him out!" Then she'd make a motion as though tearing fear from her breast.

I was never afraid when Mother Amy was with me except when she was telling ghost stories. I was never afraid of her, either. I was often afraid of Mother. Anna says that she wasn't as afraid of Mother as I was. Maybe by the time she bore Anna, she was so tired that she didn't have time to get after her.

These levees stir me up. It takes hours to get to sleep afterward, and my mind rattles on so.

Even Uncle Willy has given up and gone to sleep. He draws one leg up under him sometimes when he sleeps. I tried it, wide awake, and I wobbled. I gained new respect for Uncle Willy.

If I prattle on, I'll never get to bed.

Until the morrow, God willing.

D.P.M.

*S*howers of tiny black flies dropped from the leaves of the trees, hovered, and then rose up again like raindrops returning to the clouds.

Barely half past seven and the morning was sticky. Dolley prepared a cold late breakfast for Jemmy, who had been working since six o'clock. Whenever he could rise early, he would go straight to his desk, forgetting about food.

Cold ham, fresh mustard, corn bread, a succulent melon, and a dripping pitcher of iced coffee lured the President from his papers.

They sat in what should have been the backyard, but no one had gotten around to landscaping the presidential mansion. Had Dolley even suggested it, the Federalists would have accused her of frivolousness and financial idiocy in the face of staggering debt.

She had plans for the grounds in good time, and it infuriated her that a nation would so burden its President without making the smallest effort to provide him with pleasing quarters. What better place to share the problems of state than in a beautiful garden? She took cuttings from friends' gardens and did what she could under the dreary circumstances.

Dolley tapped her foot. Irritation rose in her throat as she thought about the situation. She employed one gardener, who doubled as a handyman, and French John. Out of her money. Not only did the President need a staff, she did, but Congress wouldn't begrudge her a penny.

"Jemmy, do you think Congress will vote itself a raise this fall?"

"Not until the war is over. They'll have to make do on fifteen hundred dollars a year." He swatted at a fly. "This ham is delicious."

"It's the honey."

"Cured in honey? When we return to Montpelier, I've got to try that." He leaned back in his chair. "How I miss home."

"Perhaps in the fall . . ." her voice trailed off.

He put the sweating glass down. "Why didn't you tell me you sold your necklace to pay for the horses?"

Dolley wriggled in her seat. "I never liked those amethysts."

"Dolley—"

"Really, Jemmy, they weren't at all becoming, and—"

"You adored that necklace."

"I did not." Her lips pursed.

"You will not go off and sell your valuables without consulting me. I won't have it."

"Jemmy, you have far more important things on your mind. I am not going to bother you with drivel. The farm needed a new team and really, truly, I had grown tired of the amethysts." She edged toward a pout. "Anyway, how did you find out?"

He smiled. "You aren't the only person in Washington with good sources of information. Now, do you promise?"

"You know, I was just thinking how titanic are the mental powers of Daniel Webster. Surely he's related to Memory, mother of the Muses." Jemmy eyed her as she rolled on. "Young Daniel has to remember everything. Such prodigious powers." She paused. "Far in excess of my meager intellectual capacities, but then I don't really need such a mighty brain. The advantage of telling the truth is that I don't have to remember what I have said."

Jemmy tipped back his head and roared.

Dolley rose to clear the table.

Still chuckling, Jemmy folded his arms over his chest. "Mrs. Madison . . ."

"Oh, all right, I promise!"

He laughed even harder.

4 August 1814, Thursday

*A*nna promised me she will leave the city if the enemy marches on us, but until such a calamitous day comes, she is staying put. We had words over this but then we both settled down. She's uncomfortable and laughs that she's at the waddle stage with this baby. Also, it wouldn't look heartening if my sister fled the city on the basis of rumors. I did get her to promise in front of Richard that she would go if the situation worsened. He was away so much in the winter. I'm glad he's home these days.

Richard has lost so much to the war already. Financial losses are hard for men to bear, far harder than for women, I think. I know Anna remembers our father's retreat when he went bankrupt, and she fears bankruptcy for herself. Fortunately, they aren't bankrupt. Should that misery befall them, I don't know what Richard would do. As for Anna, she will do as our mother did, keep working.

Jemmy received from Henry Clay a copy of a London newspaper with a story claiming that half the eighteen thousand troops assigned to attack the most important ports in America have sailed. We've known that Wellington's men were to fight here, but we haven't known the numbers. Some reports have said thirty-five thousand troops are on the way. Of course, one must be wary since inflated numbers are a certainty and Britain is paying men to tell "secrets."

Since the bill passed for more troops, we should have enough Regulars to face them, but in fact we don't. Most of the men between Baltimore and Washington are only recently mustered in, so I can't believe they will be very different from the militias. I hope they have fighting hearts.

A British squadron was sighted off Norfolk, and we've heard that enemy ships have been scouting the Patuxent River. The Patuxent, of course, leads toward Washington. When Jemmy reported the rumor to Armstrong, the Secretary of War said it was merely a feint.

General Winder still has no staff and is exhausting himself doing the work that subordinates should be doing. My husband told Armstrong today that if he wouldn't give Winder an adjutant, Jemmy would name one himself. I think Armstrong's attitude has rubbed off on General Winder, who has called up only a fifth of the Maryland Militia. Not many have responded either.

What I keep telling myself is that British ships have been sighted on trickles of water. In wartime people become most anxious, and a raft floating down a creek becomes three warships on the Mississippi.

Mother Madison wrote Jemmy, urging him to send out a declaration to the people. Tell them to throw stones if they have no ammunition. The image of Mother Madison aiming rocks at the enemy from her roof made me laugh. She'd do it, too.

How I love Montpelier in August! I look forward to each summer when we escape Washington and sink deeper into the rolling green hills of Virginia. The carriage sways back and forth on the dusty, rutted roads, and I know every shed, barn, and house between here and home. Finally we turn onto the land, past the cornfields and the hay, until we can see the stables, the horses in the fields, and then the house. By the time we reach the front door, Mother Madison is on the porch, arms outstretched, while the servants dash about and the dogs bark. It is heaven, my heaven anyway.

As soon as I'm out of the carriage, Mother Madison asks me if I want to rest; before I can answer, we're hurrying into her gardens so that she can show me what improvements she's made. Then it's off to the stables to see the foals and the yearlings. Mother Madison and I never run out of things to talk about and we're both so proud of Jemmy's farming abilities. He uses the most advanced techniques, and Montpelier gets more yield per acre than do any of the neighboring farms. When Jemmy isn't studying state papers, he's poring over agricultural treatises. Truthfully, he's far happier as farmer than as President.

Just this time of year, too, iridescent hummingbirds flock to the orange trumpet creepers, bumblebees are so laden with their booty that I don't know how they fly, and rabbits scamper everywhere. I love to sit in a pasture listening to the horses munch, smelling the sweet grass, and watching hawks laze overhead on the soft breezes. Uncle Willy accompanies me but he becomes agitated if he sees a hawk. He opens his turquoise wings, his yellow chest gleams in the sun, and how he hollers. They can hear him up at the big house. Fortunately he likes the horses, so he behaves when they're around.

I love the sound of the men and women singing in the fields, black voices so melancholy and beautiful.

I love to stroll through the stables, to smell the dark-leather odor of the traces, collars, saddles, and bridles, each bearing the name of the animal to which it belongs. Out streak the barn cats—black and white ones, one enormous calico, and, of course, tigers. The order appeals to me, the sense of purpose.

I think when people go wrong, it's because they don't have a sense of purpose. Perhaps that's what destroyed my father. The Society of Friends was his purpose and when they failed him, he couldn't find a new one. He had given his life over to ideas. Better he had given it over to people.

Mother's purpose never wavered. She had her children and she had her faith, and no group of people, liking her or disliking her, could shake that faith. It wasn't to be found in books, in rules, or under a roof dedicated to God. Her faith was inside. She was filled with the Inner Light.

In this last year I have thought much about my purpose. I am bound to my husband, and our purposes are mutual. He serves the country in his way as do I, in my small way. I will always believe that if I had been able to sit the Prime Minister of England and Jemmy at my dinner table, this cursed war would never have happened.

A country seems to be, and is, a great purpose; but I remember Mother's words about worldly vanity, and there's much of that in the politics of leading a country. There is a purpose even higher than my country, and in this all Christian peoples share.

When I am most in need of comfort, I read the Beatitudes.

I must set aside thoughts of Montpelier until we are through this ordeal.

Until the morrow, God willing.

D.P.M.

I have unraveled the Sukey mystery. When she daydreams and hums to herself, it means she's up to no good. She hummed constantly while she was enjoying the favors of Daschkov, or was he enjoying hers? Well, no matter. For the last few days she's been far more industrious than usual, attempting to get her work done before nightfall. I usually let her go about town until it's time for me to get ready for a gathering, and then she needs to be here. She's quite good with my clothes and she's the best hairdresser I've ever had. I truly do need Sukey. She may even be beginning to understand that she needs me.

While Daschkov was her object of attention, she would sneak off into the night. She hasn't been doing that, so I took her staying home at night as a sign of improvement. Staying home to trifle with poor young Paul! Oh, I could box her ears. She torments and taunts him endlessly. He's been in love with her for some time and she appears to be returning his affection. Then she pushes him away.

I found him today in a flood of tears because she told him his nose was too big. It isn't, of course; he's a handsome lad. I asked him why it should matter, who cares what Sukey thinks, and he burst out afresh, saying that he loved her and couldn't live without her.

Seducing Paul is different from toying with the Russian minister, who is a man of the world. That affair caused such eruptions in this household that I can't chastise her for this one, although I do think, morally, this is worse. Paul is so terribly innocent and young and she'll shred his heart. I love that boy. I hate to see him hurt.

Naturally I can't tell Jemmy. He believes that one must wait until finding the right partner and then marry and hold fast to that partner. Infidelity, the mere hint of it, infuriates him. He often says that he waited until his forties to find me and it was worth it.

Jemmy can be very gallant. When he began courting me, I did inquire and I was surprised to discover that he had courted only one other lady, when he was much younger, and that she had found someone else more attractive. She hinted that Jemmy was too short and not very handsome. Silly fool. Not even a hint of dalliance after that for Jemmy.

At first, when I ascertained these facts, I rejoiced. Then—and of course this was before I married him—I thought that perhaps he was a man who was not drawn to women physically. I've had occasion to observe such marriages and they seem to be fine. I shared this suspicion with Lucy and Anna. Lucy counseled me to remember that John was young when I married him and physically quite superb. Jemmy, being older and frail (I think of him as wiry but everyone else, Jemmy included, says frail), might be less robust in such matters. Anna, as always, drove to the heart of the matter. She said that I would know after we were married.

And so I did. My husband is all that I or any other woman could wish.

This reverie does not solve the problem of Sukey! I must do as Nelson did at Trafalgar and turn a blind eye.

Thinking about men and vigor: Henry Clay has eight children and yet I don't believe he really loves Lucretia. Some people seem incapable of deep love. They may be good people, but intertwining their lives with others' just isn't their way. I think this is true of Mr. Clay. He's a convivial man but he keeps the most important things to himself.

All the Payne girls married for love, and we've been most fortunate in our husbands.

I asked Lisel Serurier, who drove with me today along the river, if Europeans marry for love. She replied that it often depends on their class. She found Louis handsome. He dazzled her parents because he was a rising star in the Napoleonic firmament, but mostly because he had money. She confided that she learned to love him after they married, and that as much as she cares for him, she thinks their relationship is quite different from Jemmy's and mine.

This startled me and I said, "How?"

She replied, "You and Mr. Madison are two souls with one heart-beat."

Until the morrow, God willing.

D.P.M.

The road to Bladensburg curved across the soft hills of Maryland. A light rain during the night kept the dust down. Except for the furious rumble of bumblebees in the crape myrtle and honeysuckle tumbling along the road, it was quiet and deserted.

James Madison, riding his favorite blood bay, and James Monroe, astride his sorrel horse, walked ahead of their small military escort, which consisted of Colonel Charles Carroll and a young captain hoping to rejoin his troops outside the small town.

The pleasant temperature, not at all like that of an August day, made the war seem far away. Madison and Monroe spoke of supplies, troops, and possible entrenchments. The day was so lovely, they chatted for a few moments about the old days. James Monroe knew Madison liked horse racing. He asked the President if he enjoyed boxing, and Madison replied that he had not witnessed many such matches but they were exciting in a brutal fashion. The men recalled Tom Molineaux, a freed Virginia slave who had caused a sensation in England as a heavyweight boxer a few years before. He was finally beaten in the fortieth round of an extremely punishing match. Madison thought that as the country became more civilized, blood sports would wither and die. Monroe thought that men would always pay for the delight of seeing one man beat another insensate.

"What is it, think you, Mr. Monroe, that drives us to violence?" Madison asked genially.

"Think of our cattle and our horses. Don't the strongest stallions and the strongest bulls drive the others off? It's the nature of male animals to dominate, to kill one another, I'm afraid, and we can't suppress it entirely. Perhaps if we encouraged more boxing, we'd have less war." Monroe smiled, revealing good strong teeth stained with tobacco.

"That may be our animal nature, but didn't Christ come to free us from our animal nature?"

Monroe thought long and hard. "I would have to say that men are perverse, and by repudiating Christ, men gain earthly glory. Most men prefer earthly glory to heavenly reward. After all, they can't see heaven."

"I see it in my wife's eyes." Madison smiled. He adored mentioning his wife occasionally to other men. If he indulged in the sin of pride, then he would suffer later, in the afterlife. He simply could not resist a chance to brag about Dolley.

"You, sir, are most fortunate, as am I." Monroe smiled, too. He had known this little fellow next to him for most of his adult life. Perhaps old wounds were never completely forgotten, but there was a complacency, an easiness, in being with an old, old acquaintance.

They rode another ten minutes before Madison spoke. "General Winder seems to be encountering a host of delays in raising fortifications for our city." He sighed. "Well, the one good thing I did accomplish was in effecting military promotions by merit. We are beginning to see the result of that but, unfortunately, not here. In the last two years the age of our field generals, on the average, has dropped from sixty to about forty. And I think this new crop of generals—Jacob Brown, Winfield Scott, Edmund Gaines, Alexander Macomb, and Andrew Jackson—I think these young men will take the fight to the enemy."

"And John Armstrong will take the credit. Every time you make a decision on one of Armstrong's suggestions for a promotion, he instantly informs the officer as though he has been totally responsible for the action. If you grant the officer's promotion, the officer thinks Armstrong is his friend and he is sure Armstrong has petitioned you constantly in his favor. If you deny a promotion, you make a political enemy and Armstrong goes back to the man and wrings his hands in sympathy. I detest the ground that imbecile walks on," Monroe said.

"So do I."

A cavalry lieutenant greeted them from the opposite direction. He rode up at a trot. Seeing that it was the President and the Secretary of State, he executed a smart salute.

Colonel Carroll and the young captain hastened to catch up to the President and Monroe.

When the colonel introduced himself, the lieutenant grinned. "There are a mess of Carrolls in this neck of the woods."

"Shake a tree and a Carroll falls out," the colonel agreed with good humor.

"Then start shaking trees, gentlemen. I have need of men like Carroll," Madison said.

Colonel Carroll nodded, grateful for the praise—praise that would be heard from one end of Washington to the other, for in Washington the only thing that traveled faster than praise was bad news.

Both Madison and Monroe struggled to conceal their shock when they came to the ragged bands of militia at Bladensburg. General Winder was farther down the road, but still, this was sobering. It wasn't simply bad news, it presaged disaster. Colonel Carroll spoke sharply to the officer in charge, which produced salutes from the soldiers.

As Madison continued riding, he realized that Washington didn't have a hope in hell. Monroe knew it, too. Neither man spoke of it.

For the first time in his life, James Monroe prayed that John Armstrong was right: Baltimore was the target.

6 August 1814, Saturday

*T*onight a soft rain pats a counterpoint to the scratching of my quill. I told Sukey to sharpen the point, but she has an unlimited capacity for forgetfulness. I also asked her to be careful with Paul. He's so sweet and young, I don't want him hanging on the short end of a promise. She didn't reply, which meant she didn't want me meddling in her business. However, she was civil. That's a step forward.

Jemmy returned home from his inspection, exhausted but invigorated. No sign of the British. Armstrong stubbornly presses his case that those troops sailing to our shores will be diverted to New Orleans or to Baltimore. Control of New Orleans means control on the Mississippi, which means control of the entire West. As for Baltimore, it's in the middle of the coastal states, a thriving city, a perfect location—once conquered—from which to send out ships both north and south.

Armstrong vows he is making every effort to see that Washington is not conquered. Jemmy says that if what he saw today is Armstrong's "every effort," then we had better arm the women and children.

The British, under General Phineas Riall and General Gordon Drummond, are laying siege to Fort Erie. We've just learned of the struggle, but no one yet knows the outcome. We have two thousand men at Fort Erie. The British are rumored to have a force of at least a thousand more.

If only we knew what was happening there and in Louisiana. The news crawls to our door, or so it seems. As for the peace commission, Henry Clay writes regularly. The British still haven't appeared. If seas are smooth and winds favorable, we receive news in about one month. Usually it takes six weeks. Knowing is always better than not knowing, even if the news is bad.

Then there are the persistent rumors that the British will invade the Hudson River Valley, take Albany, and control New York City. This would dislodge the Northeast from the rest of the nation, and some people are speculating that should this happen, New England and New York will stay permanently dislodged.

When we run out of military rumors, we can always listen to the outright lies—more rumors about my "amours." Henry Clay this time, but since he's in Ghent, I am said to be consoling myself with Mayor Blake.

The only rumor I haven't heard is that the British troops will drop out of the sky. Even doomsayers and mountebanks stop somewhere this side of reality!

I think about Albert Gallatin's advice: all wars are bad, but if they can't be avoided, it is less expensive to be ready than to rush to arms unprepared. How foolish the Federalists were, and remain, to be so set against Gallatin. Never a war hawk, he worked tirelessly at the

209

Treasury, which was ultimately to their benefit as well. They could never understand that Mr. Gallatin does not suffer fools gladly, nor could they weaken his loyalty to Jemmy.

Today I made French John laugh. Rainy days provoke me to organizing. I started with the drawing room, and the more I worked and dusted, the more I thought I really must do something. So I called in French John to help me rearrange furniture. I said, "If I can't change the world, at least I can change this room." It struck him so funny that he had to put down the chair he was carrying and sit in it. Uncle Willy joined in, which only added to his amusement. He said that for just a moment I reminded him of a fat French priest. My expression must have changed. Every now and then I can get a little plump, but I lose the weight during the summer. Well, he laughed some more and said no, no, he didn't mean I was fat but that when he was a boy, a ward of the Church of Rome, one of the priests was forever moving furniture about the library or whatever room struck his fancy. One day French John and the acolytes moved a particularly heavy pew, and the priest decided he wanted it returned to its original place. French John, instead, walked over to the priest, picked him up with the help of three other boys, and threw him out the window. The second-story window! He prudently followed this action by running away from the Church.

This was not the first time he had told me the story, but I never tire of it.

Then I asked him to return the chair to its original place, and we both grew so silly that we had to sit on the floor and laugh. I do so love French John. When Payne was little, he'd roll up the sleeves of his shirt and show my little angel his tattoos. Each tattoo had a story. If Payne was a good boy, he'd get to hear a story every day.

We laughed until we ached. Then we repaired to the kitchen and the icehouse, where I cut open a delicious cantaloupe and put vanilla ice cream in the middle. The two of us ate so much we couldn't move.

French John, my eyes and my ears, never fails me. He informed me that the first panic is over. The people who are staying in Washington seem to have settled back into their routines, and the ones who have left would probably have gone to their country retreats anyway. He's putting a good face on it, but there's some merit to his view.

He brought a keg of powder to the back door. When I asked him why, he replied, "Just in case."

And we talked politics. He said he thinks Webster is a bit of an actor and that his wrath is calculated to appeal to those men who are losing money in this war. What an interesting thought.

French John is proof of Jefferson's dictum that the common man will make the correct decision if given the information. But then French John is not a common man. Perhaps no one is.

Delighted as I am to see this soft rain, I know the battle against pokeweed and dandelion will be renewed by midweek.

I'm no different from the other residents of Washington, sinking into routine. I go over the food purchases with French John. I inspect my little garden. I plan for my levee. I've decided a few small dinner parties for the Cabinet members will be good for morale. The small rituals of daily life offer solace and structure. No, I don't know what tomorrow will bring, but do we ever? Isn't the future an illusion, a kind of hallucination we call up to drive us forward? The uncertainty about the British, about our very lives, only serves to illustrate how fragile life is.

What is my life? What will I leave behind besides my handsome and gifted son? Will anyone remember the dinner parties when I'm long dead? Would they remember Mother's little house in Philadelphia where the great men of the day dropped by during the Constitutional Convention? Alexander Hamilton, doomed man; Aaron Burr, doomed too; Benjamin Franklin—oh, the list could go on, those shadows and spirits who founded this government. Perhaps they will be remembered, but I doubt that Dolley Payne will be remembered, except as a notation: wife of James Madison, fourth President of the United States.

Is it vain to want to be remembered? According to the Society of Friends I suppose it is, but to me it seems quite natural. Well, I won't be remembered. The social aspect of government is much enjoyed and instantly forgotten. I was hostess for Thomas Jefferson when he was

President and James was his Secretary of State. I especially enjoyed helping Meriwether Lewis and William Clark prepare for their great expedition. Oh, how I would have loved to make that trek with them. I've seen every great man this country has produced and most of the great women, too. Abigail Adams most impressed me, a force truly. I've met the ministers from other lands who've come here to cajole us, cheat us, or observe us. And how odd to think that it will wash away with our passing. I will wash away.

Time has greater power than any of us can imagine. John Todd has disappeared, as have my mother, Mother Amy, my brother Temple and my son Temple, beautiful sister Mary, my oldest brother, Walter, my brother Isaac, and Father. It's as if they dissolved in the silver rain outside the window. And when I'm gone, who will remember them?

How curious is this life. How curious memory, at once a caress from the past and a thorn in the heart. I have learned to live with my losses, and my losses have taught me how to cherish life. Surely, there is a kinder way to learn.

I am vain. The ladies at Pine Street Meeting House used to complain to Mother that I was overfond of fripperies. A ribbon was damnation itself.

I do want to be remembered. I was here. I lived. I cried. I laughed. I breathed. I was part of the life of my beloved country.

Well, I won't be here to know I'm forgotten! So there.

As Senator Brown would say, "Mrs. Madison, it's all a crapshoot."

I rolled my dice. Nine. I rolled nine in six tries and I didn't lose. I should have made a wish on it. A wish that if I got my number before double sixes or snake eyes, I would be remembered. Too late now. That would be cheating. Still, I rolled my number.

Until the morrow, God willing.

D.P.M.

7 August 1814, Sunday

*D*o I use rouge? Apparently this has become a question of paramount importance to certain ladies of the town. The slander of my supposed extramarital escapades has dimmed. They seek new sins. When Madame Serurier told me today, I didn't know whether to laugh or strike some wellborn names off my guest list. Of course, I would never do that. Jemmy needs their husbands' support. The utter pettiness of this to-do in the midst of a war astonishes me. Madame Serurier shrugged and counseled that women, denied a share in the exercise of true citizenship, sink into social superiority. Emotions become their province, social control their destiny. Not for us the voice that commands thousands on the battlefield or raises the roof of Congress. No, it is our place to sit around worrying about whether someone wears rouge, a sure sign of the tart or of fading charms.

To tell the truth, I never thought I had much in the way of physical charms, with the exception of my skin. Men pay attention to me, but that's because I love life. Such energy attracts and men will ever be pulled to a warm, lively soul over a cold and perfect beauty.

The rouge drama, argued hotly by my female detractors and defenders, rages. My detractors offer as proof the fact that I turned forty-six on May twentieth. How good of them to remember my birthday. No woman of my doddering years could possibly have color in her cheeks. My Grandmother Coles kept hers. My defenders trumpet as proof of my virtue that when I was given the Macedonian flag at a naval ball by a handsome officer, the color rushed and then fled from my cheeks.

Dear God, save me from my defenders!

I think I preferred the rumors of my various affairs with men to this twaddle.

Oh yes, another rumor is that I wear turbans because I'm going bald.

I think the gossip that did offend me was that I have no close friends. They say I am close only to members of my family.

If I cultivate many friends outside my family, then they say I am not paying attention to my first duty. If I cultivate male friends, well, it's obvious what they say. If I cultivate female friends, I'll be scourged as a frivolous gossip.

There are moments when the human race looks rather less than dogs or cats. At least they mind their own business.

Well, Madame and I, overlooking the Potomac on this sticky day, spoke of many things loftier than these absurd rumors.

I said, in reply to the drivel, that it is in the nature of men and women to prattle in the face of crisis.

She asked, "If so, then how can you believe in democracy, people being the idiots we know them to be?"

I replied that our discussion about the state of women answered her question. Removed from the stage, they fiddle backstage, lose interest, and make trouble.

"Men gossip worse than women do," Lisel observed.

"Supposedly their gossip is in the service of the state. It's disguised as information."

This made her laugh and we chattered on about political systems, men, and Nature. She said something that struck me. She is quite wise for one so young, and so infused with dark beauty. Lisel commented, "You can't use Nature to justify a political system. Nature is amoral and ordered. Politics is immoral and chaotic."

The French Revolution has left a bloody mark on Lisel, like the mark on the forehead of a Roman Catholic on Ash Wednesday. She has no faith in the perfectibility of man. All systems of government rest on the threat of force, and I am hard-pressed to deny her that outlook.

It's a curious thing that people can't work together in harmony naturally. A form of coercion is necessary. Why, if working together is for the common good? Some get more good out of it than others do; the Boston bankers perhaps are a case in point.

Lisel spread out a delicate handkerchief of Belgian lace. She placed it in my hands. The lace felt so cool against my skin.

"Women toil for days to make this lace, a small handkerchief; yet they can barely feed their children. If I tear this or grow tired of it, I'll buy another. I don't think I am a wasteful or an extravagant woman, by French standards anyway, but what must that Belgian lace maker think of me, if she thinks of me at all? Hatred."

I thought about that. "Someone of your own class could hate you equally, but Lisel, no one who knows you could hate you at all." True enough, for Madame Serurier shimmers with goodness.

"Knowing me might provoke a moment of communion with a lace maker but only for a moment. I'm near the top of the heap and she's near the bottom."

"Your efforts, given your station, are as diligent as the lace maker's labors are for hers. Surely, an intelligent lace maker could see that?"

"Oh, Dolley, you are so American." She laughed. "You people brim over with optimism. In Europe we trip over the corpses of hundreds of thousands of dead—not just those of the Napoleonic Wars but those countrymen we killed ourselves. And how did that happen? One day the peasants had had quite enough of the crass disregard the aristocrats showed them. Or maybe the sight of a lace handkerchief to a woman in rags was too much. I don't know. Everyone has a theory, of course, but I have yet to be convinced of facts. What *is* a fact is that we slaughtered one another. For liberty, equality, and fraternity." She leveled her gaze on mine.

"Surely, what your country experienced will produce some good. Suffering teaches many lessons."

"Mostly that you no longer want to suffer." She inhaled the heavy air. "Your New England citizens have suffered very little compared with those of France, very little, and yet for dollars they would abandon the rest of this country. What will happen if enormous suffering should befall this abundant nation?"

"Don't be misled by Federalist leaders. The Yankee farmer knows well enough why we fight."

"What's the Yankee farmer against the might of the wealthy?"

"What was the peasant against the might of the aristocracy?"

"Touché." Lisel smiled. "But consider the result."

"Touché, in turn."

In the quiet of the evening—even Uncle Willy is resting—I am drawn to wonder if it is possible to create a nation that reflects the teachings of Christ. If that is not possible, can we create a nation where simple justice is the rule and where persons can rise according to the level of their ability?

If we believe that, then we must destroy, once and forever, slavery.

The first American Revolution was against the tyranny of King George III. The second American Revolution must be against the tyranny of selfishness.

Until the morrow, God willing.

D.P.M.

*T*oday we learned that the British, under General Drummond, have captured Fort Erie. Their ability to hold on to their prize is questionable, and the fate of Fort Erie will be played out until the ice and snow return, I fear.

We receive no good news from the war or from the peace. I wonder if the British peace commission under Lord Gambier has finally arrived in Ghent. I do wish Henry Clay would write me another letter. How will the British open the negotiations? Clay, before he left in January, said they are so cynical, they will use anything to confuse us.

Today I wrote Lucy a long letter. No doubt she's sweltering in Lexington. It contained my usual chitchat about family and friends and thoughts on the war, and I signed it "love" as I always do.

Can you send love through the mail? I think you can. I think you can send it if you sit quietly and pray, too. Over the years I've sat side by side with Death. I know his ways. Even in his kindness, the relief of intolerable suffering, he leaves behind others, dumbfounded with grief. I've felt his shadow at noon, and oddly, I have learned not to fear him. He's taught me a great deal. All the getting and pushing and winning are but surface activity. Love, in its myriad forms, is the true force of life, and sometimes Love cheats even Death of his gruesome finality. And so I sign my letters "love."

Lisel, fascinated by Bonaparte's conquests, told me that when the French were in Egypt, they found a chant for the dead. It sings of a goddess, and I forget her name, but the chant says, "And she will recognize the way. She will come and go around those who love her for millions of days."

Love leading the dead toward what? Forgetfulness of life or perhaps rapture. But I was struck by Love giving those she cherishes millions of days. Isn't that what each of us has to give, time? Our days?

I observe people at my levees. Most work. A few are no-counts. Would that I had the time those no-counts squander. The hours and days and years. Would that I had that time to go around those I love for millions of days.

Until the morrow, God willing.

D.P.M.

10 August 1814, Wednesday

*U*ncle Willy proved to be the most exciting creature at my levee. The chatter was dim, the smiles were forced, and most of the women were missing. They must slip away in the dead of night, leaving their husbands to make excuses. Their health, the oppressive humidity of Washington, and so on. I can't blame them. If the worst comes, they want to make sure their families are spared.

John Armstrong still has not produced a staff for General Winder. Jemmy read him a list of duties that must be performed, including the defense of Washington. Other than a handful of militiamen and Commodore Joshua Barney's sailors and marines, about four hundred of them, to guard the river, there's little between us and the British.

In the early spring Jemmy invited Commodore Barney to Washington and asked his advice on how to defend the city. The Commodore replied, "There's no way to defend it as long as you have fools and incompetents in command." Well, at least one man spoke the truth!

Armstrong promised to execute each of Jemmy's demands. It's not my place to criticize my husband, but his virtues are sometimes his faults. Jemmy undergoes the tortures of the damned if he must censure anybody. The time he had to punish Sukey for her indiscretion, it was harder on Jemmy than it was on her. When something disturbs him, he becomes quieter. Armstrong lacks any sensitivity, much less a grain of sense. Most men would have understood by now how deeply concerned the President is. For Jemmy to be driven to read off a list of demands—you'd think Armstrong would have the grace to resign! Actually, my poor, burdened husband should have relieved him of his Cabinet post, but Jemmy believes that would be worse than keeping him. I bit my tongue when he told me of the Cabinet meeting. I could do a better job than John Armstrong!

Anna attended the levee. The night air, often cooling, kept so still tonight that we sweated as though in a steam bath. Quite hard on Anna, who should deliver next month. She wanted to be useful. I told her to sit by the table and hand me cups while I poured tea.

James Blake did tell me an amusing story. At the recent battle of Chippewa, in July, the Americans wore militia-gray since not a shred of blue cloth could be found for their uniforms. When the British general saw the Americans and their commander, Winfield Scott, he said to his men that they were only militia and not to worry about them. But our boys kept coming and they didn't flinch under fire. Finally the British yelled, "They're Regulars, by God!" We beat back the British.

This Winfield Scott impresses me. He led our troops at the battle of Lundy's Lane later in July, and Jemmy said it was the hardest-fought battle of the war to date. They fought throughout the day, without rest, up until midnight. Neither side claimed victory or defeat.

Would that we had Winfield Scott here in Washington.

Wonderful news! Louis XVIII continued Louis Serurier's diplomatic mission to our nation. Lisel and I were so happy we prattled like schoolgirls this evening. The Seruriers and the Daschkovs gave the evening whatever luster it possessed.

I had feared for Lisel. Apparently the King and his counselors aren't lopping off heads, which is heartening, and Talleyrand remains as powerful and wily as ever. Some day I must ask Lisel to tell me everything about him.

Sukey petted Paul today like a favorite puppy. She coos at him and then cuffs him. Mother Amy would have had her hide by now, but I'm not Mother Amy. There's no one like her nor will there ever be. Sukey, unusually cheerful, pressed my dress and petticoats without being asked. To what do I owe this sudden improvement in her behavior?

Mother Amy's husband died before I was born. She used to tell me that she loved him but that it was a relief when he was gone. He kept her busy as a cat's hair. "Mens is juss big babies, that's all they is. Juss mo' work," she'd say. Then she'd laugh. There are times when I'm inclined to agree with Mother Amy's assessment, except in Jemmy's case, of course.

Lisel noticed how many ladies are absent now. We agreed that when there's the right balance of men and women at a gathering, it's the liveliest. Then we mourned the gentlemen who are the liveliest: Henry Clay, James Brown, Langdon Cheves—more Lisel's choice than mine. Dr. William Thornton was here, but without the congressmen it's slow. Dr. Thornton told me he believes we should create a phonetic alphabet. It would make English easier to teach and to learn. I suppose it would, but I'm so used to the old one.

I made Lisel and even Elizabeth Monroe laugh when I told them the story of Senator Brown's losing a beautiful lady to a rival when he was a young man. Distraught though he was, he didn't lose his sense of humor. He had cards printed with a black border, *Toujours en deuil,* "Always in mourning," which he sent out to her wedding guests after bribing a slave for the guest list. The beauty stamped her foot and shook her pretty head and Senator Brown was disinvited to the wedding. Every year on her wedding anniversary he sends her the same card. Secretly he confided in me how fortunate he was not to have married her. She's fat as a tick now and a terrible nag, but he sends her the card anyway as a remembrance of youth and lost love. I doubt his wife is amused, but then again, I doubt that his wife knows about it.

And who knows what she's about? Those Louisiana people break all Ten Commandments with as much haste as possible. But oh, what delightful company they are!

I caught Sukey rubbing her lips with raspberries.

When she was out of range, I tried it. Produces quite a rosy glow. Until the morrow, God willing.

D.P.M.

*K*ing George lasciviously spied on the chickens reposing on the kitchen table, their plucked legs akimbo. The fragrance of blood enticed her. French John and Paul carried in corn, flour meal, and milky-white pattypan squash, as well as deep yellow crookneck. Mrs. Madison featured American foods at her table. Her husband's only intrusion on this national celebration was French wine. James Madison's refined taste brought him the respect of foreign ministers if not that of his own. But then, taste isn't strength.

Sukey swirled into the kitchen, her right hand in her large apron pocket. André had bestowed upon her a golden snuffbox with a bee carved on it. One of his numerous relatives sent it to him after the retreat from Moscow. The thousands on thousands of dead Frenchmen, sleepers in the deepest cold, bequeathed to the pursuing Russians many a precious bauble.

Dolley, Uncle Willy on her shoulder, came in from the garden, her basket full of cuttings, mostly roses.

"Sukey, put these in water, please. I'll arrange them later."

"Yes, ma'am," Sukey chirped and then winked at Paul, who blushed deeply.

"How far did you have to go to get provisions today?" Dolley asked French John.

"The Georgetown market. Today there was an abundance." He hesitated. "But the cost came to seventy-five dollars."

"What?" Dolley exclaimed.

Daily food supplies usually came to fifty dollars, far more than the bills under the frugal John Adams, who lacked the Southern sense of hospitality.

"The chickens alone were a dollar twenty apiece."

Dolley slammed her basket on the table. "I think the farmers ought to move to Boston. They'd fit in nicely there, except the Boston bankers make them look like pikers when it comes to profiteering."

A knock at the front door captured French John's attention. He composed himself and left to open the door. Within minutes he returned, his face strained, a letter in his hand.

"Now what?" Irritation crept into Dolley's usually soothing voice.

French John handed over the letter. Dolley opened it and read it, her face flushing with color. The President was being dunned for not paying the saddler's bill for her birthday present.

"Enough is enough!" Dolley smacked her hand on the kitchen table. King George, who had edged closer to the chickens, thought it was meant for her. She leaped off the table, scurrying down the hall to the hoots of Uncle Willy, now as upset as his mistress.

"Oh, hush this instant, Willy," Dolley commanded.

Willy screeched more. Never had his beloved Dolley scolded him.

Sukey held the roses in her hand and barely breathed.

"I'll take him." French John reached over and lifted Uncle Willy off Dolley's shoulder.

"I'm not fit to pour whiskey on a dog." Dolley charged out of the kitchen toward her private rooms.

Paul quietly slipped out the back door to haul in the sweet potatoes. The sight of his mistress so upset frightened him. He had never seen her this frustrated. No matter what happened, she kept her level head and cooled flaring tempers around her.

He pushed open the door with his foot and placed the bushel basket on the floor.

"These are difficult times for Mrs. Madison." French John noticed the expression on Paul's face.

"What was in the letter?" Sukey's curiosity raged, and she wished she could read better because she knew where Mr. Madison hid everything, including those old letters in Dolley's hand, tied together with a faded cream ribbon. The President surely prized those pieces of paper. After the diary episode, however, she stayed far away from anyone's desk.

"Trash, that's what was in that letter."

"They talking trash 'bout her again?" Paul's anger illuminated his sweet face. "If I was a white man, I'd call them out for a duel. Pistols or sabers, never no mind to me. Why don't the Master stand up for her? Why don't he call out those men spreadin' rumors about her?" Paul, taught by French John, was learning to listen in the marketplace, at the stable, wherever he found himself. In this way he would be more valuable to the Madisons. But Paul, often outraged at what he heard, still had to learn to betray no emotion when he listened to lies, filth, and scandal brewing.

"The Master is dead set against dueling. He thinks it's barbaric. Believe me, if Mr. Madison weren't so damned principled about it, I'd have fought plenty of duels by now. What's a few more scars?"

"They accusing her of—" Sukey was interrupted. She was going to say, "More men."

French John's teeth glittered. "Sneaking out of the house late at night doesn't always go unnoticed, and political enemies don't much care which female is sneaking out. All they have to say is that they saw a lovely female form hasten out the back way to a waiting carriage. Imagination takes care of the rest."

Paul stopped unloading the meal sacks and stared at Sukey. Sukey stared back.

"What's he saying?" Paul's voice rose.

"Nothing. He ain't saying nothing. French John don't like me no how, no way."

"You're a lazy, deceitful, lying bitch." French John's voice sounded almost sleepy. "And if you think I don't know you're still crawling all over that Russian, then you don't know much."

"Are you?" Paul's hands shook. "You promised you weren't. When you tore up Miz Dolley's diary—afterward, you promised me!"

"I do as I please." Sukey's reply was not calculated to make Paul feel better.

"But you promised . . ."

"So what? A promise to a man don't mean no more than a goat

223

barking. And a promise from a man ain't worth the time it takes him to make it." She turned from the heartsick boy to French John, whose eyes had narrowed in contempt.

"The whole goddamned British Army is maybe a day's march from here," French John hissed. "It preys on her mind. The ratty militia skulking about the streets couldn't defend themselves from a rabid dog, and poor James Blake, flying in and out of here like a sparrow, asking for help—" He waved his hand as if to say it's hopeless. "The last thing she needs to know right now is that you lied to her again, you lied to the President, and you're still"—he lapsed into French and used a very vulgar word for intercourse—"André Daschkov. I figure six weeks was the most rest you gave his part before you were pulling on it again."

Paul burst into tears and ran out the back door.

"Paul!" Sukey called after him.

Uncle Willy had had his fill of human drama. He hopped off French John's shoulder and walked out of the kitchen, peering intently around corners for sight of that awful King George.

"You leave that boy alone." French John got up in her face now. "He's a good boy with a good heart. Don't you go spoiling him. Ruining him for some good woman. Ruining him for himself."

"Men deserve what they get."

"So do women." He smacked her. "You get in line, girl, do you hear me? Mrs. Madison is too softhearted to take the strap to you, but by God, I'm not. You've got a job to do and you get to it. This whole world does not revolve around you, Sukey. If you don't straighten up, I will get Mr. Madison to sell you, and I mean every word."

"He'd never sell me!" She spit in his face.

"Just you wait. You aren't doing anything but making trouble. Don't you know what they're suffering? Don't you have any feeling for them at all?"

"He'll never sell me." Sukey crossed her arms over her alluring bosom. "And if the British win, they'll set me free."

For good measure French John struck her again, harder. "Free you? To do what?" he bellowed. "To starve in the streets? You think they'll take you back to England? They'll play with you because you're pretty and then cast you out. I know the British. You'd better wake up, girl, and figure out who your people are. They aren't the British!" He then went outside to find a sobbing Paul.

Sukey, with precise deliberation, put the chickens in the water to drain. That was really the cook's job, but she had no desire to go back into the rooms and see Dolley.

She hated French John's spying on her or doing whatever he did to figure out her affairs.

She fingered the gold snuffbox. It was worth it. She wanted money. She sometimes thought about buying her freedom. She knew she'd be expensive, but the Master would never sell her unless it was to herself. She was in the richest bloom of youth, accustomed to the company of powerful people, and her special skill was with ladies' clothing. Her demeanor and training would fetch a handsome price. You couldn't give away an old broken-down field hand. A mammy carried high value but not as much as she. Only a cook or a butler would bring more. She figured her market price to be between six and seven thousand, in hard cash and not the current devalued dollar.

She liked knowing her worth.

Buying her freedom, a fluttering daydream, wasn't the real reason Sukey wanted jewelry and money. She wanted them because they were proof of her power over men, white or black.

The Missus would never understand the icy thrill rushing to Sukey's temples when she recalled one of her conquests, sweating, begging her to caress him. Sometimes when she'd take a man's member in her mouth, he'd choke back tears of pleasure. For that, they'd do anything, give anything, and Sukey made sure she got what she wanted.

The President had power. Mrs. Madison had a kind of power, too, but Sukey believed she herself wielded the ultimate power. Immediate power. Tangible power. She could feel it beneath her fingertips. She could brush a man's nipples with her lips and make him burn. Raw sex was the greatest power of all.

*F*rench John, his arm around the wretched Paul, walked with him behind the flower garden Dolley so lovingly planned and tended. He spoke of good women and bad women, of love and sex, of desire and dependence, of slavery and freedom. It had never occurred to the handsome boy that one could be slave to one's own desires. Being born a slave, he thought that was the extent of it, and one learned to live with that. This was different, and more painful than a physical hurt.

"This game's not worth the candle, boy."

"But I love her."

"She's no good, Paul. No good to herself, either. You be patient. There's a woman out there who'll be good for you. She'll be worth the wait. I know I'd be half a man without my wife." He hugged the boy closer to him, feeling the shoulder muscles, feeling the developing power in Paul's young body.

How different from James Madison's small frame.

He thought about the old man and Dolley, still bursting with energy at forty-six years. Two small figures in a swirling maelstrom, the British at their doorstep, Congress adjourned, no help from any quarter save God; and God cared not for the United States of America these last few years.

He'd watched the citizens of Washington slip out of town in the middle of the night, hurrying across the river to Virginia and then to who knows where. He'd seen that before in Paris—the hunted, haunted look on people's faces and the thin shine of cowardice on their brows.

He knew, too, that Dolley was frightened more for her husband than for herself. She thought of James first. She thought of many people before herself. Hers was a giving nature. Yes, there was fear for herself—she wouldn't be human if there wasn't—but she resolutely kept going, keeping to routine, seeing people and being seen. Her cheerfulness blessed others with a bit of light piercing through the dark cloud cast by the British approach.

Still, the months of strain, the not knowing, the struggle to find a way and discovering every path blocked—all had taken their toll. Her flash of temper today, so small compared with what was arrayed against her, would seem terrible to Mrs. Madison. She expected a great deal of herself and punished herself mercilessly if she failed her expectations.

French John sighed. The Quaker upbringing. Underneath the turbans, the clothing, and the gaiety, that stringent, austere voice sounded in Mrs. Madison's head. He wished she had been raised a Roman Catholic. She wouldn't be so hard on herself. She wouldn't be troubled by the war in quite the same way, for her upbringing had taught her that it was wrong to kill, no matter what the situation. French John knew Dolley, knew and respected her in a way both tender and admiring. What did it do to her, to support the killing? What silent betrayal of faith gnawed at her? The ghosts of her mother and father must be hovering close by. He worried about her and for her.

Men kill and are killed. Thus it will always be. To beat oneself for the reality of human nature, to believe that one can improve it, seemed a cruel delusion to French John. Far better to accept the human animal and to accept oneself. Human beings hadn't changed since the Greeks fought beneath the walls of Troy. Who knows what they did before that, but he was quite sure there was killing and more killing. Human beings weren't going to change now, and no matter how much Mrs. Madison prayed and worked, the blood would flow.

He prayed hers wouldn't flow with it. And that bill. Mr. Madison's creditors were turning on him now. They figured he was lost and they wanted their money. French John spat on the ground. Vultures with dollar signs on their wings. He'd seen them in France, too, first picking over the bones of dead aristocrats and then over each other.

Paul wiped his eyes as French John released him.

"Everything will be all right. You'll see." French John said it, but he didn't believe it.

11 August 1814, Thursday

The creditors are hounding us. I have no intention of showing my husband the insulting letter from the saddle maker. And Sukey is up to no good. Armstrong flies between incompetence and insolence. Elbridge Gerry is failing in health and, I fear, so is little Dickey. Anna is overburdened and looks pale to me although her spirits are fine. Jemmy is losing weight and sleep. My son doesn't write. If it weren't for Henry Clay, I wouldn't know that Payne is still alive. The weather is oppressive. So are the British.

At this late hour, with only the sound of the crickets and the peepers, I imagine I can hear them breathing—thousands of British lungs inhaling our freedom, exhaling death. They sit miles away like a great beast, sides rising and falling, waiting and watching before it strikes. Where?

Here. I know in my heart that they are coming here.

I don't know what else I can do for my husband, my country, or even myself. My world is crumbling around my ears. If I were a man, even an old man, I'd join the Army. But I'm not a man, so I watch.

I have a splitting headache; the left side of my head is throbbing. I so rarely feel sick that I note it here.

My true sickness is in my heart. I can't stop an army. I can't stop the New England Federalists from plotting against their own country. We've heard the rumors of the secret convention they're planning. Given their disposition to contentiousness, it will take them all summer to determine a date and a place.

I can't stop John Armstrong in his headlong rush to ignominy.

I can't even stop my own husband from punishing himself by working until he drops. This war will kill him.

I don't know how I arrived at this moment in my life. Did I

purposefully reach this point or was I carried along by the current? I'm not sure it matters.

I've ransacked my past to find an answer. I've reviewed my child-hood, my mother and father, my sisters and brothers, Mother Amy, the Revolutionary War. There are no answers because, simply, I was a child. Whatever agony the War of Independence caused my mother and father, I perceived it as a child.

Well, I have put away childish things. I have no power, nor am I responsible for these current horrors. I am still responsible for myself and my family. I can only pray that I will acquit myself with honor. I still can't find the path between my own beliefs about war and peace. However much I long to hold to the faith of childhood, I do not see how it can possibly work in this world.

What images swirl out of memory, that grab bag of life, have no order. I remember the Redcoat and Mother. I remember Mother Amy pushing me on the swing and saying that youth was the up, old age the down.

I remember one summer sunset when we still lived in Virginia. The butterflies swooped toward their night's rest. A cricket signaled the end of day. The horses, back in the barn, neighed as Temple fed them. I was standing on the steps of the house looking west. The last rim of the sun disappeared and a light, so golden and pink I was sure it could only be the smile of God, suffused the landscape, the steps, my dress. I put my hand before my eyes and it, too, was golden as though drenched in butter, and I was beautiful. I was the sunset for that moment, as were the oaks, the horses, and the tea roses spilling over the zigzag fence. The world glowed golden and I felt that I could do anything, that we all could do anything if we would live within God's radiant smile. I watched until the evening star dashed onto the sky, and a luna moth, enormous with its pale mint swallowtailed wings edged in brilliant burgundy, alighted on my shoulder. I be-lieved the moth sang in my ear. I believed the moth was really an angel who sang, "God is great, God is good. All living creatures sing his praises. All living creatures are friends and life is love."

Life is love. Somehow over the years and the joys and sorrows, the beginnings and endings, the births and deaths, the light and the half-light and the night, somehow I have remembered that song . . . until now.

Now I hear the clock striking thirteen.

Until the morrow, God willing.

D.P.M.

A stiff breeze kicked up a funnel of dust. Neither Madison nor Monroe bothered to close the open window because the stifling heat would be worse than the dust. Neither man considered removing his coat or his waistcoat, or opening his shirt. It simply wasn't done. In the swelter, the dyes used to color the fabrics emitted a distinct odor, not entirely unpleasant but then not entirely pleasant either. Each man had grown accustomed to the other's scent, stronger on a day like today.

"I've heard travelers' tales that there's a desert wind that howls for months and will drive a man mad if one is not born to it." Madison allowed his mind to wander from the subject.

"One does hear strange things about other lands. Remember Herodotus."

"Indeed." Not only did James Madison remember the lively Greek historian, but he remembered his teacher, who had not been a lively man. "I really wished that Herodotus had written in Latin. At the time I found him trying."

Monroe smiled and picked up a stiff paper, then carefully placed it on the now-gritty table. "Fortunately, the Treaty of Fort Jackson is written in plain English."

"Do you think it will hold?"

"As long as Andrew Jackson is in the Army, the Creeks will honor the treaty."

On March 27, with three thousand men, Andrew Jackson and General John Coffee, his chief subordinate, had attacked the fortified position the Creek Indians and their Cherokee allies had built on the Tallapoosa River in Alabama. The place, called Horseshoe Bend, became a graveyard for nearly one thousand braves. The white men lost only fifty-one, with one hundred forty-eight wounded.

Preceded by a year of hard fighting, this defeat had convinced the Creeks to negotiate a treaty to end the slaughter. Not only did the white man kill them in great numbers, he carried off their women and children as prisoners.

The Creeks agreed to cede two-thirds of their territory to the United States and to retreat forever from southern and western Alabama. The whites referred to the territory as West Florida.

Madison, hagridden with care, glanced at the treaty drafts, which had taken almost as long to draft as the Indian Wars took to fight. "This frees our Army in the West and the South." He blinked as a new blast of dust filled the room. "Not fast enough for us to call them up here, I'm afraid."

"Not unless they ride night and day as the messengers did."

"What is it? 'If wishes were horses, beggars might ride,' " Madison said.

" 'Beggars mounted ride their horse to death.' "

"Ah." Madison, hearing another familiar expression, smiled. "It's curious what one remembers and one forgets. The British have taught me a great deal these last few years. They've taught me that in a time of war, you hurt your enemy any way you can. They've stabbed us in the back with the Indians in the North and the South, and Admiral Cochrane threatens us with a slave insurrection. They stop at nothing."

"According to André Daschkov, the British are as dangerous an ally as they are an enemy."

"Imprudent of Daschkov to say so." Madison sneezed. "The dust!" The President continued. "Tomorrow I want to ride out to the Navy Yard and beyond. If James Blake is available, I'd like him to accompany me . . . and you, too."

"Of course."

"No mention of this to Armstrong." Madison's voice dropped. "Mr. Monroe, this spring, did you find his recommendation to promote Thomas Flournoy to major general odd?"

"I took it as part of his vendetta against Jackson."

A sly expression washed over the older man's face and then evaporated. "That, too." Monroe leaned forward, so Madison added,

"Technically, Flournoy was subordinate to Andrew Jackson. Hot-headed as Jackson is reputed to be, promoting Flournoy over him would surely have driven him out of the Army." Madison inhaled and then sneezed again. "But did you ever ask yourself what was at stake?"

"Promoting Flournoy, an untested man, would have blocked the more obvious promotion—Jacob Brown. I assumed, Mr. President, that Armstrong was clearing the field of rivals." A red flush crept into Monroe's cheeks, so passionate was his hatred for Armstrong. "He doesn't want a great general to rise up out of this conflict. He'd risk losing the war rather than see it happen."

Madison's eyebrows shot upward. This vague notion, now for-mulated by Monroe, no longer shocked him. What shocked him was to hear it said out loud. "Yes, I believe that now. I took too long to see the truth about John Armstrong—"

"Remove him," Monroe interrupted, surprising himself and the President.

Madison's reply was characteristically mild. "With the British at our door? No. But I propose that you and I assume the responsibili-ties of Secretary of War and not inform John Armstrong of this deci-sion. Once the country is out of danger, I will remove him. No need to give the British added hope."

Monroe thought that removing Armstrong would send a differ-ent message to the British, not one of confusion at the top level of government but of determination to find the best man for the job and to get that job done. He kept this thought to himself, for over the decades of observing James Madison, he had learned that gentle though the little fellow was, he radiated stubbornness.

"Should we inform the Secretary of the Navy?"

"No need. Our presence will do that." Madison retrieved a lovely handkerchief from his pocket and wiped his brow, unknowingly smearing dust across his face. "Did you know, Mr. Monroe, that John Armstrong has secretly wooed Congress to create the grade of lieutenant general?"

"No." Monroe was startled. "He's mad. He's absolutely mad to think he could do such a thing."

"Randolph is mad. Armstrong is merely self-deluded. He thinks he will reserve that rank for himself, once Congress sees the necessity for it. He'll lord it over the major generals, who lord it over the brigadier generals. Armstrong—the only lieutenant general in the Army. If he had had his way, and I had accepted Flournoy, then his two rivals, Brown and Jackson, would never have been promoted to major general. Not only would Armstrong have been a lieutenant general, no other Army man would be within striking distance of him, you see."

Monroe saw very well, once he was pointed in the right direction. By driving the talented men out of the Army, and assuming an American victory, Armstrong would appear to the public as the architect of that victory. Certainly no credit would go to the President, who would follow Washington's example and decline to run for another term, or to himself, the Secretary of State. The public much prefers the illusion of a man of action to the reality of a man of negotiation. Monroe's hatred for Armstrong increased tenfold. John Armstrong would never be President of the United States. Monroe would never allow such a fool, a near-traitorous fool, to snare the party nomination. If he had to, he would drive Armstrong to the other party and let the idiot parade himself there, but he didn't think he would have to do that. The covert assumption of the duties of the Secretary of War would become overt in good time, and John Armstrong would be ruined forever.

What Monroe also felt, more by sensing it than knowing it, was that Henry Clay would return from Ghent—if they had any luck at all —as the hero of the negotiations. John Quincy Adams, a formidable man, had no stomach for pushing himself forward with the people the way Clay did. Adams expected his achievements to speak for themselves. Clay would speak with no hesitation about his achievements. This war, much to everyone's surprise, was finally producing a few winning generals. Clay, enamored of his own gargantuan gifts, would miss the fact that the voter prefers a military hero. If even one of those generals had the heart for political battles, Clay could eventually be overshadowed. As much as Monroe hated Armstrong, he recognized that Armstrong knew this and was banking his future on nipping those military men in the bud.

As these thoughts raced through his mind, Monroe struggled to say something to Madison. "What do you think Armstrong will do after the war?"

"Write his memoirs," came Madison's wicked reply, "with one of those new lead pencils, I should think. Invented by a man named Monroe. Did you know that?"

"No, no, I didn't."

"William Monroe of Concord, Massachusetts. A distant relative of yours, perhaps?" James Madison relished the comment, happy that his information was better than that of his Secretary of State. Later in the day, when he had time to reflect on this conversation, it might occur to James Monroe that if he was going to be President, he'd have to get good information fast.

Madison stood up, signaling that the meeting was over. As he walked out of the room, he thought of lead pencils. A passing fad. Nothing would ever replace a well-made quill pen.

12 August 1814, Friday

I feel much better today. Lisel Serurier accompanied me to the saddler and that lifted my spirits. She scowled at him while I gave him a partial payment, promising him that the balance would follow. If he wanted to voice his pessimism at the likelihood of the British defeating us—and of the balance, therefore, never being paid—Lisel's disapproving glances checked his tongue.

She told me she heard from friends in Ghent that John Quincy Adams berates himself for too much theater, too much conviviality, and too little exercise. Poor John, so hard on himself if he snatches a moment of enjoyment in the prosecution of duty.

Fortunately, Henry Clay can bear his pleasures with greater fortitude. His pleasures must be pleasures indeed, because Lisel also said that Adams was grumbling that Clay lived under the threat of dissipation.

If Adams becomes President someday, following in his father's footsteps, Washington will be quite dull. If Clay ever becomes President, life here will be one sumptuous extravaganza. By that time I shall be retired to Montpelier, a matron of age, prattling about the Revolutionary War, this war, Uncle Willy, my son, my grandchildren —I hope—my nieces and nephews, and my garden. I can get along anywhere, but I do like the excitement that comes from being at the center of things.

Lisel and I marveled at that comet across the skies, in the end reduced to glittering ashes: the Empress Josephine, who died this May. It's odd to think that she was only five years older than I, for in my mind she seemed much older, of another age. Lisel saw her many times and remarked that Josephine was a frivolous and flirtatious, but not malicious, woman, not domineering like Madame Mère, Napoleon's mother. I understand that despite Napoleon's eclipse, Madame

Mère is treated with respect, but poor Josephine, blessed with Creole beauty and cursed by the men in her life.

Outside a bright star is caught in the branches of a tree, like a white heart caught in black intrigue, or so it seems to me.

Foolish musings. I'm going to put the cover over Uncle Willy's cage and go to bed myself.

Until the morrow, God willing.

D.P.M.

13 August 1814, Saturday

S ukey creeps up to my door. I can hear her sigh when she sees the light shining underneath. It's past midnight and my husband still has not returned from the Army camp. If there was a great deal of business and detail to tend to, he may not return until morning. After all, seven miles take time. Yet I worry. What if the British suddenly marched westward?

I probably wouldn't worry so much if I hadn't dropped by Anna's today. As I walked down the hall, I noticed that travel cases had been packed with papers, and others contained children's clothes. Not many cases but enough to make me wonder if my sister will be leaving Washington. I think she should but I will worry about her health, with her time so near, and I so hate to be separated from Anna.

As I walked back from her house, a few militiamen were straggling about, one limping actually with a sore foot. Few people were out and I attributed that to the heat. On second thought, no, they've left. There are a handful of us left in Washington, and even our number is dwindling.

I can't stand the sight of John Armstrong, with his flabby jowls. That's hateful of me, but his incompetence and intransigence have put the full burden of the war on Jemmy's shoulders. Thank God, James Monroe is loyal. He, too, shows signs of this relentless strain. Dark circles are under his eyes, and he's lost quite a bit of weight. Nearly a stone.

I remembered that Armstrong's friend from the War of Independence was General James Wilkinson, another of General Gates's aides. Henry Clay's comment on Wilkinson is, "He never won a battle and never lost a court-martial." But as I was crossing F Street, the thought popped into my head that perhaps Wilkinson lied to

General Gates about Benedict Arnold. Arnold was never quite the same man after the Battle of Freeman's Farm.

Strange. This thought was like a flash—that Wilkinson was the agent of Arnold's undoing, and Armstrong has remained Wilkinson's friend despite all. Did Armstrong participate in obscuring Arnold's fighting prowess at Freeman's Farm? Perhaps my antipathy for the man goads me to see wrongdoing and conspiracy in his past as well as his present. I think I am a fair person; yet I cannot overcome my disquiet about Armstrong.

The older I get, the more I believe in a sixth sense and the more I trust my own. I've also learned not to talk about it.

I'm going to try and get to sleep. I'm sure my husband is fine. He chides me that I worry too much about him and laughs that I don't worry about anything else. Why should I, I tell him. He worries enough for both of us.

Until the morrow, God willing.

D.P.M.

*T*he dust, deep and dry, muffled the sound of the horses' hooves as James Madison and James Monroe rode through Washington at one o'clock in the morning. The Navy Yard was in good order, but not one trench had been dug around the city. No felled trees were fashioned into obstacles and not one cannon faced in the direction from which the enemy would approach.

Each man had tied a handkerchief around his mouth. Their eyes peered out through the layers of dust on their faces, and their hats had turned a light tan regardless of their original colors.

They passed a drunken woman, quite attractive, her décolletage revealing a sumptuous bosom. She giggled when she saw the President and the Secretary of State, not knowing who they were. She winked at Monroe, who tipped his tricorn. The dust flew off it, and she giggled some more because no one else wore such an old-fashioned hat. The President merely brought the forefinger of his right hand up to the rim of his hat.

Once out of her earshot Madison mumbled, "What's left for her husband?"

"A creature like that probably doesn't have the protection of a husband," Monroe answered. He was not a man to dally with ladies of the evening, but he was not a man immune to a beautiful bosom either.

"Ah, yes, well—" Madison coughed. "What happens to women of that sort?" He had never once thought of them until now.

"If they're fortunate, marriage to some rough country fellow, a man who wouldn't mind their"—he was delicate—"station. A Westerner, most likely."

"What if they're not so fortunate?"

"Disease and death, I should think."

Madison shuddered, then glanced up at the stars peeping out from behind huge, creamy clouds, gray and slate-blue in the night. "I had hoped that when we created our form of government, men would work hard, enjoy their labor, and contribute in some fashion. I thought democracy would bring out the best in men and I inferred from that, the best in women, too. A woman should rise and prosper with her husband. I am beginning to fear we shall always have the lower orders with us and I'm damned if I know why."

Because James Madison rarely cursed, Monroe was surprised despite the President's even tone of voice. "Perhaps some fall by circumstance, others by character."

"Yes, but not to try to better oneself no matter what—this I don't understand."

"Maybe she is bettering herself." Monroe nodded back in the direction of the young woman. "We don't know her origins."

"I do think we've made life too easy for the young." Madison grumbled. "They expect a great deal more from life than I did, and they don't want to start at the bottom and work their way up. I can't point the finger at others. I am certainly responsible."

"Not for that woman, sir." Monroe placated him.

"I was thinking of Payne. Clay has written that he drinks dangerously, loses control of himself, and gambles throughout the nights."

"The pot calling the kettle black, I should think," Monroe responded, sympathetic to Madison's plight. He had known Dolley's son since she had moved to Montpelier. He had watched the young man get in one scrape after another.

"I apologize for inflicting such information on you," Madison said wearily. "It's late. I quite forget myself."

"Mr. President, your concerns are parallel to my own. My daughter astonishes me with her demands. She has no idea what the dollar is worth and she's far too concerned with her wardrobe. Of course, she gets that from her mother. An obsessive concern with apparel is the sign of a superficial character—in a man more than a woman, I should say."

Madison laughed. "You sound like my departed mother-in-law.

241

Dolley always tried to wear a simple gray frock when her mother was around, but of course, with the demands of my work, often my wife would have to engage in fripperies as Mother Payne called them. I do think it pained her, but she tried not to criticize Dolley."

"It's bad enough here. It's worse in Paris. Be grateful you have never been an ambassador." Monroe alluded to the time he spent as minister to France.

"Ha," Madison laughed and coughed dust at the same time. "My wife manages to spend money in Paris even though she's never been there. She's the hostess to the nation and I suppose she has to keep up a certain appearance, but I want to know why a new dress of the latest fashion costs four times as much as a new coat for me."

"Elizabeth says more fabric."

"I never thought of that."

They rode on. James Monroe pulled down his handkerchief, then replaced it over his nose and mouth. "I have been riding along here for the last few minutes recounting our conversation, dwelling on my daughter, and it seems I have forgotten to consider my blessings. She's a good child and she'll learn even as we did. No doubt our parents said the same things about us that we're saying about our children."

"My mother still does," Jemmy agreed.

"I was also thinking how fortunate I am not to bear Clay's burden. He would gladly spend his fortune to save his son."

"I've heard the young man"—Madison retrieved the name—"Ted, is extraordinarily handsome and capable of random insight. Clay once told my wife there are moments when the boy is not only lucid but hauntingly brilliant."

"I have observed that in others so afflicted."

"Then there are the people who seem intact but degenerate over time. Randolph is one of those and perhaps John Lewis, as well." Madison referred to George Washington's great-nephew.

"Circumstances can drive men mad. I remember, in the first war with Britain, a fellow officer, a man of such promise, who became so deranged he would cut off the hands of the enemy's fallen. Then he would shake hands with the severed members and carry them about."

"We're right back where we started. Is it character or circumstance?"

"Mr. Madison, you have no equal in the subtlety of thought."

James Madison decided not to rebuke him for the compliment. There was nothing subtle about the thought, and besides, at this moment he would gladly exchange his intellectual powers for the gift of military prowess.

The presidential mansion rested up ahead. Both the President and the Secretary of State were bone weary.

"I can't remember when I have had such an interesting conversation, Mr. Monroe." Madison stopped his horse, took off his handkerchief and wiped his mouth. "I regret that our pasts have created some, uh, distance between us, but I am thankful to have you in my Cabinet. You are the strongest man there and I profit by working closely with you in these"—he cleared his throat—"perilous times."

Monroe also removed his handkerchief. "Thank you."

"You have provoked me to pose the question whether a nation possesses character much as an individual does."

"Yes, it does."

"Then our character is being sorely tested by harsh circumstance."

Hoarsely, James Monroe replied, "With you as our leader, we cannot fail. You will save this nation."

"God willing." Madison touched his hat and turned toward the stables. He did not want Monroe to see the tears in his eyes, tears of gratitude for a man he had not helped in this life, though he had not harmed him either. This war was not just changing the nation. It was changing him.

14 August 1814, Sunday

*J*emmy insisted on attending service today even though he didn't return until two o'clock this morning. I was sound asleep. I instructed Paul, who offered to wait through the night, to waken me if my husband returned. He's such a polite boy that he wouldn't come into my room but instead woke Sukey—never a happy riser—to waken me. We're all bleary-eyed today.

I have never observed my husband in his current state. He can take no pleasure in food or even wine, and thinks only of the war. His preoccupation is so complete that when Uncle Willy flew onto his shoulder, he didn't notice.

We have so little time alone now, I cherished the few moments we were together today before he returned to meetings with William Jones and James Monroe. While we were sitting behind the house, hoping for a cooling breeze from the river, Jemmy said that I was a source of comfort and strength to him and he regretted putting me in such a dangerous place. I told him that I feel safe and not to worry.

He replied that he's always had a sense of the future, but now when he tries to look ahead, he sees only darkness. I put my arms around him and rested my cheek next to his. A single tear rolled down his face and touched my cheek, too. I held him as tightly as I could. When I released him, he was composed.

I wonder if Washington felt this way when all seemed hopeless. I think of him often now. I draw strength from his portrait, which, while not as accurate as I would wish, does convey a sense of his calm purpose. He was such a tall, imposing man. Sometimes I think that if my James were as tall as George Washington, his mastery over other men would be easier. And yet what a silly thought. My husband desires mastery over himself alone. He truly believes that men must convene as equals, as rational beings, to plot the course of the future. Great as George Washington was, Jemmy has the better mind and a greater tolerance for the vagaries of politics.

I think of Mother and Mother Amy, my brothers and sweet Mary, who suffered so, and I think of John Todd. I wish I had them around me to help me protect my husband. Perhaps their spirits observe us. If so, I ask them for their love. I know they would willingly give it. They gave it in life, and none would give more than my handsome John, whose only desire was for my happiness. How curious that I wish he and Jemmy could be friends.

Until the morrow, God willing.

D.P.M.

*A*nna poised on the edge of her chair like a bird on a perch. If she sank backward, it was too difficult to get back up.

Dolley paced. A trickle of perspiration ran down her cheek. She held in her hand a letter from Lucy.

"There's little you can do about it now," Anna counseled.

"I know. It worries me though because we need time after this war, peaceful time, before we launch into another bitter fight amongst ourselves."

"The New England states and the South will never stop fighting," Anna said flatly.

"I know that," Dolley snapped. "But when Congress convenes, if the Federalists vote as a block for an amendment to the Constitution requiring a two-thirds vote of both houses to admit new states to the Union, it will be a nasty tangle of yarn."

"Well, the Federalists will simply block any Western state from joining the Union if they are slavers. Dolley, will you sit down? You'll wear a hole in the rug."

"There's got to be some way around slavery in the new territories."

"There is. No slavery."

Dolley crossed her arms and shot her sister a withering glance. "That's not possible—at this moment. I hate slavery. You hate it. But are you willing to see the country torn apart over it now? We've got to win this war, wipe out the terrible debt, and grow. We're like a six-year-old child. We just need to grow. Another generation will solve this problem. Not ours, sadly."

"Well, if Rufus King gets his pet amendment through Congress—"

Dolley interrupted. "Oh, that. He won't. This business of all

245

representation in the House of Representatives being based on the number of free inhabitants of each state isn't going to pass. He's tied federal funds to it. The money is based on each state's population of freemen. He's cooked his own goose."

"Someone can resurrect it later. A version not tied to federal funds."

"Perhaps." Dolley flipped back a corner of the rug with her foot. "Anna, the dogs have chewed the rug here."

"No, it's Dolley Payne."

"Aren't you feeding my namesake?"

"She eats anything she can get her hands on. Last night she chewed my stockings."

"She's like a little locust." Dolley shook her head. "Anna, I think the British will come up the Patuxent River. That way they're between Washington and Baltimore. They'll sail as far as they can in their frigates, then land and march."

"I've been studying the maps, too. If Washington was their only goal, they'd come straight up the Potomac to Alexandria."

"When did you start reading the maps?" Dolley asked.

"A month ago. You?"

"From the beginning."

"Did you know their strategy from the beginning?"

"No, but when the war started, I thought I'd best keep up with events. After a time the geography becomes obvious, even to one who's untrained."

"You could go to Montpelier." A flash of fear overtook Anna.

"No, I can't."

15 August 1814, Monday

We don't need the British to destroy us, we can do it ourselves. I am beginning to think that Armstrong, a New Yorker, doesn't mind sacrificing Washington to the British. Northerners regard Washington as a Southern city. When Jemmy demanded that

Armstrong erect defensive earthworks and trenches around the city, he replied, "Bayonets are known to form the most efficient barriers."

French John avoids Armstrong. He swears he will wring the man's neck. With his powerful build, he could do it, too. I rather wish he would.

Jemmy was so tired this morning that I combed and dressed his hair. He calls me his favorite barber. He fell asleep in his chair. If James Monroe and William Jones hadn't arrived, I would have let him sleep.

I forgot to remove my dice from my pocket. I usually hide them in my desk. Jemmy opened his eyes and asked what was rattling. No point in evading him. I fetched the dice out of my pocket. His tone was mild. "No wagering, Mrs. Madison."

"No," I said.

Then he left the room. Uncle Willy, uncharacteristically silent, cocked his turquoise-and-yellow head and looked at me as if to say, "Uh-oh."

On top of everything else I've disappointed my husband. Now he'll worry that I'm gambling again, as I once was overfond of cards.

Of all times for me to fail my Jemmy!

I wrote him a letter and put it on his pillow. He's still in meetings and I heard James Blake's voice when he was admitted over three hours past. Our mayor, once portly, is now nearly as thin as Jemmy, who is positively gaunt.

We've heard outrageous rumors about the officials of Alexandria removing gold from the banks and preparing a separate peace treaty should the British choose to strike by sailing up the Potomac.

Given that troops have harried the Chesapeake for these two years, I don't know which way they will come. Sailing up the Potomac would seem easier than marching overland from the east, but then I know little of military maneuvers. I think I've seen every political maneuver possible under the sun.

Which reminds me, now that Russia and England coo at each other, Daschkov is more circumspect in his relations with us. He's not cool, but his dispatches from Saint Petersburg must be taking a different tone. I wish I could see them. I hate Sukey's continuing duplicity over Daschkov. I haven't the strength to be bothered with her, but I find myself flying off the handle, and I know that is one reason.

I asked her to warm my curling iron this afternoon—the humidity necessitated this second torturing of my hair—and she said she was "busy." I don't know what got into me, but I stood up and, in front of Anna, too, shouted, "You'll do as I say and you'll do it now!" My curling iron appeared as if by magic. I scared Anna, too.

She said I used to yell at her to churn the butter when we were small. Anna swore I was as frightening as Mother when she had reached the end of her patience, but then hastened to add that I possess much more patience than our mother had.

I don't think I do. Mother was besieged by many more children than either Anna or myself. Anna may catch up to Mother, who bore nine children, but I won't, and my solitary specimen was no trouble at all. Willful sometimes, but Payne was an uncommonly sweet child, eager to please. I suppose he still is. I hear so little from him, perhaps he has changed. Then too, Mother for years had the burden of Father, a hermit on the second floor. I don't think I ever appreciated her life until recently. I don't know how she did it.

I'm wandering again. Am I going to be one of those old women who sit around and dream of the past? I hope not. Maybe I'm thinking about it now because it's a retreat from the present, but thinking about Mother's hardships isn't especially pleasant. I did little to help her. Oh, I worked hard—all the Payne women work hard—but I didn't understand how she felt. I didn't even think about it. My head was full of girlish foolishness—namely, myself. I hope she forgave me. She never upbraided me, but she must have felt very alone despite being surrounded by her children. How ironic that we live cheek by jowl with the mother and father who brought us into this world; yet we know precious little about them, nor do we care until we are older, and by then it's too late. Would that I could honor my mother with the love she deserved. Since I can't, I offer it to my son and my friends. Is this the compact of generations?

Until the morrow, God willing.

D.P.M.

General William Winder, a study in perpetual motion, rode between camps but issued no orders for entrenchments, roadblocks, or even, at the simplest level, felled trees. Having seen action once, briefly, he was unprepared for the command of the Potomac District, which included both Washington and Baltimore.

The more time James Madison spent with General Winder, the more he realized that this decent man was not qualified for the task of Washington's defense. However, Madison's few young fighting generals were hundreds of miles away. The one advantage of Winder's appointment was the full cooperation of his uncle, Levin Winder, the strong Federalist governor of Maryland.

The President was a politician and he needed to watch his back. Putting Winder in charge would prevent the governor from negotiating separately with the British. Much as Madison wanted to believe that Levin Winder would prove a patriot, the example set by the governors of Massachusetts and Connecticut bade him be cautious. They had scotched his every effort to raise militia within those states. He was kept current on their part in organizing a conference against the war. Keep Levin Winder in the war. Give his nephew an opportunity for glory. As glory seemed unlikely, at least William Winder would have the opportunity to do his duty. That was more than others had done, and Madison knew a live dog was worth more than a dead lion.

"Mr. President, do I have your permission to call out the militia?" Mayor James Blake's usually jolly face was drawn, making him appear ten years older.

"I would advise you to keep them in readiness, but do not assemble them publicly just yet, sir. We do not wish to spark a panic."

Blake peered at the wide blue ribbon of the Potomac, curling across the map. "The faint hearts have fled." He smiled. "Those of us left will do the best we can."

Madison nodded. "We'll throw rocks if we have to."

Blake lifted his eyes, looking into Madison's clear ones. "There's no hope for my city, is there?"

"There's always hope, Mr. Blake . . . always."

16 August 1814, Tuesday

A strange miasma of unreality enshrouds us now, like a silvery fog obscuring the landscape's beauties as well as its pitfalls. John Armstrong says any British troop movements in our direction are a feint to cover their true target, Baltimore. His vehemence is his defense against reality.

But it isn't just Armstrong, it's the city. Those remaining go about their business like dreamers. I know that I do.

And somehow, not knowing is worse than knowing. Will they come? When? By what route? Our men are fighting in New York and deep in the Mississippi Delta, and we know nothing. Have we won any battles? Have we lost any? Rumor travels with a thousand tongues, the truth with but one. Hardest of all is the waiting.

It reminds me of when my oldest brother, Walter, sailed for England in 1785. When four months had passed and we heard no word, we thought that Walter might be slow in writing. Another month passed and Mother walked down to the docks to ask the sailors and their captains if they knew of the ship. They did, but no one had had any report of the ship's ever making land. No one had seen it. As the months passed and then the years, Mother accepted that Walter had been lost at sea. But in those first months, I used to think we'd surely hear some news. We heard nothing. I couldn't stand it. Mother could, and did.

This time reminds me of then but in a different way. Thousands are waiting and watching for the glint of a bayonet, the rap of a drum, a shot, something, yet nothing happens.

French John bought a whole hog today for dinner. I go on entertaining as usual, if a bit more feverishly. The hog cost six dollars, dressed. French John reported that the butcher first asked for eight! If time is standing still for me, it certainly rushes forward at the marketplace.

Today I found myself staring out the window, Uncle Willy on my shoulder. There I stood staring, like a resident of Bedlam, I suppose, until I realized there was a crowd staring back. Once I regained my senses, I fed Uncle Willy, since that's what they like to see.

I never saw our cousin Patrick Henry's mad wife, but Isaac, Temple, and I used to scare Anna with stories about her, which we punctuated with screams because we thought all insane people screamed. Today I wondered if a touch of that blood isn't in me. I've never before lost myself like that . . . just staring into thin air . . . thinking of John.

I felt his presence like a little golden hammer tapping at my heart. I could almost hear his deep voice, "Trust in the Lord, Dolley, trust in the Lord." As he lay dying at thirty, so young, so handsome even with the fever raging through him, he didn't complain. He trusted in the Lord.

This time doesn't frighten me. That time did. I was twenty-five. Perhaps, at forty-six, I've lived long enough. The thought of dying isn't fearsome. What was it Samuel Johnson said? ". . . when a man knows he is to be hanged in a fortnight, it concentrates his mind wonderfully." I should know. I should know many things.

Back in 1793, I only knew that I loved my husband and Death held him in his white claws. John, so blessed by nature and respected by all, a lawyer with a blossoming practice, a good businessman—such wonderful things were predicted for John. And in early October his mother and father perished of the fever. He bore it with fortitude. We were all shaken. The death toll in Philadelphia was thirty-three people a day. And before the month was out, my husband and my older son had died, adding to that frightful number.

And then I, too, fell ill. I don't really know why I lived and they died. I had Payne. There were times when I was so sick I didn't even know I had a living son. I couldn't remember who I was or that my love had died or my boy. Then a piercing shaft of light would open my eyes and I would remember. Oh, that cursed memory, which pressed into my heart like jagged glass. The pain tore so deep I couldn't cry. I couldn't breathe. Then I would remember Payne, so small and helpless, fatherless. He would not be motherless. I lived.

I don't know what's before me, but I do know that I will do all I can. At least I know my enemy's name. At least my son is a grown man and far from harm's way. If I die, I can't complain that I haven't lived.

My only wish, my one regret, is that Jemmy and I never had children. God granted me two sons by a gentle and good man and one lived. If only God could have granted me another son or a daughter with the man to whom I have pledged my life, a man I first respected and then learned to love. More than my own life I love Jemmy. If only we could have left some love behind with a child.

When I turned forty, we were at Montpelier. It must have been a late spring that year, 1808, for even though my birthday is May twentieth, a few lilac bushes remained in bloom. Jemmy and I walked to the log cabin his parents built when they first came to the land. He asked me if I minded very much that we had never had children together. I replied that I would have liked to have them but it was not to be. He put his arm around me as we walked and said, "I'm grateful you have a son." Then he paused and said, "Perhaps for us, the United States is our child." That was the only time he ever discussed the matter with me. Jemmy displays a remarkable restraint. He never wants to burden another person with his feelings and yet he is willing to bear their burdens. He's bearing everyone's burdens now and I wish, more than ever, that we had children of our own. Young people to share in this woe and to give him laughter; sons and daughters to live on, should we die in this war.

I don't mind dying, but I can't bear the thought of Jemmy's dying.
"Trust in the Lord."
Well, John, I have no choice.
Until the morrow, God willing.

D.P.M.

17 August 1814, Wednesday

*F*rench John said we needed the blind, the lame, and the halt to fill up the table tonight. My levee, again attended by more foreigners than Americans, was a quiet affair, except for Uncle Willy, of course.

The cook let King George out of the kitchen, and that bold creature dashed into the dining room, jumped on the table before anyone could catch her, and stole a huge hunk of pork as big as she was. Then she tore off the table with her booty. Indeed, King George provided most of the evening's entertainment. She's quite the thief.

Even the small orchestra was flat.

Still, we enjoyed the company of friends. Dr. Thornton and his wife attended. As usual, the superintendent of our Patent Office boomed jolliness and believes the day will come when we have talking machines. Jemmy is grateful he has remained in the city, especially since Dr. Thornton is a Federalist.

Afterward Lisel and Louis Serurier, André Daschkov, French John, and I found ourselves in a most unusual conversation. Everyone avoided the subject of the British, for which I was thankful. I can't remember how the conversation started, but I know French John brought Virginia wine from Mr. Jefferson's county for the Seruriers and Daschkov to sip. I serve American foods whenever I can, although I know it will take our vintners centuries to catch up to the French and the Germans. My guests politely sampled the white wine, and André was complimentary. The Seruriers too were, naturally, polite. Now I remember how the conversation started. French John beamed as they complimented the wine and asked the Seruriers, who would have been extremely young then, if they remembered the wine before the Revolution in France—those great vintages, which then faltered as did everything during the Revolution.

The priest at the church where French John was an acolyte told him that those vintages of the ancien régime were worth more than plate, gold, or jewels, and that aristocrats employed heroic measures to save their wines. Some hid them in secret compartments on their estates. When the families were guillotined, no one was left to reveal the hiding places. Centuries from now, some individual will lean against a portrait or stumble over a key and find the treasure. Many others managed to get the wine onto ships and flee to England, those wise enough to know there was no hope in France for their kind. If the British come, I wonder what we will hide and then forget.

We listened to these tales. The Seruriers too had many to tell, of buried wine and wealth, when André asked if anyone knew who actually beheaded the King and Marie Antoinette. Louis replied that the identities of the executioners for any guillotine remained secret. Before the guillotine, the same was true for the axman. In fact, this was a profession with strict rules for practitioners and a long apprenticeship. A great executioner made certain that his victim did not suffer much pain. The beheadings, whether with the blade or the ax, were quick. We have nothing comparable here. Our condemned are hanged, which a European aristocrat would consider a vile death, a commoner's death. Beheading—by ax, broadsword, or guillotine—was a privilege of station. Naturally, an executioner needed to be strong because the neckbone is not easy to sever. The guillotine changed that, but should there be a failure, the executioner had to make a good job of it. With haste.

How curious that we lapsed into discussing executions. I suppose we are each thinking of death.

André Daschkov reminded us that no Russian Czar has ever been killed by commoners. This is certainly not true in England and France, where kings have been killed by their subjects. Now, it has always been hinted that Catherine the Great had her insane husband killed, but that's not the same as the people rising up and killing their ruler. Daschkov, passionate by this time, said, "If only you could see Russia. If only you could see how beloved the Czar and his family are. The Russian is born to obey. The idea of revolution is anathema and akin to blasphemy."

Madame Serurier complacently listened to André's outburst. She regards a Russian as most Frenchmen do: an oaf. I find this odd because the Russians speak impeccable French, and we Americans can barely speak English correctly.

Lisel touched André's glass with hers (he shivered with delight) and said, "Robespierre was the Sorcerer's apprentice, summoning up forces he could not control, but my dear Minister, any country, at any time, is capable of producing its Robespierre. And the day may yet come even in your great nation when people turn on Pharaoh."

French John and I stared at each other. My mind turned like a top. Daschkov's country, recently ravaged by Napoleon, hates France. Even more, the Russian nobility must have hated Napoleon's liberating politics.

Louis and Lisel, servants of that same Napoleon, believe that talent must rise and nations be reborn. If aristocrats won't make way or become useful to this process, then they must be removed. Not that Lisel counsels mass extermination, and she was but a child during the Reign of Terror, but the men of ability who burst forth once that dead hand was removed and Napoleon seized power—well, they were extraordinary.

No arguments or fights have ever marred my levees. I told André and Louis, "You would seem to be polar opposites in many ways; yet both your nations have offered mine steadfast friendship, and each of you gentlemen has given my dear husband wise and valued counsel. Perhaps that is the gift my country can give to you. In Europe you would not have met and profited from each other's experiences, but here you can and do and I am the richer for it, and I think you are, too."

French John drank a glass of wine straight down to celebrate the avoidance of altercation.

André bowed to me, as did Louis, and then André said, "Madam, you grace me with your compliments just as you have continually charmed me with your kindness. Your country, also, was born of revolution. Would you consider great Washington a Robespierre?"

"Never." French John forgot his place.

I smiled and replied, "Our Revolution was more in the manner of a violent disagreement between a father and his son or a mother and her daughter. Such is the nature of the young that they wish to make their own way. I think"—and I inclined my head toward the Seruriers—"that for our dear friends, the disagreement was between brother and brother, a very different thing, you see.

"You might say the first American Revolution was against the tyranny of King George. The second American Revolution must be against the tyranny of selfishness."

This is something I had written in my diary, but I didn't expect to say it publicly. Proud as I am of my country, I don't think democracy is served by cultivating illusion, and selfishness will ever be a problem in a nation such as ours. We're taught to make our own way and to bow to no man.

I don't think our guests expected me to be so honest.

After the company had left and I repaired to my room and this inviting desk, I began to think again of the executioner. No American President has ever been assassinated. I truly pray that no one will ever be killed in office, for it is barbaric, a mark on the entire people. Yet I fear that my Jemmy could be killed. Washington, Adams, and Jefferson knew little of the personal hatred that Jemmy faces daily. If this war should go from bad to worse, it could happen that some lunatic with a pistol might attack my husband.

We have lunatics enough armed with pens. Lisel informed me of the contents of more letters from John Randolph. He and his Massachusetts counterpart, Josiah Quincy, fairly screech against the war and James. How foolish are those political men who think they can scratch out the President with the stroke of a pen, but if they express their irrational passions so eloquently, there may be another man, less articulate, who expresses himself with a gun.

I am not by nature a worrier, but sometimes even I can't turn away from aching possibilities.

And Jemmy sees it all, hears it all, and keeps working. He doesn't lose his temper. He doesn't succumb to fear. He wastes no time on personal vendettas. His greatest love is this country, and I wonder that these men who hate him so don't understand that. They will never blow him off course.

Thinking of the French Revolution reminded me of taking tea with Henry Clay last year. Congress, as usual, was in a dither over raising money for the war. Endless speeches were given, and so forth. Christopher Gore and Rufus King walked into the drawing room and Clay said, "Ah yes, the Reign of Error."

King Richard III would have given his kingdom for a horse. I think I'd give mine for a man with a sense of humor.

Until the morrow, God willing.

D.P.M.

*G*ood news arrived today in the form of a dispatch. The British attacked much-contested Fort Erie with a force of thirty-five hundred men but were repulsed by General Edmund Pendleton Gaines. The enemy suffered terrible casualties. Our losses were slight. We have only two thousand men at the fort. They suffer constant bombardment. Perhaps our luck is changing.

Mother Amy used to tell me that good luck and bad luck are like one's right and left hands. One must use them both. She could produce a phrase for any situation, and she could fetch up a knot on the side of one's head, too!

I remember once when a guest gave the blessing at our dinner table, a long-winded guest who quoted nearly everything Saint Paul ever wrote. The food turned cold. After dinner Mother Amy whispered to my mother that Saint Paul surely didn't look on the bright side of life. "Why, how could a man say not to get married unlessen you can't control yourself?" Mother Amy was scandalized.

My mother laughed and said, "Paul never was partial to women."

That convinced Mother Amy that her African tales were superior to those in the Bible. Oh, what wonderful stories she could tell, stories she'd heard from her mother and grandmother, stories kept alive as her people crossed the oceans, chained in the holds of ships.

What if the situation were reversed and I was serving some powerful African princess? I wonder what stories I would be telling, what would have survived the journey. I'm sure Moses in the bulrushes would have survived. No one can forget that story. Or Christ rising from the dead. Joshua at the walls of Jericho. Ruth and Naomi; I think that's my favorite.

General Winder finally received an adjunct. A few days ago, John Armstrong managed to release an officer to the beleaguered man.

Lisel met me at Anna's today. My sweet sister can no longer move with any speed, or grace for that matter. We thought we'd call on her to see if anything needs to be done. She was in good spirits, but her four boys ran around the house like wild Indians—even little Dolley Payne joined them. Anna lost her patience and ordered them outside, which was what they wanted. They pretended it was dastardly punishment, and the minute they were out the door we could hear them whoop and holler. I do so love the children.

As Lisel has seen great societal disruption, Anna asked her, referring to our troubled state, "What would a reasonable man do?"

Lisel replied, "In a time of crisis there are no reasonable men."

Truthfully, I think we women are more reasonable in times of crisis. I said so, too. Anna agreed that she thought men lose their heads. Lisel laughed and said that in her country they do so, literally. It shouldn't have been funny but it was.

As we left Anna's, I had an urge so strong my heart was racing. I wanted to go to the stable, saddle up, and just gallop down Pennsylvania Avenue. I told Lisel and she said once the dog days were over, we could take our horses to the Virginia side of the river and run to our heart's delight. Who is there to see us?

Jemmy is exhausted. Early this morning he said he wished Washington would come back from the grave because men fell silent in his presence. He laughed—I rejoiced to see him laugh despite the reason —and said, "Mrs. Madison, my love, it's a terrible death to be talked to death."

Not only do they never shut up, this gaggle of Cabinet secretaries, generals, and officials, but their opinions are constantly in conflict. They all talk at once. The blessing about everyone's talking at once is that you can't hear what they say.

Until the morrow, God willing.

D.P.M.

*T*he thick mist of morning hugged the well-tended fields along Maryland's shore. It hung like a gray net over Chesapeake Bay, obscuring the hulls and huge white sails of His Majesty's ships.

As the sun rose, casting a pink glow over the bay and the surrounding countryside, the warships and transport ships turned into the Patuxent River. The sight of this beautiful and terrifying fleet sent watermen into the small towns and farmers into their churches. The bells pealed alarm.

One alert American counted twenty-one warships and many other transport ships. The number of enemy ships varied according to the person reporting and how long he or she had stood on the shore, how clear the sight line was.

By the time word reached Commodore Joshua Barney, the figure was as high as fifty-one warships. His small flotilla of gunboats with their naval twenty-four-pounders could not match the collected might of massed warships and troop transports. The overwhelming numbers canceled out harassment as a strategy.

Barney ordered his men to sail farther up the Patuxent and to remain vigilant. His guns, his babies, he ordered cleaned again. The gunpowder was checked. Every man's personal weapons were checked, cleaned, and checked again.

Barney had no need to check his maps and navigation charts. The warships would have to anchor in deep water. The soldiers would disembark and march along the shore. The lighter ships, carrying more men and supplies, might sail farther upriver.

Admiral Cockburn's forces, having the run of the Chesapeake, knew the area quite well. Cockburn would make few mistakes.

Barney questioned where Cockburn's troops would link up with these new troops and how long that would take. He figured two or three days at most. The new troops were the long-dreaded veterans. They knew how to move, and their officers were experienced, too.

No question now that the fight was coming. It was only a matter of when and where.

19 August 1814, Friday

*A*midst the uncertainty of the time, I can write down one happy event: little Dickey is improved. Anna was right, it was merely a summer cold. His cough has abated. I'm more relieved than Anna; she has become accustomed to his many sicknesses. The child rarely experiences a week without some ailment, and he's not inventing them.

My brother Temple realized illness spared him bookwork and chores. Mother believed him for the first few days, but she noticed his resolve to stay ill weakened when the rest of us had finished our chores. Instead of upbraiding him, she became doubly solicitous and told him he would have to stay in bed for a week. Naturally, heavy foods were too much for his digestive system in his weakened state, so soup would be his only fare. Temple improved within five minutes. How Mother and Mother Amy laughed as he shot out the door shouting, "I'm cured! It's a miracle!"

The war raged then, yet we laughed. Whatever happens, no matter how terrible or disruptive, people seek laughter. Apart from the British officer riding into the house, the worst part of our last war was our neighbors' shunning us or arguing with Father because of our faith.

I have often reflected on how the people closest to us cause the most pain. Who are the British? They are the enemy but I don't know them. I can't call out one soldier or sailor by name. They can disrupt my life or even take it, but let my sister become cross with me and it's more painful, or perhaps it's a more personal pain. Curious.

I'm so tired tonight. Unusual for me.

Until the morrow, God willing.

D.P.M.

*R*oyal British Marines had been moving in the vicinity of Nominy Creek. James Madison was certain they would meet with the troops just landed at Benedict, approximately thirty-eight miles east of Washington. He no longer consulted with his Secretary of War. He hadn't the time to listen to John Armstrong's arguments or dismissal of the situation. The formalities would be observed; if Armstrong attended meetings, Madison wouldn't cut him off, but he saw no good reason to wait for Armstrong's approval. When General Winder ordered two Baltimore regiments to Washington, Madison thought something was being done at last.

Militia cavalry rode toward Benedict to cut trees and block the roads. The sun bathed the fields, and a slight breeze made the ride pleasant. It was hard to believe anything bad could happen on such a day.

The President ordered all government papers moved to safety. This safe destination was up to the officials packing the papers. Most thought just getting the documents across the Potomac would suffice.

The President also knew that only a few hours of calm remained. As the wagons pulled up to different buildings to be loaded, the people would see the situation and panic. There was nothing he could do about that.

20 August 1814, Saturday

*T*he British landed a force of about forty-five hundred men yesterday at Benedict, Maryland. The word reached us today. The messenger was caked in dust, his legs shaking from his hard ride. He handed over the dispatch to French John, who immediately took it to

Jemmy. I insisted that the poor fellow go back to the kitchen, where he was given some decent food and drink. Paul found him a new mount. Sukey just stood in the hallway and stared at the man.

Some citizens along the Maryland shore have hung white sheets from their windows.

James Blake called out the District of Columbia Militia. What a pathetic sight. Hardly anyone wore a complete uniform, few wore swords, and even fewer carried firearms. Many of the men were barefoot.

The sight of the militia caused more sympathy than stir.

It's as though the city of Washington is holding its breath. Will the British turn northeast against Baltimore or northwest against us?

Jemmy says we should pelt the enemy from the start. Armstrong appears paralyzed by his own view of events, which is to say he utterly refuses to believe we are the goal. Even now, he does nothing.

John Van Ness, head of our District Militia, cornered Armstrong. He said that the arrival of new troops "points to a serious blow."

Armstrong replied, "Yes, by God! They wouldn't bring such a fleet without meaning to strike, but it won't be here. What the devil would they do *here*?"

"The seat of government is the most logical target." It was obvious Van Ness was furious.

General Winder had the presence of mind to order militiamen from Pennsylvania, Virginia, and parts of Maryland, but I doubt they can get here in time.

And if they do get here, how can we feed them? The supplies and medical necessities my husband requested well over three months ago were never delivered. I doubt that John Armstrong ever intended to comply with Jemmy's request.

I sent Sukey over to Anna's to tell her all I knew and then on to Madame Serurier. Alarm won't help anyone. Information will.

Jemmy ordered all government documents moved out of Washington to safety. By tomorrow everyone in the city will know what has happened and that government papers are being removed. This will cause great alarm, and I can't blame the people.

I wish there were something I could do. Failing that, at least I can remain composed. I do so hate it when people allow their fears to gain the upper hand.

We're all going to die anyway. Whether that happens tomorrow or years from now, I no longer think it's of as much consequence as we believe it to be.

I asked French John what he thought about the number of ships arriving. He shrugged. "I've seen the British before," he said.

So have I.

Until the morrow, God willing.

D.P.M.

*A*cross the city of Washington the deep ringing of church bells called the faithful to worship. Few citizens made their way to the churches dotted across the city. People ran in all directions. Traffic snarled at every intersection as men, women, and children, household valuables clutched in their hands, hurried out of the city.

Word reached the President that the cavalry had arrived too late to block the roads to Benedict. The British had moved out.

James Monroe, in utter frustration, saddled up his horse and rode toward the site where the British had last been reported. He told Madison that he would shadow them and return that evening with a report. There wasn't time to find an officer to perform this scouting duty, and the Secretary of State didn't trust anyone else to do it anyway.

At the Navy Yard, William Jones prepared for the worst.

Dolley stepped out of the house as the carriage pulled around. The call of the bells provided an eerie punctuation to what sounded like a muffled roar as thousands of human tongues shouted, cried, called, and cursed. Sukey hopped into the carriage next to Dolley.

"Come on, Paul, we've got to get to Anna's."

Dutifully Paul clucked to the two horses and they obediently started out the gate toward the street. He waited for a break in the clogged traffic so that he could wedge his way through. A fancy carriage halted right before Dolley's. A beautiful woman stood up. Dolley recognized her as the wife of Timothy Pitkin, staunch Federalist from Connecticut.

The congressman's wife shrieked at Dolley, "You! See this hair of mine?" She unpinned the beautiful hair for which she was renowned and let it cascade around her shoulders like a titian cape. "I would pray that I might part with it if it could be used to hang Mr. Madison!"

Her driver flicked his whip and Mrs. Pitkin flopped backward in her seat, screaming at Dolley all the while.

Sukey started to shake. "She's crazy. That white woman's crazy, missus; she wants to kill you."

Dolley put her hand on Sukey's shoulder to calm her, but Sukey stood up and shook her fist at the lurching, receding figure of Mrs. Pitkin. "You can't talk that way to Missus! Clabberface! You can't! You can't, you can't!"

Paul spied an opening and moved toward it. Sukey fell forward but Dolley caught her. Sukey was sobbing.

"It's all right. People say strange things when they're frightened." Dolley patted her hand.

"She's talking about killing the Master." Sukey trembled. "Are people gonna come and kill him? They gonna kill *us*?"

"No, of course not." Dolley's stomach clenched into a knot.

"They gotta get through the door first." Paul felt the same fear.

"That white woman, she—you fed her!" Sukey stood up again to catch another glimpse of the receding, hysterical figure. "Ifin she come back in the house I'm gonna poison her!"

"She didn't know what she was saying."

"Yes, she did. Her husband's one of the Master's enemies in Congress."

Dolley waved her handkerchief in front of her face to keep the dust off. "I thought you didn't pay attention to those matters."

"I know who's for us and who's against us." Sukey's voice was firm again.

"I thought you didn't mind if the British came. They'll set you free."

"Don't believe what French John says. He hates me."

"Sukey." Paul's voice put her on guard.

"I changed my mind!" Sukey hollered.

"Why?" Dolley asked.

"Better the devil you know than the devil you don't," replied Sukey.

Paul kept driving. He both hated and loved Sukey. He wished he could put his arm around her right now.

Finally the carriage reached F Street. Dolley hopped out and dashed to the door. Paul stayed behind to wipe the dust from the horses' nostrils and eyes and to bring them water. The day was warming up.

The dust cloud reflected the sunlight, making it difficult to see. It felt as if one were moving in a gritty fog.

"Anna. Anna," Dolley called as the children ran for her. "Hello, boys, where's your mother?"

James Madison Cutts, Anna's oldest at nine, grabbed his aunt's hand and led her into the back rooms. Anna and Richard were packing the children's things.

"Dolley." Anna embraced her sister, as did Richard.

"I've brought Sukey to help us." Dolley was matter-of-fact. "What's to be done?"

"Well, calming down the boys and Dolley Payne would be a step forward." Richard smiled weakly.

"They think this is a great adventure. James wants to stay and fight the British. Thomas wants to do whatever James wants to do, and Walter and Dickey are torn between emulating their big brothers and hanging on to me."

"It is a great adventure, I suppose."

"Mrs. Pitkin said she was gonna kill Mr. Madison," Sukey blurted out.

"What?" Anna's eyes grew larger.

"I hate you!" Dickey's voice, from the next room, had a blood-curdling edge.

"Oh, Richard, dear, please do something," Anna pleaded.

Her husband went into the next room and the sound of all the boys yelling at once soon followed.

"Dear God, please let this next baby be a girl." Anna rolled her eyes heavenward and then looked at Dolley. "Now, Mrs. Pitkin."

"Not quite herself, Anna—"

"Herself is bad enough." Anna smiled. "I've known few women as vain or as stupid."

"What would Mother say to a statement like that?" Dolley started putting clothes in a small valise.

Sukey picked up clothes without being told to do so.

"Our mother wouldn't have said it but she would have thought it. Anyway, I interrupted you. Whatever did she do?"

Sukey went on. "She stood up in her carriage, that fancy green-and-gold one, and she pulled her hair down and said she wanted to cut it off and hang the President with it. That woman was crazy." Sukey relished retelling the event.

"No." Anna was all disbelief.

"Crazy as someone on corn liquor. Crazy!" Sukey imitated the distressed Mrs. Pitkin.

"Did she really?"

"She did," came Dolley's crisp reply.

Walter, six, streaked through the room, Dickey in hot pursuit. The two boys ran out the other door. Richard, chasing both of them, was huffing and puffing. He hurried after them. Little Dolley Payne, on her short legs, brought up the rear.

"Richard, Richard, don't tire yourself," Anna called.

"Five wild Indians, and you tell me not to tire myself," Richard, panting, called as he kept running. "Walter and Dickey, if you don't stop this minute, I am going to tan your hides!"

Dolley started to laugh. Sukey followed and then Anna, too.

"Do you think the British would like four bad little American boys and one little American girl?" Anna, very pregnant, laughed so hard she needed to sit down and couldn't get there. Dolley helped her into a chair.

"That's why they're over here, Anna, to get away from their own," Dolley replied, and they laughed again.

Suddenly Anna started crying. "I don't want to leave you."

"I'll be fine."

"The whole world's gone mad." Anna wiped away her tears.

Richard came back into the room. "What's this?" He bent over his wife and kissed her.

"I can't leave Dolley." Anna burst into fresh tears.

Dolley, sitting on the arm of the chair, firmly told her, "You can and you will. Think of the children, Anna, and think of the one to come. You must take care of yourself and your family."

"You're my family." Anna grabbed her sister's hand. "What will happen to you?"

"Nothing's going to happen to me."

"Don't lie to me, Dolley, you're a rotten liar. You can fool other people by putting on a good face but you can't fool me. What if the British capture you?"

"I can run faster than they can."

The children entered the room and, seeing their mother's distress, went silent.

Richard spoke to James and Thomas. "Go outside, boys, and help Paul with the horses. Take Walter and Dickey and Dolley with you, please."

"I want to stay with Mommy." Dolley Payne moved toward her weeping mother.

"You will help Paul—now."

The older brothers shepherded the three smaller ones outside. Dickey and Dolley Payne cast their mother a mournful glance. She blew a kiss to them and they left willingly after that.

"Why don't you come with us to the Forrests'? They'd be delighted to offer you refuge, and the British aren't interested in that part of Maryland." Richard sat down on the other arm of the chair, which wobbled, so he stood up again. He was heavier than Dolley, who kept her seat.

"Do come with us." Anna kissed Dolley's hand.

"No, my place is here with my husband."

"For God's sake, you could be killed!" Anna was now racked with sobs.

"Anna, Anna, please." Richard tried to comfort her. "You can't allow yourself to get upset like this. Think of the baby, darling."

"He's right." Dolley got up and began packing more clothes.

"Oh, Dolley, I couldn't live without you."

Now tears crept into Dolley's eyes. "Well, I feel the same way about you. Now please, go. We both must trust in God's will." Anna quivered and Dolley pressed on. "Anna, we weren't raised to cry over what we can't control. We must each do what we can and I am the President's wife. My duty rests with him. Your duty is to your husband and family. You will get in the carriage and you will go. Take only what is absolutely necessary."

Anna stopped crying. "Are you afraid?"

"No." Dolley smiled. "I think I'm too stupid to be afraid, and I've got too much to do to take the time to be afraid."

"You're far from stupid, but you are stubborn." Anna wiped her eyes with Richard's help.

"What's left to be done here?" Dolley asked.

"I think we've got most of it." Richard glanced around the room. "Anna, can you think of anything?"

"Their toys. It will keep them occupied, I hope."

"Or give them something to fight over," Dolley said.

"All right." Richard headed for the boys' rooms. "One toy each."

"And don't forget the dog, Richard, whatever you do."

"Pepper's out with the children and Paul." Richard left.

"You know what was funny about Mrs. Pitkin's carrying on the way she did?" Dolley shook her head. "Her language. You would have thought she was addressing a convocation of congressional wives."

"The Federalists wallow in formality—and treason." Anna, with Dolley's and Sukey's help, struggled up.

"I'm trying to consider their politics a dramatic difference of opinion. What about these shoes?"

"Walter's. Leave them. He can do with the pair he's got on, which he will outgrow by the time we reach the Forrests' house." Anna blew her nose. "We'll choke to death before any of us are shot."

"You can barely see your hand in front of your face outside."

"I never thought I'd live to see something like this," Anna said quietly.

"Nor did I, but here we are, and Anna, don't give in to despair. If we do that, they've won. No matter what, we've got to keep fighting."

"Like the winter Lucy was born. Do you remember? Mother Amy used to tell us about Washington and how the war seemed lost, and then she'd say, 'But Lucy was born, and that changed everything.' " Anna smiled.

"What I would give to have her with us now—and Mother." Dolley paused for a moment.

"Mother would say the same thing you did. Don't give in. Keep going. No tears."

Then both said in unison, "Trust in God."

21 August 1814, Sunday

*A*nna left the city today, for which I am grateful. She cried that she didn't want to leave me, but in the end, good sense prevailed.

When I came back home, Jemmy was gone. Only French John and Uncle Willy remained in the house. How oddly quiet it was. Even on slow days there is usually a deputation from some part of the country wishing to see the President. French John informed me that Jemmy left for more meetings.

Events are moving so fast and yet, at the same time, so slowly. I alternate between feeling I must do everything and feeling I can do nothing at all, between wild energy and lethargy. There are moments when I am sure nothing is real, that this is a nightmare. Then I awaken.

I carry my dice in my pocket and occasionally feel their cool, pitted surfaces. I don't know why, but the touch soothes me. And then I wonder what has become of Senator Brown. Is he too staving off the British, in Louisiana? Is he alive?

Right now, only James Monroe knows where the enemy is. I hope he has returned—poor Elizabeth must have spent an anxious day. One good thing about the British. With those red coats, they're hard to miss.

What astonishes me is that men will board ships and sail across a vast ocean for the pleasure of fighting other men. The call is to duty or putting us in our place or whatever, but underneath that there must be an element of pleasure involved. Otherwise, it's quite insane.

But tonight everything seems insane. I even wonder about myself. My heart races. I have difficulty breathing. I know that I am prepared to die, but truthfully, I wouldn't mind living either.

Until the morrow, God willing.

D.P.M.

A one-hundred-man guard, under the command of Colonel Charles Carroll, surrounded the White House. Outside, bedlam turned into pandemonium. An enveloping red dust cloud obscured his view, but James Madison could hear clearly. Hoofbeats, the creaking of wagons, the crack of whips, and the continuing shouts, cries, and hollers of fleeing people haunted him. If he survived this chaos, he knew he would never forget the sounds of panic.

James Monroe had reported back that the British were moving by land and by river barges. He estimated four thousand men in columns and another thousand on the barges.

Another report from General Winder confirmed that the British had reached Nottingham, a little town halfway between Benedict and Washington, the night before. If they continued their march today, they might get within twenty miles of Washington.

The British would assume that the bridges had been blown, so they would seek the best ford across the East Branch of the Potomac. That meant Bladensburg, if Washington was their goal. Hanging along the Patuxent River, the British could still turn east toward Baltimore, but James Madison was certain they would not.

Madison wondered why they didn't sail up the Potomac. Perhaps they feared the banks of the Potomac would bristle with cannon. Whatever their reasons, they were swinging through Maryland.

He ordered all remaining government papers moved out immediately. This time he specified the destination, Leesburg, thirty-five miles west in Virginia.

He also badgered anyone who would listen to concentrate troops around Washington.

James Blake struggled to keep the looters frightened off, but he was no more successful at that than at squeezing troops out of Armstrong for his city. Of all the men caught in this spiked web, the mayor of Washington was the one for whom James Madison felt the most pity.

Distant explosions rumbled through the house. Outside, the screams intensified. Commodore Barney, ordered closer to the city, scuttled his fifteen gunboats to keep them out of the hands of the British.

James Madison decided to meet General Winder at Long Old Fields, nine miles distant, that night. Perhaps his presence would hearten the men.

Later that same afternoon, John Armstrong passed between the State and War offices. He pulled a handkerchief over his face to keep off the dust. A sturdy, middle-aged man, Mr. Pleasanton, was carefully placing George Washington's letters, the Declaration of Independence, the Constitution, and other valuable documents in a linen sack.

"What are you doing?" Armstrong demanded.

"The President ordered me to move all government papers out of Washington."

Armstrong's upper lip curled. "That's just like Madison, to screech alarm like an old woman. The British have no intention of converging on Washington."

With disgust he passed Pleasanton, who didn't even bother to reply.

Louis Serurier, spared close contact with John Armstrong, hastily wrote a dispatch to his government. Fearing the worst, he wanted to send out one last communiqué before the city was overrun. He informed His Majesty Louis XVIII that the Americans would not dispute the British in the field, owing to their inexperience; the British were battle-hardened. He believed, however, that the Americans would make a stand six miles northeast of the capital, at Bladensburg, since it was an easy fording place over the East Branch. He scribbled in haste, blotted his mistakes, and handed the dispatch to his man, who immediately headed toward the Potomac since that route was open.

Lisel held her husband's hand as the messenger mounted his horse and took off through the mob.

"Louis, do you think we are in danger?"

"No, we're more in danger from criminals than from the British. After all, a minister is protected by the laws of civilized nations."

"You have more faith in civilization than I do," Lisel said without rancor.

"The British have no wish to insult a minister of France—not now, anyway. Are you ready to go to Mr. Tayloe's?"

"Yes, I think we'd best go at nightfall. We'll not get through now." She surveyed the mass of humans and horses trudging toward Virginia. "Madame de Stahl is ready, too."

"That cat will destroy the Octagon House, and you know the very reason John Tayloe asked us to occupy it is to prevent the British from destroying it."

"We've discussed it. She promises not to claw one piece of furniture."

Louis looked at his wife with exasperation and shook his head. A war at their door and they were discussing the cat.

*T*he British reached Upper Marlboro, sixteen miles from Washington. Admiral George Cockburn joined them there. The dolorous news reached Madison as Paul was saddling his horse.

James walked back to Dolley's room. She stopped writing and rose to greet him.

"I'll return tomorrow. Will you wait here for me?"

"Of course." Dolley wrapped her arms around him and he returned the embrace. "You'll squeeze the breath out of me."

"I don't want to let go." He kissed her with all his passion and all the memory of their life together.

"Take care, Jemmy, take care." She fought back the tears. "Your country needs you . . . as do I."

"I'll be fine." He embraced her again and turned for the door. "Look to the Cabinet papers and take care of yourself." He hesitated. "If there's a change in plan, I'll get a message to you."

275

Dolley accompanied him to the door and watched him ride into the melancholy last light of evening. When she turned to go back to her room, Uncle Willy was waddling toward her, wings outstretched as though to hug her, mouth open but no squawks. Then her tears came.

22 August 1814, Monday

*M*idnight, and here I sit drinking darkness. When I go to bed at night, my mind races with the number of people I must see, things I must do on the morrow. Tomorrow. What a glorious word. It implies hope and sunrise and a fresh slate of chores, breakfast, giving the servants their orders, hot coffee and the first caller of the day, my husband's good morning kiss. Tomorrow. The word sounds different now.

My chores are to save the Cabinet papers and to not fret over my husband's well-being. He's nine miles away tonight and it feels like one thousand. Would that I could have ridden with him, out the gate onto the dusty street, occasionally passing a house with lights on inside, someone who decided to stay. We could have ridden past the Navy Yard and over the river and then into the deep meadows of Maryland, a beautiful state. I have always loved the countryside. I know the road. I would have given anything to be with Jemmy. I have no fear of soldiers or camps, and at this moment I have no fear of the British either. I'm too tired to be afraid and too amazed at what I've seen: a city, like a tortured human being, losing its mind.

These damned skirts, swishing every time I take a step! If I had a pair of breeches, I could throw my leg over a horse, stick my hair up under my turban, and go. Let anyone try to stop me. What are the proprieties at a time like this? It's quite absurd really. My place is with my husband, and my task to ease his mind as much as possible during this impossible time.

Logically, I should have been the one to ride out. I'm younger and stronger than Jemmy. But I shall stay here and pack the papers, speak with anyone who calls, and do my best to keep people calm. I sent out invitations to the Cabinet members and their wives for dinner tomorrow. I shall keep going, keep to the routine, and keep up spirits. Still, I'd much rather be at Long Old Fields. I'd rather be anywhere but here. Is it always the fate of women to watch and to wait? To have no voice in government and yet to suffer all the pains of men's actions? Abigail Adams was right.

We fight the British and yet we have slaves and keep women in a kind of purdah. The paradox of independence has not escaped me. Free from Britain and British interference, yes, but are we free from ourselves?

I know somewhere in the life of this country we must set our slaves free. And we must allow women to contribute in their fashion to the greatness of our country. I will not live to see these dreams. It's enough that I have lived to witness the first war against Britain, and I pray that I shall live through the second.

And while I live through it, what of the time it has stolen?

Jemmy and I have had so little time together these last few months that I look at him and sometimes it's as though I am seeing him anew. Oddly, he appears younger to me than he has in years. He's tired, often, but his strength of purpose lifts him up and rejuvenates him. His eyes glitter with ideas, and his voice, a light voice, sounds firm. He is as lean now as when I first met him. I know he is not a handsome man; yet he is handsome to me and when he held me tonight, he felt like fire, he felt so young.

From outside I can hear occasional shouts and even a shot. James Blake imposed a ten o'clock evening curfew, which is being rigorously enforced. The panic, for tonight at least, has lessened, but the rumors about Federalists in southern Maryland giving aid and directions to the British have inflamed emotions other than panic. Some citizens think these traitors and spies are mixing with the refugees, so people from Maryland are being roughly treated. Such conditions provide cover for the settling of old grudges. One man has only to accuse another of spying, and the damage is done.

William Jones ordered most of the gunpowder removed from the

Navy Yard. French John told me that the clerk of the Navy Yard had to hire private teams for the task, and people charged one week's wages for the use of their wagons. Six dollars!

I do not understand how anyone can seek profit from distress. Private considerations must give way to public good.

Entrenchments are being dug, but as Mother Amy would say, "It's a day late and a dollar short." The free Negroes, and some slaves as well, are helping to dig the trenches. So much for the rumor that Frederick, Maryland, was the headquarters for a slave revolt—a rumor fostered by the British.

The slaves remain loyal, more loyal in many cases than are free white men. This tears at my heart and batters my conscience. Why so strong and why now I cannot say. It's a bit like seeing Uncle Willy today as he ran toward me when Jemmy left. The sight of him splintered my shell and let the pain rush in to all the soft, hidden places.

May God bless and help every African, may God forgive us our trespasses toward these people. I don't know if I can forgive us. I don't know if I can forgive myself.

Until the morrow, God willing.

D.P.M.

*T*he haunting call of a redheaded woodpecker was the first thing James Madison heard when he awoke at five-thirty in the morning. He noticed it because woodpeckers are usually still asleep before dawn, but the men encamped outside the house, owned by a family named Williams, must have disturbed the bird. After a few more calls of disgust the woodpecker flew off, for Madison heard the throaty song once more from a distance.

At six General Winder rode over from Long Old Fields. He neglected to tell the President that at two in the morning the American Army had sounded the alarm, rushed to formation, bayonets fixed, because cattle being driven in for the commissary were mistaken for attacking British soldiers. A dragoon told the President, who gently replied that in the dark perhaps a cow and a man did somewhat resemble each other. What he wished to say was that Armstrong resembled a horse's ass.

Armstrong glowered during the morning briefing like a dog eyeing a disputed bone. General Winder ignored him.

"As the British are thirty miles from their fleet, without cavalry and without artillery, I think they will wait for reinforcements before moving. When those reinforcements arrive, I believe that General Ross will then move on the capital." Winder spoke quietly.

"A Cossack hurrah is what Washington will see," Armstrong responded. "A foray for the sake of panicking the people. That's what the British will do. From Upper Marlboro they will turn east toward Baltimore and they will have the support of Admiral Cochrane on the smaller boats. To come overland and strike west means they lose the effect of their naval guns."

"Their naval guns will be useless on the Patuxent." William Jones betrayed his profound distaste for Armstrong.

"They are perfectly capable of sailing down the Patuxent and up the Chesapeake to Baltimore and there to meet the entire fleet," Armstrong stubbornly replied.

"They are capable of that and much else, but we have no intelligence that the fleet has moved from Benedict. And if they were planning a coordinated attack, I should think they would have done so," Jones fired back, "unless their planning is as bad as our own."

"Gentlemen." Madison stepped in. "Better to dispute the enemy at this hour than ourselves."

"Well, I say that Washington is not the target. A foray into the capital *is* likely, and what we should do is place a small number of men, a brigade perhaps or even a regiment, and hide them in the Capitol. When the British exhaust themselves, our men will rush out for an all-out charge."

The crackbrained scheme elicited no response from the assembled men. Armstrong sulked as Winder discreetly moved to the possibility of having Brigadier General Tobias Stansbury shift his fourteen hundred men at Bladensburg over to the three thousand now standing at Long Old Fields. Eight hundred men sat at Annapolis, somewhat far for immediate support, and another eight hundred, a patchwork of Maryland Militia, were now marching south to meet Winder.

The meeting broke up and Madison rode over to camp to inspect the troops. The men seemed cheerful and hurrahed their President, who was pleased.

Thomas L. McKenney, a sandy-haired dry goods dealer from Georgetown, rode into camp. He had been scouting the British with James Monroe and reported to General Winder that the British stayed put in Upper Marlboro, but he felt certain they would move on Winder's camp within twenty-four hours.

Armstrong interrupted him. "They will attack Baltimore or Annapolis. Why bother with our camp? If there's movement at Upper Marlboro, it's because they have to steal food from the countryside."

McKenney stared at the Secretary of War in disbelief, but a sidelong glance from Winder prevented another useless exchange with Armstrong.

Madison returned to the Williams house and quickly wrote Dolley. He knew the British had not come this far for the benefits of the climate, but he also believed that they might not move until all their troops were assembled in a few days' time. Joshua Barney had been their target for months, and now that he had blown his flotilla to bits as he was ordered to do, the British might need to reexamine their plans. He grabbed a pencil and wrote to Dolley:

> My dearest . . . I have passed the forenoon among the troops, who are in high spirits and make a good appearance. The reports as to the enemy have varied every hour. The last and probably truest information is that they are not very strong and are without cavalry or artillery, and of course that they are not in a condition to strike Washington. It is believed that they are not about to move from Marlboro. It is possible, however, that they have a greater force, or expect one, or that their temerity may be greater than their strength.

He finished, folded the paper, sealed it, and handed it to an aide. "Speed this on to Mrs. Madison."

The aide saluted and rode off. As of that moment, General Winder possessed three thousand men, four hundred twenty-five cavalry, and twenty guns.

James Madison twisted his feet around to loosen his ankles. Constant riding had caused the joints to stiffen.

The pencil rested on the table. He picked it up and examined it. Ingenious. He much preferred his quill, but this was certainly easy to carry.

A mood of quiet, even relaxation, spread over the Williams estate. Madison called for his horse and mounted up. William Jones accompanied him as did John Armstrong. The three started toward Washington in uneasy silence.

"Get me the trunk with the leaf-pattern lining."

"Where is it?" Sukey asked Mrs. Madison.

Dolley thought for a moment, papers spread on the floor around her. "French John will know."

"Do I have to talk to him?" A faint pout hung on Sukey's perfect lips.

"Yes, you have to talk to him, and considering our circumstances, I suggest you do it right now."

Sukey caught the tone and immediately left in search of the overworked man. Dolley heard her footfall patter down the hallway.

"Willy, stop that."

Willy continued to walk over valuable state documents, his sharp little claws clicking against the heavy papers. He enjoyed the sound. Dolley put down the sheaf of papers in her hand and picked him up. He turned his head nearly upside down and clucked at her. She sighed and placed him on his perch, a location that seemed to hold little appeal for the macaw. Dolley gave up when he fluttered down on the papers again. She couldn't sort through the documents and attend to Willy too.

French John appeared with the trunk, Sukey walking a distance behind him. The two maintained a strained politeness.

"We've got one carriage," French John reminded his mistress. "But after Mr. Madison's note, perhaps we won't need it."

"Well, he told me to see to the Cabinet papers and I'd best keep at it."

A knock at the door made Sukey run to the window while French John answered the door.

"Missus, the soldiers are going."

Dolley walked to the window. Colonel Carroll and his guard were lined up smartly and were marching away.

"What's that mean?" Sukey was suspicious.

"That we don't need them, I guess." Dolley returned to her task, and French John entered with a handsome envelope on a silver tray. Dolley took the envelope, opened it, and read:

August 23, 1814

My Dear Madam,

In the present state of alarm and bustle of preparation for the worst that may happen, I imagine it will be more convenient to dispense with the enjoyment of your hospitality today, and therefore, pray you to admit this as an excuse for Mr. Jones, Lucy, and myself. Mr. Jones is deeply engaged in dispatching the Marines and attending to other public duties. Lucy and I are packing, with the possibility of having to leave; but in the event of necessity we know not where to go, nor have we any means yet prepared for the conveyance of our effects. I sincerely hope and trust the necessity may be avoided, but there appears rather serious cause of apprehension. Our carriage horse is sick, our coachman absent, or I should have called last evening to see your sister. I feel great solicitude on her account. Yours very truly and affectionately,

E. Jones

Dolley folded the letter and absentmindedly packed it with the documents.

"Eleanor Jones will not be attending dinner." She looked up at French John. "Well, have Paul set the table anyway. We don't know what's happening from one minute to the next, and if all goes well, we'll sit down to dinner sometime."

"It's too hot to eat," Sukey complained.

"Since when has that stopped you?" French John snarled at her.

"All right, you two. We've got work to do."

"Mrs. Madison"—French John, unusually serious, bent over and handed Dolley more papers—"allow me to spike the cannon at the gate and to lay a trail of gunpowder into the house. I can blow it up once the British get inside."

"No," came Dolley's surprised reply.

"Let's kill as many as we can," French John pleaded.

"They aren't here yet, and they may not come. I won't have this house turned into a tinderbox and I won't have you murdering men like that."

"It's not murder, it's war."

"No."

Help came from an unexpected quarter. "They're killing us!" Sukey spat.

"I said no, and I mean no. Now everyone get back to work."

French John left, angry, and Sukey, also displeased, tossed papers into the trunk. Dolley glanced outside and saw a man struggling to haul his bedding on his back. How long before he abandoned that prized possession?

French John strode back into the room. "If I can't blow up the house, then let me take valuables over to Monsieur Serurier."

"He's overburdened enough. John Tayloe asked him to take up residence in the Octagon House, and I heard that Ruth Barlow stored furniture over there last night."

"They have a bedsheet with hand-drawn fleurs-de-lis hanging from a pole." French John's mouth curled up at the corner. The thought of seeing a Royalist flag so humbly presented amused him.

"If the situation gets bad enough, take Uncle Willy there."

Willy squawked at the sound of his name.

"That's all?"

"That's all. The cook has agreed to take King George, so our little family will be scattered but safe."

"Who's going to take me?" Sukey clutched a beautifully inscribed paper.

"I'm going to take you. Don't crumple that paper, Sukey. Come on, we've got to keep packing."

*T*hat evening another penciled note from the President arrived. Dolley ripped it open in haste. He asked her to be ready to leave Washington at a moment's notice. She placed the note in her skirt pocket along with her dice. She said nothing to the servants. Better to wait and see.

23 August 1814, Tuesday

*J*emmy spent the day in the saddle. He's home asleep now but for how long I don't know. I wish I could sleep. Every hour brings a different story as to the whereabouts of the British. I suspect, if they have any sense, that they're asleep.

Anna finally left today for the Forrests'. I've been so busy I haven't put down her recalcitrance in my diary. I thought that she had gone on Sunday, and then I learned that she had stayed back. She lingered in town as long as possible until Richard got furious and put his foot down.

Jemmy stopped at the Cutts house and was so famished that Richard begged him to pause a moment and eat something. Bless Richard.

Then Jemmy rode over to the Monroes' at Twentieth and I streets, where he had yet another meeting with that pompous invertebrate, Armstrong. Monroe has been in the saddle even more than Jemmy. He's shadowed the enemy for days. Jemmy reported that Monroe, while fatigued, is bursting with ideas.

A Colonel George Minor of the 10th Virginia Militia has bedded down his seven hundred men in the House of Representatives. I hope they can sleep. Those awful red curtains would give me nightmares. It may be that this is the first cooperative body of men to inhabit the House of Representatives. French John told me hardly any of those men have muskets or rifles.

Dear French John, he rushes from my house to his own. I would be lost without him.

Jemmy told me that the two bridges into Maryland will be destroyed if we hear the enemy is advancing in our direction. The lower bridge is a good strong bridge, but the Stoddert's Bridge is so rickety that destroying it will be a public service.

Jacob Barker, the banker, appeared at our door not ten minutes after Jemmy dragged in. He asked permission to blow up the Capitol so that the enemy could not possess it. If our Capitol is to be destroyed, Jemmy replied, far better to let that terrible task fall to the British. It might arouse the nation.

Such questions, which even twenty-four hours ago would have seemed ludicrous, now make perfect sense.

Tonight the streets are deserted. There's not a breath of wind, and a huge, clammy hand is cupped over Washington. Mayor Blake is patrolling the streets himself with some of the militia. They seem like ghosts wandering around a graveyard.

I search people's faces now, studying their every feature, the light in their eyes, in case I never see them again.

I practice calling up their images: Anna, fair and bright; Lisel with her exotic, dark beauty; Jemmy—Jemmy's picture is both the easiest and the hardest to call up in my mind. Some moments my fear for him overwhelms me so, I can't remember how he looks. I tiptoe over to bed to stare at him. I want to remember everything. The frostbite scar on his nose. His upper lip, longer than his lower; his fine hands, such lovely hands. His hair, nearly white now with streaks of gray, like his mother's. His face is ruddy from exposure to the sun these last days, and fine veins show under his eyes. A light gray stubble covers his chin and cheeks. He's so fastidious about shaving, sometimes he'll be shaved twice a day. Not today.

I can bear anything, dear God, anything but the loss of my husband.

Until the morrow, God willing.

D.P.M.

*A*t three-thirty in the morning a scarlet glow trembled in the east like a hesitant sunrise. Dolley, sleeping fitfully, opened her eyes, lay still, and then slipped her bare feet onto the floor. No birds called. A hush, almost a reverent quiet, enveloped Washington. She hurried to the top floor of the house. From the window she saw the pinkish light. The silence, the velvet darkness around the ball of light, convinced her this was not the sun. She thought for a moment. If the Navy Yard had been torched, she would have heard explosions and the light would be much closer. It had to be a bridge burning, but which one she didn't know. She pressed her nose to the windowpane and then opened the window, breathing in the night air, heavy and moist. The August stars, so cool and distant, promised no relief. When this day dawned, the earth would fry, a steaming heat unknown to the British. Well, that was one advantage, the climate. The United States seemed to have few others.

Dolley watched until four o'clock and then tiptoed downstairs. A chirp from Uncle Willy announced that he would like the cover removed so that he, too, could see. She lifted the fabric from his cage and opened the door, and he instantly hopped out. Willy loved having Dolley to himself. She kissed him. He kissed her back while he cooed and danced. She fed him, and when he was happily cracking seeds, she went into the bedroom. Jemmy, dead asleep, had to be wakened. Dolley didn't have the heart to do it while it remained dark outside. She walked through the house to the kitchen in back, started a fire, and ground coffee. While the pot brewed, she walked back to the bedroom and gently shook her husband awake.

He opened his eyes, lay still for a moment, then sat bolt upright. "Who's here?"

"Just me."

After coffee Dolley and James climbed up on the roof and searched the area with spyglasses just as the sun came up. Dolley pointed to where she saw the fire's glow. James concurred that it was the bridge over the East Branch.

When they returned downstairs, French John was at work and a still-sleepy Sukey was tying up the last of the four trunks crammed with papers. A few changes of clothes covered the papers. When Dolley ran out of trunks, she decided to fold her clothes over the documents. Even if she found more trunks, French John didn't think he could find another wagon. This was it.

Before the sun had cleared the horizon, a messenger arrived with a note from General Winder. It was meant for Armstrong, but the messenger delivered it to Madison either by mistake or by design, since the fighting men despised Armstrong. Madison wasted no time trying to find out why the message was brought to him: Winder was asking for help. He'd broken down three horses the day before, fallen in a ditch while walking on foot in the pitch darkness, and wrenched his shoulder and turned his ankle. None of this was in the note; the messenger told it all to the President. Madison read and reread the note. The general would kill himself with exhaustion before the British reached him.

"You may tell the general that I am on my way," Madison told the now-smiling messenger as Dolley left to find his boots.

"I boned them," French John called out. "I'll get them."

"When did you have time to do that?" Dolley wondered, knowing that running a deer bone on the inside of the boot, and the outside too, was tedious labor.

"I work fast." French John smiled. "I can't have the President riding in cracked, dirty boots."

Dolley turned back to the front hall. "Jemmy, if there's a fight today, don't ride to the front. This country needs a live President, not a—"

"Dead hero." Madison finished her sentence for her, a habit that occasionally irritated her but not this morning. "My dear, I will protect myself as best I can, but my place is with the Army."

"I'm not arguing that," said Dolley, who did at that moment feel argumentative.

"Here they are." French John handed the President his boots and boot pulls.

"These boots look new." Madison complimented French John for the miracle he had worked.

Sukey and Paul peered around the corner. Would this be the last time they saw the Master?

James Madison carefully reached down and took his wife's hand and brought it to his lips.

Sukey, not remotely moved by this or any other scene of romantic devotion between a man and a woman, blurted out, "They coming? They coming, Master James?"

"I don't know but I think they will. You watch over Mrs. Madison and attend to her every need, Sukey."

Sukey nodded.

"I'll see you tonight, and if there's any change, I'll send word." Madison returned his gaze to his wife, kissed her hand again, and then stepped toward the door, which French John opened.

"Jemmy," Dolley called out, then embraced him and let him go.

He walked down the steps, mounted his horse, tipped his hat to his wife, and rode off.

*A*t seven in the morning the President was joined by Secretary of the Navy William Jones and by James Monroe, who was back from Bladensburg, in General William Winder's temporary headquarters. The conference continued until close to ten o'clock, when it seemed clear, thanks to the latest reports of enemy movements, that a stand would be made at Bladensburg. John Armstrong arrived unforgivably late, offered little advice, and seemed not to grasp the desperation of the hour.

The one verbal outburst after they left that queerly polite meeting came from Commodore Joshua Barney. General Winder had ordered Barney to guard the Navy Yard bridge and to fire it. Barney fulminated when the President rode out with the others to inspect the Navy Yard on their way to Bladensburg.

"What do you mean, leaving me here to blow up a bridge? I've got the only men who know how to fight. We're Navy men! The Army isn't worth a tinker's damn. Goddamnit, Mr. President, a corporal and five men can blow up this bridge. We mean to fight, so let us fight . . . sir."

A strained silence followed this outburst. No one had ever witnessed a man speak to the President this way.

Far from being offended, James Madison was grateful that someone wanted to fight. God knows, his Secretary of War didn't, and General Winder was exhausted and in over his head.

"Commodore, I believe you're right. Get on with it then."

An ear-to-ear grin illuminated Barney's strong face. "Get moving, men. We'll show 'em what the Navy can do. Hell, we'll do it for 'em, the ignorant, soft jackasses."

His five hundred men limbered the five naval guns, fell into formation, and began the march to Bladensburg.

George Campbell, who in February had replaced Navy Secretary William Jones as Secretary of the Treasury, had joined in the early-morning meeting because he was a Cabinet officer, though a sick one. If the government was to fall, he would fall with it. He regretted that he was not feeling better. He regretted even more that Albert Gallatin could not have remained Secretary of the Treasury. William Jones had become too burdened with the war to continue serving as both Secretary of the Navy and acting Secretary of the Treasury. Madison, Campbell knew, was plagued with sick men and incompetent men. Campbell could not find money as Gallatin could, although in less-trying times his efforts would have been sufficient. His increasing sickness lessened his effectiveness, and he was aware he lacked Gallatin's gift of seeing the entire problem. Campbell could see only bits of the problem, but he knew one of those bits was Armstrong.

Barney's direct speech encouraged him.

"Mr. President."

"Yes." Madison turned to the stricken man, so ill he held on to the pommel of his saddle for balance.

"By chance I engaged Mr. Armstrong in conversation last night. He told me the defense of Washington was none of his business. He felt strongly that it was not his place to intrude on General Winder's command." Campbell gasped for breath, trying not to groan. "Mr. President, in our present state of distress, we need every experienced man available."

Madison blinked in surprise. The war and its prosecution were Armstrong's duties wherever that war was fought. To ease Campbell's mind, Madison promised, "I will ride up ahead to Mr. Armstrong and stress that he should speed to Bladensburg to assist General Winder." Campbell smiled. "And you, sir, will return home."

"No, I can go forward."

"Mr. Campbell, I've already lost one Vice President, and I'm losing the second. Please, I don't want to lose you. Your loyalty has heartened me, your assumption of the Herculean task of finding money impresses me. You are valuable. Please return. I command it."

Dust stung Campbell's eyes. He bowed his head and turned his horse back toward Washington.

Madison called after him. "Mr. Campbell, if the city is lost, we shall meet in Frederick."

Campbell, torn by emotion, trotted back to the President. He unbuckled his dueling pistols and handed them to Madison. "For the love of God, sir, defend yourself from harm." Before the President could reply, Campbell wheeled around and moved off, clenching his teeth in pain, heartsick as well.

James Madison strapped on the pistols.

Richard Rush, the young Attorney General, also riding in the small entourage, thought the pistols were bigger than the President. Madison's horse, strongly favoring a hind leg, stumbled more frequently. "I've got to get another horse, Mr. Rush."

Fortunately, the President was able to swap horses with Charles Carroll at the Marine Barracks. Carroll promised to care for the mare. Madison loved his horses.

As Rush and Madison rode toward Bladensburg, now five miles ahead, a column of men marched before them with Barney following.

Rush, knowing Madison hated to part with his mare, talked horses with him. "You know, once this war is over, Thornton will set out and buy every blooded horse between the Atlantic and the Blue Ridge."

"He's the only man I've ever known who can buy a weanling and not make a mistake." Madison envied Thornton his legendary eye for horseflesh, and Madison wasn't a bad horseman himself. "He wastes no money breeding them. He lets someone else bear that expense and then"—he snapped the fingers of his right hand—"he buys them just as the breeder's money is running out."

"Shrewd," Rush concurred.

"And a Federalist, more's the pity." Madison shook his head.

"Well, you were shrewd yourself when you left him in charge of the Patent Office."

"I will use a Federalist as readily as a Republican if he can do the job. It's DeWitt Clinton's approach that I fear. Apart from putting unqualified men in important positions, it will only harden the other party's resolve to do the same when they're in office."

"The spoils system," Rush said.

"Apt description."

"Clay coined it."

"Ah." Madison rode in silence. "Your opinion of Henry Clay, sir?"

"If—if things turn out badly for us, Clay had better learn to plant tobacco."

"But we will win, Mr. Rush; despite all, we will win." Madison's voice was firm.

"Then Henry Clay will be President—within eight years."

"Everyone wants to be President." Madison rubbed his chin, bristling white. "You know, Mr. Rush, if I truly disliked a man, I would wish the presidency upon him."

*B*ladensburg, a tobacco town gone bust, was laid out in an L. The Potomac's East Branch rolled along at the juncture of the

L. The town itself, handsome brick homes sliding into genteel disrepair, rested on the bank of the river.

On the eastern side three roads ran out of town. The northernmost road became a turnpike to the great seaport of Baltimore, the easternmost road led to Upper Marlboro, and the southernmost road followed the twists and turns of the East Branch. The river road, if one chose the right intersection, could also lead to Upper Marlboro.

Most of the town's houses reposed along the road to Baltimore and the more direct route to Upper Marlboro.

The river road fed into the Upper Marlboro road right at the town itself. The Upper Marlboro road and the Baltimore Pike met at the Bladensburg Bridge.

This wooden span was ninety feet long and, although narrow, was securely anchored to sturdy stone abutments.

The Bladensburg Bridge provided a speedy route to Washington, for the road on the western side of the river was well maintained.

A few hundred yards from the bridge, the Washington Road forked, with the northern fork going to Georgetown. Within the arms of this Y was a handsome field.

Colonel Decius Wadsworth, with civilian volunteers, had dug earthworks in this field. Weeks ago the President and the mayor of Washington had requested this as Madison thought Bladensburg a likely crossing. John Armstrong had ignored the order.

As the reality of a British invasion of Washington came closer and closer, Wadsworth and other military men at Bladensburg started clawing dirt. By now, no one in his right mind would listen to Armstrong.

A lone tobacco barn on the Georgetown Road, near the bridge, was the only structure on the western side of the river. Next to the fence at the tobacco barn rested a small battery of Baltimore artillery. The former Attorney General, William Pinkney, crouched to the right of the guns with a battalion of riflemen.

The artillery consisted of six-pounders, not big guns but guns nonetheless, and the British were coming on with no artillery at all.

Two guns sat smack in the middle of the Washington Road.

Brigadier General Tobias Stansbury had twenty-two hundred untrained militia. After marching from Baltimore the night before, these men were blistered and sore. They awoke that morning to a pink sky announcing that Winder had burned the bridges. The British knew Bladensburg was the next bridge. Finding the lower bridges burned, they would head for the town, and if they studied their maps, they'd be coming anyway because the river was easy to ford there.

Rations were spoiling, and James Monroe had tried to move hungry men in the night. Stansbury refused. Orders came from Winder to fall back; then countermanding orders arrived. This confusion hardly helped ease their minds, but Stansbury, once he had his men back at Bladensburg, stayed put on the western bank.

As other troops arrived throughout the morning, at least the raw recruits wouldn't be facing the enemy by themselves.

Stansbury set two companies next to Pinkney's battalion.

Wisely, Stansbury put men in the orchard, only to have James Monroe come along and move them to a ravine.

As the morning wore on and men were moved about like chess pieces, the thermometer climbed past ninety degrees. The day was going to be a whistling bitch.

Farther down the Washington Road, on the western side of a creek, there was a militia unit. A wobbly bridge, Tournecliffe's Bridge, hung precariously over the creek. Joshua Barney, driving his men like the Devil himself, would bring up his guns on the Washington Road. He'd be a third line of defense, the center of that line.

General Stansbury made the most of the terrain. Furious when James Monroe, with no military authority, moved his men about, Stansbury looked south and saw a huge dust cloud hovering in the sky. When he finally found General Winder, there was no time to repair the damage. The three-hundred-eighty-man cavalry, sitting in a ravine, theoretically to protect them, was useless.

Armstrong, arriving on the scene, looked about, said nothing, and did nothing.

The Americans squinted to catch sight of the enemy. The main body of the column was heaving into view—thousands of brilliant red coats, epaulets and bayonets catching sunlight beneath the dust cloud. The distinct tramping sound of disciplined men moving in precision only underscored the woeful lack of precision on the American side of the riverbank.

A shuddering silence swept over the Americans. President Madison and Richard Rush cantered by the apple orchard and the troops, riding past the artillery and the earthworks. They assumed Winder's headquarters was in the town itself, and they were hurrying to cross the bridge.

Madison's horse bucked and the President fought the animal as it tried to bolt.

William Simmons, recently fired from the War Department, a man who hated Armstrong with murderous fury, spurred his horse from the eastern side of the river. He was only minutes in front of the British, whom he had been scouting.

He thundered over the Bladensburg Bridge, holding his reins in his left hand and waving his right.

"Get back! Get back, Mr. President. The enemy is now in Bladensburg!"

"Good God." Richard Rush hauled back on the reins.

Madison called to the advancing Simmons, "In Bladensburg?"

"Yes. Turn back." Simmons's horse almost overtook Madison and Rush as they wheeled back off the bridge.

Rush's hat flew off as he dug into his horse's flanks. The President, still fighting his horse, drew alongside him. They galloped to the earthworks, where Monroe, Winder, and a sullen Armstrong awaited the first shot.

The men in the first line of defense didn't know the other troops had arrived to assist them. Their moment of comic relief had been watching the President and the Attorney General turn back at the bridge. The relief was short-lived.

Bugles played in Bladensburg. Drums beat louder and louder. James Madison, like most of the men on the field, had never seen combat; during the War of Independence he had been considered too frail to fight. The expectation, the sounds, made his heart pound. The exhilaration was intoxicating.

The sun, high in the sky, glared down as the front of the British column turned onto the main street of Bladensburg. Like a well-oiled machine, the Redcoats marched toward the bridge.

A volley of bullets sprayed into the Bladensburg street. The British kept marching. Madison's horse, dancing constantly, pulled on the President until his arms ached in their sockets. He was behind the center of the American line, which gave him an unobstructed view of the British. Next to him was John Armstrong, who evidenced no interest in the proceedings.

General Winder, astride a large, calm gelding, was next to Colonel Joseph Sterett's 5th Regiment, in the field between the Georgetown and Washington roads. Two regiments were to the right of Winder, also in the open—Colonel Jonathan Schutz's and Colonel John Ragan's regiments. Both units were drafted militia, most of whom wore frock coats or short hunting jackets. They stood in stark contrast to Sterett's 5th, wealthy young men from Baltimore who paid a great deal of money for, and a great deal of attention to, their uniforms.

The American marksmen began to hit home as the British closed in on the bridge. Redcoats collapsed in the dust. One man spun around and fell, tripping the man behind him.

Madison noticed the British Marines setting up tripods to the right of the bridge. A warehouse gave them intermittent cover as they ran in and out. Then a burst of flame and bizarre sounds filled the air as the Royal Marines set off rockets. No one on the western side of the Atlantic had seen anything like a Congreve rocket.

Winder calmly rode over to President Madison and requested that he move farther beyond the range of British guns. The President hesitated. What he wanted more than anything was to pick up a rifle and fire. Winder pleaded with him to take care for his safety. By now the artillery opened fire and the roar was deafening. More Congreve rockets screamed overhead from the British side.

"I beseech you, President Madison, do not present our troops with the sight of their commander in chief being wounded." Winder pleaded in earnest now. He may not have been much of a general, but he was oblivious to the dirt kicking up around him. He possessed courage under fire.

Madison inclined his head toward Winder and then spoke to Monroe and Armstrong. "Gentlemen, let us leave military matters to military men. General Winder, as you wish."

The President withdrew to the rear, but slowly. The British column reached the foot of the bridge, and Wadsworth's guns, in the middle of the Washington Road, were blowing huge holes in the line. The British broke ranks and ran for the protection of the houses near the bridge.

Cheers bellowed from the Americans between the Georgetown and Washington roads. Within minutes they stopped, for the British, lashed on by their officers—seasoned professionals—reorganized to charge the bridge. A wild Redcoat, a colonel on a gray horse, drew his sword and galloped across the bridge. A brigade followed behind him, and the guns on the road were fired again, tearing nearly a dozen of the British to pieces. But the colonel, without a scratch, emerged from the smoke and called again to his men. A bugle sounded "charge" and the British raced across the bridge. They kept coming and coming, faster than the two men tending the two cannon could reload and fire. The minute the Redcoats got clear of the bridge, they fanned out in all directions and hugged the ground for cover.

One cannon, frantically ministered to by the gunners who had jammed in the wadding before the powder, rolled over like a cast-iron whale into a ditch. The first line of defense now had one gun to face the entire British Army rushing over the Bladensburg Bridge. The riflemen fired, reloaded, and fired, but the veteran British did not falter. They were close enough for the Americans to hear their officers shouting orders in that nasal accent that sounded so snobbish.

Madison watched as the gunners, nearly overrun, abandoned the remaining cannon. A solitary, grimy-faced American placed powder in the gun, jammed down the wadding, aimed the cannon, and fired. Then that courageous soul, too, left as the tide of red swirled around him. Madison saw him tear across the field to safety.

The perfect order of the British unnerved the militia. American Regulars would have stood their ground, but these men, barely trained, folded like a bad hand of cards.

General Winder perceived that his first line of defense had collapsed. He ordered the flashy Baltimore men to press forward, and as they did, the sky filled with rockets, which found their marks. Schutz's and Ragan's regiments crawled or ran out of the field. The Baltimore boys, still looking fashionable, wavered. Colonel Sterett galloped around his men and screamed himself hoarse. They stood for a moment. A fleet of rockets rained on them, and they too turned and fled. Sterett bellowed and tears of rage ran down his cheeks.

General Stansbury wanted to shoot the fleeing men, but his own men began to run away from him. Colonel Ragan, riding hard after his boys and trying to turn them back as a shepherd dog turns his sheep, fell off his horse as the animal leaned in to the turn. The horse followed the men, and Colonel Ragan, face covered with dirt, bounced back up on his feet. He spun around and saw the entire British Army heading straight for him. He didn't give a damn. He headed over to the company of Americans still firing. It was now over one hundred degrees on the battlefield.

The smell of gunpowder burned the men's nostrils, but the paucity of artillery kept the field open to view. Puffs of smoke belched out of rifles only to dissipate. If a man had a vantage point, he could see.

Sterett, miraculously, collected his men once more. The British fire grew heavier and more accurate, and the 5th couldn't see the enemy as they slithered through the apple orchard. The Baltimore men stuck out like targets, not a tree in sight. William Pinkney regrouped his retreating riflemen with Sterett's 5th. A musket ball ripped into Pinkney's right arm. He refused help and walked off the field, blood pouring down his elbow and over his hand.

A confusion of orders from General Winder to the 5th and the riflemen took the fight out of them. They started to walk backward, still firing, and then in the bat of an eye, turned around and ran for the rear.

The disorderly retreat became a rout, and men threw away their weapons as though they had caught fire. No such disorder troubled the British, who expertly bore down on the Americans.

Colonel Jacint Laval, his cavalry useless in the ravine, heard the cries of the men. He called to his troops, but before they could charge out of the ravine where they had stupidly been placed by Monroe, a company of men in reserve blocked their path. Within minutes, both the company and the cavalry were overrun by the panic-stricken first line. His men reined in their horses, rode by the onrush, and when Laval could finally count, he had fifty-five men left. The other horsemen had simply vanished.

Monroe saw his mistakes only too clearly, but there wasn't time to correct them.

The fleeing soldiers took the Georgetown Road, preventing them from running into the advancing troops from Washington. There was no hope for their being steadied and rejoining a second wave of Americans.

Reluctant to leave the battlefield even though he knew what was happening, Madison was urged to go in a note from General Winder.

He rode over to Colonel Charles Carroll. "Colonel, fly to Mrs. Madison and tell her to go to Bellevue. I will meet her there and along with the Joneses, we'll go over to Virginia together. We can cross at Little Falls Bridge and make it to Wiley's Tavern."

Carroll saluted and galloped away. Bellevue was Carroll's home in Georgetown.

With a bitter taste in his mouth, James Madison pointed his unruly horse toward Washington. John Armstrong had disappeared.

"Go to safety, Mr. President," Monroe shouted, even as he himself headed toward the battle. At this moment, being a commissioned officer was far less important than keeping a cool head, and James Monroe surely possessed that.

As Madison rode back toward the city, he encountered Joshua Barney and his five hundred men just now hauling the guns into place. They were still in the District of Columbia when the battle started. As Barney carefully placed his guns, he took note of his position. Slightly in front of him, to his left, were six cannon under the command of Major George Peter, and a knot of Army men were on their right. Almost even with Barney's left stood the District of Columbia Militia. An Army regiment under the command of Colonel William D. Beall stood next to Barney's sailors. It wasn't the best of positions, but he would make the best of it. The honor of holding the center belonged to him.

By the pathetic Tournecliffe Bridge stood a battalion of Maryland men under the command of Lieutenant Colonel Kramer. Barney recognized that they wouldn't be part of his line, but they might be able to slow the British for a while.

He placed his two huge eighteen-pounder naval guns smack in the middle of the road. In the field to his right he placed three twelve-pounders under the command of Captain Miller. For good measure, he stuck a company of marines there, too.

Satisfied with his work, Barney eagerly awaited the arrival of the British so that he might launch as many as possible to their eternal reward.

Most of Stansbury's men ran down the Georgetown Road, but enough stragglers came down the Washington Road for Barney to get the full story of the rout. He had no use for Army men anyway.

For about twenty minutes Barney heard sporadic gunfire. At two-thirty he saw the British moving smartly down the road. Just as the surge of red reached the rickety Tournecliffe Bridge, Lieutenant Colonel Kramer ordered his Maryland men to fire. One brief flurry from the British convinced the Americans that this was not a safe place. They, too, turned tail and ran. Barney wasn't surprised. These pups shouldn't be thrown into a war with real men.

As the Redcoats crossed the bridge, Major Peter's guns loosened up on the left and Barney fired one of his eighteen-pounders. The British line staggered and then surged ahead.

Peter and Barney blasted away again, and this time they were joined by Captain Miller on Barney's right. He ripped open the twelve-pounders. The British hurried off the road and ran into the field to Barney's right.

Miller dumped grape and canister on the British to good effect. The smoke thickened, the smell of sulfur dense and lingering in the brutal heat and humidity.

Barney yelled to his men, "Board 'em!"

The sailors bounded forward, rushing to meet the British, who had stalled behind a rail fence. The sailors hit them hard and the British fell back, but theirs was not a disorganized retreat. They moved backward but stopped to fire with regularity. The sailors, jubilant, ran back up the hill to their guns.

British officers, trained to be in the thick of fire, dropped by the dozens. Rear Admiral George Cockburn and General Robert Ross, seeing their line falter, brought up the rest of the British force—one thousand four hundred sixty men—and told them to move on the double. Barney swept his eyes over the field and saw Ross, in full regalia, astride a gorgeous Arabian. Unable to stay back, as it wasn't in his nature, Ross pressed his men on. The animal was shot out from under him. Ross nimbly dismounted as the animal fell and grabbed a young officer's horse.

Rear Admiral Cockburn, drenched in gold, spurred toward the front and ordered his men to plant their rockets one hundred forty yards from Barney's line.

They didn't scare Joshua Barney or his men, but eventually the British found their range and the Americans began to fall.

British reinforcements tramped into place and pounded the American right. Barney, impervious, kept to his eighteen-pounders.

Major Peter, to Barney's left, kept at his guns as well.

Riding hard through the smoke came General Winder as he ordered General Scott's and Major Peter's Regulars to fall back. They couldn't hold back the British, and they didn't know their left was totally exposed. Winder was trying to save what men he could to fight another day.

Scott's Regulars cursed the general to his face, but Winder would not be swayed. Without firing a shot, they fell back. The District of Columbia Militia too, far tougher than anyone supposed, argued violently with Winder but ultimately obeyed his orders. Two thousand men withdrew without firing a shot.

Winder never got to Barney, or maybe he didn't try because Barney was a Navy man and Winder felt no jurisdiction over the Navy. Barney, undismayed as his support evaporated, fought on like a maniac. His sailors threw everything they had at the British, even after a bullet gouged a hunk of meat from Barney's leg and lodged inside it. He didn't go down but kept shouting orders.

The entire British Army now concentrated on one fifty-five-year-old commodore and his five hundred men.

"Come on! Come on, you sons-of-bitches," Barney screamed at the enemy. "I'll kill every one of you!"

One of the gunners whistled as he swabbed the cannon.

Barney's sailing master bellowed at him, "The wagons!" before he collapsed, shot through the head.

Joshua turned to see the ammunition wagons, driven by civilians, heading for Washington. He had only a few rounds of ammunition left.

"Finish off! Finish off and then spike the guns!"

Sharpshooters, crawling through the field, came closer and closer, picking off the sailors.

Blood gushed from Barney's thigh. "I want you men out of here, out of here now!"

Charles Ball ran over to his staggering commander. "Come on. Commodore, come on."

"Hell, Charlie, I'm too heavy to carry. Get out of here."

"No, sir." Ball spied Barney's aide on the commodore's horse. "Wilson, come over here."

Wilson galloped off. Barney yelled at him too, but Wilson had had enough.

"I'll bust up Wilson later." The pain throbbed now. "As for you, Ball, go."

"No."

"You can make it."

"No, sir." Grime-streaked sweat poured over his smooth brown features.

"Ball, you're not a freeman, and I'll tell some goddamned Virginia planter."

"How do you know that?" Ball was incredulous.

"I'm no idiot, Charlie. You never showed me your papers. Now get, *get,* or so help me God I'll shoot you myself."

Ball carefully lowered Barney to the ground. Tears came to his eyes but Barney waved him off.

Joshua Barney rolled over on his stomach and pressed hard against the ground, hoping to stem the loss of blood.

A corporal of the British 85th found him.

"I'm not surrendering to a goddamned corporal," Barney hissed. "Now get me an officer of rank."

"Yes, sir." The Redcoat saluted. He returned with Captain Wainwright, who immediately left and, to Barney's surprise, returned with both Rear Admiral Cockburn and General Ross, who knew that this was the man who had held up their advance.

Captain Wainwright introduced Cockburn, pronouncing the name "Co-burn."

Barney staggered up but sank to his knees, a fresh jet of blood pouring out of his thigh. "All this time I've been calling you Cockburn. Well, Admiral, you've got hold of me at last."

In chasing Barney, George Cockburn had grown to admire the American's skill. Today he admired his incredible bravery. A handsome man, Cockburn removed his hat. "Let us not speak of that subject, Commodore. I regret to see you in this state."

Ross and Cockburn withdrew a discreet distance, spoke for a moment, and then returned to Barney.

"Sir," Ross spoke, "we wish to parole you if, upon receiving medical attention yourself, you will care for our wounded. We can't take them with us."

"You have my word, General." Barney extended his hand and Ross shook it.

"Wainwright, see that every attention is paid to the commodore. Get stretcher-bearers. Get a surgeon. Now." Wainwright dashed back for a surgeon; he could see one yards off. "Commodore," Cockburn continued, "I hope that if we meet again, it will be under more pleasant circumstances." Cockburn saluted, as did Ross.

As the surgeon rushed up to Barney, the American had time to reflect how bizarre it was that he had more respect for Ross and Cockburn than he had for Winder, Armstrong, or Madison.

*T*he windows of the presidential mansion were closed to keep out the dust and, in vain, to make the place cooler. Outside, the heat punished man and beast. The exodus from Washington continued with people growing more frantic by the minute.

To keep herself from unraveling, Dolley was writing a letter, in installments, to her sister Lucy. She started it after her husband left and she would interrupt the narrative in order to grab something else to pack or to give the servants directions.

As it was, the four trunks were bursting. She managed to squeeze in some silver, her favorite clock, and a few books.

Sukey sat by the window in a daze. She had trouble holding her head up. Dolley couldn't understand how she could laze about at a time like this unless it was nerves. Sometimes they took people that way.

French John, arms folded, sat by the front door.

Noon passed. Dolley ordered Paul, who was also calm, to set the table. He reminded her that it had been set for yesterday's Cabinet dinner and he hadn't had the time to clear it. She'd forgotten all about that. She told him to dust the plates then and prepare for dinner at three.

Paul heard a boom, then another distant boom.

Uncle Willy, shifting from side to side on his perch, let out a bloodcurdling yell. Sukey jumped to her feet. Dolley rushed to the window and opened it. A blast of sticky heat was her first sensation.

The second was a distant roar, most definitely a cannon. Uncle Willy flapped his wings and hollered for all he was worth.

Dolley lifted him off his perch and smoothed his feathers. "Uncle Willy, this is worse than King George, isn't it?"

"That bird could wake the dead," Sukey growled.

"He feels the strain." Dolley defended him. "In his own way I guess he's as worried about Jemmy as I am."

"He's worried about his own self. That's the most selfish bird in creation," Sukey pouted.

Dolley walked into the hall. "French John."

"Yes, madam."

"How far away do you reckon that cannon to be?"

"Five miles. No more than ten."

"Could this insufferable heat distort the sound?"

"I don't think so."

A loud knock on the front door was followed by Mrs. George Campbell, wife of the Secretary of the Treasury, nearly falling through the door when French John opened it.

"Mrs. Madison"—she gasped for breath—"a great battle is being fought and we must flee. Please come with me. My carriage is outside. The British can't be but two hours from the city."

"Thank you, Mrs. Campbell." Dolley smiled at the distraught woman. "I cannot leave until I am certain as to my husband's safety. I am expecting him to return."

"I'm afraid none of them will return." Mrs. Campbell recognized that Dolley wasn't going to budge.

"I thank you for your concern for me, and I shall never forget it. Now go and save yourself."

Impulsively, Mrs. Campbell hugged her and ran back down the steps.

As French John closed the door, Dolley called to Paul, "Get the silver off the table."

"Where am I going to put it?"

"We'll find room in these trunks somehow."

A bewildered Paul hurried back into the dining room.

Another pounding on the door revealed a shockingly exhausted James Blake. On seeing Dolley, he removed his hat. "Mrs. Madison, you are in great peril. As mayor of Washington, I have an obligation to see to your safety. Please leave now."

"Mr. Blake, won't you come in for a refreshment?"

"Thank you, ma'am, I can't. Please do as I say."

"I can't." Dolley felt sympathy for him. "I can't go until I have word of my husband."

"Oh God, Mrs. Madison, that word may not come in time to save you. You must save yourself."

A shout from outside caught Blake's attention. "Mrs. Madison, I must go. Please save yourself." He turned and slowly walked back outside. He hadn't the energy left to run.

"Sukey, take down the crimson velvet curtains from my sitting room."

"Why?" Sukey was amazed.

"Because I said so!" Dolley snapped at her.

French John and Dolley watched Sukey move with some speed for the first time that day.

"I still have time to lay the powder." He cocked an eyebrow.

"And I still have time to say no." She smiled at him.

A man's screaming voice and hoofbeats pulled Dolley and French John to the window. James Smith was yelling for all he was worth. "Clear out! Clear out! Armstrong's ordered a retreat!"

"Armstrong?" Dolley puzzled. "Why not General Winder? Well, I guess it doesn't matter who gave the command."

Those people remaining in the city now appeared on the streets. No one seemed to have a clear direction. People ran this way and that. A man in a tall hat fainted from the heat. No one stopped to look after him.

"Are you ready to go, Mrs. Madison?" French John inquired, his voice low.

"No, I am not. Not until I hear from my husband."

"What if the British should come into the city?"

"Then they can just come into the house and get me."

Sukey moaned from the sitting room, "I can't get these down. They're too heavy."

"Paul." Dolley called for the young man. He appeared. "Did you finish with the silver?"

"Yes, ma'am, I did."

"Sukey needs your assistance." Dolley pointed toward the sitting room.

More hoofbeats and another pounding knock on the door sent French John hurrying to open it, but Charles Carroll pushed it open first. The two men nearly collided. There wasn't time to apologize.

"Mrs. Madison!" Carroll called.

She hurried into the hall. "Colonel Carroll, have you news?"

"I left the President's side at Bladensburg, ma'am, and we are getting the worst of it. He instructed me to tell you to go to Bellevue, to meet the Joneses there. He will meet you there if he can, and you will all cross at Little Falls Bridge to go to Wiley's Tavern."

"Wiley's Tavern?" Dolley repeated.

"On Difficult Run, Mrs. Madison."

"Aptly named." She smiled ruefully. "How was Mr. Madison when you last saw him?"

"He was well."

"He did not expose himself to fire, did he?"

Carroll thought fast. "He was in more danger from a borrowed horse than from the British." Not exactly the truth but not exactly a lie. "Now, please hurry, Mrs. Madison."

Dolley looked around. "Sukey!"

"I'm finished."

Paul dragged the curtains out.

"If they won't fit in the trunks, perhaps you can wrap them around the trunks or around papers. They'll offer some protection." Dolley turned to Colonel Carroll. "Do you need anything, Colonel?"

"Water." His face was caked with dust.

"Yes, of course."

On her way to the kitchen she noticed the Gilbert Stuart painting of George Washington. "Sukey, please fetch the colonel some water." She remained in front of the painting. "French John."

The faithful Frenchman appeared. He looked at Dolley and then up at the painting. "I'll get a ladder."

Two more messengers arrived, urging her to leave, and Mayor Blake reappeared. "You've got to go! I can't have your life on my conscience," he wailed.

"I will, I will. You've done all you can do." Dolley praised him. Satisfied, the mayor left.

Colonel Carroll drank the water and wondered where Dolley was. He called to her, "Mrs. Madison."

"I'm in here."

He walked into the room to behold French John on the ladder. Paul was handing him tools. Colonel Carroll had marched, countermarched, and witnessed a crushing defeat; now he was watching a crazy woman give orders to save a painting. It was too much. "Mrs. Madison, what are you doing?"

"The British can't have it!" was her defiant answer.

"They'll have you! You've got to get out of here."

"I will, but not until this painting is safe!"

"My God, do you want to be killed?" Carroll exploded.

"I am not going to be killed," came a reply so calm and icy that French John worked faster.

Carroll, furious, backed out of the room. "I'm going to find the President."

"Good," was Dolley's terse reply.

"I can't unscrew this thing." Rivers of sweat ran over French John's face.

"The carriage is here!" Sukey shouted from the hall.

"Load the trunks, Paul, quick time." Dolley barked.

Sukey, wringing her hands, swayed from side to side. The first stragglers from the battle, those who could run the fastest, stumbled down the street. "We all gonna die."

"You've got more to fear from me than from the British! You go help load that wagon and put your back into it." Dolley bore down on her and swatted her behind.

Sukey scurried to grab the end of a trunk.

"This isn't going to work, Mrs. Madison." French John climbed down from the ladder, found an ax, climbed back up, and smashed the frame, which clattered to the floor. He handed down the painting, still on its stretcher. "What would you have done if I couldn't get it out?"

"I would have destroyed it." Dolley's eyes blazed. "The British couldn't defeat him in life. They'll not defeat him in death!"

Jacob Barker and Robert Depeyster, both bankers, came into the house, hoping to encourage the President to safety, should he be in the city. They were appalled to find Dolley still there.

"Mrs. Madison." The men bowed. "Can we be of service to you?"

"Take this painting." She pointed to the canvas. "Please get it out of the city. If you are in danger of being stopped by the British, then destroy it. Don't let them have it. It's no stain on Washington's honor if they have defeated us today. There is always tomorrow."

The two men bowed again as if in the presence of a warrior queen.

Paul dashed in. "The carriage is ready."

"Paul, grab the eagle ornaments from the East Room. Mr. Depeyster, would you take those, too, and a few boxes of papers?"

"I would be happy to do so."

Paul returned with the eagles, and the two gentlemen began organizing their own departure.

She ran back to her room and got Uncle Willy, now hysterical. "French John, take him to Lisel—he'll be safe there. And then go to your family."

French John started to protest.

"Please, you have young children. Keep Paul at your side."

She walked to the front door, then stopped. "I want to stay right here. I defy them to come into this house!"

"Mr. Madison would be sick with fear if he thought you had stayed behind. Come on." French John half escorted, half dragged her to the carriage. He glanced up at the coachman, a trusted friend of his, Joe Bolin. "Bellevue."

Paul rushed up to Dolley. "I want to stay with you."

"No. You go with French John."

"What if something happens to you?" He choked back the tears.

"If the President and I should die, then run to freedom, Paul. Go North." She put her hand on his cheek. "You stay with French John for now. You will be safe with him." What she didn't say was that she was an obvious target. Paul would be better off without her.

French John gently drew Paul away from Dolley. "We'll have everything ready for your return," he told her.

"Thank you," Dolley replied.

Sukey hopped in with her mistress.

Uncle Willy, utterly distraught, carried on wildly. Dolley leaned out the window and kissed the bird. "God bless you," she called to French John.

Bolin pulled onto Pennsylvania Avenue as French John returned to the house. He set out buckets of water, and wine in coolers, in case the President should return and for the use of American soldiers seeking their President. He hid a few valuables and then walked the three blocks to Louis Serurier's temporary residence, the Octagon House, to hand over Uncle Willy, who was not suffering in silence.

Sukey clutched Dolley's arm as the carriage swayed through the dirt and the last lurch of citizens attempting to escape the city. The beaten American soldiers were arriving in fives and sixes where earlier they had come in twos and threes. Fatigue, fear, and depression were etched on their faces.

Dolley reached Bellevue at four-thirty in the afternoon. Eleanor Jones and her children were already there. No one knew what exactly had happened other than that the Americans had been beaten and the British were on the march. William Jones arrived within a half hour of Dolley. He told them as much as he knew and that they had best move on. There was no telling what this night would bring. One wit had already dubbed the battle "the Bladensburg Races."

An older man in civilian clothes rode up to the front door of the Carroll house. He dismounted and knocked. Secretary Jones answered the door.

"William Jones, sir?"

"Yes."

"Is Mrs. Madison with you?"

"Yes."

"The President requests that you bring Mrs. Madison and your family to Foxhall's Cannon Foundry by the river."

As the man left, Jones rallied his family. Dolley and Sukey hastened to the carriage, and by five o'clock the little procession had vacated Bellevue. Once more they crawled along in traffic and chaos. When they finally reached the foundry, a mounted gentleman, Tench Ringgold, met them with yet another change of plans. In the distance they could hear the bridges over the East Branch of the Potomac being blown.

"Mrs. Madison. Mr. Jones." He was too tired to raise his voice.

"The road out is blocked. You won't make it to Wiley's Tavern to-night. He'll meet you at Reverend Maffitt's house, Salona.

"Is he all right?" Dolley asked.

"He is indeed, ma'am," Ringgold answered and urged his horse up the road.

Twilight brought no relief from the heat, and the fading light accentuated their gloom. From behind them they heard a loud explosion. It was eight-thirty.

"The Navy Yard." Dolley patted Sukey's hand as the girl clutched her arm once again. "It's our doing, not the British, Sukey." She imagined that William Jones felt a despair as deep as death at the sound of his Navy Yard being destroyed.

"How come they aren't riding after us?"

"They haven't any cavalry." Dolley sighed, revealing how much she knew about the British troops, but in their distress no one noticed. "Anyway, they're doing enough damage on foot."

Dolley turned around to look back down the road. They were just west of Georgetown when a huge ball of flame spiraled into the air. Other whirlwinds of fire swirled upward, like an evil red tornado. A distant roll of thunder shook Dolley to her bones. She reached into her pocket and found the dice. She'd forgotten about them. She turned them over and over in her fingers.

As darkness deepened and the sky east of them glowed with a lurid, destructive light, Dolley and the Jones family fled at a snail's pace. With shouting and pushing they crossed the Potomac on a bridge sure to be destroyed within hours. At last they arrived at Matilda Lee Love's house, Rokeby, around ten-thirty. More distant explosions shook the ground; a jet of fire shot up to heaven.

Matilda rushed out to greet them. "Mrs. Madison, you poor soul, please, please come into the house."

"I'm fine, my dear, really. See to the Joneses. The children are done in."

Dolley entered the beautifully proportioned house and noticed the servants regarding her and Sukey with undisguised coolness.

Matilda, followed by the Joneses, bustled into the hall and spoke sharply to the servants. "April, see to beds for the children. Janey, bring Mrs. Madison a cup of coffee immediately, please." She turned to the Joneses. "Coffee?"

Eleanor Jones demurred. "No, I'll put the children to bed and then go to sleep myself."

"Of course." The young, beautiful Matilda, a perfect hostess even during an invasion, rested her eyes on the Secretary of the Navy. "Brandy, Mr. Secretary?"

"Yes, thank you kindly, after I help Eleanor with the children." He trudged upstairs after his wife.

Dolley slumped in a chair, Sukey at her feet.

Matilda leaned over her. "Mr. Monroe left not over twenty minutes ago. I fed him supper." She paused. "It's bad."

Dolley nodded. "Yes, it's bad."

"Mr. Monroe said he thought we lost only about one hundred fifty men. The British lost hundreds more but it didn't matter to them. He said these Redcoats fought better than any he faced in the Revolutionary War."

"The British have had more practice since then. They seem to have a natural affinity for war and killing." An edge crept into Dolley's voice, an edge Matilda had never before heard.

"What's keeping that girl? Excuse me a moment." Matilda opened the door to her kitchen to discover Janey sitting like a stone.

"Miz Love," was Janey's insolent reply to a hard stare.

"I asked for coffee!" She took a step toward Janey.

"I ain't servin' that witch nothin'. I got ears. I hears. That no good husband of hers within that no good Armstrong, they sold the country to the British!"

"Janey, I am grateful that you are not in politics. They did no such thing. I will thank you not to refer to my friend Mrs. Madison as a witch, and I will remind you, with force if I must, that you will do as I say. Now, you make that coffee!"

Janey shuffled toward the stove, dragging her feet to torment her mistress. "How you know they ain't sold us out?"

"Because President Madison is the Father of the Constitution, the man who created the Bill of Rights upon which this country was founded, and because I know him. He picked a scurrilous Cabinet. He doesn't know beans about war or men, I'm afraid, but he loves his country. If there's any way to save it, he will."

"They burnin' Washington." Janey was only half convinced.

"Washington is not the United States. I *will* see you in the drawing room shortly. Bring out cold meat, biscuits, and whatever else we have."

Matilda, with a soft step, walked back into the drawing room. Sukey was already asleep on the floor.

"Mrs. Madison, the coffee will be here in a moment. I do hope you will honor me with your presence this evening."

"I have to meet Mr. Madison. He sent a message to meet him at Salona."

"I insist that you stay here." A firmness filled Matilda's light soprano. She could see that Dolley, exhausted and emotionally battered, couldn't safely continue.

"Matilda, I can't—"

"You can and you will."

Janey, suspicious but obedient, brought in the coffee and cold meats.

"Thank you, Janey." Matilda's eyes could have burned a hole in Janey's head rag.

After setting the food down with no display of friendliness, Janey, with offended dignity, left the room. She glanced over her shoulder as Matilda presented the President's wife with a cup of coffee. Dolley was so tired she could barely bring the cup to her lips. Matilda did it for her. After a restorative sip, Dolley held the cup and saucer.

"Thank you." Dolley savored the aromatic liquid.

"Now I must insist that you stay here. It's pitch black out there—"

"The fires cast a strong light."

"It's dangerous. You're tired. You know your husband would be distressed if you were injured or took ill. President Madison would hold me responsible for your welfare. I want you to eat a little something and then go to bed. You need all the sleep you can get."

Dolley dropped her head and then raised it again. A wave of

misery swept over her. "You know, when I turned to look back at the city, it was wrapped in a winding sheet of flame. I could almost feel the sparks. Everything we built and worked for is gone." Her hand shook and she put the cup back on the saucer. "We'll build it again."

"Yes, we will." The young woman soothingly agreed. "Please let me show you to your room."

Tenderly, Matilda helped Dolley up the stairs. A four-poster bed was in the center of the room and a window looked east. When Matilda Lee Love left her, Dolley was standing at the window, staring at the red rim in the east. The funnels of flame had now become a pulsating red ball.

Matilda looked in on the Joneses. Eleanor had managed to climb into bed. William was dead asleep sitting bolt upright in a chair next to his youngest child, asleep on the floor. Matilda picked up the child and carried her back to the children's room. She must have become frightened and wanted to be with her parents.

Then she walked downstairs, wakened Sukey, and took her to a sweet-smelling cot in the back.

She opened the front door and stood outside in the night. Not a breath of wind offered relief from the heat. She cast her eyes toward the city she, too, knew so well. Tears spilled over her cheeks. She looked east into the shivering light and wondered what the future would make of this heritage of flames.

24 August 1814, Wednesday

*T*he doors of Hell have slipped their hinges.

D.P.M.

A brief thunderstorm before dawn settled the dust, but the heat continued, made steamier by the storm. A sinister calm had blanketed the area since Dolley left Matilda's home.

She stopped at Salona, but the President had left early that morning. He was looking for his wife, she was told. A pain lodged in Dolley's chest. She wanted to see her husband—just to see him. She urged the driver on.

Dolley stopped at houses along the way and questioned anyone she saw on foot. One lone traveler said he had seen two men in civilian clothes—one of them an older man, in his sixties perhaps—with a pair of dragoons heading back down the road.

If the situation wasn't so painful, Dolley thought, her searching for James and his searching for her would be funny.

By two o'clock she noticed enormous thunderheads crowding the sky. They were in the northwest, the direction storms usually came from. She also noticed that dogs, which had been running out from houses and plaguing the carriages, had stopped chasing them. The horses, too, were twitching their ears.

She inhaled deeply. It was work to get the air into her lungs. Sukey, again, was sleepy, her breathing labored. Her fright had turned into a quasi paralysis.

The clouds rolled closer. Dolley realized that this was no ordinary August thunderstorm. A greenish black color blotted out the sun. The horses snorted air through their nostrils, signaling their nervousness. "Joe, we've got to find shelter," she told the huge-boned driver.

He agreed, struck by the eerie stillness of the moment. No birds sang. Not even an insect was in the air. Animal life had disappeared. There were no people on the road either.

Dolley called out to the Joneses, following behind her in their carriage, "Let's stop at the next house we find."

William Jones waved agreement, and they thought fortune was smiling on them when a house nudged into view just up ahead.

Joe urged the horses on. When they reached the small dwelling, Dolley, Sukey, and the Joneses hurried inside as a pinkish flash of lightning darted across the sky, a signature of strange color. Within seconds a deep rumble filled the air, deeper and more ominous than the explosions of the night before.

Joe led the horses into the little stable.

"Hello, hello, is anybody home?" Dolley called out. When no one immediately answered, Dolley assumed the inhabitants had fled. She walked up the stairs to look out a window, hoping to get a better view of the storm and her location.

Heavy footsteps and a buzz of voices, including those of the Jones children, filtered upstairs.

A harsh voice called, "Miz Madison, if that's you, come down! Your husband's got mine out fighting, and damn you, you shan't stay in my house, so get out!"

Dolley whirled around and went down. The mistress of the house, a small, wiry woman, hands on her hips, yelled at her again. "Get out!"

"At least let Mrs. Jones and the children stay."

As Dolley begged for the children, other women crept into the rooms. They must have been hiding in the cellar.

"Get out, all of you!" the lady of the house screamed, and as she did, another searing flash of pink lightning gave warning outside.

The women, now emboldened, cursed Dolley. One ran back into the kitchen, picked up carrots and corn, and came back to throw them at her.

Dolley ran out into the gathering storm as Sukey hurried back to get Joe. Within minutes they were in the carriage again as the women now hurled everything they could find at Dolley.

Sukey picked up an ear of corn as she got in the carriage and threw it back. "Traitors!" she hollered at them.

A worried Joe flicked the reins, and they hurried down the road as the Joneses quickly followed.

"Slow down for a moment, Joe." As the Joneses came alongside, Dolley shouted to William, "You stay in the next house. I'll go on."

"No, Mrs. Madison. I can't leave you alone out here."

"Mr. Jones, your first duty is to your wife and children," Dolley stated firmly.

"We will all seek shelter together. Wasting our time arguing just means we'll find it too late."

Jones moved ahead and Dolley, with no answer, sat down.

The lightning tore across the sky like cracks in a green-black windowpane. Still no wind, but the thunder followed more closely. The storm was within minutes of unleashing its power. A huge rain-drop splattered on the carriage. This was followed by another and another, and a slight breeze now shook the leaves.

"Missus, you ever seen the sky look like this?" Sukey craned her neck to look upward as the clouds boiled, so close she felt she could touch them.

"No."

"God's mad at us." Sukey shielded her eyes when another jag of lightning burned the sky.

"This is a blessing." Dolley, too, peered upward.

"Huh?"

"It will put out the fires in Washington."

Sukey was far less concerned about Washington at that moment than she was about finding shelter. "What about us?"

"We're going to live."

As if to prove her point, Wiley's Tavern, next to an apple orchard, came into view.

There, finally, Dolley and her people were safe. Joe unhitched the horses and trotted them back to the stable, where he would rub them down and feed them once they'd cooled out. The wind howled, a constant low shriek.

Inside the tavern, Dolley pulled one of the children away from a window. Branches were torn off trees with a terrible cracking sound.

A haywagon turned over and skidded across the field as though a giant's finger pushed it for play.

She wondered where her husband was in this black cauldron. Outside, deep groaning added to the horror; whole trees were bending, groaning, fighting to stay alive.

The door flew open and as William Jones ran over to shut it, James Madison, Richard Rush, and a Navy clerk, Mordecai Booth, all sopping wet, rushed into the tavern.

Before Richard Rush could ask for room, Dolley ran into her husband's arms. Sukey, to her surprise, was overjoyed and ran over to Madison, too. The President hugged them both with a fierce tenderness.

Two other refugees from the storm politely allowed the Madisons the use of their room. The President informed them he would be leaving at midnight, and all hoped the storm would have blown itself out by that time.

The innkeeper brought food. After meetings with Rush and Jones, James finally yielded to Dolley's persuasions to come upstairs and rest for a few hours.

"It's no use." Madison opened his eyes again. "I can't sleep."

"Well, lie there and talk to me then. You've been in the saddle for three days, fifteen to twenty hours a day, Jemmy."

"I've got my leg back." He smiled. "I think I could ride one of Dr. Thornton's blooded horses now."

"Bet you could." She stroked his cheek; three days of white stubble made him look fuzzy.

"I'm so glad to find you here. We left Salona and rode to Wren's Tavern and then back to Salona, where you'd passed on your way here." The wind devolved from a howl to a steady hiss. "Dolley, I couldn't live without you."

She bent over and kissed him. "Nor could I without you."

"You'll have to, my dear. I'm seventeen years older and I can't go on forever."

"No one's calling you an old man now."

"They're calling me worse. When I rode back from Bladensburg, men shook their fists at me, and the filth they called me . . ." His eyes searched hers imploringly. "I could say nothing in return."

"You did everything you could." Her voice was soothing.

"Those soldiers were beyond the refinements of politics. I couldn't blame them. I was as angry and as confused as they were. John Armstrong was worse than useless, he was an obstruction. And poor Winder, he did what he could. There's not an ounce of cowardice in the man. Even after the rout he tried to reform the lines. I've got to get to him." He sat up.

"Later. Lie down. You'll find him. An Army doesn't just vanish."

"Ours did."

"Officers will round them up; you'll see."

"What impressed me, Dolley, were the British. I always believed that a freeman will fight better than will the servant of a king or a hired soldier. Well, I was wrong. There's no substitute for professional soldiers. Cannon didn't deter them. Nor heavy fire. They kept coming and they knew what to do. And the discipline held under fire. The way they closed ranks each time we blasted a bloody hole in them—"

"What were you doing close enough to see all that?" Dolley interrupted.

"I was safely out of range." Madison told a white lie. He shifted. "I don't know what's left of Washington."

"If the Russians could rebuild Moscow after Napoleon, we can rebuild Washington."

"I think they'll head for Baltimore now. We can't lose Baltimore." He turned his head to the wall. "You know, there will be people who will want me to resign as President. There will be those who will want to impeach me. There will be people who will want me to make peace with the British. I won't, you know. These are terrible times, but we haven't lost the war. Jackson is in the South and we're having some success in New York. I won't give in, Dolley."

"I know that." She smiled. "Uncle Willy is with the Seruriers. He missed you."

Madison looked back at her, a light in his eyes. "I seriously doubt that Uncle Willy missed me, but I'm quite sure he misses you. No one can spoil him as much as you do. Or spoil me."

"I love you."

"Love at first sight—for me. I know it wasn't for you. There I was, a short man with a funny nose. Not a handsome man at all, forty-three years old, never married. I did, however, wear a handsome coat. My shoes were shined, too."

"I noticed."

"I have often wondered how I must have seemed compared with John Todd. I'd inquired about him, you know." She didn't know that. "I heard he'd seen to it you and the children were safely away from Philadelphia, and about the way he continued to travel back into the city to care for his parents and to help those he could. I heard, too, what a fine, strapping fellow he was. And young. Everyone who knew John Todd said two things about him: how handsome he was and what a good Quaker he was, a true Christian man." He sat up and leaned against the headboard. "He would have to be handsome to win you, you're so beautiful. And you are as beautiful today as the day I met you. Your skin and your eyes, those merry blue eyes. They were the first things I noticed about you. You will never grow old to me, and I still don't know why you married me."

"Oh, Jemmy, I love you. I learned to love you. You were a rather quiet and reserved man. I had to get to know you."

"Quiet. Yes. I was . . . nervous."

"Now, I don't believe that." She pushed his arm. "You were such an important man. Everyone in the nation knew who you were, and I was an impoverished widow with a son."

"A beautiful widow besieged by many men. When I used to wonder how I would compare with John Todd, I knew I would be found lacking."

"This may sound strange to you, but I never compared you with John. I didn't want to marry John. I told my mother and Mother Amy I would never marry."

"You did?"

"I couldn't imagine being married, but John did have good prospects and Mother was so burdened. I helped with the boarders and the other children and my father." She paused. She rarely spoke of her father at the end of his life. "But she needed more. I knew that John would honor me and honor her, too. And so I married him. He was good to me and good to my whole family."

"You did love him?"

"Yes, but Jemmy, I was so young, so young compared with now. I can't compare you with John; I can only compare me, now, with my younger self. I love you in a way I have never loved another human being. I love your white beard." She brushed his stubble and kept her hand there. "I love your sense of humor."

"People outside the family don't think I have one."

"Well, you are—reserved with acquaintances, but no man loves his country more, and no man has loved me more. I love you for everything you have given me, not just things, not just the jewelry and the horses, but our talks. You were my teacher."

"You were mine." He smiled.

"What did I know when we married?"

"You knew how to love and you knew how to make people feel loved. I used to watch you when you would meet a new person. Within minutes that person was your best friend. I think all eight million Americans are your best friends—even John Randolph." He held up his hand. "You know, if he walked into this room, you'd be chatting with him like a blue jay. He'd forget to be hateful. Oh, how I envy you that, and how I adore being the recipient of that warmth."

"Really?"

"Really. You taught me how to love. I'll always have a hard time showing it, I fear, but I feel it, Dolley. I do feel it, and I try to let you and those I love know. Often I let you do it for me—talk to people, I mean."

"Well, I often let you think for me. Too often, I'm afraid. I add to your burdens."

"You have never been a burden to me in all the years we've been married."

"I must sometimes have been an irritation." She smiled. "I wish I could do better with money."

He kissed her forehead. "I wish I could do better, too. You know,

I would give up my five thousand acres in Orange County, my holdings everywhere, even my library, if we could be young together and live to be old together. I saw men die today, Dolley, young men, brave men—on both sides. In an instant. I don't care about the money or the land. I care about you. I care about *life*."

"You're going to live to be a hundred."

"My mother certainly is." He smiled again, then became intent. "I will never be the same man again."

"I hope that you are."

"I mean that I will never take anything for granted, not even the next breath, and I will never, ever hold another human life in light regard. I know now, if I never knew it before, that life is a gift from God, and to despise that gift, to take that gift from another man, woman, or child is a blasphemy so terrible that God has every right to turn His back on us."

They sat quietly together for a long time after that. The large clock in the hall struck eleven-thirty, then twelve, and James Madison, taking his Secretary of the Navy and a renewed sense of purpose with him, bade his beloved wife goodbye and rode into the battered night to search for his Army.

25 August 1814, Thursday

*P*raise God, my husband is safe! We have been playing tag for nearly two days, crisscrossing paths until tonight. He's drawn but in better spirits than I expected. He so desperately needed sleep, but he was wound up like a top and couldn't stop spinning. I'm afraid he will drive himself into a relapse of last summer's illness. I know these times are desperate, but that summer I thought I would lose my mind with worry over him. Now my worries are of quite a different order.

He talked constantly. I could not keep him quiet. His mind raced, he jumped from one subject to the next. He surprised me when he confessed that he compared himself with John Todd when he first courted me. I would never have dreamed that he would worry or wonder. To think that we've been married nineteen years—it will be twenty on September 15—and I didn't know this about him. I wonder if one truly ever knows another person. I think I know my husband better than anyone alive and yet, who knows the secrets he keeps, what fancies and fears he shows no one?

I usually say whatever pops into my head. Once married to Jemmy, I had to break that habit. Jemmy used to laugh at me when I would blurt something out, and chide me: "In politics, think before you speak, and if you intend to say what you really mean, then think twice." That used to make me laugh because he is not a dissembler, although he does keep a great deal to himself.

A tremendous storm ripped up trees, the sky was pitch-black with a greenish cast, and if it had poured any harder, I would have expected the animals to march two by two. I stopped at a house where I was driven out by the proprietress and other women who had fled

Washington and the storm. They threw vegetables at us and Sukey threw one back at them.

When we drove off in the carriage, apples were hurled at us, too. If I am the recipient of this hatred, what will happen to Jemmy? He's riding around with the tattered remnants of his Cabinet and two dragoons. At this point I am more concerned with angry citizens than I am with the British.

I don't know if the British are crossing the Potomac. Jemmy said before he left that he believed they were still in the city and regrouping after the battle.

He told me to stay here until he sends word. He left at midnight. I don't know how he can cross the river because the bridges have been destroyed, and after that torrent the waters must be flooding. I'd rather go with him than stay. He won't even hear of it. He stops me before I can finish my sentence. I know I could be useful to him, but he refuses to expose me to danger. I don't care about the danger. I care about him. Jemmy can be a very obstinate man in his way. So here I sit.

William Jones departed with Jemmy, so Eleanor and I are left with Sukey and the children. Eleanor has been so solicitous of her children that I don't think she has had time to realize all that has befallen us.

Sukey has risen to the occasion and been much stronger than I could have believed. I do hope that French John and Paul are safe. And Uncle Willy. I'm sure that King George is safe because she's too mean to be killed. And Lisel. I pray the British respect foreign legations.

I am rattling on. I'm as bad as Jemmy and probably nearly as tired. I can't slow down.

I can smell another thunderstorm coming up, too. I do hope Jemmy finds shelter. Worrying about him won't change anything, but I can't help it.

When I walked outside to kiss him goodbye, I noticed a bush near the mounting block. As he rode off into the darkness, the light from the inn spilled into the yard and I again noticed the bush. I could not take my eyes off a raindrop on a black thorn. It was so beautiful, a moment of perfection in the midst of human debacle.

How curious what we remember.

Until the morrow, God willing.

D.P.M.

*A*t dawn James Madison crossed the turbulent waters at Conn's Ferry. His destination was Montgomery Courthouse in Maryland, where he would link up with the Army. As he and his party rode along, he struggled to separate rumor from fact.

The fact was that the British had burned Washington, although he heard private buildings had been spared. Frightened citizens said the enemy was marching on Frederick, yet no Redcoats had been seen in that direction.

General Winder had reached Tenleytown, seven miles northwest of the Capitol, on the night the city was burned. That seemed like years ago to the President as he changed to yet another fresh horse. Thinking the British would push west from Washington, Winder had pulled back to Montgomery Courthouse, and that was Madison's last report of his whereabouts.

The United States Army of six thousand, shattered and demoralized, had never regrouped. Whatever Madison's hopes were for re-forging the Army, that hope was fading. Soldiers milled around. Some looked for their units. Others disappeared. The President heard that Colonel Beall had found only one hundred of his eight hundred Annapolis men, and Madison figured that was probably the rule of thumb.

Even if the Army had managed to re-form, how would they be fed? Because Armstrong never believed Washington would be attacked, he had never attended to food, supplies, and shelter in the area.

Madison didn't know which of his Cabinet officers had made it to Frederick. He didn't know where anyone was, other than the people riding with him. The government of the United States of America happened to be in the saddle.

Richard Rush, faithfully riding with Madison since the trip to Bladensburg, suggested that the government might move to Philadelphia.

"No," Madison answered the Attorney General. "The government will reconvene in Washington as soon as possible. Tomorrow, I hope."

"What if all the public buildings are destroyed?" William Jones asked, shifting in his saddle. Unaccustomed to riding regularly, he was quite sore.

"We'll use private buildings." Madison paused. "We'll sit in the streets if need be. We aren't abandoning Washington."

That was the end of it, and Rush and Jones decided that if the President could make do, then so could they.

The sky was crystal clear after yesterday's titanic storm. The sultry heat wave was broken and the air sparkled.

At six in the evening Madison reached Montgomery Courthouse only to discover that General Winder had moved on. Picking up a troop of dragoons, the President forced himself into the twilight.

By nine o'clock Madison realized he couldn't catch Winder. He halted at a small Quaker community, Brookville.

Overrun with soldiers and refugees, the town greeted the President with calm dignity. Mrs. Caleb Bentley took the President into her white clapboard house and allowed the soldiers to sleep outside around the house. Mrs. Bentley had served five unexpected suppers that night, so one more wasn't a problem, nor was she cowed by the sight of the President at her table.

When Madison apologized for the inconvenience, she replied, "It is against my principles to have anything to do with war, but I receive and relieve all who come to me."

"You remind me of my departed mother-in-law"—Madison smiled—"a devoted Quaker." And a formidable woman, he thought to himself.

"I had heard that your esteemed wife was raised in a Friends household." Mrs. Bentley stuck her hands in her apron. "I also heard that she has a beautiful complexion, her Grandmother Coles's complexion, people say."

As Mrs. Bentley and Madison chatted, her family was spreading beds in the parlor, fetching kindling for campfires outside, finding more room in the stable for men and horses, and doing everything possible to see to the comfort of their guests.

"Do you attend services, Mr. President?" Mrs. Bentley was curious.

"I have attended your faith's services. My mother took me to the Episcopal Church."

"I imagine you found the two quite different."

"Yes, but my wife had carefully prepared me. She herself feels the Inner Light strongly, and I think she wanted me to experience it also."

"And did you?" came the forthright question.

"I'm afraid I did not. Mrs. Madison says I think too much and in order to feel the Light, one must open one's heart. I do though, Mrs. Bentley, experience great peace and fulfillment in my wife's presence, so perhaps her Light has reflected on me."

Mrs. Bentley smiled broadly. "I'm sure it has." She paused. "You know, of course, that we are opposed to all killing, to all war."

"Yes." Madison accepted a piece of sponge cake when Richard Rush passed the plate.

"You have a good wife, indeed, Mr. Madison," Mrs. Bentley said with conviction, leaving Madison to consider the full weight of her meaning.

26 August 1814, Friday

*I*f government were a game of marbles, then you could say that the British shooter has knocked the American pieces every which way. Our government has scattered. Jemmy, Richard Rush, and William Jones are somewhere in Maryland. Where is Monroe? With Winder, I hope. Where is Armstrong? I won't say where I hope he is.

It's important for people to know that the men they elected to lead them are doing just that. I know that Jemmy will do his utmost to collect everybody. Otherwise, all manner of internal mischief could occur. The rumors are—once more—that the slaves will revolt. I'm far more worried about looters than slaves.

I'm returning to Washington tomorrow whether I hear from my husband or not. My place is in the capital and the moment I am assured the British have left it, I am going back.

Sukey will stay in Virginia and guard what few possessions I have. She fussed and moaned, but she knows that I will send for her as soon as it's safe for her to return. I think the girl needs a few days of relief. Her nerves are strained . . . and should she choose to use the confusion of war to flee, so be it. I know Jemmy won't put out a warrant for her. I will pray for her and wish her well.

I must find out if Anna and the children are all right. I'm sure they are, but I won't rest until I know. And I won't rest until I can repay those people who helped us during this terrible time, most especially the Seruriers and Matilda Lee Love.

I just remembered that Paul left the table set at the house. I do hope he's safe and sound, and French John, too, but I think French John can survive anything. I'm so accustomed to his presence that it's disquieting to be without him.

Changing into fresh clothes this morning felt more wonderful than I can describe. How we learn to be grateful for the little things. I took the dice out of the pocket of my other dress and rolled them. I don't know why, but I just did, and I rolled seven! Everything will be fine.

It doesn't matter whether it's true or not, rolling seven helped me through this day.

I can't concentrate on what I'm writing. Sometimes I feel as if I'm in a dream. I'll be better tomorrow.

Until the morrow, God willing.

D.P.M.

*D*olley held on to the sides of Mr. Parrott's carriage. The road, never good in the best of circumstances, was washed out in parts because of the violent storm. Potholes had become craters. Every tooth in her head rattled, but Dolley pressed on, determined.

James Madison had sent a note to her at Wiley's Tavern early in the morning, telling her to return to the capital: the British had retreated. Not wishing to draw attention to herself, she was fortunate enough to be able to hire a carriage from Mr. Parrott, a friend from Georgetown who happened, like many refugees, to be on the Virginia side of the Potomac. He was prudently remaining in Virginia for a while, but he was happy to rent his carriage.

Joe Bolin stayed back at the tavern, but Edward Duvall, a Navy Yard clerk, accompanied her. A junior officer came along, too. Dolley missed Sukey already. Dolley was a good conversationalist, but under these conditions talking was hard work.

As they jolted along, they occasionally met other people on the road. Surprisingly few were on their way back to the ruined city. Dolley assumed that by tomorrow they would know what she knew and there would be a traffic jam flowing back into Washington.

The sun, high and hot overhead, caused the fields to shimmer. Each time they passed a new person, Dolley would lean out and ask questions.

What she heard was that the British had left Washington as they had entered it, by Maryland Avenue. They herded cows out of the city and were also laden with their ill-gotten gain.

The revolting news was that the bodies of those fallen at Bladensburg remained unburied. The storm, with its torrential rains, had bleached the corpses, already stripped naked by looters, and then the sun had bloated them. It must have been a paradise for flies, vultures, and stray dogs. Dolley shuddered at the thought.

Edward Duvall chattered on about his work, his feelings about John Armstrong, which were hostile, and his hopes for the future. He dreaded seeing the Navy Yard. They'd rebuild it somehow, though.

Dolley listened indulgently. She had long ago learned that the more one listens, the more one learns, and there are few people who won't take the opportunity to talk about themselves, given the chance. Edward Duvall, unexciting and a trifle fussy, was eager to get to work. He knew the task of rebuilding the Navy Yard would be gargantuan. He knew Congress and therefore realized that the task would be made even more difficult by their foolishness. A trickle of pennies would come his way, but he wanted to work. He liked William Jones. He liked the Navy men.

As he rattled on, Dolley thought that it was men like Edward Duvall and thousands of men and women like him—unexceptional, able to see only their own corner of the world, hardworking—who would rebuild the country. Genius was rare and perhaps that was for the better. The Edward Duvalls of America made the country and proved that America worked.

Unexceptional as he was, he earned a decent living, he enjoyed his work, and he played his part.

She wondered if she had played her part. Could she have done more?

As she swayed, bumped, and slammed into the ever-cheerful Edward Duvall, the Potomac rolled into view on her left as the sun was setting. The waters were much higher than when she had crossed the river before, but at least they weren't turbulent, just brown as chocolate. They would not get over the river tonight. Better to press on and find lodgings.

27 August 1814, Saturday

*L*ate. I couldn't cross the Potomac tonight. I don't think there's a bridge left standing on the Virginia side of the river. I'll get over somehow tomorrow, early.

A strange lassitude overwhelms me. Not just because it's late. I've felt this way throughout the day, drowsy and dull. It's an effort to listen to Edward Duvall, likable though he is.

These last four days my husband and I, and our city, have been the playthings of chance. One doesn't know what will happen from one minute to the next. In one sense that's liberating and in another, exhausting.

I remember faces—faces I will probably never see again—of people fleeing the city, of those women who threw vegetables at me, of people staring out the windows of their homes as we rode by, of workers in the fields. And each face asks the same silent question: Why? What have you done?

It's as though the hammer of fate aimed a blow at my heart.

Until the morrow, God willing.

D.P.M.

A shroud of dense fog covered the Potomac. Dolley could see, as she came closer, the blackened skeleton of Long Bridge looming through the thick mists. The abutments still stood on either side of the river. Grunts wafted out of the fog and a barge slid into view. Four African men pushed the long poles as a single white colonel kept his hand on the rudimentary rudder. The barge hit the land with a thud.

Dolley, her bonnet covering most of her face, walked down to the barge with Edward Duvall. She noticed a pile of munitions on the bank.

Edward spoke to the colonel. Dolley overheard the colonel's name, Fenwick, as the two men introduced themselves. Edward asked for passage for himself, the lady, and the carriage. The colonel shook his head adamantly. He wouldn't take a lady into what lay on the other side of the river. Edward kept talking and the colonel kept refusing as the watermen appraised the fancy carriage.

Dolley stepped up to the men, sweeping her bonnet off her head. "Colonel Fenwick."

The stern man recognized her instantly. He removed his hat and bowed. "At your service, Mrs. Madison."

The horses balked at the barge as they were being loaded. Dolley grabbed the bridle of the left horse, Edward grabbed that of the horse on the right, and a waterman got behind each animal. With a cluck, a tug, and a slap, the animals clambered onto the barge, which rocked back and forth under its new load.

Dolley stood, still holding the horse's bridle, as the watermen poled across the river. She knew every gesture, every expression would be reported.

"You say all the British are gone, Colonel?"

"Not all of them, ma'am. They left behind over one hundred dead and maybe fifty wounded for whom the good Dr. Thornton is caring."

"Dead? When I left Washington, none of our troops were left in the city."

"Oh no, nothing like that." The colonel smiled despite himself. "You know where Delaware Avenue runs down into Greenleaf Point, right where the East Branch flows into the Potomac?"

"I do." She patted the horse's neck, calming the animal.

"The fort was destroyed, as you might suspect, but the magazine remained, you see, with a good one hundred fifty barrels of powder, and so the British general figured that it would be better not to leave any powder for us. Now I grant you, those British can fight, but when the fighting is over I'm not sure just how smart they are, Mrs. Madison, because what they did was dump the powder into the well. There wasn't enough water to cover the powder." A big grin covered Colonel Fenwick's face. "Some limey fool threw a cigar down the well, and BOOM! No well. No buildings. No more powder and no more British, at least at Greenleaf Point."

"Good heavens."

"Between that cigar and the storm, the British had had enough of our fair city."

"You say Dr. Thornton has been caring for the wounded?"

"He has. Saved the Patent Office too. He ran out just as soldiers were ready to throw a torch into the building and said that burning such a place would be like burning Alexandria, a mark against any civilized nation. So they spared it."

"He is an amazing man."

"He's been a second mayor to the city."

"What happened to James Blake?" Dolley liked Blake.

"Oh, nothing, but as you know, Dr. Thornton is not a shy man and he thought that in the crisis more leadership was needed." A sly smile played over his lips. "And, well, those two are fighting now like two boxers."

"Oh dear." Dolley sighed, knowing she'd be drawn into the middle of the quarrel. Wasn't there enough to do?

The closer the barge floated to Washington, the faster Dolley's heart pounded. As the horses gingerly stepped off the barge, Dolley turned and thanked the colonel and the four black polemen. She kept her bonnet in her hand and climbed back into the carriage. Together with Edward Duvall she set off into the city.

By the time Dolley reached Pennsylvania Avenue, she recognized that most private houses had indeed been unmolested by the British, although many had been damaged by the storm. The public buildings, however, had been looted and destroyed.

As the horses clopped down the dusty road, the buildings on either side stood lifeless, like dead trees. Few persons moved about. The desolation was as affecting as the devastation. The smell of charred wood assailed her nostrils. "I want to go home," Dolley said quietly.

"Oh, Mrs. Madison, wait. You don't want to see that now."

"I do."

"It will break your heart."

"Is there anyone in this city who hasn't had her heart broken?" Dolley set her jaw.

In the distance she could see the presidential mansion. A first glance revealed little damage, although the windows were blackened, but as the carriage drew closer, the full extent of the British depredations became obvious.

"Stop the carriage."

"Don't go in there. It might be dangerous," Edward warned her.

"The British are gone." She hopped out of the carriage.

"Yes, but with all the structural damage, Mrs. Madison—what if a wall should come down? Please don't expose yourself to unnecessary risk."

Dolley patted his arm. "Mr. Duvall, I appreciate you and your concern. I will be safe. Wait for me, I won't be long. I promise."

Edward held the horses and Dolley walked into what had been her home for thirteen years, since the time she had acted as Jefferson's hostess when he was President.

The roof was gone. The acrid smell of smoke lingered over everything. She stood in the hall, the shock so profound that tears would have seemed superficial. She just stood and stared.

What the flames hadn't gutted the British had. The furniture, that gorgeous, expensive furniture, had been smashed and piled up for firewood. Some of it had burned totally, leaving huge heaps of ashes. In other corners whole pieces of furniture had survived, and she could identify a chair leg, a desk top. Books must have delighted the British for their ability to burn. Jemmy's library had been ransacked. One morocco-bound book, the gilt still shining, lay open like a wound, the corners of the pages brown and curled from the heat. The remaining curtains, pulled off their rods, had been shredded. Most had burned up.

She wandered about and noticed a huge hole in the northeast wall. She took a deep breath and walked back through the house, leaving by the front door.

She climbed into the carriage. Edward Duvall, not without sensitivity, said nothing and drove her to F Street.

As he pulled up before the Cutts house, Dolley fought to compose herself. Richard opened the door and rushed out to help her.

"My dear Dolley! Thank God you are safe and well."

"And you too, Richard." Dolley embraced him, both of them crying. She thought his face one of the most beautiful sights she had ever beheld. "This is Edward Duvall of the Navy Yard."

"Pleased to meet you, Mr. Duvall." Richard shook his hand. "Won't you come inside and rest? Or take some refreshment?"

"Thank you, but I need to press on and deliver this team back to Mr. Parrott."

"Ah, you know they burned his rope bridge," Richard informed him.

Edward shook his head. There wasn't much to say. "Let me know if I can be of further service to you and Mrs. Madison. She is . . ." He paused, and the sight of that small figure going into the ruined presidential mansion came to him. She seemed so tiny. The ruined house seemed to engulf her. "She is a credit to our people."

Dolley turned from Richard and reached up to take Edward's

hand. "So are you, Edward Duvall, so are you." She pressed his hand to her cheek and then released it.

Tears ran down Edward's face. He didn't want to leave her. He didn't like what he saw, what was left of the city. He didn't know what he would do next or what the city would do. He remembered his mother's fierce etiquette training, but he could recall no rules for situations such as this. He wiped his eyes, nodded, and drove off.

Richard shepherded Dolley into his house, telling her that James had spent the previous night there. Yes, he was quite well and didn't look nearly as tired as Richard thought he would. His spirit was strong. Anna remained in Maryland. He was debating whether to call her back or to wait until the baby was born because her time was so near. James would be back later in the day. He was rallying all the Cabinet members, and George Campbell was growing more and more ill. As far as he knew, Campbell was in Frederick with John Armstrong.

At the sound of Armstrong's name, Dolley spoke sharply. "I don't want to hear that name."

Richard, making allowances for her state of mind, said, "Few do, Dolley, my dear, few do."

Dr. William Thornton and his wife paid a call on Dolley. She was listless and drawn. The Thorntons had never seen her this way. Even so, she was solicitous of their health.

"What a rude shock for you, Mrs. Madison. We have had a few days to adjust." Mrs. Thornton tried to be sympathetic.

"You'll feel a little better tomorrow," Dr. Thornton advised.

"I heard you saved the Patent Office."

Dr. Thornton smiled. "I did what I could. Not all of them were savages."

"They gave a good imitation. I saw our house." Dolley sounded uncharacteristically bitter.

"Yes, that was tragic," Mrs. Thornton agreed. "And Mrs. Madison, things would have been far worse if my William hadn't taken charge. He posted citizen guards at every government building that had been burned, and at some that were still burning. He closed th

Navy Yard gates. He visited the wounded, theirs too, and he went over to dear Dr. James Ewell and thanked him for all his good efforts on behalf of the physically distressed. William told Dr. Ewell that given the fact that the British wounded were suffering, we could no longer consider them our enemies." Anna Maria Thornton would have continued to sing the praises of her energetic husband if he had not gently put his hand on her shoulder and squeezed.

"Dear, Mrs. Madison has had quite a difficult few days." Then he smiled at Dolley. "We can't contain our joy at your return. Now you get some rest, Mrs. Madison. For everyone's sake. You are dear to the nation."

Dolley rose and ushered them out. As she closed the door, she leaned against it and shut her eyes for an instant.

Richard waited until she opened them to speak. "Have you heard about the Thornton-Blake feud?" He noticed her vacant look. "Dolley, here, come on, sit down."

"I did hear about it, in part."

"Well, sit down. We can discuss that later. You looked peaked."

"Richard, I feel so peculiar. I know who you are. I know where I am but it seems . . . it seems . . ."

"Unreal." He finished her sentence for her.

"Yes. Unreal."

"We may feel that way for a long time." He ran his fingers through his hair and sat opposite his beloved sister-in-law, who looked nothing like his wife, yet reminded him of her: the same voice, the same mannerisms, the same sense of humor. "Did you hear about John Lewis?"

"George Washington's great-nephew, that John Lewis, or the carpenter in Georgetown?"

"Washington's great-nephew."

"What happened to him?"

"He charged a column of British as they marched on the State, War, and Navy Department building. Screaming and firing at them. No one knows what he was screaming, but the British officer called for him to stop and he wouldn't, so the British knelt down and fired

and just riddled him, Dolley, just riddled him. Didn't touch the horse. He was dead by the time he hit the ground."

Her hand went to her mouth, an involuntary gesture. "My God." She thought and then spoke again. "He never was quite right in the head, you know, but I think he did it to avenge his great-uncle. The burden of being a relative of President Washington's must have been very heavy indeed."

Richard wanted to say, "And so can being the son of Dolley Madison," but he bit his tongue and kept to the story of Lewis. "The British declared that he smelled of whiskey. But remember, he had been impressed by the Royal Navy when he ran off to sea and his ship was overtaken. He swore vengeance."

Dolley recalled the story but wasn't entirely convinced. "He was always unbalanced, from the time he was little. Still, what a terrible end, or perhaps a glorious end, a better end than he could have hoped for had he lived on. Sometimes I wonder, Richard, if the human animal can improve itself or if whatever is in the blood recurs from generation to generation—the same mistakes, the same behavior in a different time."

"I don't know. Dolley, you look exhausted. Why don't you see if you can take a nap?"

Dolley awoke two hours later when her husband kissed her on the lips. She threw her arms around him, hugging him with all her might.

He sat on the edge of the bed for a few moments and told her that the British were in Alexandria—not the same troops that had burned Washington but a command that had sailed up the Potomac. From what he had learned, the citizens of Alexandria couldn't hurry fast enough to pay off the invaders.

The commander of Fort Washington had blown it to smithereens without firing one shot at the British. He was stinking drunk at the time, which further added to the embarrassment.

As Madison had ridden in from the Maryland side of the city yesterday, he told her, he'd seen the type from the *National Intelligencer* scattered all over the streets at the corner of Seventh Street and

Pennsylvania Avenue. The newspaper's offices had been ransacked, too. The gossip was that Admiral Cockburn had smashed all the letter *C*'s so the newspaper could no longer print his name. The Library of Congress had been burned, and the looters were a scourge of ravenous hyenas. A curfew had been imposed, but there was not a business that had not been attacked by the lowest elements of the city.

As Dolley listened, she stretched and walked over to the window. In the twilight she saw the eleven dragoons guarding her husband bed down in Richard Cutts's yard. "I wish I had ten thousand such men to sink our enemy to the bottomless pits!"

James had never heard his wife use that tone of voice, nor had he ever heard her wish harm on another human being. He came up behind her and put his arms around her. He held her until he felt her shoulders drop and her back relax.

28 August 1814, Sunday

*T*he British descended on us like a cloud of carmine locusts, eating everything. Little is left of the public buildings. Our house stands as but an empty shell. Everything of value was burned or stolen, even the love letters Jemmy and I wrote to each other.

I haven't seen the Capitol. I don't know if I want to see it but of course I must.

Over the city hangs the rancid, stale odor of smoke and shame. Even now there's a fleet of British ships at Alexandria. Every bedsheet in that town must be hanging from the windows, a summer snow of white flags.

Jemmy and Monroe want to line the Potomac with guns and blast the British when they sail down the river. Monroe has already set up artillery at the Navy Yard. I don't think a single building is standing there, and Dr. Thornton told me the looters even stole the lock off the gate.

Dr. Thornton and Mayor Blake won't speak to each other. This is a sorry time for a foolish feud.

A few people have suggested to Jemmy, since we have no government buildings, that he move the government to Philadelphia. He refuses this just as he forbade any citizen to surrender to the British. Unfortunately, this steely resolve is having little effect on the city of Alexandria.

I keep blinking to remind myself that what I am seeing is real. I'm at Anna and Richard's house. That seems real, although lonesome without Anna. But step outside and the burned buildings, the roofs torn off by the wild storm, the debris in the streets—it can't be Washington.

I remember when Mother Amy died, I thought a butterfly had folded its wings. Until that time I had never felt sorrow to such depth. Then I lost John and our son, and that shattered my heart. I thought I would never be whole again. Then Mother died.

But this is a city dying; this pain is both personal and communal. Some moments the grief makes it hard to breathe, and I find myself gasping and inhaling more stale smoke.

I am struggling to find Christian charity in my heart. Right now I hate every British soldier who ever walked. I hate the officer who rode into Mother's house. I hate the men who smashed my furniture and used it for kindling. I hate the sound of their accents, the color of their uniforms. I should pray for their dead and comfort their wounded. I can't. I want them all dead.

No church bells rang in Washington today.

Until the morrow, God willing.

D.P.M.

"Keep your head down," Dolley commanded.

"You're drowning me!" Anna sputtered as Dolley dumped another pitcher of water over her hair.

Anna had returned early that morning, and after the sisters had embraced and swapped adventures, she asked Dolley to wash her hair. She'd become so big that she couldn't bend over, and kneeling was difficult also. So Dolley, ever practical, sat her in a chair and made James hold the washbasin while Thomas fetched pitchers of water.

"Only another minute and that hair will shine."

"Mother, are you really drowning?" Thomas asked solemnly.

"No, Thomas. Now bring more water for Aunt Dolley." Anna directed him as little Dickey sent up a whoop in the other room along with Walter and tiny Dolley Payne, who was into everything. Anna sighed. "I don't want to know."

"Neither do I." Dolley doused her sister's hair again. "Towel, Thomas."

"Can I go now?" James asked.

"Throw the water out the back door first." Anna hadn't finished her sentence before he was out the back door. "You too, Thomas."

He, too, was out like a shot.

Another moan and a scream from the adjacent room signaled child warfare. Anna, with the towel wrapped around her head, waddled to the doorway. "Enough!"

That scared them silent for a few minutes anyway. She sat back down and toweled her hair as Dolley cleaned the brushes and comb. "You don't fool me." Anna's voice was muffled with the towel flopped over her mouth.

Dolley lifted the towel. "I'm not trying to fool you—just everyone else."

"It's a shock. I know I was shocked even though I knew much would be burned. I think the sight of the Capitol was the worst. I heard that Admiral Cockburn held a mock session of Congress and asked his troops if this 'citadel of foolishness' should be burned. It's hard to believe he would have had the time for such playacting, and yet it does sound like the man." Anna loathed Admiral Cockburn's insolence, his cocky sense of humor. "And people are frightened that the British will come back."

"This time I won't leave, and I don't care what Jemmy says. I want a rifle, and if I can't find a rifle, then I want a sword. I'll kill as many as I can before they kill me."

Anna, stunned at her sister's outburst, let the towel drop to the floor. "You don't mean that. You're upset."

"I do mean it, Anna." Dolley's deep blue eyes caught the light.

"We weren't raised that way, Dolley, and I don't want to hear that kind of talk from you."

"Well, I don't want to hear that kind of talk from you." Dolley crossed her arms over her chest. "I am still your big sister."

"And you're still wrong." Anna's voice was now raised. "Our mother would turn over in her grave to hear you talk like that."

"Let her spin like a top!" Dolley snapped.

"Don't you dare talk like that about our mother." Anna snapped right back. "She was a saint, a true Christian woman."

"She was a bossy saint." Dolley paced. "You got the sweet side of Mother. Those of us who were older got the fierce side." She stopped pacing. "I feared her and loved her, but I don't believe I ever felt close to her. I felt much closer to Mother Amy."

"Because she doted on you. She was all the time petting and praising you and fussing over your glossy black curls. Mother didn't indulge you. You like to be indulged, dear sister. You married men who indulged you."

"This is a fine kettle of fish. The city's smoldering outside this door. My husband is out there somewhere trying to keep our government alive. Your husband is out there doing what he can. And what are we doing? Fussing at one another."

"I'm not fussing." Anna's mouth was set hard.

"Fine." Dolley uncrossed her arms and put her hands on her hips as Anna began brushing her hair. The tangles proved a challenge, so Dolley picked up a comb to help.

"Oh no you don't." Anna pushed her hand away. "You'll yank my hair out by the roots. You did that the other time you were mad at me."

"When?" Dolley was incredulous.

"When I was six. You were horrible. I had a bald spot for weeks."

Suddenly Dolley laughed. It was the first time she had truly laughed in weeks. The gay, infectious sound carried over to Anna, and their mutual laughter dissolved their quarrel.

"I don't remember pulling your hair out, but I remember the bald spot." Dolley wiped her eyes.

"You were horrible."

"I guess I'm pretty horrible now. I feel so mean I'd break a stick just because it had two ends."

Anna laughed again. "You might have your chance."

"To break a stick or make you bald?"

"To let out some of that meanness. You know Mrs. Thornton will complain to you as soon as she thinks it decent to do so."

"Oh that." Dolley shook her head. "Before we discuss that, tell me, honestly, do you not feel any hatred at all for the British? Honestly, Anna."

"Honestly, I do not," Anna muttered. "Hate doesn't solve anything, really. I do believe we must love our enemies. I don't always know how but I believe we must try."

Dolley hugged and kissed her sister. "Oh, I wish I were as good as you are. I'm just not, you know."

"I think of the two of us, you're . . . fiercer. I think you are good, Dolley, but you want more than I do, and you love politics. I don't. Our minds are so different. You could run the government. You *could*," she repeated because Dolley was shaking her head. "And you'd like that. You've always wanted to be out in the world. You played with Temple and Walter when we were small. You rarely played with Mary or me. You belong in the world of men."

"Anna, I played with Walter and Temple because we were close in age. You're eleven years younger than I am, and Mary was younger still."

"Well, what about Lucy?"

"Lucy? I played with Lucy sometimes, but she had a different set of friends and then she ran off and married so young. Anna, I loved you when you were little. When you came to live with me, it was wonderful."

"It was." Anna nodded, and another vile sound was emitted from the adjoining room. "Dolley, will you?"

Dolley strode into the next room where Walter, playing a British soldier, was pretending to stick a fire poker into Richard's stomach. "Walter! Put that down this instant!"

"But Aunt Dolley, I'm a Redcoat and I'm going to burn Dickey alive."

"And I'm going to skin you alive. Put that poker down. No one in this family is ever going to be a Redcoat! Even in a game! Do you hear me?"

A surprised and chagrined Walter replaced the poker. "Yes, Aunt Dolley."

"Why don't you three go outside? Watch out for your sister."

"We can't go outside."

"Why not?"

"Because James said he'd take us down to the Capitol and lock us up with the dead bodies inside." Walter's eyes grew very large.

Anna, wondering why this was taking so long, came into the room.

"There are no dead bodies in the Capitol—or what's left of it," said Dolley.

Little Dickey piped up, "Then he's going to drag us down to Greenleaf and we'll have to pick up the arms and legs lying on the ground. He said so, Aunt Dolley, and I don't want to pick up no arms and legs."

"They've got flies on them." Walter's mouth pursed in disgust. "And worms."

"Where in the world do you boys hear these things?"

Walter and little Dickey retreated into the time-honored shrug of the child. Little Dolley toddled around, too young to know the trick. "Dead bodies!" she shrieked.

"There are no dead bodies. Dr. Thornton and Dr. Ewell buried the dead." Anna's voice rang with authority.

"What about the arms and legs?" Little Dickey was somewhat relieved, and somewhat disappointed, at not having a chance to see dead bodies.

"Those, too, have been buried. Now I want you to go outside with your sister and give us some peace."

Both Walter and little Dickey viewed their three-year-old sister with obvious distaste.

"Now!" Anna ordered, and they obeyed. She looked at Dolley. "Would you like something to drink?"

"Not after that discussion, no." Dolley smiled.

The two women sat down in the front room. The heat seemed less severe there.

"Now, about Dr. Thornton. What are you going to do?" Anna questioned.

"The colonel who ferried me over told me what happened. Thornton appointed himself mayor and accused James Blake of abandoning the city, which he did not. It's a more pressing topic in Washington than the enemy! I just believe Dr. Thornton did the best he could, and so did Mayor Blake, even if they did clash. Yesterday, when Dr. Thornton asked for a private meeting with Jemmy and said we really ought to surrender the city before the British march in again from the Alexandria side, that was a mistake. He doesn't understand Jemmy. After that meeting and Jemmy's telling him in plain words what he would do to any delegation that tried to reach the British and treat with them—well, Dr. Thornton went home and buckled on his sword, ready to fight if they come over the river. As far as I'm concerned, that's the end of it."

"You know it won't be."

"I know, but I'm not contributing to the fuss, and as soon as I can get to James Blake, I will do my utmost to calm him down."

"Men are like fighting cocks. At this point I don't think what happened to the city is what matters. They're mad at one another and they don't want to settle down. Each one wants to rule the roost."

"I'd much rather talk to Dr. Thornton, Mrs. Thornton, and James Blake than to John Armstrong."

"Oh." Anna squinted.

"*Oh* is right." Dolley folded her hands together. "You heard what General Samuel Smith said to Jemmy this afternoon. Every officer in his command would rather resign than serve under Armstrong. They believe him to be the willing cause of Washington's disaster. Poor Jemmy. I suspect he's riding around now trying to find Armstrong."

"General Winder will come in for his share of the blame"—Anna leaned back in her chair—"but I think most people know he did as much as he could with what he had, and, well, he had so little experience. I don't think his reputation will be ruined."

"They'll turn on Armstrong and he deserves it, but they'll turn on Jemmy, too." Dolley's voice lowered. "The Federalists will use this military horror ruthlessly. Of course, if they'd raised the men they were supposed to supply for the state militias, perhaps things would have turned out differently."

"Richard says the burning of Washington is the end of the militia. We have to have a standing Army, true professionals."

"Jemmy, too. I fear that. Look at Europe. Some fiery general captures the public's attention, and he pushes aside the civilian leaders because, of course, the Army is with him. Then what do we do, Anna?"

"It doesn't happen that often, and France is . . . volatile." She paused, then her voice rose. "The British honored the Seruriers as ministers of France. They are somewhat civilized, Dolley."

"You know what the British are?" Dolley leaned forward. "They're frightened of democracy. This war isn't about seamen and shipping. That's the excuse. They want to smash democracy. I believe that with all my heart and soul. We have to win this war even if it means that women and children must fight. We must win."

"I will not kill another human being." Anna said this quietly, with no fuss.

"Neither would our father." Dolley stared at her sister, noting her lustrous eyes. "I admired Father's convictions and I admired Mother's courage, but it's too hard, Anna, too hard being a Quaker. I don't want to kill anyone, not really, not deep down, but if the wolf is at the door, I'll kill, at least I think I will. What we are trying here is new; it's better than kings and queens and—"

"I know that," Anna snapped. "You understand politics in a way I do not. I know that, too, but Dolley, I do not believe we ever have the right to take another human life."

"You'd let the British kill you?"

"If it came to that, I guess I would. I couldn't live knowing that I'd violated what I most believe."

They sat in silence for a long time.

Dolley broke the silence. "Do you remember in 1781 when Tarleton's raiders rode on Scotchtown? You were very little then. Like Dolley Payne."

"I remember Mother Amy fighting with Mama and then Mother Amy crying and taking us back to her cabin. I don't know if I really remember or if I think I remember because everyone else told me about it."

"The thing was, Anna—and I never told you this, or anyone—I believe Mother would have killed that Redcoat if he had tried to harm her or any of us. She was like a tiger protecting its cubs. You could feel her power."

Anna pondered this. Mary Coles Payne was a staunch Quaker but yes, there was something about her, a touch of the warrior. But could their mother really kill?

"We will never know." Anna spoke at last.

"The funny thing was that as soon as the colonel rode out of the house, Mother took her apron and tried to clean up the dirt and the marks the horse's hooves had made on the pine floor. She just started working."

"You're a great deal like Mother, Dolley."

Dolley half hoped that was so and half hoped it wasn't.

29 August 1814, Monday

I have alternated between euphoria and anguish, between bursts of energy and troughs of such lassitude that I wonder if I am in full possession of my mind. The only thing that keeps me from thinking that I'm mentally undone is that I also observe this fluctuating state in those around me, except for Jemmy. Despair and rage grip him, too, but he won't give in to it. He keeps working, and where I was formerly concerned that a British bullet would kill him, I am now concerned that he will quite simply work himself to death.

Anna returned, and we flew from rapture to fussing with each other and then to happiness again. I'd like to blame this on her pregnancy, but I'm as bad as Anna and with no pregnancy to answer for my behavior.

I wept like a baby when French John sailed through the door with Uncle Willy and Paul Jennings, carrying Uncle Willy on high. I kissed him and petted him and he would not leave me when I put him on his perch. He would hop off and walk over with his funny rocking gait. So I let him sit on my shoulder and in my lap for hours.

French John wants to go back to work immediately, and I do need him. Anna and Richard are more than generous, but we must find a place to live where Jemmy can carry on the business of government. As French John was relating his experiences during the brief but vile occupation, who should appear at the door but Louis and Lisel Serurier. Dr. Thornton had just left them. The Seruriers are still staying in the Tayloes' Octagon House, which Dr. Thornton designed, and they at first thought he had visited them to see if there had been any damage. The British had respected the Seruriers' status and all was well. But no, Dr. Thornton had come to ask the Seruriers if they would return to their ministry and allow Jemmy and me to live at Octagon House until the presidential mansion can be restored. He said that he had inspected their house and it was habitable and that he had spoken to John Tayloe, the Octagon's owner, who would defer to our wishes.

Lisel blurted out that Dr. Thornton is doing everything to make up for asking Jemmy to surrender to the British, who at last report are merrily fleecing the inhabitants of Alexandria, who are turning somersaults to please them. Shame. I don't want ever to set foot in Alexandria again.

Anyway, Louis shot his wife such a searing glance, I thought she would combust on the spot. She should not have interjected her opinion about Dr. Thornton. Well, Louis doesn't know that Lisel and I discuss everything. She lowered her head. Dear Lisel will have endured a sulfurous conversation on the carriage ride home.

When Jemmy came back later, after another dreadful day, I relayed both the Seruriers' good wishes and their willingness to move, as well as Dr. Thornton's part in this decision. He said if I thought I could live there, he would be happy to go over to Octagon House as soon as possible.

We'll move over tomorrow. Anna will try to help and I won't allow it, so I hope we don't get cross with each other.

Jemmy asked John Armstrong to visit his family immediately. That's the long and short of it. And since Armstrong's family lives in Red Hook, New York, this solved a complicated problem with as much dignity as Armstrong can muster. I hope he has the sense to keep his mouth shut. However, I am sure that once he is surrounded by the warmth of his family, his passions will become excited and a flurry of letters or even a book will be forthcoming in which he will place the blame for this disaster on my husband. I guess General Winder will come in for a share of his hatred, too, and James Monroe, about whom Armstrong is nearly irrational.

Since Admiral Cockburn and General Ross's soldiers have evacuated, where will they strike next? We hear they boarded their ships. Most of us believe that Baltimore is the next target. I pray that Baltimore has better fortifications and better generals than Washington did.

Jemmy blames himself. He believes he made a punishing mistake in trying to maintain peace with everyone in his Cabinet. He upbraids himself for this, but I told him, "What's done is done. Let's look to the future." I also told him that he did the best he could and that we must keep in mind he is not a military man. He'll kick himself over Armstrong, but the one good thing about his crushing array of tasks is that he won't have much time to do so.

I do think trying to keep everyone happy with one another is a worthy goal, but there are times—many times, I suspect—when it isn't possible. Then placating and pacifying become a fault, and it's a fault I have in abundance. I can't very well criticize my husband for it.

Or my son, who wants everyone to be happy and becomes deeply distressed when someone takes issue with him. Not a word from Payne but then the mails have been disrupted, so I may yet receive a letter. I have written him to assure him that Jemmy and I are safe.

I fear the effect of Washington's disgrace on the peace negotiations. It will only harden the British in their desire to wrench as much from us as they can. I know Clay won't budge and Adams, well, he's more likely to make some concessions because he understands diplomacy. I don't think he will suggest anything damaging to our true interests. As to the other delegates, they will follow Adams. Jemmy and I haven't had a minute to talk about what might happen in Ghent. I know he has thought about it and is probably fearful.

With the British still on our soil and on our rivers, it's rather difficult to concentrate on anything other than driving them out.

French John, as usual, had the best gossip. Apparently General Ross is a milder man than Admiral Cockburn, who by all reports is marvelously handsome, the very image of Mars. Anyway, Ross told his men they mustn't touch a drop of our newfangled whiskey. He said it was too sweet and too crude, and since Americans seem to drink it in great quantities, perhaps we had poisoned our whiskey to accomplish by stealth what we couldn't accomplish by arms.

The other thing French John told me was that someone hiding in a building shot Ross's horse right out from under him in front of Robert Seawell's house. The poor creature lay unburied until today. I hate it when animals are hurt because of the transgressions of their masters.

One hero did emerge from Bladensburg, Commodore Barney. He was badly wounded in the thigh but French John says he will recover.

And Louis—without disclosing his sources, but we know they are reliable—said that conditions in the British camps are worse than battle. Fevers and dysentery have been raging. The British, unaccustomed to our sizzling summers, are coming down with all manner of sickness. Because they moved so quickly, there are no hospitals and precious few medical supplies. I suppose few doctors, too.

Sukey came back late this evening. She has become a far more helpful person. She was actually glad to see me and I was happy to see her. We embraced and all she said was, "Missus, we got to put the pieces back together." Bless her.

Oh, French John assured me that King George is safe with the cook. So Uncle Willy's nemesis will return to torment him, or is it the other way around? I can never remember which animal started that fight.

And how French John made me laugh! He told us all with such glee that the pothole in front of the presidential mansion claimed many British victims, sprained ankles mostly.

Paul seems quite sobered by his experiences. He is no longer a boy. When he apologized for not getting all the plate and silver off the table, I embraced him and said, "What are things compared to people?" We are all together. And as soon as we can possibly go, probably not until the fall, we will visit Mother Madison and enjoy some quiet days at Montpelier. He's a sweet young man, Paul, a sensitive soul, far more sensitive than are many women.

Which reminds me: Daschkov, believing discretion to be the better part of valor, left for Philadelphia before the British marched in. But French John put the keys to the presidential mansion in his house, thinking that because of the relationship between Russia and Great Britain at this time, they would be safe. Sukey appears to care not a whit that André has left. I have not spoken to her about her indiscretions. It seems like a hundred years ago now.

This has been a season of sorrow and anguish, and yet I feel more love for my family and friends than ever before. I look at their beautiful faces, perhaps not beautiful to others but certainly to me, and I am happy to be alive, so happy to know these people with all their qualities, good and bad. I think of people like Matilda Lee Love and others I will never know who helped along the way or just gave a smile instead of reviling me.

I cannot say the burning of our capital was a benefit, but it did teach us how strong we can be when tested and how loving we can be in brutal circumstances.

Until the morrow, God willing.

D.P.M.

*f*or the entire day Dolley, French John, Sukey, and Paul planned how to use the rooms of the Octagon House at Eighteenth Street and New York Avenue.

The pie-shaped lot had excited Dr. Thornton when he began working on plans for the house in 1800. He thought himself a peer of Thomas Jefferson, another self-taught architect. Fortunately for Dr. Thornton, his client was wealthy and the house was made of brick instead of sandstone, its appointments handsome and detailed.

The drawing room on the first floor boasted a gorgeous chandelier and a sensuous mantelpiece. The floorboards, long and unbroken, had gained a rich patina over fourteen years of waxing and use.

Madison took a circular room above the vestibule for his office. As Dolley was bustling about, planning, Louis and Lisel Serurier were packing; this prompted merriment between them, punctuated by Uncle Willy, who just wanted sunflower seeds and life to get back to normal.

Dolley made Lisel and Sukey stand downstairs while she made a grand entrance descending the elegant staircase.

"*Très magnifique!*" Lisel applauded.

"Well, thank you, but I won't be so *magnifique* if I don't get some clothes. I have next to nothing."

"Still got your turbans," Sukey chimed in.

"Yes, but I think I will have to wear more than that."

Lisel laughed. Dolley was returning to her old self.

Dolley turned to Sukey. "I believe I'll receive tomorrow first thing in the morning. We saved the best curtains, the crimson velvet ones. Let's put them in the drawing room, a touch of the familiar for Jemmy. And the clock we saved—yes, the clock, let's put that in there, too. A dressmaker . . . I wonder if my dressmaker remained in the city? Sukey, tell Paul to see if she's here and if she is, to bring her back with him. I can't go around in this dress forever."

"We put dresses on the tops of the trunks to protect the papers," Sukey mentioned.

"Yes, air those out, but really, I need more clothes."

Sukey smiled slyly and left the room. Her mistress would use any excuse for a new dress.

"Do you need any help?" Lisel inquired.

"No, I'm fine."

"I meant with—" She didn't finish.

"Money? Oh, Lisel, what would I do without you? Oh, I'm so glad you were spared." Dolley impulsively embraced her friend and then released her. "I still have a little left over from the necklace you sold."

"Where are the horses?"

"French John hid them from the British. They're back in the stable."

"Where did he hide them?"

"He's not telling, not even me. A man must have some secrets. Very French."

"Very French." Lisel laughed.

"I need a purse with a lock on it, I know. I appreciate your offer to assist me, but I am going to economize—seriously economize now." Dolley rattled on in this vein as she flew about the house, moving this piece of furniture and that.

Lisel smiled. How many times had she heard that vow from Dolley, only to see the economizing measures cost more than before.

A ruckus outside caused them to step through the front door. A wagon wheel had broken and the driver struggled to right the wagon. French John and Paul rushed out to help. The women observed for a moment, and then Dolley studied the remains of the unattractive house across the street, one of the few private dwellings burned by the British.

Lisel noticed. "Oh, don't distress yourself. Let's go back in."

Dolley put her arm through Lisel's. "Perhaps the British had the right idea."

30 August 1814, Tuesday

Such work today. I'm bone weary and it will take some time before we are established at Octagon House, which is lovely. How good it was to have Lisel with me, and Sukey and French John and Paul. I want to cover my eyes when I pass a ruined building, but I am feeling better and I owe much of it to my friends.

Jemmy named James Monroe acting Secretary of War. There are still British in Alexandria, but we're confused as to how many. We do know their ships are still there. Monroe instantly ordered up men, Navy men especially, to haul in batteries and to find the best positions downriver. We heard that there isn't a barrel of flour or a leaf of tobacco left in Alexandria. The British have taken everything.

I think everyone feels better now that Mr. Monroe is publicly recognized as acting Secretary of War. Since George Campbell is so ill, Jemmy feels certain that within weeks he will need to appoint a new Secretary of the Treasury. What we would give to have Albert Gallatin back, but he's so valuable at the peace negotiations. If he needs to go to another European city and find more money for us there, he does so. I find myself wishing he had an equally talented twin.

And poor Elbridge Gerry falters, too.

The fighting continues in New York. There appears to be no clear victory and Fort Erie remains a contest.

No word from the South. I pray daily that we will hear news of victories. We need a victory.

And I need silverware. Tonight we used steel utensils; those three-pronged forks will puncture one's tongue. French John and Paul saved some of our silver, but we haven't enough for a decent dinner setting.

Food prices are even worse than before the burning. We must pay them. We have no choice. I'm tempted to take a fishing pole and try my luck in the Potomac. It's one way to save money.

Sukey and I carefully inspected what little I have left in the way of clothes. I haven't even a pair of gloves or a handkerchief. As for shoes, if these on my feet wear out any time soon, I'll go barefoot.

The British took Jemmy's shirts, too. Apparently one British officer bragged about it and showed around his booty. My dear husband has as little as I do. We are going to have to borrow discreetly from friends outside the capital.

When I told Jemmy about my shoes and his—he has only boots on his feet—he laughed and said it was not as much a hardship for me. When I asked why, he said I can make certain my skirts sweep the ground. No one will see my feet.

He told me about staying in Brookville with a Quaker lady, Mrs. Caleb Bentley. He admired her lovely white frame house and her well-kept land. Then he asked me if my conscience was torn because of the war.

"Pine Street Meeting House expelled me when I married you and I have never looked back." That was my answer and it satisfied him.

After my discussion, or was it an argument, with Anna yesterday, I don't know what I think. I don't want to kill anyone; I think it's wrong and horrible, but the Redcoats brought the war to us.

In the stillness of this summer's night, though, I do think about this. I know that I am a good wife, but am I a good Christian?

Until the morrow, God willing.

D.P.M.

*J*ames Monroe's handsome features were haggard. As they rode past the ruins of the presidential mansion, he reported to the President.

"Captain James Gordon demands from Charles Simms that the city of Alexandria must hand over all public and private naval supplies, every vessel—down to a raft—all supplies intended for export trade, and furthermore, the good citizens of Alexandria are to retrieve everything that has been sent out of the town since August nineteenth." Monroe paused. "One more thing. Captain Gordon wanted the sunken boats, too, but was apparently dissuaded from this, uh, request."

"Sugar, tobacco, liquor, flour, cotton, and money." A sarcastic grin crossed Madison's face. "Good!" Before James Monroe could question his response, the President clarified his ambiguous optimism. "It means this raid on Alexandria is a plundering mission. The British will stay on the other side of the Potomac. That ought to calm the businessmen."

"The Hydra-headed Rumor." Monroe took liberties with the classics. "You know, I've heard people say that John Armstrong allowed Washington to be burned so that we would be forced to move the government to a Northern city."

"Well, at least the rumors are moving John Armstrong. He can't pack up fast enough."

Had they been true friends, Monroe would have laughed out loud. Instead he nodded in agreement.

Madison surprised him with his next remark. "They hate me too, you know."

"No they don't—"

Madison interrupted. "The people don't hate me as much as they do Armstrong. I think my work on the Bill of Rights mollifies their hostility a bit." He guided his horse around a wagon still overturned in the dusty road.

"You proved your courage at Bladensburg. The only men who hate you are men who hate our government."

"Yes, well," Madison sighed, "they regard you as a hero. You and Barney. You were a hero in the first war, too. I stayed in politics. Now I wish I had fought. Oh, I wished it then, too."

"Why didn't you?" Monroe was uncharacteristically blunt. "You didn't fear the shot, the fire, at Bladensburg."

"Everyone, including Washington, told me I was more valuable bending over parchment with a quill. And I've never enjoyed robust health." He breathed in deeply. The acrid smell, still very strong, filled his lungs. "The past is the past and the present is yours when we win." He smacked his hands together, indicating an end to this part of their discussion. "The British will be vulnerable sailing down the Potomac. Far better to attack them with artillery from the banks than to send over troops."

"Not only do they need to get their own ships out, they'll be burdened with the boats they've stolen and laden with booty."

"All right then. Let's see if we can catch the monkey with his paw in the jug." Madison halted and turned his horse in the other direction. The sight of his city dismayed him. He tried to suppress his feelings. "Did you know that someone painted on a blackened wall of the Capitol: 'George Washington founded this city after a seven-year-war with England—James Madison lost it after a two-year-war.' "

Monroe lowered his voice. "I had heard that, Mr. President."

"What I want to know"—Madison exploded—"is how, in the midst of all this destruction, they managed to find the paint?"

This time James Monroe did laugh. "Mr. President, don't let one rotten apple spoil the barrel. The people are with you—you and your lady."

The President smiled. "I've also heard that the *National Intelligencer* staff is working around the clock to put their press back together. The British threw the type in the road but left the ledgers unmolested, so war or no war, subscribers can be billed for their newspaper."

"Perhaps the spirit of cooperation we've found in our citizens, and I include Dr. Thornton, is due to the fact that the press is out of commission."

"Mrs. Madison always says that the free press works in such a way that not one of us is free from it."

"Mrs. Madison, as usual, is right. Well, sooner or later the British will go, but we'll still be here and then"—Monroe smiled ruefully—"other battles will begin."

"Government, imperfect, is but a reflection of its imperfect creators. Still better to be equals with other imperfect men, far better, than to be a subject of King George and the Prince Regent."

The President leveled his gaze on the overturned wagon, spurred on his horse, and jumped it for a lark.

James Monroe, mouth hanging open, watched in astonishment. The President, rather than being crushed by cares, was rejuvenated by them.

Monroe pushed his horse into a trot and caught up with Madison. The President turned in his saddle and spoke in a voice that for him was loud. "The British miscalculated by burning our capital. They have only strengthened our resolve."

31 August 1814, Wednesday

*I*t's a midnight beyond thought. Outside it's deathly still. Before the British came, I would often hear dogs barking or peepers, but now it's silent as a tomb. Perhaps the animals, offended by human stupidity, have left.

Daniel Webster used to complain about the "profound dullness of the place, *semper idem*." It's not always the same and I have little doubt that when young Webster returns here, he and his Federalist cronies will seize upon our misfortune for their political gain—if they can.

I started this diary to escape corruptive reflection. Years soften the edges of events. We place ourselves center stage when we are but a small player. So I kept my diary to write down events as they happened as accurately as I could. I didn't want the years to transform the events of my day into something dishonest or into a form of self-advertisement. I realize that all politics are a form of self-advertisement except for the politics of men like Washington, Jefferson, and my husband.

And I believe that ignorance is a form of censorship. Future generations must know what happened, how it happened, and why it happened. The truth, not contorted versions of events to evade responsibility or to assume responsibility in case of success, rarely gets told. I became so entangled in my thoughts that I don't think I put that down right. My quill needs sharpening. Must be the quill's fault, not mine.

As I was trying to say, people need to know the truth. Although I am just a pinprick in time, I have eyes, I have a mind, I have a heart. I can see my time and the people in it and I want to describe them as accurately as I can. If the United States is a democracy, then that democracy can flourish only if its citizens are informed. You can't make a decision if you don't have the facts. And you can't really make decisions for the future if you don't understand the past.

But my diary wanders. I wind up writing down memories of my family. My purpose is like a garden overtaken with weeds. I haven't the time to clear out the weeds—although Sukey certainly took a whack at it—but every now and then a rose pops up, its head lifting toward the sun. Which reminds me, tonight the sun looked like a paper lantern. I wondered why it looked so theatrical and strange. French John said that the air was full of dust particles and ashes, and for whatever reason this made the sun appear redder and much larger as it set.

Then French John made a pun and said Washington looked like Hell with the fires out. He makes me laugh. He always makes me laugh, and he's clever in two languages. I struggle with just one!

We're all busy as a cat's hair. Not a minute to rest and Sukey hasn't complained yet or lazed about. Mirabile dictu!

Tonight is my levee night, but I will need to wait a few weeks before reinstituting my parties. It's just as well; my eyes need a rest from the glare of diamonds.

Which reminds me, when I asked Lisel where she had hidden her fabulous jewelry, she said, "In the downspout." When the deluge came, however, Lisel raced outside to catch her valuables as they hurtled down the spout. Fortunately, no British saw her. She prayed as she became soaked to the skin, and she said she ought to thank the British for leading her back to the religion of her childhood.

People talk of the great storm as much as they talk of the British. It was as though that wind issued from the mouth of God to blow our enemies away. And the rain stopped the fires from spreading.

I wish the good Lord would help us find our better selves, help us understand that war is not choosy about its victims. The innocent and the soldier die alike. Surely there must be a better way to settle our differences, or we can't call ourselves civilized. If all else fails, I recommend throwing dice. Why not? It makes just as much sense as what I've seen and it's far less destructive. Winner take all.

Jemmy went to bed before midnight tonight. I regard that as a miracle.

I'm tired but I can't sleep. I lie down and my mind races. I may as well write in my diary as long as the quill and the candle hold out. Uncle Willy chirped so pitifully that I removed his cover. He's peering at me now as though I haven't a grain of sense and don't know it's too late. He wants to go to sleep, but he can't stand the idea that I'm doing something without him.

One week ago today I fled this city at my husband's request. Can it be that so much has happened within the span of seven days? The world has been turned upside down. I think death must be like this, in that it's unexpected. Even if one is elderly and dying, I think it must come as a surprise. We never truly believe we will die. We know it in our heads. We don't believe it in our hearts. I lived through this cataclysm. Others didn't. Death is a loud call to the living. Every moment is precious to me, and on that last lurch of the dice I want to close my eyes knowing that I truly lived, that I truly thanked God for the precious gift of life by enjoying it, celebrating it, and sharing that joy.

I remember once when I was twelve, a sober age as I recall, I was pondering the great questions of life with little result. I sometimes think that sitting in the Friends' Meeting House on those hard planks, in that silence, provoked me to such weighty thoughts. That's the purpose of dispensing with a liturgy and a sermon, I know, but sitting there with no obvious guidance, the strangest thoughts gallop across the mind. I got it into my head that there was no purpose to life. We made up a purpose to justify our puny existences. Whether our purpose was religion or politics or even the family, it was something we grabbed because it gave us a reason for living, and since everyone else was happy to tell us how to think and act, we did not need to think of our special purpose. Soon we were so overwhelmed with work and the petty detail of living as others wished us to live, our purpose quite escaped us. Or perhaps I should say the fact that there is no purpose.

I nearly drove myself wild with this. Did I have a purpose? Was it a true one? Did I just make it up? Did I believe what someone else told me my purpose would be? Well, I knew better than to bring this up with Mother or Father. One glance would have branded me a silly fool.

After weeks of torture and barely touching my food—if I don't eat, something is very wrong—Mother Amy asked me to her cabin. She was making candles, and I remember the tallow odor and the petals she had saved for the scents. She saved lilacs, roses, and even some lemon rinds. Lemons were rare then. One had to have an orangery to grow them or be rich to buy them. I helped her as she hummed and poured tallow into the molds.

I worked up my courage and told her of my dilemma. She listened gravely as I rambled on and even cried. Then I blurted out, "Mother Amy, why are we here?"

She put down her small ladle and said in a voice like music, "Why, Dolley, honey, we're here for each other."

And so we are.

Until the morrow, God willing.

D.P.M.

AFTERMATH

On September 2, 1814, the British began to leave a fleeced Alexandria. It took the town fathers another day to hoist the American flag.

The British fought their way down the Potomac, and Captain James Gordon, in command, proved an imaginative foe. When he discovered his guns wouldn't reach the American cannon on the banks of the Potomac, he weighted his ships to port. In this way the starboard guns had a high enough trajectory to reach their target. As Gordon had sixty-three naval guns to the Americans' thirteen, it wasn't much of a contest.

The British escaped, without further molestation, to the Chesapeake Bay.

General Samuel Smith, with thirteen thousand Regulars and militia, defended Baltimore. One thousand men were in Fort McHenry. The Americans prepared a defense of Baltimore while the British were burning Washington. They sank old ships so that the British fleet could not enter the harbor.

General Robert Ross unloaded his men fourteen miles from Baltimore and marched on the city. He met resistance from General John Stricker and his thirty-two hundred militia. The militia retreated but did not panic. The British general, Ross, was killed by a sniper in this engagement.

The British fleet bombarded Fort McHenry but were unsuccessful in subduing Baltimore by land or by sea. Baltimore remains unsubdued as any current resident can testify.

The British gave up on September 14 but remained in the Chesapeake Bay until October 14, when they sailed for Jamaica. They took with them General Ross's body, which had been placed in a cask of rum for preservation.

During the bombardment of Fort McHenry, Francis Scott Key, a Federalist from Georgetown, a rather well-liked and dreamy fellow, wrote "The Star-Spangled Banner." He was held hostage on a British ship during the attack. Francis Scott Key was attached to a volunteer company of artillery and had willingly boarded the enemy vessel to obtain the release of an American prisoner, only to find himself one, for his own safety. The British released him on September 14.

Earlier, Key was at the Battle of Bladensburg, but nothing in that sorry spectacle moved him to poetry.

In the North, Fort Erie was saved when General Peter B. Porter took sixteen hundred men and daringly demolished the British siege guns. The British withdrew. Losses were severe for both sides, and in early November the Americans at last relinquished the hope of conquering Canada.

The Battle of Lake Champlain, also in September, resulted in a smashing victory for the American sailors.

As men died, the peace commission in Ghent struggled to reach an accord. Clay refused to be depressed by the behavior of Lord James Gambier, Henry Goulburn, and William Adams. Often the talks stagnated. John Quincy Adams, never quite grasping Clay's vision of the West as the nation's future, nonetheless remained formidable in the exchanges, counterexchanges, and intrigues. When news of the burning of Washington reached England, it provoked as much shame as celebration. The British public was now sick of war and taxes. This probably had an effect on the British delegation. The Americans and British in Ghent finally signed a peace agreement on Christmas Eve 1814. Clay joked that the negotiations lasted almost as long as the war.

Although the Treaty of Ghent was not a diplomatic success by any standard, the news of this agreement reached the United States after General Andrew Jackson's tremendous victory at New Orleans on January 8, 1815. The fighting started on December 23 and continued intermittently until the large battle on January 8. The British sustained losses of two thousand thirty-six men killed or wounded. Miraculously, the United States suffered only eight men killed and thirteen wounded.

Andrew Jackson became a national hero, the next great American general in the public's imagination. His career, like a cue ball in a game of pool, smashed into the careers of John Calhoun, Daniel Webster, and, most especially, Henry Clay, who was being hailed as the bearer of peace.

The Federalists did call a secret convention in December 1814 at Hartford, Connecticut, where they fell just short of calling for New England's secession. However, Jackson's victory, just weeks after this convention, made its outcome less alluring to its participants.

The public, starved for a great victory, unleashed a torrent of celebration, and those men who had been at Hartford realized their careers might be in jeopardy. By the time news of the peace reached America on February 14, 1815, the Hartford Convention appeared traitorous to many people.

The War of 1812 broke the back of the Federalist Party. Daniel Webster prudently did not run for a second term in Congress from New Hampshire but moved to Boston, where he acquired wealth by serving the wealthy as a lawyer. He then reentered Congress and became a leader of the Whig Party, a forerunner in many respects of our current Republican Party. He was elected to the Senate in 1827. Like a moth to the flame, he flew near the presidency in his middle age but fell to earth, wings scorched.

This, too, happened to Clay, who made an implacable enemy in Andrew Jackson. The machinations of this hatred are worthy of a separate book. The daggers were drawn during Jackson's first run at the presidency in 1824. Clay controlled a bloc of votes, which he threw to John Quincy Adams. Whether he had actually promised those votes to Jackson is still a subject of debate. Whatever was said in smoky rooms and on outdoor walks has evaporated. The hatred of Jackson for Clay did not evaporate.

When Jackson was inaugurated as President of the United States in 1829, Clay had his hands full. The Star of the West was constantly tarnished by Jackson's minions, who were intent on destroying Clay, now in the Senate.

Clay survived and remained a power but never became President.

Calhoun's genius blistered in the service of slavery. His works are worth reading today because his extraordinary mind still impresses. But his defense of slavery cost him the presidency also, even though he was Vice President under John Quincy Adams. He, too, became a senator and remained politically powerful throughout his life, a magnificent if mutilated relic.

John Randolph reentered politics after the War of 1812 and rose to new heights of spite. His March 30, 1826, speech in the Senate remains the nadir of vituperation in Congress, much of this directed at Henry Clay. They fought a duel on April 8 on the Virginia side of the Potomac—at ten paces. In the first round both men missed. Dueling is governed by etiquette. The contest was over, but Clay insisted on a second round and fired through Randolph's coat, although the rail-thin Lynchburg man was untouched. Randolph fired in the air, then shook Clay's hand and told the startled man that he owed him a coat.

This duel did not help Clay's image even as it proved his courage. Everyone knew Randolph was erratic, which is a euphemism. Now Clay looked like a hothead. He should have known better than to aim a pistol at John Randolph.

When Randolph died in 1833 at age fifty-nine, he was buried facing west to keep an eye on Henry Clay—or so he told his friends before departing his extraordinary but ravaged life.

John Armstrong announced his resignation from the post of Secretary of War by writing a hot letter to the Baltimore *Patriot and Evening Advertiser*. He spent the remainder of his life contending that he was made the scapegoat of the war in order to advance Monroe to the presidency.

Commodore Joshua Barney survived his wound but never totally recovered. He retired from the Navy in early 1815 with a pension of six hundred dollars per year.

In May 1815, Madison asked Barney to carry dispatches to the peace commissioners still in Europe. This he did despite his chronic pain. On his return he applied for a consulship because he needed the money such a post could bring, but he was turned down. In light of Barney's services to his nation, this rejection was unconscionable.

Joshua Barney died in October 1818. The British bullet, still in his leg, was removed and sent to his oldest son, William, as Barney wished. As he was traveling when he died, his grave is in an Allegheny County, Pennsylvania, cemetery. The city of Pittsburgh, where he died, gave him a hero's funeral. They gave him more than the United States government ever did.

DeWitt Clinton finally got his canal; the Erie Canal was completed in 1825. He was another man—a fascinating personality—who remained pivotal all his life despite attempts to curb his power. Clinton proved what we now take as common knowledge: controlling New York State is a position of tremendous power.

Immediately after the war Madison faced a national debt of $81,487,846 plus some odd cents. This was a crushing sum, but he attacked it. Unfortunately, the effects of this debt extended beyond his presidency.

He was more than happy to leave office when James Monroe defeated Rufus King in 1816 and became President.

James Madison retired to Montpelier, where he constantly gave of himself to his community and his friends. He helped Thomas Jefferson build the University of Virginia, truly the great love of Jefferson's life.

Madison remained an innovative farmer and was much admired by other men of agriculture. He continued to participate in politics as a kind of professor emeritus: his responses to the doctrine of nullification (states can nullify any act of the federal government that offends them) remain a clear statement of the purpose of the Constitution. In his advanced years he began to fear civil war between the North and the South.

Mother Madison lived, although a confirmed hypochondriac, to the glorious age of ninety-seven, dying February 11, 1829. Nell Conway Madison clearly impressed everyone who knew her with her force of character. It would appear that Mother Madison did not suffer fools gladly in her near century of life.

She loved Dolley and was always grateful that her adored son had married so wisely, even if Dolley came to the altar an impoverished widow. During her day this was a gratifyingly liberal attitude because marriage was serious business and ought to enlarge one's estate. Mother Madison wished only for James to be happy.

He was.

James Madison left this earth on June 28, 1836, his mind quite clear. He was eighty-five. Sukey and Paul Jennings, who had married, were there, as well as a servant named Nelly.

Dolley had been with him every waking moment when he began to fail in the late spring. That day she had stepped out, and he chose this moment to die, possibly because he knew she couldn't bear to see him die. She'd seen so much death in her life. Sukey and Nelly tried to get Madison to eat. He put the food in his mouth but didn't swallow. Nelly asked him if anything was wrong, and he replied, "Nothing, my dear, but a change of mind." Then he dropped his head.

Dolley was a strong sixty-eight years old when the man she loved was buried in a black walnut casket made from trees at Montpelier. A huge crowd attended the fourth President's funeral, and she conducted herself with the warmth and dignity for which she was justly famous.

Little Dickey had died in October 1815—hard to bear, but harder still was the loss of her sister Anna Cutts on August 14, 1832.

Fate was not through with Dolley Payne Madison. Her son, who should have been the comfort of her life, found his solace in dissipation. He bounced in and out of jail for debt. Once a luminous, handsome youth, he became bloated, a caricature of his former self. Dolley did not know that friends around her, including Richard Cutts, were lending Payne money and did not press when he welshed on his debts. Some people said even James Monroe, out of affection for Dolley, had lent the man money. Those not close to Dolley did not forgive Payne, hence his visits to jail.

James Madison had paid Payne's debts. He had been paying Payne's debts for decades. Knowing that Dolley probably couldn't bear the truth about Payne, who was her Achilles heel, he hid everything from his wife regarding this.

Time told the tale because after James's death, Dolley discovered, slowly, that she had no money. She owned Montpelier and a house on Lafayette Square in the District of Columbia.

Dolley lacked James's great gift for farming.

In 1842 she mortgaged the Washington house to John Jacob Astor. In November of that year she sold some of Montpelier's lands to a Richmond businessman. The Cutts-Madison house, as the Lafayette Square house is now known, is still standing today.

Payne was no help nor was her brother John, who was drinking heavily again.

Despite her troubles, her need to sell her husband's papers for money, she did not lose her delight in life.

On January 8, 1844, Congress granted Dolley, now viewed as the heroine of the burning of Washington, a permanent seat in Congressional Hall by the House of Representatives.

The winter after Washington was burned, Dolley had worked tirelessly to restore social life, to raise money to rebuild the city, and to renew the people's faith in their government. Dolley and Marcia Burnes van Ness, a wealthy citizen, created an orphanage for the homeless children of Washington. She made clothes for the children and gave her own money and a cow to the orphanage.

The Capitol had been rebuilt by this time at a cost of $687,126. Reconstruction was completed in 1819. Consequent modifications, however, continued until 1826.

The cost of rebuilding the presidential mansion was great as well. Between September 30, 1816, and October 1, 1817, the accounts for expenditures to rebuild the public edifices indicate that almost $120,000 was spent on the president's house, compared to only $104,000 spent on the Capitol's reconstruction during this same period. After 1901 the presidential residence became known as the White House by executive order of President Theodore Roosevelt.

Dolley's activities, plus her courage when the British invaded and her saving Washington's portrait, made her a legend not only in her own country but throughout Europe as well.

Unfortunately, in those days former Presidents and their wives received no stipend from the government for their past services.

Financial pressures continued for Dolley.

In December 1844 Dolley was forced to sell Montpelier, a blow that would have crushed a weaker person. She insisted that the slaves stay with Montpelier and not be sold. During this difficult time Paul Jennings, James Madison's former slave, gave her his savings. He had loved Dolley for all his life, and in turn she loved Paul as a son. He was more responsible to her than was Payne, and after her death Paul was, in a sense, the keeper of her memory.

On July 15, 1845, Dolley became a member of the Episcopal Church of Washington. She had not joined any congregation since 1794, when the Pine Street Meeting House expelled her for her marriage to James Madison.

On February 19, 1848, Lucy, Dolley's sister in Lexington, Kentucky, died. Dolley was now the last of the Payne women.

Throughout her life, French John remained her right-hand man. When she had no money, he worked for free, finding ways to make a little money elsewhere, exhibiting that celebrated frugality of the French.

Like Paul and Sukey, he loved Dolley without reservation, as did the Seruriers, who remained friends.

Dolley inspired love as she inspired people to work for the good of all. At seventy-eight and seventy-nine, she was out raising money for the Washington Monument, and on July 4, 1848, she stood upright and jolly as the cornerstone was laid. She could raise money for projects for the public good but could never quite bring herself to raise money for herself. She never considered herself that important, perhaps, and her needs (except for clothing) remained modest.

She never reproached her son. Whatever anguish she felt, she kept it to herself.

371

Clay continued to visit her no matter where she lived. He utterly adored Dolley. Even Webster made a point to call on her, and Calhoun, never a social man, admired her and made no secret of it.

Her cousin, Ned Coles, freed his slaves as he had promised and moved to the Illinois Territory, where he became governor.

As with any far-flung network of relatives—the Cutts, Payne, Coles, Winston, Madison, and other families—some flourished, some failed. She loved them all and criticized no one. She never believed she had the right to judge. That was up to God.

She spoke rarely of her Inner Light, especially as she aged, but her peace and radiance bathed everyone who ever saw her or spoke to her. She bore witness. She had no need to preach. She lived what she believed, and in that respect she was like her indomitable mother.

Even as a young woman she realized that slavery would tear this country apart. The older she became, the more she despised our "peculiar institution."

She died before the War Between the States, on July 12, 1849, at the age of eighty-one.

No First Lady has ever been so tested as Dolley Madison. As there were few women in public life (women did not vote until 1920, a shocking fact when reflected upon), she became the example, the shining inspiration, to generations of women. She fulfilled our longing for an American heroine, and despite the twists and turns of our nation's life, her image has never lost its luster.

She is buried next to her husband in the small graveyard at Montpelier, where this author often brings to her grave the cut flowers that Dolley so loved.

ACKNOWLEDGMENTS

Since the British burned a huge number of our records in 1814, the research for this novel was a combination of detective work, years of reading, and visits to the various sites. My researcher, Claudia Garthwaite, and I were suspicious of many published memoirs because who would admit to being a coward when the Redcoats marched into Washington? Not only did Claudia and Gordon Reistrup, my saintly assistant, help me read, we all learned to read between the lines.

I am especially grateful to Carol Carruthers Sims-Jones, Jane Porter Fogleman, and Martha Foss for allowing me to study their family archives. As Carol Sims-Jones is a direct descendant of Jean Pierre Sioussat (French John), this generosity proved invaluable.

Colonel Joseph Mitchell was on standby, and any time I had a military question, he stepped in as he had done for so many writers over the years. His death in February 1993 is a loss for anyone who is a student of military history. Joe was a combat officer in World War II. One of the reasons I can pursue my career in freedom is because of men like Joe.

Sally Dohner and Dr. Trudy Wade were especially helpful during my trips to North Carolina because the majority of Anna Cutts's papers are in that state. Patrick Flynn of the Massachusetts Historical Society shared his knowledge of Elbridge Gerry.

The staff at Montpelier was ever ready to assist me, and I encourage you to visit the home of the Madisons.

The Library of Congress, that treasury of record and literature for America, once more was wonderful as was the University of Virginia Library. The Virginia Historical Society also fielded my inquiries. I am fortunate to live in a state where history is regarded as a part of our living present.

Hoping to bring more of Virginia's rich and varied past to light, and in this case an often overlooked historical aspect, Governor L. Douglas Wilder proposed a slave museum. At the Second African/African-American Summit in Libreville, Gabon, early in 1993, Governor Wilder, as the keynote speaker, unveiled his plans for this new institution. The Jamestown Slave Museum will be a freestanding facility located near the historical Jamestown site. The initial planning group met for the first time in August 1993.

I am also extremely lucky that Senator John Warner fought in Congress to alter the tax laws that caused staggering financial hardships for those of us writing historical novels; the laws caused hardships for other categories of artists, too. I have always known that the handsome senator was a bold rider, but his courage in this issue was both refreshing and applauded.

I'd like to thank Juts and Liska for accompanying me on eight years of field trips. We felt a bit like Saint Paul describing his journeys: first we were set upon by thieves and then a great storm came up, etc., etc. Both dogs happily shared in the hardships as long as I gave them a Frosty for their efforts.

The cats proved helpful, too. The teethmarks in the original manuscript bear testimony to their careful proofreading.

AUTHOR'S NOTE

Montpelier, in the process of reconstruction, needs money. Any contribution from you would be manna from heaven. During these times of economic duress—euphemistically called a recession—national landmarks are not high on the list to receive funds, regardless of their importance to the cultural and political life of our country. Please send whatever you can to Friends of Montpelier, Box 67, Montpelier Station, VA 22957.

BIBLIOGRAPHY

Adams, Henry. *History of the United States during the Second Administration of James Madison.* Vol. 1. New York: Charles Scribner's Sons, 1904.

———. *History of the United States of America during the Administration of James Madison.* Books 5 and 6. New York: Albert and Charles Boni, 1930.

Alden, Robert Ames. *The Flights of the Madisons.* Fairfax, Va.: Fairfax County Council of the Arts, 1974.

American Historical Review. Vol. 2. "The Negotiations at Ghent." A. T. Mahan. Vol. 1, No. 1. October 1895.

Anthony, Katharine. *Dolley Madison: Her Life and Times.* New York: Doubleday & Company, 1949.

Arnett, Ethel Stephens. *Mrs. James Madison: The Incomparable Dolley.* Greensboro, N.C.: Piedmont Press, 1972.

Barnett, Richard J. *The Rockets' Red Glare: When America Goes to War, The President and the People.* New York: Simon & Schuster, 1990.

Baxter, Maurice G. *One & Inseparable: Daniel Webster & the Union.* Cambridge: Harvard University Press, 1984.

Beirne, Francis F. *The War of 1812.* Hamden, Conn.: Archon Books, 1965.

Blumenthal, Henry. *France and the United States: Their Diplomatic Relations 1789–1914.* New York: W. W. Norton & Company, 1972.

Bradford, Gamaliel. *Wives.* New York: Harper & Brothers, 1925.

Brant, Irving. *James Madison: The Virginia Revolutionist.* Virginia Edition. Indianapolis: Bobbs-Merrill Company, 1941.

———. *James Madison: Secretary of State, 1800–1809.* Indianapolis: Bobbs-Merrill Company, 1953.

———. *James Madison: Commander in Chief 1812–1836.* Indianapolis: Bobbs-Merrill Company, 1961.

Bruce, Philip Alexander. *The Virginia Plutarch*. Vols. 1 and 2. Chapel Hill: University of North Carolina Press, 1929.

Bruce, William Cabell. *John Randolph of Roanoke, 1773–1833*. New York: G. P. Putnam's Sons/Knickerbocker Press, 1922.

Buckley, William Edward. *The Hartford Convention*. Hartford: Tercentenary Commission of the State of Connecticut Committee on Historical Publications, 1934.

Caffrey, Kate. *The Twilight's Last Gleaming: Britain vs. America, 1812–1815*. New York: Stein and Day, 1977.

Capers, Gerald M. *John C. Calhoun—Opportunist: A Reappraisal*. Gainesville: University of Florida Press, 1960.

Chandler, David G. *Dictionary of the Napoleonic Wars*. New York: Macmillan Company, 1979.

Clark, Allen C. *The Life and Letters of Dolley Madison*. Washington, D.C.: Press of W. F. Roberts Company, 1914.

Clay, Thomas Hart. *Henry Clay*. Philadelphia: George W. Jacobs & Company, 1910.

Coit, Margaret L. *John C. Calhoun: American Portrait*. Boston: Houghton Mifflin Company, 1950.

Colman, Edna M. *75 Years of White House Gossip: From Washington to Lincoln*. New York: Doubleday, Page & Company, 1925.

Curran, Louise C. *McLean Remembers Again*. McLean, Va.: Sound Publications, 1976.

Curtis, George Ticknor. *Life of Daniel Webster*. Vol. 1. New York: D. Appleton & Company, 1870.

Cutts, Richard. Original Letters.

Dangerfield, George. *The Era of Good Feelings*. New York: Harcourt, Brace and Company, 1952.

Daniels, Jonathan. *The Randolphs of Virginia*. New York: Doubleday & Company, 1972.

Davidoff, Robert. *The Education of John Randolph*. New York: W. W. Norton & Company, 1979.

Dean, Elizabeth Lippincott. *Dolley Madison: The Nation's Hostess*. New York: Lothrop, Lee & Shepard Co., 1928.

Desmond, Alice Curtis. *Glamorous Dolley Madison*. New York: Dodd, Mead & Company, 1946.

Dictionary of American History. Rev. ed. Vol. 7. New York: Charles Scribner's Sons, 1976.

Dictionnaire des Maréchaux de France: du Moyen Âge à nos jours. Coordination de Genevieve Maze-Sencier; avec collaboration de Christophe Brun et al. Paris: (Librarie Academique) Perrin, 1988.

Ellet, Mrs. *The Queens of American Society*. New York: Charles Scribner & Company, 1868.

Fall, Ralph Emmett. *The Diary of Robert Rose: A View of Virginia by a Scottish Colonial Parson, 1746–1751*. Verona, Va.: McClure Printing Company, 1977.

Footner, Hulbert. *Sailor of Fortune: The Life and Adventures of Commodore Barney, USN*. New York: Harper & Brothers, 1940.

Frary, I. T. *They Built the Capitol*. Richmond, Va.: Garrett & Massie, 1940.

Gerson, Noel B. *The Velvet Glove: A Life of Dolley Madison*. Nashville, Tenn.: Thomas Nelson & Sons, 1975.

Goodwin, Maud Wilder. *Dolley Madison*. Vol. 2 of *Women of Colonial and Revolutionary Times*. New York: Charles Scribner's Sons, 1896.

Grant, Matthew G. *Dolley Madison: First Lady of the Land*. Chicago: Publications Associates/Creative Education, 1974.

Grun, Bernard. *The Timetables of History: A Horizontal Linkage of People and Events*. (Based on Werner Stein's *Kulturfahrplan*.) New York: Simon & Schuster, 1979.

Hickey, Donald Robert. "The Federalists and the War of 1812." University of Illinois, Doctoral thesis, 1972.

———. *The War of 1812: A Forgotten Conflict*. Urbana: University of Illinois Press, 1989.

Hopkins, James F., ed. *The Papers of Henry Clay*. Vol. 1, *The Rising Statesman*. Lexington: University of Kentucky Press, 1959.

Hunt, Gaillard. *The Life of James Madison*. New York: Doubleday, Page & Company, 1902.

———. *Life in America 100 Years Ago*. New York: Harper & Brothers, 1914.

Hunt, Gaillard, ed. *The Writings of James Madison, 1769–1836*. Vols. 1–9. New York: G. P. Putnam's Sons/Knickerbocker Press, 1910.

———. *The First Forty Years of Washington Society*. Portrayed by the family letters of Mrs. Samuel Harrison Smith (Margaret Bayard Smith) from the collection of her grandson J. Henley Smith. New York: Frederick Ungar Publishing Co., 1965.

Hunt-Jones, Conover. *Dolley and the "Great Little Madison."* Washington, D.C.: American Institute of Architects Foundation, 1977.

Johnson, Gerald W. *Randolph of Roanoke: A Political Fantastic.* New York: Minton, Balch & Co., 1929.

Journal of Southern History. Vol. 21, 1955.

Ketcham, Ralph. *James Madison: A Biography.* New York: Macmillan Company, 1971.

Kirk, Russell. *John Randolph of Roanoke: A Study in American Politics, with Selected Speeches and Letters.* Chicago: Henry Regnery Company, 1964.

Koch, Adrienne. *Madison's "Advice to My Country."* Princeton, N.J.: Princeton University Press, 1966.

Lawson, Don. *The War of 1812.* New York: Abelard-Schuman, 1966.

Lord, Walter. *The Dawn's Early Light.* New York: W. W. Norton & Company, 1972.

Madison, Dolley Payne Todd, 1768–1849. *Memoirs and Letters of Dolley Madison, Wife of James Madison, President of the United States.* Edited by her Grand-niece. Boston: Houghton Mifflin Company, 1886.

Madison, Dolley Payne Todd, 1768–1849. Original letters.

Martineau, Harriet. *Retrospect of Western Travel.* Vol. 1. London: Saunders and Otley, 1838.

Minnigerode, Meade. *Some American Ladies: Seven Informal Biographies.* New York: Knickerbocker Press, 1926.

Moore, Virginia. *The Madisons: A Biography.* New York: McGraw-Hill Book Company, 1979.

Morgan, Helen L. *Mistress of the White House: The Story of Dolley Madison.* Philadelphia: Westminster Press, 1946.

Morison, Samuel Eliot. *Harrison Gray Otis: The Urban Federalist.* Boston: Houghton Mifflin Company, 1969.

Morris, Richard B., ed. *Encyclopedia of American History.* New York: Harper & Row, 1976.

Muller, Charles G. *The Darkest Day: 1814 The Washington-Baltimore Campaign.* Philadelphia: J. B. Lippincott Company, 1963.

Napoleon I, Emperor of the French, 1769–1821. *Napoleon Self-revealed, in*

Three Hundred Selected Letters. Translated and edited by J. M. Thompson. Boston: Houghton Mifflin Company, 1934.

Napoleon I, Emperor of the French, 1769–1821. *Letters and Documents of Napoleon.* Vol. 1. Selected and translated by John Eldred Howard. London: Cresset Press, 1961.

The Negro Soldier: A Select Compilation. New York: Negro University Press, 1970.

Niven, John. *John C. Calhoun and the Price of Union.* Baton Rouge: Louisiana State University Press, 1988.

Padover, Saul K., ed. *The Complete Madison: His Basic Writings.* New York: Harper & Brothers, 1953.

Peterson, Merrill D. *The Great Triumvirate: Webster, Clay, and Calhoun.* New York: Oxford University Press, 1987.

Randolph, John, 1773–1833. *Letters of John Randolph to a Young Relative.* Philadelphia: Carey, Lea & Blanchard, 1834.

———. *Collected Letters of John Randolph of Roanoke to Dr. John Brockenbrough, 1812–1833.* Edited by Kenneth Shorey. New Brunswick, N.J.: Transaction Books, 1988.

Rives, William Cabell. *History of the Life and Times of James Madison.* Vol. 3. Boston: Little, Brown & Company, 1868.

Robbins, Allan W., ed. *Alexandria History.* "Alexandria in the War of 1812." Vol. 6. Alexandria, Va.: Alexandria Historical Society, 1984.

Rogers, Joseph M. *The True Henry Clay.* Philadelphia: J. B. Lippincott Company, 1902.

Royall, Mrs. Anne. *Mrs. Royall's Southern Tour, or, Second Series of the Black Book.* Washington: 1830–1831.

Rutland, Robert A. *James Madison: The Founding Father.* New York: Macmillan Company, 1987.

Schlesinger, Arthur M., Jr. *The Almanac of American History.* New York: G. P. Putnam's Sons, 1983.

Schurz, Carl. *Life of Henry Clay.* Boston: Houghton Mifflin Company, 1893.

Springer, Mary Elizabeth. *Dolley Madison: A Story of the War of 1812.* New York: Bonnell, Silver & Company, 1906.

Tully, Andrew. *When They Burned the White House.* New York: Simon & Schuster, 1961.

Urdang, Laurence, ed. *The Timetables of American History*. New York: Simon & Schuster, 1981.

Van Deusen, Glyndon G. *The Life of Henry Clay*. Boston: Little, Brown & Company, 1937.

Wharton, Anne Hollingsworth. *Social Life in the Early Republic*. Philadelphia: J. B. Lippincott Company, 1903.

Whitcomb, Edward A. *Napoleon's Diplomatic Service*. Durham, N.C.: Duke University Press, 1979.

White's Conspectus of American Biography. A Tabulated Record of American History and Biography. 2d ed. Compiled by the Editorial Staff of the National Encyclopaedia of American Biography. New York: James T. White & Company, 1937.

White, Patrick C. T. *A Nation on Trial: America and the War of 1812*. New York: John Wiley & Sons, 1965.

Williams, John S. *History of the Invasion and Capture of Washington, and of the Events which Preceded and Followed*. New York: Harper & Brothers, 1857.

Wilson, Dorothy Clarke. *Queen Dolley: The Life and Times of Dolley Madison*. Garden City, N.Y.: Doubleday & Company, 1987.

Woodson, Henry Morton. *The Woodsons and Their Connections*. Columbia, Mo.: H. M. Woodson and E. W. Stevens Publishing Company, 1915.